BARBARA HOWARD

Love, Lies, and Local News

First published by Barbara Howard Media 2024

Copyright © 2024 by Barbara Howard

All rights reserved. No part of this publication may be reproduced, stored or transmitted in any form or by any means, electronic, mechanical, photocopying, recording, scanning, or otherwise without written permission from the publisher. It is illegal to copy this book, post it to a website, or distribute it by any other means without permission.

This novel is entirely a work of fiction. The names, characters and incidents portrayed in it are the work of the author's imagination. Any resemblance to actual persons, living or dead, events or localities is entirely coincidental.

Barbara Howard asserts the moral right to be identified as the author of this work.

Barbara Howard has no responsibility for the persistence or accuracy of URLs for external or third-party Internet Websites referred to in this publication and does not guarantee that any content on such Websites is, or will remain, accurate or appropriate.

First edition

This book was professionally typeset on Reedsy.
Find out more at reedsy.com

Contents

Acknowledgments v
1 Prologue: Chaos in Caracas 1
2 Finding Refuge 24
3 Homeward Bound 43
4 Old Wounds, New Scars 57
5 Familiar Streets, Foreign Feelings 70
6 Echoes of Dissent 80
7 Wedding Bells and Old Flames 97
8 Borrowed Romance 120
9 Whispers and Warnings 143
10 Conflict and Chemistry 167
11 Digging Deeper 183
12 Protest and Passion 194
13 Vincent's Return 212
14 Swept Away 227
15 Beneath the Surface 240
16 Between Two Worlds 252
17 Noah's Dilemma 260
18 Fault Lines 279
19 Uneasy Alliance 288
20 Heart vs. Head 294
21 Breaking Boundaries, Tangled Hearts 306
22 Vincent's Last Stand 333
23 The Price of Truth 338
24 Epilogue: A New Chapter 346

Cast of Characters	357
Book Club Discussion Questions	367
About the Author	369
Also by Barbara Howard	370

Acknowledgments

To Patricia Sargeant, thank you for your unwavering support and inspiration—you've been instrumental in helping me grow as a writer. Your insights and encouragement have meant the world, and I'm so excited to see all the amazing things ahead for you in your own career. I'm deeply grateful for your friendship and all the moments we've shared on this journey.

1

Prologue: Chaos in Caracas

Elizabeth's heart raced as she stood in the center of Plaza Bolívar, the air thick with tension and the acrid smell of tear gas. The once-peaceful square had transformed into a battleground of ideals, with protesters flooding in from every direction. She gripped her microphone tightly, her dark eyes scanning the chaotic scene before her.

"We're live in Caracas," Elizabeth began, her voice steady despite the turmoil surrounding her. "What started as a peaceful demonstration has quickly escalated into a full-scale riot."

Behind the camera, Vincent's steady hands kept her in frame as he expertly navigated the surging crowd. Elizabeth felt a flutter in her stomach that had nothing to do with the danger around them. She pushed the feeling aside, focusing on the task at hand.

"The streets are filled with thousands of protesters," she continued, gesturing to the sea of people behind her. "Makeshift barricades have been erected, and the air is thick with smoke from burning tires."

A sudden explosion nearby made Elizabeth flinch, but she didn't break eye contact with the camera. Vincent's unwavering gaze behind the lens gave her strength.

"The Bolivarian National Guard has begun using tear gas to disperse the crowd," she said, her voice growing hoarse from the irritants in the air. "But the protesters show no signs of backing down."

As if on cue, a group of young men rushed past them, their faces covered with bandanas. One of them stumbled, nearly knocking Elizabeth off her feet. Vincent's free hand shot out, steadying her with a firm grip on her arm. The touch sent a jolt through her, and for a moment, their eyes met.

"You okay?" Vincent mouthed, concern etched on his face.

Elizabeth nodded, swallowing hard before turning back to the camera. "The situation here is escalating rapidly. We'll continue to bring you updates as-"

Her words were cut short by a deafening roar. The crowd surged forward, and Elizabeth found herself swept up in the tide of bodies. Panic gripped her as she lost sight of her videographer.

"Vincent!" she called out, struggling to keep her footing in the crush of people.

Elizabeth's heart pounded as she fought against the surge of bodies, desperately scanning the crowd for Vincent. The cacophony of shouts and explosions made it impossible to hear if he was calling for her. She clutched her microphone like a lifeline, using it to create a small buffer between herself and the pressing mass of protesters.

"Vincent!" she called again, her voice lost in the chaos.

A flash of movement caught her eye, and relief flooded through her as she spotted Vincent's familiar form pushing through the crowd toward her. His camera was held high above his head, protected from the jostling bodies around him. As he drew closer, Elizabeth could see the worry etched on his face. He reached out, grabbing her arm and pulling her close.

"Liz, we need to get out of here," Vincent shouted over the din, his breath warm against her ear. "It's getting too dangerous."

PROLOGUE: CHAOS IN CARACAS

Elizabeth nodded, the adrenaline that had been fueling her reporting suddenly giving way to fear. Vincent's grip on her arm tightened as he guided her through the throng, his body shielding her from the worst of the pushing and shoving. They made their way to a narrow side street, the press of bodies lessening as they moved away from the main square. Vincent lowered his camera, his finger hovering over the stop button.

"I'm cutting the feed," he said, his eyes meeting Elizabeth's. "We've got enough footage. It's time to prioritize our safety."

Elizabeth hesitated for a moment, her competitive nature warring with her sense of self-preservation. But as another explosion rocked the air behind them, she nodded in agreement.

"You're right," she said, her voice a strained whisper, choked by the stinging tear gas. "Let's get out of here."

Vincent pressed the button, ending their live broadcast. The red recording light blinked off, and Elizabeth felt a weight lift from her shoulders. They were no longer journalists on assignment; now, they were just two people trying to survive in a city torn apart by unrest.

Elizabeth's heart hammered in her chest as she and Vincent sprinted through the chaotic streets of Caracas. The acrid smell of tear gas stung her nostrils, and the deafening roar of angry protesters mixed with the sharp crack of gunfire filled the air. Military vehicles rumbled past, their treads crushing the pavement with a menacing authority. Inside, soldiers gripped their weapons, eyes scanning the surging crowd. The tension in the air was palpable as the presence of the armed forces intensified the atmosphere, leaving Elizabeth acutely aware of the precarious balance between chaos and control. She could feel her heart pounding, her breath coming in short, sharp bursts as she took in the scene around her. The soldiers' stern faces and rigid postures only added to the sense of unease that permeated the streets. Elizabeth's keen journalistic instincts kicked in, and she mentally cataloged every detail, every nuance of the unfolding situation. The weight of her camera felt reassuring in her hands, a reminder of her purpose amidst the tumult. As she watched the interplay between the protesters and the military, Elizabeth sensed a volatile situation, a powder keg teetering on the brink of detonation.

"We gotta move faster, Liz!" Vincent shouted over the din, his camera equipment jostling against his back as they ran. Elizabeth could hear the urgency in his voice, barely audible above the shouts and sirens that filled the air. She felt another surge of adrenaline course through her veins as she pushed her legs to move quicker, her own gear bouncing uncomfortably with each hurried step. The turmoil around them seemed to intensify, driving home the importance of Vincent's words. They needed to reach a safer vantage point, and fast.

They weaved through the throng of panicked civilians, dodging flying debris and pushing past frenzied looters. Each breath she took hitched in her chest, a frantic rhythm against the backdrop of the city's escalating chaos. The airport, their beacon of escape, seemed impossibly far away, swallowed by the sprawling urban landscape and the suffocating fear that pressed in from all sides.

A surge in the crowd suddenly separated them again. Elizabeth spun around, searching frantically for her partner. "Vincent!"

She spotted him stumbling, his feet tangling with those of the fleeing masses. Time slowed as she watched him fall, disappearing beneath a sea of stampeding feet. A wave of panic gripped her. The crowd pressed forward, a relentless tide that threatened to swallow him whole. She pushed through the throng, her own body a weapon against the brutal force of the crowd, her mind screaming his name.

"No!" Elizabeth struggled through the crowd of people, pushing and shoving her way back to where Vincent had fallen. She found him curled on the ground, his face contorted in pain.

PROLOGUE: CHAOS IN CARACAS

"My ankle," he groaned as she helped him to his feet. "I think it's broken."

Elizabeth slung his arm over her shoulder, supporting his weight as best she could. "We're almost there. Just hang on."

They limped forward, Vincent gritting his teeth with each step. The crowd pressed in around them, jostling and shoving. Elizabeth felt Vincent's grip on her tighten as he used his broader frame to shield her from the worst of it.

At the airport, chaos reigned. Desperate travelers clamored at check-in counters, security personnel struggled to maintain order, and the air crackled with tension and fear.

"Our equipment," Elizabeth gasped, eyeing the long lines at customs.

Vincent's face was pale with pain, but his jaw was set. "We'll make it. We have to."

They inched forward in the queue, Vincent leaning heavily on Elizabeth. She could feel him trembling with the effort of staying upright. When they finally reached the customs officer, the man barely glanced at their credentials before waving them through.

"Wait," the officer called as they started to move away. Elizabeth's stomach dropped. But the man only nodded at Vincent. "You need medical attention. There's a first aid station near Gate 3."

Elizabeth exhaled sharply, her shoulders sagging with momentary relief. They weren't safe yet, but they were one step closer to escape. The bustling airport around them seemed both a blessing and a curse - a crowd to blend into, but also potential eyes watching their every move. She glanced at Vincent, silently willing him to hold on just a little longer. They still had a ways to go before they could truly breathe easy. Elizabeth knew this all too well, her emotions on high alert as they navigated the crowded airport. Every passing face, every announcement over the loudspeaker, every security guard in sight seemed to hold potential danger. Her shoulders were weighed down by the gravity of their situation, a continuous reminder of the obstacles ahead. She fought to keep her composure, knowing that appearing calm and collected was crucial to their escape plan. Still, a large part of her longed for the moment when they could finally relax, when the threat would be behind them, and they could process everything that had happened. But for now, vigilance was their only option.

Elizabeth guided Vincent through the crowded airport, her eyes constantly scanning for potential threats. The first aid station near Gate 3 was their immediate goal, but she knew they couldn't linger long. Every second they remained in Venezuela increased their risk of being trapped there indefinitely. As they approached the station, a harried-looking nurse glanced up from tending to another patient. Elizabeth felt a flicker of impatience as the woman slowly finished applying a bandage before turning to them.

"What happened?" the nurse asked, eyeing Vincent's swollen ankle.

"He fell during the protest," Elizabeth explained, her voice low and urgent. "We have a flight to catch. Can you just wrap it quickly?"

The nurse nodded, gesturing for Vincent to sit. As she worked, Elizabeth kept watch, her nerves fraying with each passing minute. She could hear announcements echoing through the terminal, some in Spanish, others in broken English. Each one made her flinch, half-expecting to hear their names called out.

Elizabeth watched Vincent's face closely as the nurse worked on his ankle. His jaw was clenched tight, a muscle twitching in his cheek as he fought to contain his pain. Sweat beaded on his forehead, and his normally warm brown eyes were clouded with discomfort.

"How bad is it?" Elizabeth asked softly, her heart clenching at the sight of his suffering.

Vincent attempted a smile, but it came out as more of a grimace. "I've had worse," he said through gritted teeth. "Remember that time in Syria when-"

He broke off with a sharp intake of breath as the nurse manipulated his ankle. Elizabeth instinctively reached out, placing her hand on his shoulder. She could feel the tension in his muscles, coiled tight with pain.

"Sorry," the nurse murmured, not looking up from her work.

Vincent shook his head. "It's fine," he managed. "Just do what you need to do."

Elizabeth admired his stoicism, but she could see the toll it was taking on him. His normally rich olive complexion had paled, and his breathing was shallow and rapid.

"Vincent," she said, her voice hushed and urgent. "You don't have to play tough. If you need a moment-"

"No," he cut her off, his voice firm despite the pain. "We can't afford to waste time. We need to get on that plane."

The determination in his eyes was recognizable to Elizabeth. It was the same look he got when they were chasing a story, refusing to give up no matter the obstacles. But this time, it worried her. She knew Vincent would push himself beyond his limits if he thought it was necessary.

With a sense of urgency, Elizabeth turned to the nurse, speaking in a hushed tone. "Something for the pain? Surely, you have something you can give my friend."

The nurse glanced up, her brow furrowed. "I can administer a local anesthetic or provide some painkillers-"

"No," Vincent interjected firmly, his jaw set. "I don't want anything."

Elizabeth whirled to face him, surprise etched on her features. "Vincent, you're in pain. It's okay to-"

He shook his head, cutting her off. "We can't risk it, Liz. I need to keep my head clear."

Elizabeth understood his reasoning immediately. Any medication could potentially impair his faculties, making their already uncertain situation even more dangerous. Moreover, carrying or being under the influence of medication could give customs and airport security a reason to detain them - a risk they couldn't afford to take.

She nodded reluctantly, respecting his decision even as concern gnawed at her. "Okay, if you're sure."

Vincent's eyes softened, recognizing the worry in her voice. "I'm sure. We've come too far to jeopardize our exit now."

"Okay," the nurse said, finishing up the bandage. "That should hold you for now, but you really should see a doctor as soon as possible."

Vincent nodded, already pushing himself to his feet. He swayed slightly, and Elizabeth quickly moved to support him.

"Thanks," he muttered, leaning heavily on her. "I can manage."

"Keep it elevated when possible," the nurse advised. "And try not to put too much weight on it."

Elizabeth helped Vincent to steady himself, supporting him as he tested his weight on the injured ankle. She felt the tension in his body, the way he leaned into her more heavily than before. But his face remained stoic, betraying no sign of the pain she knew he must be feeling.

"Ready?" she asked softly.

Vincent nodded, his eyes scanning the bustling airport crowd around them. "Let's get out of here."

But as they took a few steps, Elizabeth could feel him trembling with the effort. His face was drawn, lips pressed into a thin line as he fought against the pain.

"Vincent," she started, concern evident in her voice as she helped him back to his seat and entreated the nurse once more.

He shook his head, cutting off her protest. "We keep moving," he said, his voice strained but determined. "We're not safe until we're in the air."

PROLOGUE: CHAOS IN CARACAS

"All set," the nurse said, re-fastening the last of the elastic bandage. "You should really have this properly examined-"

"Thanks," Elizabeth cut her off, already helping Vincent back to his feet. She felt a twinge of guilt at her brusqueness, but there was no time for niceties.

They made their way to their gate. Elizabeth's eyes darting from side to side, scanning for any signs of trouble. She could feel Vincent's labored breathing against her side, his determination matching her own as they pushed forward, one step at a time. The gate number loomed ahead, a beacon of hope in their desperate flight, Vincent's limp slowing their progress. Elizabeth's mind was in a frenzy, reliving the events that brought them to this moment: the interview that had gone sideways, the damning footage they'd captured, the frantic dash through the city. It all seemed surreal now, like a fever dream.

As they settled into the worn plastic seats near their gate, Elizabeth allowed herself a stolen moment to breathe, the tension slowly ebbing from her shoulders. She noticed how Vincent was trying to hide his pain, but she could see it in his eyes. His hand rested protectively on his injured leg, and Elizabeth felt a pang of guilt, knowing she'd pushed him too hard. She reached out, covering his hand with hers, offering a silent apology and a small squeeze of reassurance. He returned the pressure, a flicker of a weary smile touching his lips.

"How're you holding up?" she asked softly.

Vincent managed a weak smile. "Been better. But hey, at least we got the story, right?"

Elizabeth nodded, her hand instinctively moving to the hidden pocket where she'd stashed their memory cards. The burden of what they carried -both literally and symbolically -weighed heavily on her.

A commotion near the security checkpoint caught her attention. Two uniformed men were speaking urgently with the guards, gesturing animatedly. Elizabeth's heart rate spiked as one of the men produced a photo, showing it to the security personnel. She watched the uniformed men at the security checkpoint. She knew all too well how the authorities viewed journalists, especially outsiders like herself and Vincent. In Venezuela, as in many other places they'd reported from, journalists were often seen as threats rather than truth-seekers. The government's distrust of the media had only intensified in recent years, making their work increasingly dangerous.

She leaned closer to Vincent, her voice barely above a whisper. "We've got company. Security checkpoint. Two men showing photos."

Vincent tensed beside her, his eyes scanning the area without moving his head. "Think they're looking for us?"

Elizabeth's mind raced through possibilities. Their confrontation with the local officials during the protest had been brief, but heated. Had someone recognized them? Or worse, had their equipment been spotted during the chaos?

"It's possible," she murmured, her hand unconsciously tightening on the strap of her bag where her credentials were hidden. "We need to be ready to move."

She watched as one of the uniformed men pointed toward the gates, his expression grim. The security guard nodded, speaking into his radio. Elizabeth's pulse quickened. They were running out of time.

"Vincent," she said, her voice low and cautious, "can you walk if we need to move?"

He nodded, his jaw set. "Just give the word."

Elizabeth's eyes darted between the approaching security personnel and their gate. The boarding hadn't started yet, but she could see the gate agents bustling around, preparing for the rush of passengers. If they could just hold out a little longer...

She was acutely aware of how dangerous their situation was. As foreign journalists in a country gripped by political turmoil, they were walking targets. The footage they carried could be damning to those

PROLOGUE: CHAOS IN CARACAS

in power, and Elizabeth knew the authorities would stop at nothing to prevent it from leaving the country.

Elizabeth's pulse quickened as she leaned closer to her partner. "Vin," she whispered urgently as she nudged him gently with her elbow. "We might have company." Her eyes darted back to the checkpoint, where the uniformed men were now pointing in their general direction. A cold knot of dread formed in the pit of her stomach as she realized their carefully laid plans might be unraveling before their eyes.

Elizabeth's mind whirled, searching for a way out. She scanned the terminal, her eyes landing on a maintenance door tucked away in a corner. Without a word, she helped Vincent to his feet, trying to appear casual as they moved away from their gate.

"What's the plan?" Vincent whispered, his face taut with pain and worry.

"We need to disappear," Elizabeth said, guiding him toward the maintenance door.

As they approached, she glanced over her shoulder. The uniformed men were now speaking with the gate agent, their backs turned. She seized the moment, quickly ushering Vincent through the door and pulling it closed behind them. They found themselves in a narrow service corridor, dimly lit and eerily quiet compared to the bustling terminal. The stark contrast made Elizabeth's ears ring as she tried to get her bearings.

"This way," she said, leading Vincent down the corridor. Her heart hammered in her chest, each beat seeming to echo off the bare walls. They turned a corner and nearly collided with a startled maintenance worker. The man opened his mouth, likely to question their presence, but Elizabeth cut him off.

"Por favor," she said, her Spanish tinged with desperation. "We need help. My friend is hurt."

The worker hesitated, his eyes shifting between them and the corridor behind them. For a moment, Elizabeth feared he would turn them in. But then his expression softened, and he nodded toward a door at the end of the hall.

"That leads to the tarmac," he said in accented English. "Be careful."

Elizabeth felt a rush of gratitude as they hurried past him. As they reached the door, she paused, her hand on the handle. She turned to Vincent, suddenly aware of how close they were standing. His breath mingled with hers, warm and quick.

"Ready?" she asked, searching his eyes.

Vincent nodded, his gaze intense. "Always, with you."

The moment stretched between them, charged with unspoken emotions. With a deep breath, she pushed open the door, and they stepped out into the unknown. The cool night air rushed in, carrying with it the faint scent of diesel and spices. Elizabeth squinted, taking in their surroundings.

Crouched behind the crates, they held their breath, their eyes darting across the tarmac, every muscle tense, listening for the telltale sound of approaching footsteps. The atmosphere was permeated by the distant rumble of jet engines and the strong odor of fuel. Elizabeth's pulse quickened as she strategized their next move.

"Psst! Hey, you two!" A low voice caught their attention.

Elizabeth whirled around, her hand instinctively reaching for her camera. A man in his mid-forties with salt-and-pepper hair and weathered skin stood a few yards away, gesturing urgently for them to follow.

"You look like you could use a ride," he said, his accent thick with local inflections.

Vincent shot Elizabeth a wary glance. She hesitated, weighing their options. The stranger seemed to sense their reluctance.

"Name's Carlos. I've got a small plane that can get you out of here, no questions asked." He jerked his thumb toward a hangar in the distance. "But it'll cost you."

Elizabeth's mind raced. They were out of options, and time was running out. She could hear shouts in the distance, growing closer.

"How much?" she asked, her voice barely above a whisper.

Carlos named a figure that made Elizabeth's stomach drop. It was steep, but not impossible. She glanced at Vincent, who gave a slight nod.

"Fine," Elizabeth said, her jaw set. "But we need to leave now."

Carlos grinned, revealing a gold tooth. "Follow me and stay low."

As they made their way across the tarmac, ducking behind vehicles and equipment, Elizabeth's mind whirled with possibilities. Was this a trap? Or their only chance at escape? They reached the hangar, and Carlos ushered them inside. A small, battered plane lay hidden in the shadows, its propellers catching a faint glimmer from the dim light.

"Where can you take us?" Vincent asked, his voice strained with pain and exhaustion.

Carlos shrugged. "Anywhere within range. But the farther we go, the more it'll cost you."

Elizabeth bit her lip, calculating. They needed to get far enough to ensure their safety, but close enough to still break their story. She locked eyes with Vincent, a silent conversation passing between them. The distant shouts were growing louder, and time was running out.

"Colombia," she said firmly, locking eyes with Carlos. "Can you get us to Bogotá?"

Carlos raised an eyebrow, considering. "It's doable. But it'll cost extra."

Elizabeth nodded, her hand unconsciously moving to the hidden pocket where she kept their emergency funds. "We can manage. Let's go."

As Carlos began his pre-flight checks, Elizabeth helped Vincent into the small aircraft. The interior was cramped and smelled of old leather and aviation fuel. Vincent winced as he settled into his seat, his injured ankle clearly causing him discomfort.

"You okay?" Elizabeth asked, her voice low.

Vincent managed a tight smile. "I'll live."

The sound of approaching vehicles caught their attention. Elizabeth peered out the small window, her heart racing as she saw flashing lights in the distance.

"Carlos," she called urgently. "We need to leave. Now."

The pilot nodded, his face set in concentration as he flipped switches and adjusted dials. The propellers sputtered to life, their rhythmic whirring drowning out the chaos outside.

As the plane began to taxi, Elizabeth felt a mixture of relief and anxiety wash over her. They were escaping, but at what cost? The story they carried with them could change lives and expose corruption, but it had also put them in grave danger.

The small aircraft picked up speed, racing down the runway. Elizabeth gripped the armrests. She glanced at Vincent, whose jaw was clenched tight, his eyes fixed on the path ahead.

Just as they lifted off, Elizabeth caught sight of several vehicles screeching to a halt at the edge of the runway. Figures poured out, gesticulating wildly, but it was too late. They were airborne. As the lights of Caracas faded behind them, Elizabeth allowed herself a moment to breathe. They weren't safe yet, not by a long shot, but they had cleared the first hurdle. She turned to Vincent, finding him already looking at her.

"We did it," he said softly, a mix of disbelief and exhaustion in his voice.

Elizabeth nodded, reaching out to squeeze his hand. "We're not done yet. But yeah, we did it."

PROLOGUE: CHAOS IN CARACAS

***

The small plane touched down on a dimly lit airstrip outside Bogotá, its wheels screeching against the tarmac. Elizabeth's heart skipped as the aircraft slowed to a stop. Her eyes briefly met Vincent's, who offered a grim nod. They had made it this far, but their journey was far from over.

As they disembarked, Carlos handed Elizabeth a crumpled piece of paper. "My contact," he muttered. "He can help you get to the States. But be careful."

She pocketed the paper, her mind already swirling with plans. They needed to move quickly, but Vincent's injury complicated matters. She surveyed the surroundings, and a sigh of relief escaped her lips as she spotted a lone taxi idling nearby. They approached the cab, Elizabeth supporting Vincent as he limped along. The driver eyed them suspiciously but said nothing as they climbed in.

"El Dorado International Airport, por favor," Elizabeth said, her voice steady despite her frayed nerves.

As they weaved through Bogotá's early morning traffic, Elizabeth pulled out her phone, grateful for the international plan she had insisted on. She dialed a number she knew by heart, her fingers trembling slightly.

"Sarah? It's Liz. I need a favor," she said quietly, conscious of the driver's presence. "Can you book us two tickets to Miami? The earliest flight possible. Use the emergency fund."

She listened intently, jotting down details on her notepad. "Perfect. Thanks, Sarah. I owe you one."

Hanging up, Elizabeth turned to Vincent. "We've got a flight in three hours. It's not ideal, but it's the best we can do."

Vincent nodded, his weary eyes showing the signs of his silent suffering. "And once we're in Miami?"

"One step at a time," Elizabeth murmured, squeezing his hand reassuringly.

At the airport, they moved as quickly as Vincent's injury allowed, keeping their heads down. They made it through security without incident, a small miracle given their circumstances.

As they settled into their seats at the gate, Elizabeth felt the tension melt away, and she took a deep breath. They weren't safe yet, but they were closer. The bustling airport around them provided a strange sense of anonymity, a temporary shield from the dangers that had been nipping at their heels. She pulled out Carlos's crumpled note, studying the name and number scrawled there in hasty, barely legible handwriting. Her eyes traced each curve and line, committing the information to memory. Their next move would be crucial, but for now, all they could do was wait. Elizabeth's mind filled with possibilities and potential pitfalls, her thoughts refusing to let her fully relax. She glanced at Vincent, who sat beside her with his injured ankle propped up on their carry-on luggage, silently hoping that their gamble would pay off.

"How're you holding up?" she asked quietly, leaning in close to avoid being overheard.

Vincent managed a tight smile. "I could use a drink."

Elizabeth nodded, her hand instinctively finding its way to the hidden pocket where the precious footage was tucked away safely. The gravity of their story pressed against her, a constant reminder of their motivation and the risks they had endured.

As the minutes ticked by, Elizabeth replayed the events of the past few days in her mind. The clandestine meetings, the heart-stopping chase through Caracas, the desperate flight with Carlos. It all seemed surreal now, sitting in the fluorescent-lit normalcy of an international airport.

PROLOGUE: CHAOS IN CARACAS

A burst of laughter from a nearby group of tourists made Elizabeth flinch. She took a deep breath, trying to calm her nerves. They still had a long way to go before they were truly safe.

"Flight 237 to Miami now boarding," crackled the announcement over the intercom.

Elizabeth straightened, her heart rate picking up. "That's us," she said, helping Vincent to his feet.

As they made their way to the boarding gate, Elizabeth couldn't shake the feeling that they were being watched. She resisted the urge to look over her shoulder, knowing it would only draw attention. Instead, she focused on guiding Vincent through the crowd, her hand steady on his arm. They handed their boarding passes to the attendant, Elizabeth holding her breath as the woman scanned the documents. After what felt like an eternity, she smiled and waved them through.

"Enjoy your flight," the attendant said.

Elizabeth nodded, a wave of relief washing over her as they ascended the jet bridge. They were one step closer to safety, one step closer to breaking their story. But as they boarded the plane, she knew their journey was far from over. The real challenge would begin once they landed in Miami.

She settled into her window seat, their usual routine playing out as Vincent gestured for her to slide in first. Her muscles ached from the tension of their escape, but the cushioned seat offered some relief.

"Here." Vincent draped the thin airplane blanket over her legs, his movements practiced and automatic. The scratchy fabric wasn't much, but it was their ritual - one they'd developed over countless flights together.

"You're hurt. You should take it," Elizabeth protested, though she knew it was futile. Vincent never budged on this.

"Keep it, Liz." He eased into the seat beside her, favoring his injured ankle. "You know how you get cold on these flights."

She did get cold, and he always noticed. Elizabeth pulled the blanket up to her chest, breathing in the sterile airplane scent mixed with a trace of Vincent's cologne from where he'd handled it. The familiar scent helped calm her racing thoughts.

"Try to rest," Vincent whispered, his voice soft and intimate, as if sharing a secret. "I'll keep watch."

Elizabeth nodded, knowing he meant it. Even injured, Vincent remained vigilant -it was part of what made them such an effective team. She turned to gaze out the small window as the plane began to taxi, watching the lights of Bogotá blur into streaks of color.

* * *

The Miami air hung heavy and humid, a stark contrast to the crisp Andean air they'd left behind. Elizabeth hailed a cab, giving the driver the address of a small, unassuming motel near the airport. As they pulled up to the faded pink building, Vincent leaned against her, his breath warm against her ear.

"Kitten," he murmured, his voice rough with exhaustion, "we made it."

A flicker of something more than relief sparked in Elizabeth's chest. She met his gaze, the intensity of his dark eyes momentarily stealing her breath. She wanted to lean into him, to let the tension of the past few days melt away, but the importance of their mission kept her grounded.

"For now," she replied softly, her voice barely above a whisper.

Inside the cramped motel room, the air conditioner sputtered, struggling to combat the oppressive heat. Elizabeth tossed their bags onto the worn floral carpet, the sound oddly loud in the small space.

Vincent sank onto the bed, exhausted.

"I need to make some calls," Elizabeth said, pulling out her phone. "Confirm our story. Make sure Fred's got everything lined up."

Vincent nodded, closing his eyes. "Wake me when you're done."

As Elizabeth paced the room, speaking in hushed tones to her contacts, the reality of their situation sunk in. They had escaped Caracas, but the threat still lingered, a shadow lurking just out of sight. The footage they carried was a ticking time bomb, and they needed to detonate it carefully, strategically. They needed a flight west as soon as possible.

"El Paso," she murmured, more to herself than to Vincent. A plan was forming, a way to use their pursuers' assumptions against them. El Paso. A city on the border, a place where they could blend in, disappear amongst the flow of people crossing back and forth between countries. A perfect red herring.

Elizabeth finished her calls, a sense of purpose settling over her. She looked over at Vincent, his face relaxed in sleep, the gentle rise and fall of his chest the only sign of life in the quiet room. A wave of tenderness washed over her, a stark contrast to the adrenaline that had been coursing through her veins for days. She kneeled beside him, gently brushing a stray lock of hair from his forehead.

"Vin," she whispered, her voice soft. "We need to move."

He stirred, his eyes fluttering open. He looked at her, a question in his gaze.

"El Paso," she explained, her voice low. "It's our next stop."

He sat up, a flicker of understanding in his eyes. He reached for her hand, his grip firm. "Let's go, then."

* * *

In the dim glow of the early morning, Vincent and Elizabeth settled into the backseat of the cab, the hum of the engine a low, steady rhythm beneath them. Vincent leaned back against the seat, eyes heavy with fatigue, his hand resting limply on his injured ankle. Elizabeth watched him, her eyes filled with worry, but he gave her a small, reassuring nod, his gaze lingering on her as if gathering strength from her presence.

Outside, the city was just beginning to wake, streetlights casting long, sleepy shadows over quiet sidewalks and empty storefronts. The cab weaved through the early dawn, leaving behind the flickering neon lights and muted chatter of the city. The silence between them felt almost reverent, each of them lost in thoughts they weren't quite ready to voice.

As they neared the airport, Elizabeth reached over and covered his hand with hers, giving it a gentle squeeze. He turned to her, his exhaustion momentarily softened by a grateful smile. In that silent exchange, they both felt the weight of what lay ahead, knowing that this ride was the beginning of a journey that would test them both in ways they couldn't yet imagine.

Elizabeth walked close beside Vincent, supporting him as they wove through the crowded terminal toward their gate. He moved with a stiff, determined pace, his jaw clenched as he fought to keep the weight off his injured ankle. The pale, exhausted look in his eyes told her everything she needed to know—he was running out of time and strength.

She squeezed his hand, catching his gaze as she promised, "As soon as we land in El Paso, I'll get a car, and we'll drive the rest of the way to L.A. No more airports, no more layovers."

He gave her a weary smile, his voice barely a murmur. "I trust you, Liz."

As they settled into their seats on the flight, Vincent gestured toward

PROLOGUE: CHAOS IN CARACAS

the window with a faint smile, letting Elizabeth claim her spot. She nestled in beside him, taking his hand in a quiet gesture of support. She stared out the small window as Miami's coastline disappeared beneath the clouds. The weight of Vincent's hand in hers anchored her, a constant amid the turmoil of the past few days.

"Some unfinished business I need to handle in Texas," Vincent said, his voice low. "Don't worry about it. Might need to drop out of sight for a minute when we land."

She turned to study his face, noting the tension in his jaw. Before she could press him for details, he shifted in his seat and winced.

"Your boot's coming loose," Elizabeth said. "Let me fix it."

Vincent started to protest, but she was already bending down. As she reached for his laces, she noticed the dark stain spreading across the bandage. Blood had pooled around his ankle, seeping through the gauze that had been hastily applied during their escape. He shifted his foot and glanced over her shoulder.

"Fuck."

She kept her voice steady despite the concern tightening her chest. "This is bad, Vin."

"It'll hold until we land."

Elizabeth frowned as she carefully retied his boot, trying not to disturb the injury further. The blood worried her -it was too much, too fresh. Whatever he had planned in El Paso would have to wait. He needed medical attention, and soon. She straightened in her seat, still holding his hand. Vincent's eyes were closed, his breathing shallow. She watched him pretend to sleep, knowing he was trying to mask the pain. The façade might fool others, but not her. Not after all they'd been through together.

Elizabeth watched as the last rays of sunlight faded through the airplane window. Her thumb traced absent circles on Vincent's hand, still clasped in hers. The weight of the hard drive containing the footage pressed against her side, tucked safely in her jacket's hidden pocket.

"Ladies and gentlemen, we're beginning our descent into El Paso International Airport. Please return your seats to their upright position and ensure your tray tables are stowed."

She gently squeezed Vincent's hand. His eyes opened, dark with pain.

"Almost there," she said.

Vincent nodded, shifting in his seat. The movement caused him to grimace, and Elizabeth noticed fresh blood seeping through his boot. Her stomach clenched. They needed to find help fast. The plane touched down with a jolt, taxiing to their gate. Elizabeth gathered their minimal belongings, supporting Vincent as they made their slow way through the terminal. The evening air hit them like a wall of heat as they stepped outside.

She flagged down a taxi, helping Vincent into the backseat. As she slid in beside him, she noticed his face had grown pale, his skin clammy. The driver asked for their destination, but before Elizabeth could respond, Vincent leaned forward and muttered an address she didn't recognize.

"No." Elizabeth's voice cut through the humid evening air. "Take us to the nearest E.R.," she told the driver, her tone leaving no room for argument. She felt Vincent tense beside her.

"Liz, I told you -"

"You're bleeding through your boot, Vin." She kept her voice low but firm.

Vincent's jaw clenched, a muscle twitching beneath his skin. She recognized that look -the same stubborn determination that made him an excellent videographer could also make him impossible to reason with.

"The footage -" he started.

"Is safe." Elizabeth patted her jacket pocket. "But it won't matter if you lose that foot to infection."

The taxi merged into traffic, the lights of El Paso's downtown blurring past their window. Vincent slumped back against the seat, his resistance fading as the pain seemed to catch up with him. Elizabeth watched his face in the passing streetlights, noting the sheen of sweat on his forehead, the tight lines around his mouth.

She pulled out her phone, checking the time. They'd been running for nearly forty-eight hours straight. The adrenaline that had kept them going was wearing thin, but they couldn't rest. Not yet.

"Ten minutes," the driver announced, catching her eye in the rearview mirror.

Elizabeth nodded, her hand finding Vincent's in the darkness of the backseat. His fingers were cold, his grip weaker than usual. Whatever business he had planned to handle in El Paso would have to wait. The only thing on her mind was finding help for him as soon as possible.

2

Finding Refuge

Elizabeth paced the sterile hallway of Kincaid Medical Center, her gaze shifting between the closed door of Vincent's room and the bustling nurses' station. The harsh fluorescent lights cast a sickly pallor over her exhausted features. She ran a hand through her tangled hair, wincing as her fingers caught on a knot.

The events of the past few days played on a loop in her mind. Their narrow escape from Caracas, the tense flight to Bogotá, and the mad dash to Miami. They had thought they were in the clear. Now, here they were in El Paso, their journey interrupted by an unforeseen complication.

A doctor emerged from Vincent's room, clipboard in hand. Elizabeth adjusted her posture, feeling her heart pounding.

"Ms. Nelson?" the doctor asked, glancing at his notes.

Elizabeth nodded, her throat dry. "How is he?"

"Mr. Rivera has suffered very serious damage to his ankle," the doctor explained. "We've scheduled the surgery. He'll need to stay with us for at least five more days. Longer if there are complications—"

"Surgery? Are you sure?"

Elizabeth followed the doctor to a row of light panels mounted on the wall. Her stomach churned as he pulled out a dark film from a manila envelope.

"Since Mr. Rivera has authorized you as his medical proxy, I can show you the extent of his injury." The doctor clipped the x-ray to the panel and flipped a switch. Light illuminated the ghostly image of Vincent's ankle bones. "As you can see here, this is what we call a comminuted fracture."

Elizabeth leaned closer, her eyes tracing the spiderweb of fracture lines across the bones. Multiple fragments, like pieces of a broken puzzle, scattered through the joint. Her chest tightened at the sight.

"The impact shattered the bone into several pieces," the doctor continued, using his pen to point out the worst areas. "Here, and here. The displacement is significant."

Elizabeth's fingers pressed against the cool surface of the light panel, as if she could somehow reach through and piece the bones back together. The image brought back flashes of their escape -Vincent's stumble as they rushed through the Miami airport, the way he'd tried to hide his pain until he couldn't anymore.

"Without surgery," the doctor said, "these fragments won't heal properly. The risk of chronic pain and limited mobility would be substantial."

Elizabeth nodded, forcing herself to look away from the x-ray. The magnitude of Vincent's injury made their situation even more complicated. They couldn't run anymore - not with his ankle in pieces. She struggled to process the medical terminology as the doctor continued his explanation. Her tired mind latched onto fragments of information, trying to piece them together but with no luck.

"Think of it like this," the doctor said, pulling out an X-ray and holding it up to the light. "Mr. Rivera's ankle bone didn't just break - it shattered into multiple pieces. Like dropping a ceramic plate on concrete."

"But he was walking on it," she protested weakly.

"Adrenaline is a powerful painkiller," the doctor explained. "And sometimes these injuries don't immediately show their full severity. The swelling and pain he experienced were warning signs, but without an X-ray, there was no way to know the extent of the damage."

He tucked the X-ray away. "Without surgery to realign these bone fragments properly, he risks permanent disability. We'll need to use pins and plates to hold everything in place while it heals."

Elizabeth wrapped her arms around herself, suddenly cold despite the warm hospital air. "And recovery time?"

"The surgery itself is just the beginning. He'll need extensive rehabilitation afterward - physical therapy, exercises, the works. We're looking at a minimum of six weeks before he can put any weight on that ankle. Longer for the PT."

Elizabeth's stomach dropped. Six weeks. Their story couldn't wait that long. She forced herself to focus on the doctor's words.

"Can I see him?" she asked, already moving toward the door.

The doctor nodded. "Of course. He's a bit groggy from the pain medication, but he's awake."

Elizabeth slipped into the room, her eyes immediately finding Vincent. He lay propped up in the hospital bed, his right leg elevated and encased in a bulky white bandage. His face was pale, dark circles under his eyes portraying his exhaustion.

"Hey," Vincent croaked, managing a weak smile.

Elizabeth crossed the room in three quick strides, sinking into the chair beside his bed. "Hey yourself," she replied, her voice thick with emotion. "How're you feeling?"

Vincent grimaced. "Like I picked a fight with a cement truck and lost." He paused, his eyes searching her face. "The footage?"

Elizabeth patted her bag, feeling the reassuring weight of the memory card and camera pack inside. "Safe," she confirmed, her voice low and urgent. "But Vincent, you can't stay here. It's too exposed."

Her eyes glanced toward the door, then back to Vincent's pale face. The adrenaline from their earlier escape still pulsed through her veins, like liquid fire, making her heart pound in her chest. The sterile hospital room suddenly felt like a trap, its white walls closing in around them with an oppressive weight. The harsh fluorescent lights buzzed overhead, casting stark shadows that seemed to dance and flicker with each passing moment. She knew they had to move, and soon, but the sight of Vincent's injured leg, swathed in bandages and propped up on a pillow, made her stomach clench with worry. The steady beep of the heart monitor beside his bed only served to heighten her anxiety, each sound a reminder of how precarious their situation truly was. Elizabeth's fingers twitched nervously at her side as she fought the urge to grab Vincent and run, knowing that any hasty movement could worsen his condition.

Elizabeth's mind raced, trying to find a solution to their predicament. She knew they couldn't risk moving Vincent, but staying put felt equally dangerous. She leaned in close, her voice barely above a whisper.

"Alright, look. We need to stay here, just for now. At least until you're stable enough to move. Maybe a month or so."

He started to protest, but she cut him off with a gentle squeeze of his hand. "I know it's not ideal, but we don't have much choice. I'll figure something out."

Vincent's eyes searched her face, then he nodded reluctantly. "Okay, Liz. I trust you."

Elizabeth stood, determination setting her jaw. "I'll be right back."

She strode out of the room, her eyes scanning the hallway until she spotted a nurse. "Excuse me," Elizabeth called out, her voice steady despite her nerves. "I need to speak with someone about staying here with my partner."

The nurse, a middle-aged woman with kind eyes, looked at her quizzically. "Visiting hours end at 8 PM, ma'am."

Elizabeth shook her head. "No, you don't understand. I need to stay overnight. In his room."

The nurse's expression softened. "I'm sorry, but that's not typically allowed-"

"Please," Elizabeth interrupted, her voice cracking slightly. "He's been through a traumatic experience. I'm all he has right now. I can't leave him alone."

The nurse hesitated, then sighed. "Let me speak with the doctor on call."

Elizabeth waited anxiously, her fingers drumming against her thigh. After what felt like an eternity, the nurse returned with a doctor.

"Ms. Nelson?" the doctor asked. Elizabeth nodded. "I understand you want to stay with Mr. Rivera overnight. While it's not standard protocol, given the circumstances, we can make an exception."

Relief washed over Elizabeth. "Thank you," she breathed.

"We'll have an extra bed brought in," the nurse added. "But please understand, this is a temporary arrangement. Short term."

Elizabeth nodded gratefully, already planning their next move. She returned to Vincent's room, a small smile on her face.

"Good news," she said, settling back into the chair beside him. "I'm bunking here tonight."

Vincent's eyebrows shot up. "How did you manage that?"

Elizabeth shrugged, a hint of her usual spark returning to her eyes. "I can be persuasive when I need to be."

As an orderly wheeled in another bed, Elizabeth felt some of the tension leave her body. They weren't out of danger yet, but at least for tonight, they were together. But she couldn't shake the feeling of unease that clung to her like a second skin. Even with Vincent safely tucked away in his hospital bed and her own temporary accommodations secured, her instincts screamed that they were far from safe.

She paced the small room, her eyes constantly checking the door, the window, and back to Vincent's sleeping form. The weight of the memory cards and camera pack in her bag felt heavier with each passing moment, a constant reminder of the dangerous information they carried.

As she settled onto the edge of her makeshift bed, Elizabeth's mind retraced the events that had led them here. The clandestine meetings in Caracas, the whispered confessions of corruption at the highest levels, the heart-stopping chase through the city streets. They had uncovered a story so explosive, so far-reaching, that powerful people would stop at nothing to keep it buried.

Her gaze lingered on Vincent's face, softened in sleep, and a wave of protectiveness washed over her. They had started this journey years ago as colleagues, but somewhere along the way, amidst the danger and adrenaline, something had shifted. Elizabeth felt her heart quicken at the thought, a mixture of excitement and fear.

A soft knock at the door made her jump. She tensed, her hand instinctively reaching for her bag. The door creaked open, revealing a night nurse with a gentle smile.

"Just checking in," the nurse whispered. "Everything okay?"

Elizabeth nodded, forcing a smile. "Yes, thank you."

As the door closed, she let out a shaky breath. Every interaction, no matter how innocent, felt like a potential threat. She knew their pursuers had resources, connections. How long before they traced them to El Paso? To this very hospital?

Elizabeth moved to the window, peering out at the dimly lit parking lot below. The shadows seemed to writhe and shift, hiding potential dangers. She pressed her forehead against the cool glass, closing her eyes for a moment. When she opened them, her gaze met Vincent's in the reflection. He was awake, watching her with concern.

"Liz," he said softly, his voice still rough with sleep. "Come here."

She turned, drawn to him like a magnet. As she perched on the edge of his bed, Vincent reached out, his fingers intertwining with hers.

"We've been through a lot together," he murmured, his thumb tracing circles on her palm. "Whatever comes next, I can handle it. Don't you worry about me."

Elizabeth felt some of the tension leave her body at his touch, at the warmth in his eyes. She knew the danger was still out there, lurking beyond the hospital walls. But in that moment, with Vincent's hand in hers, she allowed herself to believe that maybe, just maybe, they stood a chance.

She walked over to close the door, her eyes scanning the dimly lit corridor outside Vincent's room. The nurses' station, usually a hub of activity, stood eerily quiet. Only a single nurse hunched over paperwork, the harsh glow of a computer screen illuminating her tired face.

As the minutes ticked by, Elizabeth realized just how deserted this wing of the hospital seemed. No squeaking wheels of medicine carts, no hushed conversations between staff members, not even the distant echo of footsteps. The silence was almost oppressive, broken only by the steady beep of Vincent's heart monitor and the occasional rustle of sheets as he shifted in his sleep.

She moved away from the door, padding softly across the room. The extra bed they'd brought in for her looked more inviting by the minute, but Elizabeth couldn't shake her vigilance. She perched on its edge, her gaze alternating between Vincent's sleeping form and the closed door.

As the night wore on, the absence of any hospital staff became more apparent. No routine checks, no night rounds. It was as if they'd been forgotten in this corner of the medical center. The realization should have set Elizabeth's nerves on edge, but instead, a strange sense of calm settled over her.

This wasn't a bustling hospital room anymore. It felt more like a private sanctuary, a hidden pocket of safety in the midst of their chaotic flight. The privacy afforded by the short-staffed night shift was an unexpected blessing. Here, in this quiet bubble, they could breathe, plan, and recover without constant interruptions or prying eyes.

Elizabeth allowed herself a small smile as she sank back onto her bed. For the first time since they'd fled Caracas, she felt like they might actually have a moment to catch their breath. The hospital room had transformed into an unexpected haven, more akin to a secluded hotel suite than a medical facility. She reached across and took his hand.

Her hand felt small within Vincent's grasp, her slender fingers enveloped by his rough, calloused palm. The contact was a fleeting moment of calm amidst the tempest that had swept them from Caracas to this sterile hospital room in El Paso. The room felt miles away from their worries. The rhythmic beep of the heart monitor, the sterile scent of antiseptic, the pale moonlight filtering through the window—it all conspired to create a strange sense of peace. But Elizabeth's inner world was a maelstrom.

Despite the pain medication clouding his senses, whenever Vincent's dark eyes focused on her there was an intensity that made her pulse quicken. Even weak and hurt, his face pale and drawn, he was still the sexiest man she knew. His brow ridged as he slept, his chest rising and falling in the rhythmic cadence of breath. The way his temple dipped as if carved by some Greek sculptor–even unconscious, that grace shone through like an Aztec king. It wasn't just a rugged, broad-shouldered kind of sexy. It was the way he moved, how his dark eyes held such a hidden depth, how the music of his voice could soothe a screaming asylum. He was like a finely tuned instrument, all vibration and hidden notes.

The few nights they'd spent together, she hadn't been able to fight the pull. Each lingering look, every touch, ignited a fire in her that threatened to consume her. It was always a battle of wills, Elizabeth struggling to maintain control while Vincent effortlessly drew her in. And she always lost. This time, the temptation to lean down, to brush a stray hair from his forehead, to feel his rough skin beneath her fingertips, was almost unbearable.

But he was vulnerable now, broken in a way that made her stomach twist. She couldn't even imagine what he'd been through. And she didn't want to marvel at his captivating features while their lives were precariously balanced on a knife's edge. She needed a plan to get them out of danger. Out of El Paso.

"Vincent?" Elizabeth whispered, but he didn't stir. She traced the line of his jaw with her thumb, his skin warm beneath her touch. His eyes fluttered open and locked with hers, a glimmer of longing in their depths.

"Come here," he whispered, his voice a low rumble that seemed to vibrate through her. He pulled her closer. She hesitated, her gaze flickering to the door and then back to him. The rational part of her brain screamed caution, reminding her of their risky situation, the dangers that lurked beyond the hospital walls. But her body ached with a need that she couldn't suppress, a hunger that only Vincent could sate.

With a resigned sigh, Elizabeth leaned in, her face inches from his. His breath was warm against her skin, stirring the loose strands of hair that framed her face.

"What?" she breathed, a plea and a surrender wrapped in a single word.

In response, Vincent reached up, his hand gently cupping the back of her neck, his fingers tangling in her hair. He pulled her closer, his lips brushing against hers in a kiss that was both tender and demanding. Elizabeth's resolve crumbled under the heat of his embrace. She pressed herself against him, the cool, impersonal fabric of the hospital gown a stark contrast to the burning heat of his skin. Her hands roamed over his chest, tracing the contours of his muscles, the terrain of his body eliciting a wave of desire that left her dizzy.

Vincent's good leg wrapped around hers, anchoring her to him as their kiss deepened. The world outside their small bubble of need and urgency ceased to exist. All that mattered was the taste of his mouth, the insistent pressure of his lips, the quiet groans of pleasure that escaped from deep within his chest.

His fingers fumbled with the hem of her shirt, slipping beneath the fabric to explore the soft skin of her lower back. Elizabeth shivered at his touch, her own hands sliding lower, tugging the edge of his gown, daring to venture beneath it.

As she watched him fight for his usual dominance, her heart throbbed in her chest. She pulled back slightly, studying Vincent's face in the soft light. His normal commanding presence was subdued by pain and medication. The tables had turned -tonight, she needed to be the protector, the strong one.

"Let me," she whispered, brushing her lips against his temple. Her fingers traced gentle patterns across his chest, mindful of his injuries.

Vincent's breath hitched as he tried to shift position, a grimace crossing his features. "Kitten, I -"

"Shhh." Elizabeth pressed a finger to his lips. "Just rest. You're always taking care of me. It's my turn now."

His dark eyes met hers, vulnerability mixing with trust in their depths. It was a side of Vincent she rarely saw -this willingness to relinquish control, to let someone else lead. Her heart swelled with tenderness. She cradled his face between her palms, drinking in every detail: the scar above his eyebrow, the slight stubble along his jaw, the way his breath fluttered beneath her fingertips.

"I've got you," she murmured, and meant it with every fiber of her being.

Vincent relaxed under her touch, surrendering to her care. Elizabeth felt the shift in their dynamic like a tangible thing - delicate yet powerful. She would be his anchor tonight, his safe harbor in the storm.

She was grateful for the trust he placed in her and took a deep breath, removing her jeans slowly, letting them form a pile at her feet. With a tender smile, she climbed onto the bed, aligning their bodies. The palpable tension between them made her shiver with excitement as she leaned forward, ready to claim him. She reached for the hem of Vincent's hospital gown, her fingers grazing against his skin with a feather-light touch as she eased it up, inch by inch, exposing more of his sculpted torso.

"Oh my god," she breathed, her eyes drinking in every detail revealed to her hungry gaze. His chest was a tapestry of scars and bruises, the marks telling a silent story of the ordeal he'd endured. A jagged line marred his left pectoral muscle, still pink and raw, while deeper purple blooming along his ribcage spoke of cruel blows.

She traced each mark with reverent fingers, mapping the topography of pain he'd suffered. Vincent hissed softly through clenched teeth as her touch brushed over particularly sensitive areas but didn't pull away. Elizabeth knew that for him to let her see this side of himself -vulnerable and marked -was an offering in itself.

"I'm sorry," she whispered, pressing gentle kisses along the path cleared by her fingertips. "I'm so damn sorry." Tears pricked at the corners of her eyes, but she blinked them back fiercely. She needed to focus on him now, not dwell on what they'd both been through.

With agonizing slowness, Elizabeth worked Vincent free from the confining fabric. She tugged it up and over his head in one smooth motion before letting it fall to join her jeans on the floor with a soft rustle.

Vincent lay before her then, bared except for a thin sheet draped across his hips. The light filtering through the window painted long shadows down his body and Elizabeth swallowed hard around a sudden thickness in her throat. She wanted nothing more than to taste him right then -all that beautiful skin just waiting for her mouth and hands to explore. Her palms skittered over his chest once more before trailing lower, tracing abs honed from years spent behind a camera.

"Kitten..." Vincent groaned when she reached the waistband of his boxers. The heat in his gaze matched the flush appearing high across his cheekbones despite how pale he remained otherwise.

"Shhh." Elizabeth leaned forward until their foreheads touched and breathed him in deeply. "Let me take care of you."

His free hand grasped her hip and squeezed almost desperately even as he nodded mutely at her words. That small show of trust made something inside Elizabeth twist almost painfully tight with an emotion so sharp it felt like its own form of ache. Her unsteady fingers caught in the waistband of those troublesome boxers next, yanking them down to settle around Vincent's thighs. As the cool air caressed his newly bared flesh, he stirred restlessly but remained still when Elizabeth grazed her nails over it once more.

Elizabeth felt her heart pounding as she looked down at Vincent, her breath catching in her throat. The sight of him beneath her, his body a map of scars and injuries, filled her with a mixture of emotions -desire, concern, and a deep-seated need to protect him. His dark eyes watched her from beneath heavy lids, the usual intensity softened by the pain medication but still filled with unmistakable heat.

She took a moment to appreciate the sight before her -Vincent's strong shoulders tapering down to lean hips, his chest rising and falling with each shallow breath. And nestled between his muscular thighs, his arousal jutted proudly against the white sheet, a silent testament to the effect she had on him even in this state.

"Liz," he rasped out her name. His hand came up to cup the back of her neck, fingers threading into her hair as he pulled her down for another searing kiss. She melted into it willingly enough but made herself pull back after only a moment.

"Slowly," she breathed against his parted lips. "We have all night."

The words sent a visible shiver through Vincent's body and when he opened his eyes again, they were so dark with lust they looked almost black. "You're killing me, Nelson." he groaned a second later.

Elizabeth stifled a moan as his hand grazed her hip before gliding up underneath the bunched fabric of her shirt, which had crept higher to expose more of her bare thighs.

"I said I'd take care of you." Her teeth grazed his lower lip before she drew back, her tongue gliding over the spot to ease the ache as she shifted until their chests no longer met.

"Come on." He bucked hips up into hers and Elizabeth gasped outright at the sudden pressure along her already throbbing center. The evidence of what she did to him made her insides clench hard in answering response.

She ignored it in favor reaching between their bodies instead. She felt her cheeks flush as she traced her fingers along the ridges and valleys of the seemingly endless tattoo that wound its way down Vincent's body. Despite the heat rising within her, she was captivated by the intricate artwork and the stories it told of Vincent's past. Her fingers danced along Vincent's body, tracing the lines of his tattoos and scars. The intricate designs seemed to tell a story of their own, each marking a piece of his history that she longed to explore further. She leaned down, her lips brushing against the inked skin as she mapped the contours of his chest.

"Oh, fuck," Vincent exhaled, his voice husky with need. His hand tangled in her hair, urging her lower. "Lizzz—."

Elizabeth smiled against his skin, reveling in the power she held over him in this moment. Slowly, she trailed kisses down his abdomen, her tongue darting out to taste the salt-sweat mixture that clung to him. Vincent's stomach clenched beneath her touch, a silent testament to the desire building within him.

She paused at his hip bone, nipping gently before soothing the sting with a soft lick. His hips jerked up involuntarily and Elizabeth hummed in approval. "Patience," she murmured as she pushed herself up until they were face to face once more. Vincent's dark eyes met hers, pupils blown wide with lust and a hint of pain from the strain on his injuries. She cupped his cheek tenderly before leaning in for another deep kiss.

As their tongues tangled together, Elizabeth shifted until she was straddling him fully. The heat of him pressed insistently against her. She had to bite back a moan at the sensation. Breaking away from the kiss with a soft gasp, she reached between their bodies again. Vincent bucked into her touch as soon as her fingers made contact with his arousal and he hissed through gritted teeth. "Fuck."

"You said that already," Elizabeth teased breathlessly as she stroked him from base to tip.

He growled low in response but remained still otherwise as she continued exploring him with reverent touches. The feel of velvet skin stretched tight over steel beneath it had her clenching around nothing in anticipation.

When Vincent tugged impatiently at her shirt next, it didn't take much encouragement for Elizabeth to pull it off herself instead and let it fall carelessly onto the growing pile of clothes on the floor behind them.

"Damn." His curse turned into something unintelligible when Elizabeth arched her back for him after letting go, so he could get a good look at her newly bared breasts before leaning forward again.

His uninjured hand cupped one breast while his fingers toyed with the other, the aching tightness of her nipples intensifying under his touch until they throbbed with equal parts longing and exquisite ache.

"Yes, Kitten," he moaned once he had thoroughly mapped out each contour and hollow with his fingers and lips.

Elizabeth's breath hitched as Vincent's hand slid up her back, his fingers gripping her hair into a tight fist. The heat of his gaze made her skin prickle with desire. She arched into his touch, the aching tightness of her nipples intensifying under the friction of his tongue.

"Tell me what you want," she breathed, her lips brushing against his temple.

Vincent's eyes darkened with lust and something else -a vulnerability that made Elizabeth's heart ache. He cupped her face between his palms, holding her gaze steady, his breath hot against her mouth. "I want to make you forget everything but my name."

She shivered at the promise in his words, her core clenching with need. "And how do you plan on doing that?" Elizabeth teased, tracing the line of his jaw with one finger.

His teeth grazed her lower lip before he nipped it sharply enough to sting. "Slowly."

With deliberate slowness, he trailed kisses along her jawline and down the column of Elizabeth's throat while one hand kneaded a breast almost reverently. Elizabeth wove her fingers through his hair, anchoring him as she directed him downward. Her other hand guided him until his breath caressed a hardened bud. His tongue flicked out languidly at first, lapping gently before enveloping the sensitive peak in searing wetness.

"Vin -" Elizabeth broke off into a fractured moan as he bit down just hard enough to send sparks shooting through nerves already raw with need. She relished the tender relief as he eased her throbbing need with soft, wet strokes of his lips, gradually moving across the valley between her breasts to lavish attention on its neglected twin. The exquisite sensations sent molten heat coursing through her core, causing her inner muscles to tighten around emptiness and driving her hips up in instinctive search for that deep pleasure.

Elizabeth's breath caught as Vincent positioned himself at her entrance, the blunt head of his arousal nudging insistently against her slick folds. She braced herself on his shoulders, her fingers digging into firm muscle as she raised her hips slightly.

The first few inches of him filled her so perfectly it stole the air from her lungs -a delicious stretch that had her biting down hard on her lower lip to keep from crying out in equal parts pleasure and pain. Her eyes fluttered shut at the sensation of being opened up so thoroughly. "Vin." She breathed his name like a vapor when he rolled his hips shallowly instead of pushing further inside. The friction sent sparks shooting through already over-sensitized nerves.

"Hmm?" His murmur was accompanied by another tiny flex of his hips, barely more than a tease but enough to have Elizabeth squirming down onto him with desperate need.

She opened her glazed eyes to meet his dark pupils blown wide with lust. "I want-." Elizabeth swallowed hard around a suddenly dry throat and tried again when words failed her the first time around. "I need you to-"

"Shh." Vincent cupped one ass cheek while the other hand came up to anchor on her hip bone before tugging both down forcefully onto his arousal. He didn't let her adjust for more than a heartbeat before starting up a slow, torturous roll of his hips, pulling almost all the way out only to plunge back in deeply.

"Oh, fuck," she gasped, her nails digging crescent shapes into his skin as he drove himself deep inside her.

Vincent grunted his appreciation through gritted teeth as he adjusted the angle of his hips, his next thrust striking that perfect spot just behind her pelvis.

Her sob echoed through the room as over and over, he sped up until all she could do was cling to him fiercely and meet his momentum with frantic passion. She forced her heavy lids open, molten heat pouring over her skin as they watched each other, lost in the escalating heat.

A sharp hiss of pain tore from Vincent's throat, the sound a sobering reminder of his injury. Elizabeth pulled back instantly, her eyes wide with concern.

"Sorry," she gasped, her hands retreating as if scorched. "I forgot -"

Vincent shook his head, his eyes shining with determination. "Don't apologize," he said, his voice gruff with unspent desire. "Just... be careful with me, Kitten."

That nickname, tenderly spoken in the heat of passion, made something inside Elizabeth melt. She nodded, her movements slow and deliberate as she resumed her exploration, mindful of his bandages and the tender flesh around them.

They found a new rhythm, a dance of desire tempered by the reality of their situation. Each touch, each kiss, was a silent promise, a declaration of trust and shared strength. In that moment, they were not a foreign correspondent and her videographer, not two people on the run from powerful enemies. They were simply Elizabeth and Vincent, two halves of a fractured whole, seeking solace and connection in the shadow of uncertainty.

The roughness of his skin against hers sent shivers down her spine. She could feel his warm breath against her neck, and the gentle brushing of his beard against her cheek sent tingles down her arms.

She closed her eyes, focusing on the sensations washing over her.

As their bodies moved together, the sounds of the hospital—the distant chimes of call buttons, the hushed whispers of night staff—faded into the background, replaced by the symphony of their own making. The beep of Vincent's heart monitor kept time with the beating of their hearts, a steady drumbeat that underscored their quiet surrender to the moment.

The need for silence added an edge of intensity to their lovemaking, every moan caught behind clenched teeth, every gasp muffled against the other's skin. They were a tangle of limbs and heated whispers, a testament to the depth of their connection, the unspoken understanding that had grown between them over countless shared adventures and narrow escapes.

As their passionate dance continued, Elizabeth felt the tension coiling tighter and tighter within Vincent's body. His breathing became more ragged, his grip on her hips almost painful. She knew he was close, and a surge of tenderness welled up inside her.

"Let go," she whispered in his ear, her voice barely audible above the soft rustle of the sheets and the hum of the hospital machinery. "I've got you."

Vincent's response was a hoarse groan, but she felt him relax infinitesimally beneath her, as if her words had given him the permission he needed to release. His hips bucked once, twice more, and then he stilled, his entire body tensing as he reached his climax.

Elizabeth felt a wave of relief wash over her, grateful for the momentary peace that had settled upon Vincent. His willingness to yield, if only for a fleeting moment, carried a significance beyond words. As their breaths steadied and pulses returned to normal, Elizabeth pushed aside the pang of longing that she hadn't experienced her own orgasm. In this fleeting instant, it held no significance. Besides, there would be other opportunities—safer, quieter moments—when they could lose themselves in each other.

As the night wore on, their movements slowed, the urgency giving way to a languid, bittersweet tenderness. They clung to each other, the bond between them solidifying with each passing second, each shared breath. Finally, with the first hints of dawn creeping through the blinds, they lay spent and sated, their bodies cocooned in the narrow hospital bed. Elizabeth's head rested on Vincent's chest, the steady thrum of his heart a soothing lullaby that lured her toward sleep.

He stroked her hair, his fingers tracing idle patterns on her scalp. "We're going to get through this," he murmured, the conviction in his voice resonating in the silent room, deposited into the depths of her heart. Elizabeth closed her eyes, allowing herself to believe his words, if only for tonight. With the warmth of Vincent's body beside her mixed with the musky scent of their shared passion, she drifted into a restless sleep, the echoes of their intimacy lingering in the air like a promise of hope and resilience.

3

Homeward Bound

Elizabeth stepped out of Vincent's room, wheeling the breakfast cart just outside the door. She glanced up and down the quiet hospital corridor before slipping into a small waiting area. Her fingers trembled as she pulled out her burner phone, dialing a number she knew by heart.

"New York Citizen, this is Fred Stein," a gruff voice answered.

"Fred, it's Elizabeth Nelson," she said, keeping her voice low. "I've got something big."

There was a pause on the other end. "Liz? Jesus, where have you been? There are rumors you've gone missing in Venezuela."

"It's a long story," Elizabeth replied, her eyes darting to the door. "But I've uncovered something huge. It's the story of a lifetime, Fred."

She could almost hear Fred leaning forward in his chair. "I'm listening."

Elizabeth took a deep breath. "I can't say much over the phone, but it involves top government officials, multinational corporations, and a cover-up that spans continents. We've got video evidence, documents, everything."

"We?" Fred questioned.

"Vincent Rivera and I," Elizabeth explained. "He's... injured. We're laying low for now."

Fred was silent for a moment. "This sounds dangerous, Liz. Are you sure about this?"

"More sure than I've ever been about anything," she said firmly. "But we need protection, Fred. And resources to get this story out before they can bury it."

"Okay," Fred said, his voice taking on a determined edge. "Here's what we'll do. I'm sending a secure courier to you. Don't tell me where you are over the phone. Text the address to this number." He rattled off a string of digits.

Elizabeth quickly jotted it down. "And then?"

"Send copies of everything you have with the courier. Keep the originals safe. Once we verify your information, we'll move you both to a secure location and start working on the story."

Elizabeth felt a wave of relief wash over her. "Thank you, Fred."

"Don't thank me yet," he warned. "This isn't going to be easy. But if what you're saying is true—"

"It is." she said.

As Elizabeth ended the call, she felt a potent cocktail of emotions swirling within her -fear and exhilaration chief among them. Her heart raced, and her palms were slick with nervous sweat. They were one step closer to breaking the story, a realization that sent a thrill of excitement through her. Yet, she couldn't shake the nagging dread that settled in the pit of her stomach. The most dangerous part of their journey was just beginning, and Elizabeth knew that from this moment on, every move they made could mean the difference between exposing the truth and becoming another silenced voice. She took a deep breath, steeling herself for what lay ahead, acutely aware that the path they'd chosen was as treacherous as it was necessary. Her fingers trembled slightly as she reached for her notebook. The familiar feel of pen and paper grounded her, reminding her of why she had become a journalist in the first place -to uncover the stories that needed to be told, no matter the cost.

Elizabeth leaned against the hospital wall, her mind winding back to the chaotic streets of Caracas. The acrid smell of tear gas and burning rubber filled her nostrils, a phantom memory so vivid she could almost feel it. She closed her eyes, letting the flashbacks wash over her.

It had started innocently enough. A tip from a local activist about unusual health issues in a small village near an oil refinery. Elizabeth and Vincent had driven out there, expecting to find a simple story about corporate negligence. What they uncovered was far more sinister.

The village was a wasteland. Children with rashes and respiratory problems played in muddy streets, while adults spoke in hushed tones about mysterious illnesses. Elizabeth remembered the haunted look in one mother's eyes as she cradled her sickly infant.

"We've tried to speak out," the woman had said, her voice barely above a whisper. "But they silence us. Always."

Their investigation led them to a labyrinth of shell companies and offshore accounts. Multinational corporations were not just ignoring environmental regulations; they were actively suppressing information about the devastation they were causing.

Elizabeth's hands clenched as she recalled their confrontation with a corporate representative. The man's smile had been shark-like, his threat, thinly veiled.

"Ms. Nelson," he had said, his voice dripping with false cordiality. "I'd hate to see such a talented journalist meet with an unfortunate accident. Perhaps it's time you found a new story to pursue."

But they had pressed on, gathering testimonies, collecting water samples, and filming the environmental destruction. Each piece of evidence felt like a ticking time bomb in their possession.

The night of the riot, everything had come to a head. The roar of the crowd was still echoing in Elizabeth's ears, and the feel of countless bodies pressing against her lingered, a reminder of the chaos she had just escaped. They had been so close to their safe house when a group of men in unmarked vehicles had cut them off. Her heart raced as she relived the harrowing moments of their escape from Caracas. The memory of Vincent's quick thinking and her own desperate scramble for safety sent a shiver down her spine. They had barely made it out alive, their precious evidence clutched tightly to their chests.

Now, standing in the hallway of the hospital, Elizabeth felt the impact of their discoveries weighing down on her. She glanced back toward Vincent's room, a mix of emotions swirling within her. The moment of intimacy offered a temporary escape from the danger that still loomed over them, but it had also complicated things in ways she wasn't quite ready to confront.

She pulled out her phone again, her fingers hovering over the keypad. The number Fred had given her seemed to taunt her, a lifeline and a risk all at once. She knew that sending their location, even through secure channels, could potentially expose them. But what choice did they have?

With a deep breath, she began to type out the address of the hospital. Her mind scrolled through contingency plans, trying to anticipate every possible outcome. Would the courier be intercepted? Could they trust Fred completely? What if their enemies had already infiltrated the *New York Citizen*?

As she hit send, Elizabeth felt a rush of determination. They had come too far to back down now. The truth they had uncovered was too important, the lives at stake too numerous. Whatever came next, she knew they had to see this through.

Elizabeth pocketed the phone and made her way back to Vincent's room, her steps quiet but purposeful. They would need to be ready to move at a moment's notice. As she pushed open the door, she steeled herself for the challenges ahead, knowing that the real fight was only just beginning.

As she glanced at her companion, their eyes met in a silent exchange of determination and apprehension. They both understood the gravity of their situation, the potential consequences that loomed on the horizon. Elizabeth's mind filled with possible scenarios, contingency plans forming and dissolving with each passing second. She knew that from here on out, every shadow could hide a threat, every friendly face could potentially mask an enemy. The thrill of the chase mingled with a cold dread in her gut, creating a hurricane of emotions that threatened to overwhelm her. But she pushed it all down, focusing instead on the task at hand. They had come too far to turn back now, and the truth they sought was worth any risk they might face.

Elizabeth's phone buzzed, startling her from her thoughts. She glanced at the screen, her brow furrowing at the unfamiliar number. Cautiously, she opened the message.

> **Liz! It's Stacy. I got a new number.**
> **And you'll never guess what happened - I'm getting married!**
> **Please tell me you can come back to Sweetwater Springs for the wedding.**
> **I need my best friend here ASAP!**
> **Love you girl!**

Elizabeth's heart skipped a beat. Stacy Harris, her best friend since childhood, was getting married. For a moment, the weight of her current situation lifted, replaced by a flood of memories from their small Ohio town. Lazy summer days by the river, homecoming dances, late-night confidences shared over milkshakes at the local diner.

She stared at the message, her thumb hovering over the reply button. The idea of returning to Sweetwater Springs, of stepping back into a world that now seemed so far removed from her current reality, was both tempting and ridiculous.

Elizabeth glanced at Vincent as he drifted in and out of sleep. Their situation was uncertain, the danger far from over. How could she even consider leaving now, when they were in the middle of the biggest story of their careers? When their lives might still be at risk?

But Stacy's words tugged at her heart. "I need my best friend here!" Elizabeth could almost hear Stacy's voice, filled with excitement and a touch of pleading. She thought of all the milestones they had shared, the promises they had made to always be there for each other.

With a sigh, Elizabeth began to type a response, her fingers hesitating over each word. She wanted nothing more than to be there for Stacy's big day, to celebrate with her friend and forget, even for a day, the madness that had become her life. Elizabeth grappled with articulating her thoughts as the gravity of her decisions weighed heavily on her. The life she had left behind in Ohio seemed like a distant dream, a universe apart from the risky reporting and global intrigue she'd become entangled in. Yet Stacy's message served as a poignant reminder of the connections and relationships she had sacrificed in pursuit of her career.

Elizabeth's fingers froze over the phone screen again, her heart torn between duty and friendship. After a long moment of internal struggle, she began to type:

Stacy! Congratulations!
I'm so happy for you.
Of course I'll be there for your big day.

Wouldn't miss it for the world.
Can't wait to see you and catch up.
Love you too!

She hit Send before she could second-guess herself. A mix of emotions washed over her -excitement at the prospect of seeing her best friend, guilt at potentially putting her mission at risk, and a hint of fear at the dangers that might follow her back to Sweetwater Springs.

Elizabeth glanced at Vincent, still sleeping peacefully. She'd have to tell him about this new development, figure out how to make it work with their current situation. But for now, she allowed herself a small smile, remembering happier times with Stacy in their hometown.

She began to formulate a plan in her mind. They'd need to be careful, of course. Perhaps they could use this as an opportunity to throw off anyone who might be tracking them. A small town in Ohio would be the last place their pursuers would expect them to go. Elizabeth's thoughts were interrupted by a soft groan from Vincent. She moved to his bedside, taking his hand in hers.

"Hey," she said softly as his eyes fluttered open. "How are you feeling? Fred's sending a courier."

Vincent managed a weak smile. "Good. Hey, did we do it last night? Or was I hallucinating?" His expression turned serious as he studied her face. "What's going on, Liz? You look… conflicted."

Elizabeth took a deep breath. "We need to talk about our next move. I think I might have found us a temporary safe haven. But it's going to complicate things."

She hesitated, unsure of how to explain the sudden change in plans to Vincent. She squeezed his hand gently, gathering her thoughts.

"My best friend from back home is getting married," she began, her voice low. "She wants me there for the wedding in Sweetwater Springs."

Vincent's eyebrows shot up. "Ohio? Liz, we can't just -"

"I know, I know," Elizabeth cut in, holding up a hand. "But hear me out. It might actually be the perfect cover. Who would expect us to go to a small town in the Midwest right now?"

Vincent frowned, considering her words. "It's risky," he said finally. "But you might have a point. We'd be hiding in plain sight."

Elizabeth nodded, relief washing over her. "Exactly. Plus, it gives us a chance to regroup, plan for our next assignment. We can't stay in this hospital forever."

"What about the courier Fred is sending?" Vincent said.

"We'll meet them before we leave," Elizabeth said. "Send off the copies, keep the originals with us. Once we're in Sweetwater Springs, we can figure out our next steps."

Vincent was quiet for a moment, his eyes searching Elizabeth's face. "This is important to you, isn't it? Going back for your friend's wedding?"

Elizabeth felt a lump form in her throat. "Yeah," she admitted softly. "It is. Stacy's been there for me through everything. I can't let her down now."

Vincent nodded, a small smile playing at the corners of his mouth. "Then we'll make it work. But Liz, we have to be careful. Our story, what we uncovered in Venezuela -it doesn't stop being dangerous just because we're in small-town Ohio."

"I know," Elizabeth said, her expression turning serious. "We'll be on high alert the whole time. No one can know the real reason we're there."

As they began to hash out the details of their plan, Elizabeth felt a mix of excitement and apprehension. Returning to Sweetwater Springs would be a risk, but it also offered a chance at normalcy, however brief. She just hoped they weren't making a terrible mistake.

A soft knock at the door interrupted their conversation. Dr. Rossi, a tall, slender man with kind eyes, entered the room, a clipboard in hand. He greeted Elizabeth and Vincent with a warm smile before turning his attention to the patient.

"Mr. Rivera, I have the results of your scans," he began, his voice calm and professional. "The good news is that the surgery to repair your injuries is relatively straightforward. However, the recovery process will be lengthy."

Vincent frowned, glancing at Elizabeth before turning back to the doctor. "How lengthy are we talking? I've got a plane to catch, Doc."

Dr. Rossi consulted his notes. "After the surgery, you'll need to undergo extensive physical therapy and rehabilitation. We're looking at a minimum of three to four months before you'll be able to travel safely."

Elizabeth's heart sank. *Four months.* The thought of being separated from Vincent for that long, especially now, was almost unbearable. She reached for his hand, intertwining their fingers. Vincent, however, seemed lost in thought. He turned to Elizabeth, his expression serious. "Liz, you have to go to Sweetwater Springs without me."

"What? No," Elizabeth protested immediately. "I'm not leaving you here alone."

"You have to," Vincent insisted, his voice firm. "Your friend needs you, and we can't put our lives on hold indefinitely. I'll join you as soon as I'm able, but you need to go now."

Elizabeth shook her head, tears welling at the corners of her eyes. "Vincent, I can't just leave you. What if something happens? What if they find you here?"

He squeezed her hand reassuringly. "I'll be okay, Liz. The hospital is secure, and I'll have Dr. Rossi and the staff looking out for me. But you need to go, to keep up appearances and throw off anyone who might be watching."

Dr. Rossi cleared his throat gently. "If I may, Ms. Nelson, Mr.

Rivera is right. The best thing for his recovery is to focus on his treatment here. And if you have obligations elsewhere, it's important that you attend to them. We'll take excellent care of him in your absence."

Elizabeth looked between the two men, torn. She knew they were right, that splitting up was the logical choice. But the thought of leaving Vincent behind, injured and vulnerable, tore at her heart.

Finally, she nodded, blinking back tears. "Okay," she whispered. "I'll go. But you have to promise me you'll stay safe, Vin. And that you'll come to Sweetwater as soon as you're able."

Vincent brought her hand to his lips, pressing a soft kiss to her knuckles. "I promise, Liz. Nothing will keep me from you."

She left the hospital room feeling weighed down, her mind filled with both plans and anxieties. She made her way to the designated meeting spot, a quiet corner of a nearby park, to rendezvous with Fred's courier.

Elizabeth's heart pounded in her chest as she neared the designated bench. A nondescript woman in a crisp gray suit stood up, her movements precise and controlled. Their eyes met, and the woman gave a subtle nod of recognition. Elizabeth felt a mixture of relief and apprehension wash over her as they exchanged a few predetermined phrases, their voices low and careful. The coded words rolled off their tongues with practiced ease, confirming their identities and the legitimacy of their clandestine meeting. She marveled at the bizarre reality of the moment -there she stood, in a secluded section of the green space, participating in what seemed like a scenario plucked from an espionage thriller.

"The package, please," the courier said, her voice low and businesslike.

Elizabeth handed over a sealed envelope containing copies of their evidence. Her hands trembled slightly as she relinquished the documents, acutely aware of the weight of what she was passing on.

"The Citizen will be in touch," the courier said, tucking the envelope into her briefcase. With that, she turned and walked away, disappearing into the crowd.

Elizabeth exhaled slowly, and pulled out her phone, her fingers hovering over the screen for a moment before she began to type. She sent Fred the hospital's information, providing him with a secure way to contact Vincent during her absence. Next, she checked the flights out of El Paso through the closest airport.

Finally, she opened her conversation with Stacy. Elizabeth's heart clenched as she thought about her best friend's excitement and the complicated situation she was walking into. She typed out a message:

> **Hey Stacy! Just booked my ticket.**
> **I'll be arriving in Sweetwater Springs next Tuesday.**
> **Can't wait to see you and hear all about the wedding plans!**
> **Love you!**

Elizabeth hit Send, then stared at the screen for a long moment. She was committed now. There was no turning back.

She made her way back to Vincent's room. The burden of their separation weighed heavily on her heart. The smell of antiseptic filled her nostrils as she pushed open the door.

Vincent lay propped up in bed, his dark eyes fixing on her the moment she entered. "How did it go?"

"Clean exchange. The courier got everything." Elizabeth crossed to his bedside, settling into the chair next to him. Her fingers found his, intertwining naturally. The warmth of his skin against hers, a gentle and familiar sensation, offered a small comfort in the midst of their worries.

"Good." Vincent's thumb traced circles on the back of her hand. "When's your flight?"

"Tuesday." She studied his face, memorizing every detail -the thick eyebrows, the scar above his left eye, the slight stubble darkening his jaw. "I still don't like leaving you here alone."

"Hey." Vincent's grip tightened on her hand. "I'll be fine, Kitten. Focus on your friend's wedding. Try to enjoy yourself a little."

Elizabeth managed a weak smile, but worry still gnawed at her insides. The thought of being states away while Vincent recovered made her stomach churn. Yet she knew they had no choice -this was the safest option for both of them.

Her phone buzzed. Fred's name flashed across the screen. She left the room and headed into the hospital waiting area.

"Your Venezuela piece is solid gold, Nelson." Fred's gruff voice came through. "We're running it next Sunday, front page digital edition with a print follow-up."

Elizabeth leaned forward, suddenly energized despite her exhaustion. "The footage Vincent got of the military's involvement?"

"Damning stuff. Our legal team cleared it. The stills from the protest are particularly powerful." Fred paused. "How's our guy doing?"

"Fractured ankle. He's lucky it wasn't worse." Elizabeth glanced toward Vincent's room. "The doctors say he'll need a few months of rehab."

"Listen, this story's going to make waves. Big ones. You might want to lay low for a bit after it drops. Both of you." Fred's tone grew serious. "We've already gotten some pushback from unofficial channels about the military corruption angle."

Elizabeth felt a chill run down her spine. "That's why we need to run it, Fred. The people deserve to know—"

"Oh, we're running it alright. Just make sure you and Rivera stay safe. I've got a contact in El Paso who can help if things get dicey."

After hanging up, Elizabeth walked back to Vincent's room, where he was adjusting his position on the hospital bed.

"Fred's running the story next Sunday," she said, settling into the chair beside him.

Vincent's eyes lit up despite the pain medication. "Full package?"

"Everything. The corruption, the military involvement, the civilian casualties." She reached for his hand. "We did it, Vin."

"We always do," he squeezed her fingers, then grimaced as he shifted his ankle. "Though next time, let's try to avoid the dramatic exit."

Elizabeth smiled, however, her thoughts were already contemplating the implications of the story's publication for both of them. They'd exposed a dangerous truth, and soon the whole world would know it.

Her phone buzzed again -this time a message from another journalist colleague congratulating them on the Venezuela coverage. The story hadn't even run yet, but whispers were already circulating through the industry. Words like "groundbreaking" and "Pulitzer-worthy" floated around, making her stomach flip with equal parts pride and anxiety.

She peeked at Vincent, who had dozed off again. The steady rise and fall of his chest provided little comfort against the gnawing worry in her gut. They'd been through countless dangerous situations together, but this felt different. This time, she wouldn't be there to watch his back.

"I have to pack up," she whispered, though he couldn't hear her. Standing up, she gathered her things, her movements slow and deliberate. "The nurse will be in soon to check your vitals."

Vincent stirred slightly but didn't wake. Elizabeth leaned down and pressed a gentle kiss to his forehead, lingering for just a moment. They'd earned their biggest story yet, possibly the kind that could define careers and change lives. But standing there in the hospital room, she would have traded it all to ensure his safety.

Elizabeth straightened up and walked to the door, forcing herself not to look back. He would be fine. He had to be fine. She took a deep breath and slowly exhaled. They both knew the risks associated with their line of work, Vincent more experienced than she. If anyone could rebound from a setback and recalibrate a way forward, it was Vincent Rivera. The hospital staff knew their protocols, and Fred's people would keep watch around the local area. She had to trust that would be enough.

Elizabeth's footsteps echoed on the linoleum as she walked down the corridor. Each step felt heavier than the last, carrying her further from Vincent and closer to Sweetwater Springs. She pushed through the hospital's main doors, escaping the sterile air and stepping into the warmth of the El Paso afternoon. She shielded her face from the blazing sun as she flagged a cab, the scent of exhaust fumes permeating the air.

It was time to go home.

4

Old Wounds, New Scars

Elizabeth stepped off the commuter bus from the Ohio Valley Regional Airport, her worn backpack slung over her shoulder and dragging her wobbly carry-on bag along the cobblestone path. The familiar sight of Sweetwater Springs' public square greeted her, unchanged since she'd left years ago. The clock tower chimed noon, its resonant tone echoing through the sleepy town. She inhaled deeply, the scent of freshly mowed grass and blooming flowers filling her lungs. It was a stark contrast to the smoke and tension-filled air she'd left behind in Venezuela.

"Liz! Oh my god, you're here!"

Stacy's excited shriek pierced the quiet afternoon. Elizabeth barely had time to brace herself before her best friend crashed into her, pulling her into a tight hug. Stacy's dark chestnut curls bounced as she pulled back, her warm brown skin glowing with joy. Her curvy figure was wrapped in bright purple scrubs—clearly just off her shift at the hospital where she worked as a registered nurse.

"I can't believe you made it! When you texted me, I thought for sure something would come up and you'd cancel."

Elizabeth patted Stacy's back awkwardly. "Yeah, well, here I am."

Stacy pulled back, her eyes shining with unshed tears. "I've missed you so much. Come on, let's get you settled."

As they walked toward Stacy's car, Elizabeth's gaze swept across the square. The same old businesses lined the streets, their storefronts barely altered. A pang of nostalgia mixed with unease settled in her stomach.

"So, how long are you staying?" Stacy's key fob chirped, unlocking her car.

Elizabeth tossed her backpack in the backseat and stowed the rest in the trunk. "Just until after the wedding. I've got leads to follow up on for my next story."

Stacy's smile faltered for a moment. "Oh. Well, we'll make the most of it then!"

As they drove through town, Elizabeth's attention drifted to the passing scenery. The rolling hills, the patchwork of farmland, the lazy Ohio River in the distance - it all felt suffocating now. She'd outgrown this place, hadn't she?

"I hope you don't mind, but I've got you staying at my place," Stacy said, turning onto a familiar street. "It'll be just like old times! We can stay up late, watch movies, talk about boys-"

"Stacy, I'm not-"

"I know, I know. You're all grown up and sophisticated now." Stacy's tone held a hint of something Elizabeth couldn't quite place. Disappointment? Resentment? "But humor me, okay? It's my wedding month, after all."

Elizabeth sighed, forcing a smile. "Of course. Whatever you want, bride-to-be."

As they pulled into Stacy's driveway, Elizabeth steeled herself. She could do this. It was just a few weeks in her hometown, getting some desperately needed rest, and attending her best friend's wedding. How hard could it be?

She stepped into the house, the cozy scent of cinnamon and vanilla enveloped her. The living room was a whirlwind of toys and colorful artwork pinned to the walls.

"Sweetie, come say hello," Stacy called out as she gathered up random toys and tossed them in a plastic bin.

A small boy with large, inquisitive brown eyes and a short, neatly trimmed afro appeared from behind the plush, floral-patterned couch. Elizabeth noticed his hesitant movements as he slowly emerged, his gaze darting between her and Stacy. His tiny hands gripped the edge of the couch, as if seeking reassurance from its texture. The child's presence immediately softened the atmosphere in the room, and Elizabeth felt a gentle tug at her heart, recognizing this must be Pierson, Stacy's son she'd heard so much about but had yet to meet in real life. His eyes shifted around the room, never quite meeting her gaze.

"Hi there, Pierson," Elizabeth said softly, crouching down to his level.

The boy didn't respond, instead fixating on a toy truck in his hands.

Stacy gently guided Pierson closer. "Remember what we practiced? Wave hello to Auntie Elizabeth."

Pierson's hand moved in a jerky approximation of a wave, his eyes still on the truck.

"He's a little shy," Stacy explained, her voice tinged with a mix of love and something else -worry? "Pierson is... our special boy. He doesn't always communicate the way other kids do."

Elizabeth nodded, understanding dawning on her. She'd encountered non-verbal children in her travels before.

A gruff voice from the adjacent room caught her attention. "Stacy, who's that at the door?"

"It's just Liz, honey," Stacy called back. "Come on, I'll introduce you to Mark."

They entered the den where a stocky man slouched in a recliner, his eyes glued to the TV. A news report showed protesters gathered outside the town hall.

Mark grunted a greeting, barely glancing at Elizabeth. "Can you believe this nonsense? Bunch of tree-huggers trying to shut down our only chance at decent jobs."

Elizabeth's instincts perked up. "What's going on?"

Stacy sighed. "There's talk of expanding the concrete plant on the outskirts of town. It would bring in a lot of jobs, but some people are concerned about the environmental impact."

"Concerned?" Mark scoffed. "They're trying to ruin us. If that expansion doesn't go through, half the town'll be out of work."

Elizabeth's mind raced, piecing together the conflict. A struggling small town, desperate for economic growth, pitted against environmental concerns. It was a story she'd seen play out before, but never so close to home.

"How long has this been going on?" she asked, unable to mask her curiosity.

Mark turned, eyeing her suspiciously. "Why? You're not here to write some hit piece on us, are you?"

"No, of course not," Elizabeth assured him quickly. "I'm just here for the wedding."

But as she watched the protesters on the screen, their signs waving in the Ohio breeze, she could feel the pull of a story waiting to be told. She followed Stacy into the kitchen, grateful for the escape from Mark's suspicious glare. The room was filled with wedding paraphernalia -swatches of fabric, floral arrangements, and stacks of invitations covered every surface.

"So, what do you think?" Stacy beamed, gesturing to the clutter around them.

Elizabeth forced a smile. "It's... something."

Stacy laughed, pulling out a chair for her. "I know it's a lot. But wait till you see this!"

She rummaged through a nearby drawer, extracting a well-worn sketchbook. Flipping it open, she revealed a detailed drawing of a wedding dress.

"Isn't it perfect?" Stacy gushed, pushing the sketch toward her.

Elizabeth studied the design. It was a classic A-line silhouette with delicate lace sleeves and a sweetheart neckline. Simple, elegant - everything Stacy had dreamed of since they were kids playing dress-up.

"It's beautiful, Stacy," Elizabeth said softly, a genuine smile tugging at her lips.

Stacy clasped her hands together, eyes shining. "I'm so glad you like it! And speaking of the wedding..." She took a deep breath, her expression turning serious. "Liz, I was hoping... would you be my maid of honor?"

The question hung in the air, heavy with expectation. Elizabeth felt a knot form in her stomach. She'd suspected this was coming, had wished against it since she'd agreed to come back for the wedding. The plan was to lay low for a few weeks, hang out at home with her bestie, and get buzzed at the reception. Then afterward, she would bug out back to El Paso once Vincent was released from Kincaid to start his PT. She wasn't looking for a wedding "assignment" to deal with. But seeing the hope in Stacy's eyes, she found herself nodding.

"Of course," Elizabeth heard herself say. "I'd be honored."

Stacy squealed with delight, enveloping Elizabeth in another tight hug. "Oh, thank you, thank you! This means so much to me. You have no idea."

As Stacy rambled on about dress fittings and bachelorette party plans, Elizabeth's mind wandered. She thought of Vincent, still recuperating in that Texas hospital. Of the story waiting to be written about the concrete plant controversy. Of all the reasons she'd left Sweetwater Springs in the first place.

But for now, she pushed those thoughts aside. This was Stacy's moment, and she was determined to be the friend Stacy needed her to be. Even if it meant confronting the past, she'd tried so hard to leave behind. Elizabeth blinked, suddenly aware that Stacy was still talking. Her friend's excited chatter had faded into background noise as Elizabeth's mind wandered, but now Stacy's words snapped back into focus.

"... and of course, we'll need to get you fitted for your dress before the rehearsal dinner next week," Stacy was saying, her eyes bright with enthusiasm.

"Wait, what?" Elizabeth raised an eyebrow. "You've already picked out a dress for me?"

Stacy nodded, oblivious to Elizabeth's discomfort. "Oh yes! It's perfect, Liz. A lovely lavender number that'll look amazing with your complexion. You'll love it, I promise."

Elizabeth forced a smile. She'd been back in Sweetwater Springs for less than an hour, and already she felt overwhelmed. The pressure of expectations -her own, her friend's, and the news team at the *Citizen* -was all bearing down on her.

"That's... great," she managed, her voice strained. "Listen, Stacy, I'm feeling a bit tired from the trip. Would you mind if I rested for a bit?"

Concern flashed across her friend's face. "Oh, of course! I'm sorry, I got carried away. Come on, I'll show you to your room."

Elizabeth followed Stacy up the narrow staircase, her backpack feeling heavier with each step. The climb was a maze of family photos and children's artwork, a testament to the life her friend had built here while she had been chasing stories across the globe. She was arrested by a small black-and-white photograph, a poignant portrait of Stacy with her son, hanging askew in a simple frame. Elizabeth studied the picture as she reached out to realign it on the wall, drawn in by the tenderness of their expressions; the use of light and shadow made them seem angelic.

"I'm so disappointed that you didn't bring your guy with you," Stacy said over her shoulder as she reached the top step.

"Vincent?" Elizabeth blinked back to the moment. "Oh, he's not the plus one type." She noticed the incredulous look on Stacy's face. "We're not ... it's not like that with us. We're just ... it's complicated." She made her way up the remaining steps between them.

"Ah, gotcha. Well honey, whatever keeps you warm at night," Stacy giggled. "That's all I'm gonna say."

"Yeah, he's a great videographer. I'm lucky to get to work with him." Elizabeth cleared her throat marking the end of the discussion concerning their arrangement. She shrugged off the remark. Sure, working so closely with Vincent had forged an undeniable bond between them. But anything beyond that was too ... inconvenient.

"Here we are," Stacy announced, pushing open a door at the end of the hall. "I hope it's okay. It's not much, but-"

"It's perfect," Elizabeth interrupted, eager to be alone. The room was small but comfortable, with a single bed pushed against the wall and a small desk by the window. It reminded her of her old bedroom, before... She shook her head, pushing away the unwelcome memories. "Thanks, Stacy. I think I'll lie down for a bit, if that's alright."

"Of course," Stacy said, hovering in the doorway. "I'll be downstairs if you need anything. We're so glad you're here, Liz. Really."

Elizabeth sat on the bed and closed her eyes as the door shut behind Stacy, bracing herself against the flood of emotions. She was back in Sweetwater Springs, surrounded by reminders of a past she'd tried so hard to escape. And now, she was expected to play a starring role in her best friend's wedding, as if nothing had changed. *You can handle it,* she thought. *It's only for a couple of weeks. How bad could it be?*

She exhaled, reaching for the remote control on the nightstand. Maybe some mindless TV would help quiet her racing thoughts. She flipped through the channels, pausing briefly on regular network logos before continuing her search. Suddenly, a grainy image caught her eye. It was a local channel, one she didn't recognize from her childhood. The amateur quality of the broadcast was immediately apparent - shaky camera work, unpolished graphics, and a nervous-looking anchor sitting behind a makeshift desk.

"... and now we turn to our top story," the young woman on screen said, her voice slightly too loud for the microphone. "The ongoing controversy surrounding the proposed concrete batch plant and its potential impact on our beloved Centennial Community Center."

Elizabeth sat up straighter, her interest piqued once again. This was the issue Mark had mentioned earlier. The camera cut to footage of the community center, its red brick facade and white columns a stark contrast to the modern equipment surrounding it. A group of protesters stood on the steps, their signs visible even through the low-quality video.

"As we've been reporting," the anchor continued, "Ohio Valley Aggregates Corporation has proposed building a new concrete batch plant on the site currently occupied by our town's historic Centennial Community Center. Supporters argue that this will bring much-needed jobs to Sweetwater Springs, while opponents fear the loss of a cherished landmark and potential environmental risks."

The screen split to show two interviewees: a man in a hard hat and safety vest, and an elderly woman clutching a framed photograph.

"This plant could revitalize our economy," the man insisted. "We're talking about dozens of good-paying jobs. The town needs this."

The woman shook her head vehemently. "At what cost? This building has been the heart of our community for generations. My great-grandfather helped build it. Are we really going to tear down our history for some greedy corporation?"

Elizabeth leaned forward, her mind tracking the scene. This wasn't just small-town politics -it was a microcosm of issues she'd seen play out across the globe: economic desperation versus environmental concerns, progress at the expense of heritage. And right in the middle of it all was the community center where she'd spent countless hours as a child, where she'd first dreamed of becoming a journalist.

She turned off the TV, her mind buzzing with questions. The controversy over the concrete batch plant seemed to encapsulate everything she'd left behind in Sweetwater Springs -the struggle between tradition and progress, the complex web of small-town relationships, the weight of history choking out every decision that promised a new direction.

She flopped back onto the bed, staring at the ceiling. Why had she come back? The thought nagged at her, insistent and uncomfortable. She'd spent years building a life far from here, chasing history makers around the world. And now, in just a few short hours, she felt like she was being pulled back into the very world she'd fought so hard to escape.

Her thoughts drifted to Vincent. She should be there with him, she realized with a pang of guilt. They'd been through so much together in Venezuela, and now she'd left him alone to heal. What kind of friend did that make her? Sure, they were free to go their own way. But every assignment they took together meant they were a team until the end.

And the story -their story. Would Fred keep his word when the pressure heats up to squelch it? She reached for her phone, tempted to check her emails for any updates from the assignment desk. But she hesitated, her finger hovering over the screen. What if their agreement at the *New York Citizen* fell through, all their hard work and risk for nothing? Sitting in this small wood paneled guest room in Stacy's attic, she felt like a fish out of water. *Check yourself, Nelson.* Why was she freaking out all of a sudden? Everything would be fine.

She set the phone aside. She'd made a commitment to Stacy, to be here for her wedding. Whatever else was happening in the world, she owed her oldest friend that much.

But the concrete batch plant controversy... that was something she couldn't ignore. It was the kind of story she lived for, a complex issue with no easy answers. And it was happening right here, in her hometown.

Elizabeth sat up, that razor-sharp determination settling over her. She'd be Stacy's maid of honor, play her part in the wedding. But she'd also dig into this story, uncover the truth behind the dispute. It was what she did best, after all.

She sank into the soft embrace of the twin bed, the familiar creaks and groans of the old house settling around her. She propped her phone against the pillow and dialed the Kincaid Medical Center. She smiled at the sight of Vincent's face illuminated by the harsh fluorescent lights of his hospital room.

"You look better," she said, studying the lines of fatigue creasing around his eyes.

He shrugged, wincing slightly at the movement. "Getting there. How's small-town life treating you?"

Elizabeth hesitated, then launched into a description of the concrete batch plant argument. "It's fascinating, Vin. The whole town is divided over it. I'm thinking of reaching out to that local news station, see if I can dig deeper."

Vincent's brow furrowed. "Liz, be careful. You don't want to get too wrapped up in local drama. Remember why you left in the first place?"

"I know, but -"

"Your next assignment could come any day. You need to be ready to move, not bogged down in some Sweetwater crap. Take this time to relax."

Elizabeth felt a flicker of irritation. "It's not just local drama. This is the kind of story that matters, Vincent. Environmental concerns, economic anxiety - it's all here."

Vincent sighed, running a hand through his hair. "I get it, I do. But your career as a foreign correspondent... that's what you've worked for. Don't let this distract you."

Elizabeth bit her lip, torn between the pull of the story and the truth in Vincent's words. "I'll be careful," she promised, not entirely sure if she meant it.

His face clouded over. "Liz, there's... something that," he glanced around the hospital room, then leaned closer to the camera, his voice dropping to a low murmur. "I need to ask you for a favor."

Elizabeth straightened and turned up the volume, her brows furrowed. "Of course. Anything."

He hesitated, picking at the edge of his hospital blanket. "You know my family left the Ohio Valley decades ago, but... there's one person who stayed behind. My Uncle Leo."

Elizabeth nodded, recalling snippets of stories Vincent had shared about his childhood summers spent in the Appalachian foothills.

"He practically raised me," he continued, his voice thick with emotion. "Whatever good traits I have, they came from him."

A wave of clarity struck her. Vincent, despite his outward bravado, was deeply connected to his family roots, customs, and rituals.

"He taught me how to track deer, how to fix a busted engine, how to tell a good story from a bad one. He taught me how to be a man." Vincent paused, his gaze distant. "He's the only family I have left."

"What happened?"

"We lost touch after... well, after everything happened with my parents. I was young, angry. I pushed everyone away." He looked up at her, a flicker of vulnerability in his eyes. "I haven't heard from him in years, and with everything that's happened... I need to find him. I need to know he's okay."

Elizabeth didn't hesitate. "I'll find him, Vincent. I promise."

He seemed surprised by the immediacy of her response. "It won't be easy. He's... off the grid. Lives up in the hills somewhere. No phone, no internet."

"Tell me everything you remember. Where he lived when you were a kid, what he did, anything that might help."

Vincent's shoulders relaxed slightly, a glimmer of hope replacing the worry in his eyes. "Thank you, Liz. This... this means more than you know."

As they said their goodbyes, Elizabeth couldn't shake the feeling that she was standing at a crossroads, with Sweetwater Springs pulling her in one direction and her hard-won career in another. After she ended the call with Vincent, a mixture of emotions swirled in her chest. Setting her phone aside, she lay back on the bed, her mind preoccupied with thoughts of the concrete plant debate and Vincent's warnings.

With a sigh, she pushed herself up and padded to the bathroom. As she went through her nightly routine, the familiar scents of old toiletries Stacy had stocked for her brought back a flood of memories. She caught her reflection in the mirror, noting how different she looked now compared to her awkward teenage years.

Back in her room, Elizabeth slipped into her favorite oversized t-shirt and settled cross-legged on the bed with her laptop and scanned surface maps of the region. She opened a new browser window and typed "Echo Ridge Trailer Park" into the search bar. It was the farthest stretch of land that could barely be classified as "residential" for districting purposes.

The results were sparse, but she managed to find a few local news articles mentioning the park. It was located on the outskirts of town, tucked away from the more affluent neighborhoods. Elizabeth scrolled through the limited information, piecing together a mental image of the place Vincent's Uncle Leo had once called home.

As she read, a strategy started to take shape in her mind. She'd drop by the trailer park tomorrow, maybe find Uncle Leo if she was lucky. It could be an opportunity to learn more about Vincent's past and perhaps setup a way for them to be reunited.

Elizabeth closed her laptop and set it aside, her anticipation already kicking into gear. She'd need to approach this carefully. Leo was likely to be as guarded as his nephew. But the challenge only fueled her curiosity. She settled back against her pillows, her mind buzzing with questions and possibilities. As sleep gently pulled her under, her final thoughts lingered on what tomorrow's visit might uncover.

5

Familiar Streets, Foreign Feelings

The rental car, a compact and unremarkable sedan, felt alien beneath her hands. Sweetwater Springs had always been a walking town for her. Although Stacy had offered to shuttle her around, Elizabeth opted to have her own set of wheels during the trip. She navigated the familiar streets, the once-charming downtown now tinged with a layer of neglect she hadn't noticed before. Past the quaint storefronts, the road began to climb, winding toward the outskirts of town. The landscape shifted, manicured lawns giving way to overgrown weeds and dilapidated fences.

A sudden, sharp curve brought her to the crest of the ridge, and there it was –Echo Ridge Trailer Park. The name, painted on a faded wooden sign, seemed ironic. The only echo here was the quiet hum of neglect. Rows of trailers, varying in states of disrepair, lined the narrow gravel roads. Some boasted small, struggling gardens, while others seemed abandoned, windows boarded up, metal siding rusting in the afternoon sun.

As she drove deeper into the park, a memory, sharp and unwelcome, pierced through her. The screech of metal, the ground trembling beneath her feet. The acrid smell of smoke and the frantic shouts of rescuers. The train derailment. She'd been walking home from school, the distant rumble growing louder, then the horrifying crescendo of crashing metal. Her parents, driving home from work, had been caught in the path of the derailed cars. The failed recovery efforts, the agonizing wait for news, the crushing finality of their loss—it all came flooding back, a wave of grief threatening to drown her.

Elizabeth gripped the steering wheel, forcing herself to breathe. The past was the past. She was here for Vincent, for answers. She pulled up to the trailer number she'd gleaned from Vincent's vague memories, a small, single-wide with peeling paint and a crooked porch. A man sat on the steps, his back to her, a worn straw hat shading his face. He was whittling a piece of wood, the rhythmic scrape of his knife the only sound in the oppressive stillness. This had to be Leonard Montoya. Elizabeth took a deep breath, steeling herself for the encounter, and stepped out of the car. As she drew closer, he looked up, his weathered face etched with lines of suspicion.

She approached the old man cautiously, her eyes scanning the old trailer and its surroundings. The small yard was a patchwork of dry grass and bare earth, dotted with rusted car parts and forgotten tools. A rickety clothesline sagged between two metal poles, a few faded shirts fluttering halfheartedly in the breeze.

Leo's appearance matched the worn-down aesthetic of his home. His skin was deeply tanned and creased, like old leather left too long in the sun. Silver-gray hair spilled out from beneath his straw hat, falling past his shoulders in unkempt waves. His hands, gnarled and spotted with age, moved with surprising dexterity as he worked the piece of wood.

His features, a blend of Native American and Hispanic heritage, held a certain stoicism, a quiet strength that seemed rooted in the earth itself. His eyes, dark and deep-set, watched her with an unnerving intensity, as if assessing her worthiness, then looked away.

"Mr. Montoya?" Elizabeth asked, her voice a little hesitant.

Leo didn't answer immediately. He continued whittling, the knife scraping against the wood, a slow, deliberate rhythm that seemed to stretch the silence. Finally, he looked up, his gaze meeting hers.

"You the girl from Sweetwater that run off a while back?" His voice was rough, gravelly, like stones grinding together.

Elizabeth nodded, shifting her weight from one foot to the other. "Yes, sir. Elizabeth Nelson. I'm a friend of Vincent's."

The mention of his nephew's name didn't seem to soften his expression. If anything, his eyes grew colder, more guarded. He spat a stream of tobacco juice onto the dry earth, the brown liquid disappearing into the dust.

"Vincent," he repeated, the name sounding foreign on his tongue. "He's caused me enough trouble."

Elizabeth's brow furrowed. This wasn't the warm welcome she'd hoped for. "I understand he's been...," she began, carefully choosing her words. "I'm not here to cause any problems. I just want to talk to you about something important."

Leo finally set down his whittling, the piece of wood—a small, intricately carved bird—resting on his calloused palm. He looked at it for a moment, then back at Elizabeth.

"Talk," he grunted, gesturing toward a rickety chair on the porch. "But make it quick. I got things to do."

As Elizabeth drew closer, she noticed his eyes beneath bushy brows, dark and watchful, held a wariness that made her pause mid-step. Leo's clothes were well-worn but clean—a faded flannel shirt rolled up at the sleeves and sturdy work boots caked with mud.

The porch creaked ominously as she placed a foot on the bottom step. To her left, an ancient rocking chair swayed gently, its peeling paint matching the trailer's exterior. Pots of withered plants lined the railing, a failed attempt at brightening the space.

"Mr. Montoya," her voice sounded unnaturally loud in the stillness of the trailer park. "Umm, how have you been?"

Leo's eyes narrowed, his hands still on the wood. He didn't respond immediately, instead studying her with an intensity that made Elizabeth shift uncomfortably. Finally, he spoke.

"Ain't had visitors in a long time. What brings you out here?"

Elizabeth swallowed hard, steeling herself. "I'm here because Vincent asked me to find you and check up on you."

At the mention of Vincent's name, Leo's expression hardened again. He set aside his whittling and stood slowly, his joints creaking audibly. Despite his age, he still cut an imposing figure, broad-shouldered and solid.

"Vincent? He did, huh?" He spat the name like it left a bad taste in his mouth. "Ain't seen that boy in years. What's he done now?"

After a moment's hesitation, Elizabeth rose and perched on the edge of the step, careful to maintain some distance. She tried to formulate how to move on with their conversation, but it felt like every line of questions she proposed would be filled with booby traps. "Well—"

"So, you're back in Sweetwater," Leo said, his tone flat. "Didn't think anyone came back once they got out."

Elizabeth chuckled nervously. "It's for a friend's wedding. But I've been hearing some... concerning things about what's going on here. Especially with OVAC so I thought I might—"

Leo's face darkened. "Ain't nothing good coming from that place. New folks running the town, they don't care about us. Just lining their pockets."

"What do you mean?"

"Trucks coming and going at all hours. Strangers poking around, asking questions. Something ain't right." Leo picked up his whittling knife again, running his thumb along the blade. "You ask me, they're hiding something big out there."

Elizabeth wanted to press further, but she reminded herself why she was here. Vincent. The urge to tell Leo about his nephew's condition gnawed at her, but as she looked at the old man's face and tense posture, she hesitated. He already seemed burdened by the changes in Sweetwater. News of Vincent's injury might be too much.

"I appreciate you sharing this with me, Mr. Montoya," she said instead. "I'll keep my eyes open while I'm in town."

He grunted, returning to his whittling. Elizabeth stepped forward, brushing off her jeans. As she turned to leave, Leo's gruff voice stopped her.

"You tell Vincent... tell him to watch himself out there. World ain't kind to folks who ask too many questions."

Elizabeth nodded, a lump forming in her throat. If only Leo knew how right he was.

* * *

Elizabeth steered the rental car away from Echo Ridge. The gravel crunched beneath the tires, kicking up dust in her rearview mirror. Leo's words replayed in her mind, but another thought pulled at her as she drove the same route she'd purposely avoided for seventeen years. Again.

Her car seemed to turn on its own, following the old access road that ran parallel to the railroad tracks. The summer heat shimmered off the asphalt, distorting her view of the twin steel rails that stretched endlessly toward the horizon.

The memory hit her without warning. She was twelve again, walking home from school, her backpack heavy with books. The ground had rumbled first—not the usual vibration of a passing train, but something violent and wrong. The screech of metal against metal tore through the air. Then came the crashes, one after another, like giant dominoes falling.

Elizabeth yanked the wheel, pulling onto the shoulder. Her chest constricted as the images flooded back. The twisted metal of train cars. The angry smoke that burned her lungs. The desperate voices of first responders. Her parents had been driving home along this same road, crossing these same deserted tracks at exactly the wrong moment.

She fumbled with her seatbelt, practically falling out of the car. The hot air hit her face as she doubled over, hands on her knees, fighting back waves of nausea. The sound of cicadas filled her ears, just like they did that day. She could still hear the crackle of emergency radios, the shouts of rescue workers, the horrible silence that followed when they realized it was too late.

"Not now," she whispered through quivering lips, pressing her palms against her eyes. "Please, not now."

But the memories wouldn't stop. The weight of her mother's favorite necklace being pressed into her hand by a somber police officer. The empty chairs at the kitchen table. The pitying looks from neighbors who brought casseroles she couldn't eat.

Elizabeth slid down against the car door, the metal hot against her back. She hugged her knees to her chest, letting the tears come as trucks rumbled past on the distant highway. She wiped her eyes with the back of her hand and pulled herself up using the car door. The metal burned against her palm, but the sharp pain helped ground her. She drew in a deep breath, steadying herself.

As she turned to get back in the car, something caught her eye—a glint of metal through the trees. She squinted, making out dark shapes beneath heavy tarps, stretched across what looked like construction equipment. The site sprawled across the valley floor, surrounded by a chain-link fence topped with razor wire.

Her feet carried her to the edge of the ridge before her mind caught up. The overlook provided a clear view of the valley below, where Ohio Valley Aggregates' concrete plant dominated the landscape. But this wasn't normal construction equipment. The tarps didn't quite cover everything, revealing glimpses of specialized machinery she didn't recognize.

Guards patrolled the perimeter, their uniforms bearing no company logos. Two men stood by what appeared to be a makeshift security station, checking papers as trucks rolled through the gate. The whole setup felt wrong—more military than industrial.

Elizabeth crouched behind a scrubby bush, her reporter's instincts firing. This wasn't just a concrete batch plant. The security, the hidden equipment, the unmarked vehicles—it all pointed to something else entirely. She pulled out her phone and snapped several photos, making sure to capture the guard station and the covered machinery.

The sun beat down on her neck, prickling her skin with an uncomfortable heat as she studied the valley below. Ohio Valley Aggregates Corporation, or OVAC as the locals called it, sprawled across the landscape like a concrete octopus. Its imposing towers cast long, ominous shadows that stretched across the valley floor, while dust kicked up by the constant flow of trucks created a hazy veil, obscuring the full extent of the operation. A metallic tang hung heavy in the air, a gritty reminder of the cement dust swirling around her. She squinted, trying to see past the haze, her gaze sweeping over the perimeter fence and the glimpses of covered machinery she'd photographed earlier. Something felt deeply unsettling about this place, an instinct that gnawed at her gut and urged her to dig deeper.

A flash of movement caught her eye. A small group of people gathered near the main gate, holding signs and chanting slogans she couldn't quite make out from this distance. protesters. She'd been following the reports in town about growing unrest, concerns over OVAC's expansion and its impact on the environment. Now, seeing them firsthand, a sense of unease settled over her. These weren't just disgruntled locals; their organized presence suggested something more serious. And they might be onto something.

She zoomed in with her phone camera, trying to decipher the signs. "Stop OVAC," one read. Another: "Protect our water." A third, more ominous: "They're hiding something." Her heart pounded in her chest. Leo's words, "Something ain't right," reverberated in her mind, each syllable a chilling warning. The protesters, Leo's suspicions, the strange activity at the plant—the pieces began to fit together, forming a disturbing puzzle she felt determined to solve.

Elizabeth considered her options. She could return to Stacy's, pretend she'd never seen anything, and focus on the wedding. But the journalist in her, the same instinct that had driven her to Venezuela, wouldn't let her ignore this. This wasn't just a local story; it felt bigger, more significant. And if the protesters were right, if OVAC was indeed hiding something, it was a story that needed to be told.

The image of Vincent flashed in her mind, his face pale against the hospital pillow. His repeated advice to her echoed in her mind: *"Be careful, Kitten. Some things are best left buried."* A shiver ran through her. Had he encountered something similar and not told her? Was this connected to his warning?

She had to know.

Elizabeth returned to her vehicle, her thoughts racing. She needed a strategy. The protesters were her best bet. They might have information she couldn't get anywhere else. They might be the key to understanding what was happening in Sweetwater Springs, and maybe, just maybe, the key to understanding Vincent's warning. She decided to drive closer, park discreetly, and record them. It was a risk, but a risk she felt compelled to take.

Elizabeth grabbed her phone and pulled up Vincent's number. She needed to share what she'd uncovered—both finding Uncle Leo and witnessing the mysterious activity at the overlook, especially about his uncle's deteriorating situation.

The call connected on the first ring.

"Bad timing." Vincent's voice was tight, strained. Hospital sounds echoed in the background—the squeak of wheels, muted voices, the beeping of monitors.

"Vincent, I found your—"

"I'm headed into surgery right now." He cut her off, his words clipped. "Can't talk."

"But there's something you need to know about—"

"Señorita, we need to prep the patient," a nurse's voice interjected from the background.

"Listen," he interrupted again, his voice softening slightly. "Enjoy your down time. This is supposed to be a break for you, remember? I'll get in touch when they spring me from this place."

"Mr. Vincent, you need to end the call now," the nurse's voice came through more clearly.

"No need to keep checking in," he said quickly. "Take care of yourself, Liz."

"Vincent, wait—"

"Gotta go. They're wheeling me in."

The line went dead before Elizabeth could protest further. She stared at her phone for a moment, then let out a slow breath. This wasn't the first time they'd gone their separate ways for a while–it was part of their dynamic, part of what made their partnership work. Vincent needed space to heal, and she... well, she had a potential story to investigate.

She started to type out a detailed message about Uncle Leo's situation, then stopped, deleting the draft. Vincent's words echoed in her mind: *No need to keep checking in.* He'd contact her when he was ready. They both knew the drill. She typed out a quick text instead:

Found your uncle. Something's not right here. Call when you can. Good luck with surgery.

The message stayed undelivered, a small exclamation point appearing next to it. She tried again. Nothing. The hospital's thick walls were probably interfering with the signal now that Vincent was in pre-op. She pocketed her phone, her mind already shifting to the task at hand.

Uncle Leo clearly knew something about what was happening at that overlook, and those armed guards weren't there for show. If there was indeed a story brewing in Sweetwater Springs, she'd find it.

For now, she'd keep an eye on Uncle Leo, dig deeper into whatever was happening with those shipping containers, and let Vincent focus on his recovery. They'd reconnect eventually –they always did. After all, some of their best stories had started this way: with one of them stumbling onto something while the other was temporarily out of the picture. When Vincent was ready, she'd have more than just suspicions to share with him. She'd have answers.

6

Echoes of Dissent

The squeak of the community center's heavy oak doors echoed in Elizabeth's ears, a sound she hadn't heard in years. The air hung thick with the combined scents of stale coffee and pine scented floor wax. Every seat was filled, bodies spilling out into the aisles. A low hum of conversation filled the room, punctuated by the occasional outburst. Elizabeth squeezed into a spot near the back, her notebook and pen at the ready.

"Quiet down, folks, quiet down!" A booming voice cut through the noise. Councilman Noah Montgomery, Sweetwater Springs' golden boy, stood at the podium.

Noah? Elizabeth shifted in her seat to get a better vantage point.

His confidence radiated from him, an aura of ease, his smile wide and practiced, like a well-rehearsed performance. A rush of heat flushed Elizabeth's cheeks. She pushed a stray strand of hair behind her ear, suddenly self-conscious. He looked...different. Older, of course, but filled out, the boyish charm replaced by a polished, almost unsettling, air of authority. *Councilman Montgomery.* The words felt alien in her mind. *My Noah... a politician?*

Elizabeth unlocked her phone's screen, pulling up search results for Noah Montgomery. The local news articles painted a picture of Sweetwater Springs' groundbreaking political figure -the first African American elected official in the town's history, with an impeccable reputation. His credentials were impressive: Wharton School of Business graduate who'd returned to serve his community, transforming his role as councilman into a platform for positive change. His social media profiles showcased his involvement in numerous charitable organizations, including youth football coaching and sponsorship of a girls' tennis club. The Alpha Phi Alpha fraternity brother seemed to be at every major community event, his million-dollar smile lighting up photos as he handed out scholarships or cut ribbons at charity functions. The town's newspapers praised his diplomatic approach to controversial issues, describing him as "highly esteemed" and "a unifying force in local politics."

Despite scrolling through countless images of Noah at black-tie galas, Elizabeth noticed one glaring omission -no wife, no children, not even hints of a serious relationship, though she did spot him escorting a variety of socialites to charity events. She caught herself lingering on a recent photo of him in a perfectly tailored suit at a hospital fundraiser, looking even more handsome than she remembered.

She lifted her gaze from her phone as Noah stood at the podium, commanding the room's attention with an effortless grace that years of public service had clearly honed. The photos hadn't done him justice -his broad shoulders filled out his suit perfectly, and that relaxed, devastating smile still had the power to make her pulse quicken. He carried himself with the same athletic confidence she remembered from high school, but now tempered with a polished professionalism that spoke of boardrooms and political savvy. When their eyes met across the room, she saw a flash of recognition, followed by that slow, warm grin that used to make her teenage heart somersault -and apparently still did. Noah subtly adjusted his silk tie, a gesture she remembered from their youth when he was trying to maintain his composure, and for a moment, beneath the successful politician's veneer, she glimpsed the boy who used to call her "Lizzy" and make her believe anything was possible.

He launched into his speech, a carefully worded address about community values and economic progress. The concrete batch plant, predictably, took center stage. Noah spoke of jobs, growth, and Sweetwater Springs' bright future. Elizabeth's pen scratched across her notepad, capturing his words, but she was thinking of a million other things. She remembered Noah the quarterback, Noah with the shy smile and the clumsy attempts at flirting. *He never looked at me like that*, she thought, watching him command the room.

A woman in the front row, impeccably dressed and radiating a subtle but unmistakable air of importance, caught Noah's eye. He offered her a special smile, a brief, private acknowledgment that didn't escape Elizabeth's notice.

Victoria, she recalled. Head cheerleader, prom queen, Noah's on-again, off-again girlfriend. The same Victoria who had once, with a saccharine smile, "accidentally" spilled a cherry slushy down Elizabeth's brand new white sweater at a football game. *Some things never change*, Elizabeth thought, a taste of bitterness rising in her throat.

Noah finished his speech to a wave of polite applause. The hum of conversation resumed, louder now, charged with a nervous energy. Elizabeth closed her notebook, a knot forming in her stomach. She needed air. She slipped out of the community center, the squeak of the heavy oak doors now an unsettling, sound.

Elizabeth felt a flicker of something she hadn't felt in years, a dormant ember of high school infatuation. He looked even better now than he did back then. A wave of warmth, unwelcome and unexpected, spread through her chest. She quickly shoved the thought away, tucking it into a dark corner of her mind. *Focus, Elizabeth. You're here for a story, not a trip down memory lane.*

She flipped open her notebook and slipped back into the community center, the swell of angry voices hitting her like a wave. The room had transformed in her brief absence. Gone was the polite audience, replaced by a sea of red faces and jabbing fingers.

"You can't just bulldoze over our concerns, Councilman Montgomery!" A man in overalls stood, his calloused hands balled into fists. "My well water's already showing signs of contamination."

Noah's practiced smile wavered. "I understand your concerns, Mr. Jenkins, but our environmental impact studies -"

"Studies paid for by Ohio Valley Aggregates!" A woman near the front interrupted, her voice sharp with accusation.

Elizabeth's nerves sparked. She scribbled furiously in her notebook, capturing every heated exchange. The room crackled with tension, reminding her of protests she'd covered in South America - minus the tear gas and rubber bullets.

"Please, let's maintain order." Noah's charm slipped further, replaced by something harder, less familiar. "The plant will bring jobs, growth-"

"At what cost?" Another voice cut through. "My kids can't play outside anymore without breathing in concrete dust!"

Elizabeth watched Noah's transformation with fascination. Gone was the smooth-talking politician from earlier. His jaw clenched, a muscle twitching beneath his perfectly trimmed facial hair. He gripped the podium edges, knuckles flexing against the dark wood.

"The council has thoroughly reviewed all proposals," Noah's voice strained with forced patience. "Ohio Valley Aggregates has met every requirement-"

A chorus of angry voices drowned him out. Elizabeth recognized faces from her childhood -teachers, neighbors, parents of old classmates -all wearing expressions she'd never seen in this sleepy town before. The air felt electric, charged with something that went beyond simple civic disagreement.

Noah's gaze swept the room, landing briefly on Elizabeth. Recognition flickered across his face once more, followed by something else -uncertainty? She held his stare, pen poised above her notebook. For a moment, she saw the boy she'd known in high school, caught in the headlights of unexpected opposition.

"Now, I know we're all here tonight with strong feelings about this proposed concrete plant expansion." Noah gestured toward a large map displayed on an easel behind him, dotted with red and green markers. "Ohio Valley Aggregates Corporation assures us this project will bring much-needed jobs to our community."

A man in a worn flannel shirt jumped to his feet. "Jobs that'll poison our water and choke our kids to death with dust!"

"That's just fear-mongering, Jed!" another voice shouted back. A woman with tired eyes cradled a baby in her arms. "We need those jobs. My husband's been out of work for six months."

"Order! Order!" Noah pounded his gavel on the podium. "We'll have none of that. Everyone will have their chance to speak." He pointed to the man in flannel. "Jed, you first."

Jed stepped forward, his face flushed with anger. "This town's been dyin' a slow death ever since the train derailment. Now they want to finish the job by poisoning our air and water. For what? A few lousy jobs?"

The woman with the baby spoke next, her voice trembling. "My kids need to eat, Jed. We can't afford to be picky."

The room erupted in a cacophony of voices, accusations and counter-accusations flying across the room like angry hornets. Elizabeth scribbled furiously, capturing snippets of conversation, the raw emotion in the room palpable.

"This town is divided," a voice next to Elizabeth murmured. She turned to see an older woman with kind eyes and a worried frown. "Torn between survival and... and everything else that matters."

Elizabeth nodded, her gaze sweeping across the room, taking in the raw, desperate faces of her neighbors. Survival, she thought. A primal instinct that could make people compromise their values, their beliefs, even their health. She understood. She'd seen it before, in other countries, other communities ravaged by greed and corruption.

And then she saw him. Uncle Leo. He stood near the back of the room, his face a mask of quiet fury. His earlier stoicism had crumbled, replaced by a simmering rage that radiated from him like heat from a furnace. He clutched a crumpled piece of paper in his hand, his knuckles bulging against the thin, yellowed sheet. He hadn't seen her yet. He was focused on Noah, his gaze burning into the young councilman's face.

Elizabeth hesitated. Should she approach him? He'd been so closed off, so suspicious when she'd visited him at the trailer. Would he even want to see her now? But something in his face, beneath the anger, compelled her forward. She threaded her way through the crowd, the angry voices washing over her. As she drew closer, she saw that the paper in his hand was a photograph. A faded, dog-eared picture of a younger Leo, standing beside a smiling woman with kind eyes and long, dark hair. Elizabeth recognized her instantly. Vincent's mother.

She reached his side, placing a gentle hand on his arm. He flinched, his eyes widening in surprise as he turned to face her. "You..." he began, his voice rough with emotion. He looked down at her hand on his arm, then back up at her face. The anger in his eyes softened, replaced by a deep, aching sadness.

"It's me, Elizabeth," she said softly. "Vincent's...friend."

He nodded slowly, his gaze drifting back to the photograph. "Maria," he whispered, his voice thick with unshed tears. "My brother's wife. Vincent's mother."

Elizabeth's attention snapped away from Leo as a sharp cry cut through the heated debate. A burly man in a hard hat shoved past her, charging toward the front of the room where a young activist clutched a stack of environmental impact papers.

"You tree-hugging little shit!" The man's meaty hands grabbed the activist's collar, slamming him against the wall. Papers scattered across the floor like startled birds. "My family needs these jobs!"

The room exploded. People leaped from their seats, some rushing forward to intervene, others backing away from the violence. Chairs scraped against hardwood floors, creating a horrible screech that mixed with the shouts and gasps.

"Get your hands off him!" someone yelled.

"Fight! Fight!" another voice called out.

Elizabeth's heart hammered in her chest as she raised her phone to record the chaos. The activist struggled against the wall, his face red with fear and rage. Two other men pulled at the construction worker's shoulders, trying to separate them.

Noah's gavel cracked against the podium. "Order! Security!"

But his words disappeared into the mayhem. The crowd surged forward and back like a turbulent ocean. Elizabeth felt Leo's grip on her arm, pulling her away from the worst of it. A woman screamed as someone stepped on her foot. An elderly man stumbled and caught himself on a chair.

"This is what happens!" a voice rose above the din. "This is what your concrete plant brings to our town!"

The security guards finally pushed through the crowd, their uniforms stark against the sea of casual clothes. Elizabeth kept recording, her journalist senses overriding her fear. This wasn't just about jobs anymore. This was about a town tearing itself apart.

She weaved through the churning crowd, her phone held high to capture the unfolding altercation. The construction worker still had the activist pinned against the wall. Despite her natural instinct to retreat, she felt a wave of adrenaline as she inched closer.

"Why did you attack him?" she called out, her voice steady despite her racing pulse.

A sharp elbow caught her ribs as someone pushed past. She stumbled, nearly dropping her phone, but caught herself against a chair. The room spun with motion -security guards shoving through the masses, people screaming, Noah's useless gavel cracking against wood.

"Get that camera out of here!" The construction worker released one hand from the activist's collar to swat at Elizabeth's phone. She ducked, years of field experience kicking in as she sidestepped his reach while keeping her lens trained on the scene.

A woman grabbed Elizabeth's arm, her fingers digging in. "You saw it -he attacked first! The activist, he -"

"That's a lie!" Another voice cut through. "Reynolds threw the first punch!"

Elizabeth's reflexes sparked, drinking in every detail -the sweat beading on Reynolds' forehead, the activist's crooked glasses, the scattered papers bearing Ohio Valley Aggregates' letterhead. She needed to document everything, every angle, every voice.

Someone crashed into her from behind. Elizabeth stumbled forward, her shoulder slamming into the wall. Pain shot through her arm, but she kept her phone steady, recording. This wasn't Venezuela, but the surge of adrenaline coursed through her - that electric mix of fear and purpose that made her feel most alive.

"Clear the room!" Security guards pushed through the crowd. "Everyone out!"

Elizabeth pressed herself against the wall, continuing to film as the guards separated Reynolds from the activist. The crowd's energy shifted from aggressive to anxious, people backing away from the officers. She caught glimpses of faces she recognized -old teachers, neighbors, faces from her past now contorted with anger and fear.

His face betraying nothing, Noah raised his hands in a calm gesture. "Please, everyone, calm down! This isn't how we solve things in Sweetwater." His voice, though strained, projected across the room, a desperate plea for order amidst the chaos.

"Easy for you to say, Montgomery!" Jed's voice boomed from the back. "You ain't the one breathin' in that grit and dust!"

Noah's jaw tightened. He took a deep breath, visibly struggling to regain control. "I understand your concerns," he said, his voice regaining some of its earlier smoothness, "and I assure you, the council is taking them very seriously. We're not going to let anything jeopardize the health and safety of our community."

"Then shut down the plant!" someone yelled.

"We need the money!" another voice countered.

Noah's gaze swept across the room, landing briefly on Elizabeth. Their eyes met for a fleeting moment, and she saw a glimmer of... what? A plea? Frustration? He looked trapped, caught between the warring factions of his town. His carefully constructed image of the small-town hero was cracking under the pressure.

The scuffle near the back of the room escalated. The construction worker, Reynolds, broke free from the men trying to restrain him and lunged toward the activist again, his fist raised. The activist cowered, shielding his face. Elizabeth, still filming, found herself caught in the crossfire. Reynolds, enraged, turned on her. "You little bitch! Delete that video!" He swiped at her phone, his face contorted with fury.

Suddenly, a body slammed into Reynolds, knocking him off balance with a meaty thud. Elizabeth stumbled back, her phone clattering to the floor and skidding across the polished hardwood. She looked up, her heart pounding against her ribs like a trapped bird, to see Noah standing between her and the enraged construction worker. He provided a reassuring presence, his broad shoulders shielding her as she leaned into him, breathing in the alluring aroma of his cologne -something woodsy and expensive.

"Leave her alone!" Noah's voice was low and dangerous, a stark contrast to his earlier attempts at diplomacy. His eyes blazed with a protective fire. Elizabeth felt her breath catch in her throat at this unexpected display of chivalry.

Reynolds, momentarily stunned, snarled, "Get out of my way, Montgomery. This ain't your business." Spittle flew from his lips as he clenched and unclenched his meaty fists.

"It is now," Noah said, his stance firm. He stood, his arms slightly spread, shielding Elizabeth from the construction worker's rage. The muscles in his back tensed beneath his tailored shirt, ready to respond to any sudden movement. Elizabeth could see a slight tremor in his hands - not from fear, she realized, but from barely contained anger.

The crowd thinned as security escorted Reynolds out, his threats echoing off the community center's walls. Elizabeth retrieved her phone from beneath a folding chair, checking for damage. The screen remained intact -she'd seen worse in war zones and invested in the best protective gear for her devices.

Noah's shoulders relaxed as the last stragglers filed out, muttering and shaking their heads. He turned to face her, his brow furrowed and his eyes filled with worry. "You okay?"

"I've handled worse." Elizabeth brushed dust from her jeans, trying to ignore how his cologne still lingered in the air between them.

"You shouldn't have provoked him like that." Noah ran a hand through his hair. "This isn't Venezuela, Lizzy. We do things differently here."

The old nickname caught her off guard. Heat crept up her neck as memories flooded back -stolen glances in high school hallways, the way he'd never quite seen her back then.

"Different how? By letting bullies silence the truth?" She met his gaze, noting how his brown eyes still crinkled at the corners when he frowned.

"That's not what I -" He stepped closer, lowering his voice. "Things are complicated here. More than you know."

Elizabeth felt the familiar pull, the magnetic tension that had always existed between them, but now charged with something new. Adult. Dangerous.

"Then explain it to me." She didn't back away, even as he moved closer. The empty room seemed to shrink around them.

Noah's hand twitched, as if he might reach for her, but he stopped himself. "I can't. Not yet." His expression softened. "But thank you. For recording everything. Maybe it'll help people see…" He trailed off, leaving the thought unfinished. The air grew thick with unspoken words, years of missed opportunities, and fresh complications.

"Well," Noah said, a small smile playing on his lips. "It's really good to see you again."

A warmth spread through her chest, a pleasant contrast to the lingering adrenaline from the near-brawl. "You too, Noah," she said, surprised by the genuine pleasure in her voice. It had been years since they'd last spoken, a lifetime ago, back when she was a gawky teenager with a hopeless crush on the star quarterback. Now, standing here in the echoing silence of the community center, the years melted away, leaving a strange mix of familiarity and nervous anticipation.

"It's…different," she said, gesturing vaguely at the room, the scattered chairs, the lingering tension in the air. "Sweetwater Springs isn't exactly how I remember it."

He chuckled, a low rumble in his chest that sent a shiver down her spine. "No, I suppose it isn't. Things change." His eyes met hers, and she saw a trace of something unreadable in their depths. Sadness? Regret? Or was it just the lingering stress of the evening?

"So," he said, shifting his weight, a hint of awkwardness creeping into his demeanor. "What are you doing back in town after all this time?"

"Stacy's wedding," she said, glad to have a simple answer. "Maid of honor duties."

"Right, of course." He nodded, then hesitated, as if debating his next words. "We should...catch up sometime. It would be good to hear what you've been up to. Over coffee, maybe? Or dinner?"

Elizabeth's heart skipped a beat. Was he asking her out? It felt like a date, but maybe she was reading too much into it. "Sure," she replied, her voice carefully nonchalant, though her pulse betrayed her excitement. "Dinner would be great."

"Okay, great." He smiled, and this time, there was no mistaking the warmth in his eyes. It was the same smile that had made her knees weak in high school, the same smile that had haunted her dreams for years afterward. "How about tomorrow night? There's a new Italian place downtown. Or we could go to the old diner, if you're feeling nostalgic."

"The diner," she said, a smile playing on her lips. "Definitely the diner." The thought of revisiting that old haunt with Noah, after all these years, filled her with a strange mix of excitement and trepidation.

"Perfect," he said, his voice a rich, velvety baritone that captivated her. "I'll meet you there at seven?"

"Seven sounds good," she said, trying to ignore the butterflies fluttering in her stomach.

A charged silence hovered between them as Noah walked her to her car, the unspoken questions hanging in the air, filling her with a mixture of intrigue and nervousness. The streets of Sweetwater

Springs took on a mysterious, alluring quality under the long shadows cast by the streetlights. Their eyes locked, and in that instant, it felt as if the entire world outside their small town had vanished, leaving only the electric energy crackling between them.

A young woman in a crisp blazer hurried toward them, her heels clicking against the community center's floor. "Councilman Montgomery, sorry to interrupt, but there's an urgent call from Columbus waiting."

Noah's shoulders tensed. "I'll be right there." He turned to Elizabeth, regret crossing his features. "I have to take this. Tomorrow at seven?"

She nodded, watching him follow his aide down the sidewalk, his confident stride masking the strain she'd glimpsed earlier.

As Elizabeth turned to leave, she spotted Leo among a cluster of protesters near the entrance. His face looked drawn, tired. The photograph of Vincent's mother was still clutched in his hand, though now it trembled slightly. She approached the group, catching fragments of their heated discussion about water contamination and property values. Leo stood slightly apart from them, his eyes distant.

"Can I give you a ride home?" Elizabeth touched his arm gently. The old man startled, then focused on her face.

"You don't need to trouble yourself," he mumbled, but she noticed how heavily he leaned against the wall.

"It's no trouble. I'm heading toward Echo Ridge, anyway." A lie, but she couldn't bear the thought of him walking all that way in the dark.

Leo studied her for a long moment, his tired eyes searching her face. Finally, he gave a slight nod. "Much obliged," he said quietly, tucking the photograph into his shirt pocket.

Elizabeth guided him toward the parking lot, feeling the weight of curious stares from the remaining protesters. She recognized the same protective instinct she'd felt earlier at his trailer. There was something about Leo's quiet dignity, his stubborn independence, that reminded her of Vincent.

She steered the car along the winding road toward Echo Ridge, stealing glances at Leo in the passenger seat. His hands fidgeted with the photograph in his lap, uncreasing and smoothing the edges.

"Something ain't right about this whole business," Leo muttered, breaking the tense silence. "That concrete plant, OVAC - they're moving too fast, pushing too hard."

Elizabeth kept her voice neutral, though her journalist's gut feeling perked up. "What makes you say that?"

"Been watching them trucks coming and going at all hours. More equipment than any small batch plant needs." Leo's eyes narrowed as he stared out the windshield. "And Montgomery, he's changed. Used to be one of the good guys, looked out for the little folk. I'm afraid he's turning into just another suit, telling us what's good for us while his friends get richer. I hope I'm wrong. He's from a great family. I do hope I'm wrong about him."

The car's headlights caught a pothole, and Elizabeth swerved to avoid it. "You think Noah's involved in something questionable?"

Leo's laugh was harsh and bitter. "Money talks. And somebody's spending an awful lot of it to rush this thing through. Those council meetings?" He shook his head. "Just theater. Decisions were made long before any of us got to speak our piece."

Elizabeth thought of Noah's strained expression earlier, the way he'd avoided direct answers. "Have you tried talking to him directly?"

"Yes, we all have. Each time the council secretary says he's too busy." His fingers tightened around the photograph. "My family's lived on this ridge for four generations. Vincent grew up here. Now they want to tell us the air might not be safe to breathe, but trust them, they'll fix it?" He scoffed. "I may be old, but I ain't stupid."

They arrived at Leo's trailer. The porch light flickered, casting long, dancing shadows across the overgrown weeds that choked the small yard. Leo paused before the steps, his hand resting on the railing. "Come in. Have some tea."

She followed him inside. The air hung thick with the scent of dried herbs and wood smoke. Bundles of sage, sweetgrass, and other plants Elizabeth couldn't identify hung from the ceiling. Every surface seemed covered with small jars filled with dried leaves, roots, and powders. Bottles of tinctures and oils lined the windowsill, their dark glass glinting in the lamplight. A worn mortar and pestle sat beside a stack of well-thumbed books, their spines cracked and faded. Despite the clutter, it felt strangely ordered, each item placed with deliberate care. A faded rug covered the floor, its intricate geometric patterns worn smooth with age. On one wall, a framed photograph of a younger Leo, dressed in traditional Native American regalia, hung beside a dream catcher woven with feathers and beads. A small, wood-burning stove stood in the corner, radiating a comforting warmth that battled the evening chill.

Leo shuffled into the kitchen area, his movements slow but deliberate. He filled a kettle with water and placed it on the stove, the metal clanging against the burner. "My grandmother taught me about these plants," he said, gesturing toward the hanging herbs. "Their power to heal, to protect."

Elizabeth took a seat at the small table, her eyes scanning the room, taking in the details. A worn leather pouch lay open on a shelf, revealing a collection of smooth, polished stones. A small clay bowl filled with burnt embers sat on the floor, sending a thin wisp of fragrance curling toward the ceiling.

"Vincent, he always scoffed at these old ways," Leo continued, his voice tinged with a hint of sadness. "Said it was all superstition. My Vincent. Always curious, always questioning." He poured the boiling water over a handful of dried leaves in a teapot. "People need to understand the connection, the way these plants speak to us, if only we listen."

Elizabeth nodded, feeling a strange sense despite the unsettling events of the evening. The trailer, filled with the scent of the warm herbs and the quiet murmur of the stove, felt like a sanctuary, a world away from the noise and confusion of the town.

The night deepened around them as Leo poured a third cup of tea, the blossoms releasing their earthy aroma into the cramped trailer. Elizabeth wrapped her hands around the warm ceramic, letting the heat seep into her fingers. Her phone lay forgotten in her purse, the outside world fading away as Leo's stories swept over her.

"Vincent was maybe six when he caught his first fish," Leo said, his expression softening at the memory. "Wouldn't let me help him. Stood there in the creek for hours, determined to do it himself."

Elizabeth smiled, picturing a tiny Vincent with that same stubborn determination she knew so well. "Sounds like him."

"He ever tell you about the summer we tracked that mountain lion?" Leo's eyes gleamed like polished stones in the dim light. He reached for an old tin box, pulling out a stack of faded photographs.

Time slipped away as they shared stories deep into the night. Elizabeth learned about Vincent's first attempts at photography, his childhood adventures, the quiet strength he'd inherited from his uncle. In return, she told Leo about their work together, carefully editing out the more dangerous parts but sharing the moments of triumph, of connection, of purpose they'd found with each assignment.

The clock on the wall ticked past midnight, then one, then two. Neither seemed to notice or care. Leo brewed more tea and brought out homemade bread and honey. They talked about the land, about loss, about belonging. Elizabeth felt the walls she usually kept so firmly in place begin to soften.

"You're good for him, you know," Leo said quietly, as the first hints of dawn began to creep through the window. "He needs someone who understands his restless spirit."

Elizabeth felt tears prick at her eyes, touched by the simple acceptance in Leo's voice. Here, in this small trailer filled with herbs and memories, she'd found an unexpected connection -a piece of family she hadn't known she was missing.

7

Wedding Bells and Old Flames

Elizabeth startled awake to her phone's buzz. Her heart pounded as fragments of the dream slipped away -Noah's warm smile, his fingers brushing her cheek, the way he'd looked at her back in high school when she'd been too shy to hold his gaze. She pressed her palms against her eyes, willing the images to fade.

Sunlight streamed through Uncle Leo's trailer window, casting patterns on the worn linoleum floor. She'd fallen asleep on his lumpy couch after hours of talking about Vincent, the protests, and the changing face of Sweetwater Springs.

"Damn it," she muttered, grabbing her phone. Three missed calls from Stacy and a text from Vincent that made her stomach twist:

> **Need to talk**
> **Important**
> **Call when you can**

The clock read 9:47 AM. She was supposed to meet Stacy and the wedding planner at 10:30. No time to return Vincent's call now - she'd have to catch up with him later.

Uncle Leo shuffled out of his bedroom in plaid pajama pants and a faded t-shirt. "Made some coffee if you want it."

"Thanks, but I've got to run." She gathered her laptop and notebook. "Wedding stuff with Stacy."

"Don't forget - protest today. Those kids from the cable station'll be there."

Elizabeth nodded, trying to shake off the lingering warmth of her dream about Noah. The real Noah had made his position clear yesterday, choosing politics and people pleasing over principles. Just like always. The patchwork star quilt slipped from her shoulders as she fumbled for her phone on the coffee table.

"Hello?" Her voice came out raspy from lack of sleep.

"Where are you?" Stacy's worried tone cut through the morning haze. "I've been texting you all night."

Elizabeth rubbed her eyes, taking in the trailer's cramped living room. Empty cups and scattered papers from her late-night discussion with Uncle Leo littered the scratched coffee table. The old man's weathered recliner sat empty, but the scent of fresh coffee wafted from the kitchen.

"Sorry, I crashed at Vincent's uncle's place. Lost track of time going through some documents about the OVAC plant."

"Girl, you had me worried sick." Stacy's voice softened. "Next time send a text, okay?"

Uncle Leo shuffled into the living room, carrying two steaming mugs. His long silver hair hung loose around his shoulders, and his dark eyes held the same intensity from their midnight conversation about the town's changes.

"Thanks for letting me stay," Elizabeth whispered, covering the phone.

He nodded, setting down the coffee. "Least I could do after keeping you up with my ramblings."

"Stacy, I'll head back soon." Elizabeth reached for the fresh cup. "Just need to grab my notes and -"

"The wedding planner's coming at noon. Don't you dare be late." Stacy scolded.

Elizabeth glanced at her watch and cursed under her breath. "I'll be there."

The quilt slid to the floor as she stood, her muscles protesting from sleeping on the lumpy sofa. Her notebook had fallen beneath the coffee table, its pages filled with Uncle Leo's detailed accounts of suspicious activities around the trailer park. She gathered her papers and camera, tucking them into her worn leather messenger bag. The aroma of bacon and eggs drifted from the small kitchen where Uncle Leo stood at the ancient stove.

"Got time for breakfast? Making my specialty." He gestured at the crackling pan with his spatula. Deep creases formed around his eyes as he smiled, a rare sight that made her pause.

"I really should get going." Elizabeth slung her bag over her shoulder, fighting the guilt that crept in as his smile faded. "But I'll come back tonight. I want to hear more about what you've seen."

Uncle Leo turned off the burner and wiped his hands on a faded dish towel. "If you want the real story, make it to the rally today." He moved to the window, pushing aside the thin curtain. "Down by Saint Gregory's Church. Noon sharp."

"The protesters are meeting at the church?"

"Pastor lets them use the parking lot." He dropped the curtain and faced her. "They're good people, Elizabeth. Not troublemakers like Noah and his friends want everyone to think."

She pulled out her notebook again. "Who's organizing it?"

"Local college kids mostly. Environmental group. Don't remember the name of it." He crossed his arms, his expression hardening. "They've done their homework on OVAC. Have proof of what that plant will do to our water, our air."

"I'll be there." Elizabeth touched his arm. "And I'll bring dinner when I come back tonight. Chinese okay?"

The hint of a smile returned to his weathered face. "Get the hot and sour soup from Golden Palace. Only place that makes it right."

* * *

Elizabeth left the keys in the glove box for the rental company to pick up the car. Then she climbed into her "new" ancient Subaru, that she picked up from a guy in the trailer park for one hundred and fifty bucks, and rattled down the gravel road, kicking up clouds of dust in her wake. The morning sun glinted off the rusty mailboxes that lined the trailer park's entrance, their crooked posts marking her escape back to civilization.

Her phone buzzed against the passenger seat. Vincent's name flashed across the screen, along with a missed call notification and a text message from an hour ago. Her heart skipped. She hadn't told him about finding his uncle yet. Time zone differences and dropped cell signals around Echo Ridge made their communication sporadic. Elizabeth pulled onto the main road and hit the call button on her steering wheel. The phone rang once before Stacy's incoming call cut through.

"Where are you?" Stacy's voice filled the car's speakers.

"Ten minutes away." Elizabeth merged onto Main Street, passing the old movie theater with its faded marquee. "Just leaving Leo's place now."

"The planner's coming early. She called from the highway."

"Shit." Elizabeth pressed harder on the gas, watching the speedometer climb. "I need to shower and change."

"I laid out some clothes for you. Just get here."

"Thanks, I -" Elizabeth glanced at Vincent's unread message again. She'd have to call him back later. "Be there soon."

The Subaru's tires squealed as she turned onto Maple Drive, where Stacy's red brick house sat waiting. Time to switch gears from investigative journalist back to maid of honor. Vincent would understand -he always did. She pulled into Stacy's driveway, her mind drifting back to Noah. Maybe she'd been too quick to write him off. When he looked at her during the protest, he seemed genuinely concerned -not like a typical politician.

She killed the engine and sat for a moment, drumming her fingers on the steering wheel. The Noah she remembered from high school had been idealistic, passionate about making their town better. That fire still burned in his eyes when he spoke at the town meeting, even if his methods had changed. She dashed inside for a quick shower and tugged on the outfit Stacy had carefully laid out for her. Not a bad choice, considering.

"Councilman Montgomery," she murmured, testing the title. It suited him, she had to admit. His demeanor now radiated a quiet authority that sharply contrasted with the cocky quarterback she remembered from the hallways. Her phone buzzed with another text from Stacy:

Where are you? Wedding planner's here!

Elizabeth made a beeline down the street, parked, and grabbed her bag before racing up the path to the venue. But she paused with her hand on the door handle, her mind still wrestling through her feelings. Perhaps she was letting old hurts cloud her judgment. Noah might have valid reasons for wanting to keep the protests contained. As a journalist, shouldn't she hear all sides before drawing conclusions?

The memory of his warm hand on her arm, pulling her to safety during the town hall scuffle, had sent an unexpected shiver through her. Maybe it was worth getting to know this new version of Noah - not as her teenage crush, but as a community leader trying to navigate complex issues. She stepped inside and was immediately met by Stacy, who grabbed her arm and practically dragged her to their seats.

Elizabeth stifled a yawn behind her hand as the wedding planner flipped through another leather-bound portfolio. The Heritage Inn's ornate meeting room blurred at the edges of her vision, crystal chandeliers and gilded mirrors melting together in a haze of wedding details she couldn't focus on.

"What do you think about these centerpieces, Liz?" Stacy held up two nearly identical flower arrangements.

"They're both beautiful." Elizabeth reached for another petit four from the silver tray, hoping the sugar would keep her alert. The tiny cake melted on her tongue, almost making up for missing Uncle Leo's strong coffee this morning.

Her watch read 11:15. Forty-five minutes until the rally started at St. Gregory's.

The wedding planner's voice droned on about table linens and place settings. Elizabeth nodded at what seemed like appropriate moments while her mind wandered to the shipping containers she'd spotted near the trailer park, to Vincent's unread message, to the protest signs she'd helped Uncle Leo paint last night.

"Elizabeth?" Stacy touched her arm. "Are you okay?"

"Just tired." She forced a smile, watching her friend's face light up as she described her dream wedding cake. Even though Elizabeth was preoccupied, she couldn't ignore the warmth radiating from Stacy's joy. Her friend deserved this happiness.

11:30. Elizabeth shifted in her chair, calculating how long it would take to drive across town.

"One last thing," the wedding planner pulled out another folder. "Let's discuss the rehearsal dinner seating chart."

Elizabeth's stomach growled, reminding her that petit fours weren't a proper breakfast. She glanced at her watch again. The protesters would be gathering soon, their voices ready to rise against the concrete plant expansion that threatened to change everything about their small town. But for now, she watched Stacy beam over wedding details and reached for another tiny cake.

Ten minutes later, Elizabeth rose and made her apologies, kissed Stacy on the cheek and exited the meeting. She burst through the Heritage Inn's double doors, her heels clicking against the polished marble floor. The sound of Stacy's cheerful wedding planning chatter faded behind her. She dug through her purse for her car keys, head down, mind already at St. Gregory's -

"Oof!" She collided with a solid chest, stumbling backward.

Strong hands steadied her shoulders. "Whoa there, Lizzy."

Her heart lurched at the familiar voice. Noah Montgomery stood before her in a crisp charcoal suit, his delicious fragrance wrapping around her like a memory. Behind him, several men in business attire occupied a corner booth at the bar.

"Noah, sorry, I wasn't looking -"

"Always in a rush." His hands lingered on her shoulders before dropping away. His smile carried her to another flashback when he'd been the star quarterback and she'd been the awkward school newspaper photographer pining after him from afar.

"Some things never change." Elizabeth shifted her weight, too aware of how close they stood.

"Remember that time you literally ran into me outside chemistry class? Knocked all your books and science project supplies everywhere." Noah said.

"And you helped me pick them up even though you were late for practice." Heat crept up her neck. "Coach Bennett was furious."

"Worth it." Noah's eyes held hers. "We had something special back then, didn't we? Well, almost. Before you left for college and never looked back."

Elizabeth's throat tightened. She remembered their almost-kiss at senior prom. And the way he'd started dating the head cheerleader two weeks later again. "Ancient history."

"Maybe." He stepped closer, his voice dropping. "Or maybe we just had terrible timing. I've thought about you, Lizzy. About what might have been if -"

"Councilman Montgomery?" one of the men called from the bar. "We need your input on these projections."

Noah sighed. "Duty calls. But I'd love to catch up properly. Find out where that spark went."

Elizabeth backed away, her skin tingling. "I have to go. I'm late for-" She stopped herself before mentioning the rally. Something."

"Story of our lives," Noah said softly. "Always running in opposite directions."

Elizabeth's pulse raced as she stepped out into the morning sun, Noah's cologne still lingering in her senses. Her hands trembled slightly as she fumbled with her car keys. The way he'd looked at her, touched her shoulders -it brought back a fresh flood of memories she'd buried years ago.

"Hey Lizzy," Noah called after her. "Don't forget -dinner tonight at seven?"

She turned, catching his warm smile through the Inn's glass doors. "I'll be there."

Back in her car, Elizabeth pressed her forehead against the steering wheel and took a deep breath. The teenage version of herself would have swooned at this moment -dinner with Noah Montgomery, the guy whose yearbook photo she'd kept hidden in her diary all through high school. But she wasn't that girl anymore. She'd grown up, built a career, seen the world. So why did her stomach flutter like she was sixteen again?

"Get it together, Nelson," she muttered, starting the engine. The protest at St. Gregory's waited, along with Vincent's unread message. Important things. Real things.

Yet as she pulled onto Main Street, Elizabeth couldn't stop the smile spreading across her face. Maybe Stacy was right -coming home didn't have to be all bad memories and old wounds. Maybe it could be second chances too.

She raked her fingers through her hair and laughed at herself. One touch from Noah Montgomery and she was already daydreaming like a schoolgirl. The weight on her shoulders felt a little lighter. She checked her reflection in the rearview mirror. The awkward teenager with braces and bangs was long gone. In her place sat a woman who knew her worth, who'd traveled the world and carved out her own path. She started the engine, already mentally sorting through the outfits she'd packed. For the first time since arriving in Sweetwater Springs, she felt a spark of excitement about being home.

**

Elizabeth's car lurched into the last parking spot along Oak Street, half a block from St. Gregory's. She grabbed her phone and notebook, checking the time - 12:10. Late, but the crowd's energy told her she hadn't missed anything crucial.

The church lawn bustled with activity. Hand-painted signs bobbed above heads: "No Concrete Plant!" and "Protect Our Water!" A group of college students huddled near the church steps, their laptops balanced precariously as they typed updates for their news blog. The student station director, Maya, waved Elizabeth over while adjusting her camera equipment.

"Perfect timing," Maya said. "We're about to go live."

Elizabeth scanned the growing crowd. Young faces dominated - students she'd seen from pictures of their planning meetings, environmental science majors, aspiring journalists. A flash of silver caught her eye. Uncle Leo stood apart from the main group, his long gray hair pulled back, watching the scene unfold with arms crossed over his worn shirt. He looked out of place among the youth, yet his presence seemed to anchor the protest, giving it weight beyond student activism.

Their eyes met across the lawn. Leo nodded once, his face set in grim determination. He'd told her this would happen -the community rising up, refusing to stay silent. Elizabeth pulled out her phone to capture the moment, but her hand froze mid-motion.

This wasn't just another story anymore. These weren't anonymous protesters in a foreign country. This was her hometown. These were her neighbors from childhood. And there stood Vincent's uncle, the man who'd raised him, standing up against forces that threatened to reshape their community.

Maya's voice cut through Elizabeth's thoughts. "We're starting in five minutes. Want to do a quick interview?"

Elizabeth nodded, smoothing her hair back. "Of course. Let me know when you're ready."

Maya positioned the camera, adjusting the frame to capture both of them with St. Gregory's white clapboard walls as a backdrop. A student held up a makeshift reflector - what looked like aluminum foil taped to cardboard - to soften the harsh midday shadows.

"Rolling in three, two-" Maya pointed at Elizabeth.

"We're here with Elizabeth Nelson, the Truth Mercenary, an award-winning foreign correspondent who's covered the recent social movements across South America. Ms. Nelson, what brings you to this protest?"

The familiar rhythm of an interview settled over Elizabeth, but this time from the other side of the lens. "These students understand something crucial -local journalism matters. When communities lose their voice, they lose their power to shape their future."

"Any advice for aspiring journalists covering controversial issues?"

Elizabeth thought of Vincent, of the stories they'd chased together. "Stay focused on the facts. Document everything. And remember -behind every protest sign is a person with a story worth telling."

Maya beamed, lowering her camera. "That was perfect. Would you mind if we did a longer piece later? The students would love to learn from your experience."

"I'd like that," Elizabeth said.

Maya's calm, authoritative voice as she directed her crew filled Elizabeth with pride. Here was the next generation of truth-seekers, armed with smartphones and determination. They evoked memories of her younger self, before she experienced international missions and the horrors of war, back when she only had a borrowed camera and unresolved questions about a train collision that had devastated her life.

The sound of approaching sirens cut through the crowd's chatter. Elizabeth's head snapped toward the noise, her instincts as a journalist instantly awakening. Two police cruisers rolled slowly past the church, their presence a silent warning.

Elizabeth pulled Maya aside as the cruisers disappeared around the corner. "Listen, I've covered protests like this before. Your students need to know their rights if things escalate."

Maya's dark eyes widened. "You'd help train them? Most of them have never done field reporting."

"We'll start with the basics. How to document safely, what to do if confronted by authorities." Elizabeth glanced at the students clustered around their laptops. "And proper fact-checking protocols. A story like this needs rock-solid sourcing."

"We meet Tuesday and Thursday afternoons at the campus media center." Maya pulled out her phone. "Could you come tomorrow? The team's working on a deep dive into the environmental impact reports."

Elizabeth checked her calendar - wedding preparations with Stacy weren't until evening. "Count me in. Three o'clock?"

"Perfect." Maya hesitated. "There's something else. We found some discrepancies in the permit applications, but we're not sure how to verify them without getting shut down by OVAC."

The familiar thrill of investigation tingled through Elizabeth's spine. This wasn't just about teaching - these students had stumbled onto something real. "Show me what you've got. I might know some ways to cross-reference public records that won't raise red flags."

Maya's face lit up. "Really? That would be amazing. The team will be so excited to learn from someone with your experience."

Elizabeth watched the young reporter hurry back to her crew, remembering her own early days chasing leads and building sources. She hadn't planned on getting involved, but these students' dedication struck a chord. They weren't just covering a story - they were fighting for their community's future.

Her phone buzzed with a text from Vincent. She sent him a quick canned text message promising to call him back, then she tucked her phone away. He'd understand. Some stories demanded more than just observation. Sometimes you had to step in, share what you knew, help others find their voice.

A familiar laugh cut through the crowd's chatter. Elizabeth turned to see Harper Martinez, her black hair now streaked with bold magenta, weaving through the protesters.

"Oh my God! Elizabeth Nelson? What are you doing in this backwater?" Harper pulled her into a tight hug.

"My best friend's wedding. But I could ask you the same thing."

"Following leads, as always." Harper's eyes sparkled. "Last time I saw you was at the Stellars—still can't believe that they passed on your coverage of the wildfires in Tasmania. You deserved to win."

"Thanks, I had a great team with me. And look at you, moving up from the Crimson Call-Out gossip columns. I used to live for your celebrity dirt, but taking down that criminal, Robert Gaines? That's next level."

Harper's expression turned serious. "That story was unexpected. And it's ongoing. I want you to know that you were my inspiration. Watching you tackle those international stories, it made me realize I could do more. You're the 'Truth Mercenary'- that's so bad ass!"

"Please, you were already a force of nature." Elizabeth pulled out her phone. "We should grab drinks while I'm here."

"Definitely. I'm live over in Clover City, just a few miles southeast." Harper's face lit up. "Oh, and you have to come to The Boat House - my fiancé's the executive chef."

"Fancy. Moving up in all ways, I see." Elizabeth watched as Harper typed in her number.

"Says the woman who's been dodging bullets in South America." Harper glanced at her watch. "I've got to go, but let's not wait years to catch up again."

Elizabeth shook her head and leaned back against the church's white fence. "Anyone wanting to follow in my footsteps should know -it's not all press passes and breaking news. Most nights are spent in cheap motels with spotty Wi-Fi, eating stale granola bars."

"Oh please." Harper's magenta-streaked hair caught the sunlight as she laughed. "You've exposed government corruption in three countries. The *New York Citizen* and *Washington Sentinel* fight over your stories. And that piece about the diamond smuggling ring? Pure genius."

The praise warmed Elizabeth more than she expected. For days she'd felt like an outsider in Sweetwater Springs, but Harper spoke her language -deadlines, sources, the thrill of uncovering truth. Here was someone who understood the drive that kept her chasing leads across borders.

"Takes one to know one." Elizabeth nudged Harper's shoulder. "Your Gaines investigation had real teeth. Not many reporters would've dared take on a mob boss."

"I learned from watching the best." Harper pulled her into another tight hug, her designer perfume. a stark contrast to the earthy scent of perspiration and grass that shrouded the protesters. "Don't be a stranger, okay? The journalism world needs more women like you showing us what's possible."

Harper strode off into the crowd, her hand lifted in farewell. Elizabeth felt a lightness in her being. Maybe she wasn't so out of place here after all. She turned and spotted Noah inside of a gleaming black SUV idling across from St. Gregory's. He caught her eye through the open passenger window and beckoned her over with a slight tilt of his head. The crisp lines of his tailored suit seemed out of place against the backdrop of protest signs, students and construction workers. She crossed the street, keeping one eye on Maya's crew as they packed up their equipment.

"Quite the scene you've got going here." Noah's smile didn't reach his eyes. "Listen, Lizzy, you might want to keep your distance from all this. Things could get complicated."

"Complicated how?" Elizabeth leaned against his car door, studying his face. The same handsome features but there was something different in his expression -a careful neutrality that hadn't been there before.

"Those activists don't understand the bigger picture. The plant expansion means jobs, progress." He drummed his fingers on the door. "Getting involved could make things... awkward for you. For us."

"I'm a journalist, Noah. Getting involved is what I do." She straightened up, stepping back from his car. "The community deserves to know what's happening."

"I see. Well, about dinner tonight -" He adjusted his tie, glancing at his watch. "Something's come up with the council. Rain check?"

"Sure." Elizabeth kept her voice neutral, but her jaw tightened. "Rain check."

The SUV pulled away from the curb, leaving Elizabeth standing on the sidewalk. The same old Noah -trying to please everyone, avoiding hard conversations. Some things hadn't changed since high school.

***

Elizabeth pushed open the door of Golden Palace, the familiar jingle of bells and scent of ginger and garlic washing over her. The cramped interior hadn't changed since childhood -same red paper lanterns, same faded zodiac placemats lining the counter.

Mrs. Chen looked up from her crossword puzzle, her face brightening. "Elizabeth! Long time no see."

"Hi Mrs. Chen. Could I get the hot and sour soup to go? For two. Mr. Montoya highly recommends it."

"Uncle Leo's favorite." Mrs. Chen winked, already reaching for takeout containers. "I add extra mushrooms, just how he likes."

Elizabeth settled onto one of the worn vinyl stools at the counter, pulling out her phone. She had left her number with the council secretary. No new messages from Noah, not that she expected any. His quick retreat from their dinner plans stung less than she'd anticipated. Maybe because deep down, she'd known he would find a reason to cancel.

The kitchen doors swung open, releasing a cloud of steam and the rhythmic sound of chopping. Mr. Chen's voice called out in Mandarin, followed by Mrs. Chen's reply. Some things in Sweetwater Springs remained constant -the Chens' banter, the way the soup could warm you down to your bones on a cool evening, Uncle Leo's quiet wisdom.

She found herself looking forward to another night of Leo's stories about Vincent as a boy, about the town before everything started changing. There was something comforting about sitting in his small trailer, watching the sun set over the hills while he talked about the old days.

Mrs. Chen placed two containers of steaming soup on the counter. "Extra crackers for Leo. Tell him to come visit sometime, not just send pretty girls to pick up his dinner."

Elizabeth laughed, pulling out her wallet. "I'll tell him. Though I think he prefers having dinner delivered by pretty girls."

* * *

Elizabeth sat in the cramped but cozy trailer, the scent of Uncle Leo's freshly brewed coffee mingling with the faint smell of motor oil and pine from the woods nearby. She was leaning forward, engrossed in Leo's stories about Vincent as a kid catching tadpoles, when her phone buzzed to life in her hand.

"It's him!" she said, her face lighting up as she quickly answered and put the call on speaker.

"Hey there," Vincent's voice crackled through the speaker, sounding distant yet unmistakably warm. "Just wanted to let you know, I'll be seeing you soon. And, Elizabeth, I'll even bring you some of that black licorice you're always asking for. In the meantime, take care of Uncle Leo for me."

Elizabeth's smile faded instantly, her stomach sinking. She forced herself to respond lightly, "Sure, Vincent. See you soon." She ended the call, her fingers lingering on the phone as she processed what she'd just heard.

Leo clapped his hands together, beaming. "Well, that's good news, don't you think? He sounds like he's feeling much better."

But Elizabeth's face was tight with worry. "No, Uncle Leo. I hate black licorice," she murmured. "He knows that."

Her eyes lingered on her phone, Vincent's words looping in her mind. She looked up at Leo, her voice in a soft whisper. "He's not coming. The licorice... it's a signal." The coded message that he wouldn't join her in Sweetwater Springs, or maybe ever again, left her stunned. *What's going on?* She shot him a quick text, wanting to know why he was ghosting her. Upon seeing the notification, her heart sank.

Message Not Delivered

Leo's face softened, his eyes full of understanding and a quiet strength. He motioned toward the small kitchen table, where the takeout containers were waiting. "Come on, sit and eat," he said gently. "Things will work out, one way or another."

She hesitated, then nodded, sinking into the chair across from him. Leo took her hand in his, a reassuring warmth that steadied her, if only for a moment.

***

Elizabeth sat back in the worn leather armchair, savoring the last spoonful of Mrs. Chen's hot and sour soup. The empty containers sat on Leo's coffee table beside a collection of small glass bottles filled with various colored liquids.

"What are all these?" She pointed to a dark amber bottle.

Leo picked it up, holding it to the light streaming through his trailer window. "Elderberry tincture. Good for colds, building immunity." He set it down and grabbed another, this one filled with pale green water. "This one's yarrow. Nature's bandaid - stops bleeding, fights infection."

Elizabeth leaned forward, picking up a bottle of deep purple liquid. The glass felt cool against her palm. "You make all these yourself?"

"Everything grows right here on these hills." Leo gestured toward his window. "Learned from my grandmother. She knew every plant, every root that could heal."

The passion in his voice reminded her of Vincent when he talked about getting the perfect shot. Same intensity, same devotion to their craft.

"I could show you, if you want to stay another night. Best foraging's early morning, when the dew's still fresh."

Elizabeth glanced at her phone. No urgent messages, nothing from Vincent, and Stacy wouldn't need her until tomorrow afternoon. "I'd like that. Though I warn you, my plant knowledge stops at 'don't eat the red berries.'"

Leo's face crinkled with amusement. "Good rule to start with. We'll work on the rest tomorrow."

* * *

Dawn painted the hills in soft pastels as Elizabeth followed Leo along a narrow dirt path behind his trailer. Her boots, borrowed from a box of Vincent's old things, were a size too big but comfortable enough for gardening.

"Vincent used to help me plant these rows every spring." Leo kneeled beside a patch of rich soil, his seasoned hands working the earth with practiced ease. "Always wanted to know the story behind each plant. Why this one heals, why that one hurts."

Elizabeth settled beside him, watching as he demonstrated how to space the transplants. The morning air carried the scent of damp earth and wild bergamot.

"He never told me about the garden." Elizabeth gently pressed a cabbage plant into the soil, mimicking Leo's technique.

"No? Well, he was different then. Before the cameras, before he started chasing his wild ideas around the world." Leo reached for another plant. "Used to sit right here, helping me sort herbs for drying. Said the quiet helped him think."

They worked in companionable silence, moving down the row. Elizabeth's fingers grew dirty, her back ached, but there was something satisfying about working the land.

"Your parents," Leo said suddenly, "they were good people. Used to bring me soup when I was sick, even though we barely knew each other."

Elizabeth's hands stilled in the dirt. "You knew them?"

"Small town." Leo nodded toward a patch of purple flowers. "Your mother loved echinacea. Said it reminded her of her grandmother's garden in Mexico. After the accident, I planted these for her."

Elizabeth touched a purple petal, her throat tight. All these years, and she'd never known this connection existed. Her mother's favorite flowers, blooming in Leonard Montoya's garden.

"Vincent would sneak over here sometimes," he continued, "He'd gather a bunch and leave flowers on their graves. Never told you that either, did he?"

Elizabeth shook her head, unable to speak. The image of young Vincent, carrying purple flowers up the cemetery hill, filled her body with an unexplainable calm. They finished planting the leeks and onions, then returned inside for the rest of the day's tasks.

She surveyed Leo's small trailer, noting the stack of newspapers in the corner and the thin layer of dust on the windowsills. The morning's gardening had shown her a different side of Vincent's uncle -not just the suspicious old man warning about corporate schemes, but someone who carried deep wisdom and unexpected connections to her past.

"This place could use a woman's touch," she said, running her finger along a dusty shelf.

Leo looked up from his herbs, a hint of tenderness crossing his hardened features. "Vincent used to help keep things tidy when he visited. These days, well..." He shrugged, turning back to his work.

Elizabeth watched him methodically sorting the leaves into small piles. The thought of him here alone, tracking suspicious activities at that corporation while living in this neglected space, tugged at her heart.

"I've been thinking," she said, moving to help him with the herbs. "After Stacy's wedding, I don't have any immediate assignments lined up. Maybe I could stay here for a while, help fix this place up."

Leo's hands stilled. "You'd want to stay here? In this old trailer?"

"Why not? It's quiet, perfect for writing. And someone needs to document what's happening with this concrete plant situation everybody's riled up about." She gestured toward his collection of notes and newspaper clippings. "Plus, I could learn more about these herbs of yours."

A slow smile spread across Leo's face. "Well, the spare room needs clearing out. Been using it for storage since Vincent left. But if you're willing to help clean it up..."

"I'd like that," Elizabeth said, realizing she meant it. "It feels right."

Leo nodded, reaching for another bundle of herbs. "Then it's settled. Welcome."

Her phone buzzed against the coffee table. Vincent's name flashed across the screen, making her heart skip.

"Hey stranger," she answered, trying to keep her voice light.

"What's this I hear about you getting mixed up in protests?" Vincent's typical protective tone crackled through the line. "I thought you were staying with your friend for a wedding."

"Actually, I'm staying here in Echo Ridge." She didn't know how to read him. How did he find out about the protests? "With your uncle. I found him!"

Silence filled the line. "That's not a good idea, Elizabeth. That area's never been safe. A lot of transients camp out there."

"I've gathered some interesting leads here. Besides, your uncle could use the company —"

"Let me talk to him."

Elizabeth handed the phone to Leo, who took it with trembling fingers. He shuffled onto the small porch, his voice a low murmur through the screen door. She busied herself organizing her notes, trying not to eavesdrop.

When Leo returned several minutes later, his eyes were red-rimmed and glistening. He pressed the phone back into her hand, turning away quickly to wipe his face.

"Vincent?" she asked softly.

"Be careful, Liz. Promise me." His voice was tight with concern.

"I will. Look, I need to head out -Stacy's rehearsal dinner." She ended the call and grabbed her purse, watching Leo sink heavily into his chair. "I'll be back tonight, Uncle Leo. We can finish sorting those herbs together. Okay?"

Leo nodded without looking up, his shoulders hunched as if carrying an invisible weight.

She paused at the door, torn between her commitment to Stacy and the urge to stay, to understand what had transpired between uncle and nephew. A heavy silence filled the air, punctuated only by the fragrance of the earth and Leo's medicinal concoctions. As she walked to her car, her emotions overflowed with regret, like she was walking away from something precious and rare. She glanced back at the trailer, where Leo stood watching her departure with a gentle wave, and felt a familiar tug at her heart–his silhouette reminding her of the father she'd lost. And she made a silent promise to return right after Stacy's rehearsal dinner. The drive away from the trailer park felt like leaving a piece of herself behind, but the comforting fragrance from the small bag of aromatic herbs Leo had insisted she take offered a tangible connection to this newfound peace.

* * *

Elizabeth smoothed her sapphire blue cocktail dress and stepped into the rehearsal venue. The alluring scent of gardenias filled the air, Stacy's signature flower choice for all occasions. Her breath caught as she spotted Noah across the room, his tall frame cutting an elegant figure in a classic black suit. *Damn, he's fine.* His eyes met hers. That magnetic pull hit her full force as he crossed the room.

"A little birdie told me you'd be here." Noah's smile lit up his face.

Elizabeth's heart skipped. "Let me guess - Stacy?"

"She might have mentioned it." He touched her elbow, steering her toward a quiet corner. "Listen, about canceling dinner yesterday -"

"It's okay." She surprised herself by meaning it. His hand on her back, warm through the delicate fabric of her dress, sent a jolt through her, scattering her thoughts like leaves in a wind.

"No, it wasn't. I got caught up in town politics." His brown eyes held genuine regret. "But seeing you at that protest... brought back memories of that fierce girl who always fought for what she believed in."

Heat crept up Elizabeth's neck. "Still do."

"Some things never change." The scent of Noah's cologne hit her senses as he drew nearer, a luscious aroma of citrus and warm woodsy notes. "Makes me wonder if we could pick up where we left off." His words were drawn out in that mesmerizing, slow tone. And that smile... "Before graduation launched us into different worlds."

Elizabeth's pulse quickened. "That was a lifetime ago."

"Maybe. But this connection?" He gestured between them. "That feels pretty current to me. How long are you staying in Sweetwater?"

Elizabeth thought of Leo's trailer, the mysterious concrete plant, the stories waiting to be uncovered. "As long as it takes."

Noah's smile widened. "I like the sound of that."

8

Borrowed Romance

The historic community center glowed with afternoon sunlight streaming through tall windows. Elizabeth adjusted her lavender maid of honor dress, watching Stacy fuss with her veil in the antique mirror. The scent of gardenias filled the air, mixing with the excited chatter of guests filtering into the main hall.

"How do I look?" Stacy turned, her lace gown catching the light.

"You are ... beautiful. Just perfection." Elizabeth blinked back unexpected tears. Her best friend radiated joy.

The ceremony unfolded like a dream, bathed in the warm glow of candelabras along the dark oak-paneled walls of the community center. She stood beside Stacy, holding the bouquet of white roses and baby's breath as the couple exchanged heartfelt vows. Her throat tightened watching their tender expressions, their fingers trembling as they slipped on rings. The way they gazed at each other, so full of hope and promise, stirred something deep within her -a longing she usually kept buried beneath her independent spirit. As Stacy's voice wavered with emotion, Elizabeth blinked rapidly, determined not to let her mascara run. *No one wants to see panda eyes in their wedding photos.*

Outside, the garden provided a stunning backdrop for photos. Elizabeth snapped candids on her phone while the photographer positioned the newlyweds, directing them with gentle commands to tilt their heads just so and shift their shoulders. The late afternoon sun cast everything in honey-gold light, transforming ordinary flowers into glowing jewels and making Stacy's white dress shimmer like spun sugar. *Breathtaking.*

"Lizzy," a familiar voice called. "You're all over the place!"

She turned to find Noah approaching, devastatingly handsome in his dark emerald green tailored suit. Her pulse quickened.

"Guilty as charged," she said, managing a smile despite the butterflies in her stomach.

The reception filled the building with music and laughter. Elizabeth watched couples twirl across the dance floor, lost in thought until Noah's hand found the small of her back. Her breath hitched as his hand moved smoothly around her body and settled on her waist, guiding her into the slow dance. His scent stirred her intensely, filling her senses, creating a dangerous pull that she couldn't resist.

"Remember our last school dance here?" His voice rumbled low near her ear.

"When you danced with Jessica Cortez all night?" The words slipped out before she could stop them.

Noah pulled back, his brown eyes searching her face. "I wanted to dance with you." He rested his cheek against her temple as he pulled her closer. "But you looked too pretty to touch."

Her heart skipped a beat. As they swayed to the music, the heat from his hands on her body sent shivers down her spine, a thrilling mix of warmth and anxiety. Their bodies moved as one, their motion fluid and synchronized, like magnets pulled together after years of being apart.

"You should've asked me." Elizabeth leaned back, focused on the knot of his tie, avoiding those intense eyes that seemed to see right through her carefully constructed walls.

"I was an idiot back then." His fingers traced small circles along the curve of her hip. "Too caught up in what everyone else thought."

The dance floor faded away. All she could sense was Noah's steady heartbeat against her body, the strength in his arms as he held her close. His touch, the flex of his muscles tightening around her, sent a wave of goosebumps across her body. Part of her wanted to melt into him, to forget everything else -the concrete plant expansion plans, her investigation, where her next assignment would send her. But another part remembered the sting of watching Noah date other girls in high school, of never feeling like she was quite enough.

His fingers intertwined with hers, and she leaned closer, breathing in the scent of him–something distinctly Noah that transported her back to their high school days. She tilted her head to fit perfectly under his chin, like they were two pieces of a puzzle finally clicking into place, and the warmth of his broad chest against her cheek made her heart flutter in a way she hadn't felt since she was seventeen. As they swayed to the music, his other hand resting possessively at the small of her back, Elizabeth found herself fighting the urge to press completely into his embrace, knowing that doing so would make it impossible to maintain the professional distance she'd been trying so hard to keep. The gentle pressure of his thumb tracing circles on her hand sent warm pulsating shockwaves through her body. And when he softly murmured "Lizzy" into her hair, she closed her eyes and eased her muscles, momentarily forgetting about deadlines, stories, and all the reasons why this was probably a bad idea.

"You know, back in the day some people thought that would be us." Noah nodded toward Stacy and her new husband sharing their first dance. He pulled her even closer, his touch electric. Elizabeth flowed with him, letting herself imagine the possibility. For a moment, she could see it all - the white dress, the rings, the life they might have shared if things had been different. The fantasy was as exhilarating as it was dangerous.

Noah whispered in her ear, "It could still happen, don't you think?"

Her heart whispered, Yes.

* * *

Elizabeth followed Leo onto his small back porch, carrying two steaming mugs of chamomile tea. The wooden boards creaked beneath their feet as they settled into mismatched lawn chairs. Above them, stars pierced the velvet darkness, far brighter than any she'd seen in the cities that had been called home in past years.

"Vincent used to sit out here for hours," Leo said, accepting the mug she offered. "Said the stars helped him think clearer."

Elizabeth traced the Big Dipper with her eyes, remembering nights in Venezuela when she and Vincent had camped under the open skies. "He still does that, you know. Finds the highest spot he can whenever we're on assignment in the remote areas."

"Some habits stick." Leo's voice carried a hint of pride. "Like caring about this place. These hills. The water that runs through them."

The night air carried the sweet scent of honeysuckle and the distant chorus of crickets. Elizabeth wrapped her hands around her warm mug, letting the peaceful moment wash over her.

"I used to think I had to leave to make a difference," she admitted. "That the important stories were always somewhere else. Out there."

"Sometimes the biggest fights happen in the smallest places." Leo pointed to a cluster of stars. "See that? Cassiopeia. The queen who defied the gods to protect her people."

Elizabeth smiled at the parallel. Here she was, a journalist who'd covered revolutions and wars, finding herself drawn into a small town's battle for survival.

"This land," Leo continued, "it's more than just dirt and trees. It's stories. Memories. Future possibilities. When they threaten that, they threaten everything about us."

The truth of his words settled deep in Elizabeth's heart. She'd traveled the world discovering tales of communities fighting for their rights, never imagining she'd find herself in the middle of one back home.

"I understand now," she said softly. "Why Vincent told me about this place. And why it mattered so much to find you."

Leo nodded, his eyes fixed on the starlit horizon. He shifted in his chair, the wood groaning beneath him. "Saw you talking to Noah Montgomery at the rally."

Elizabeth's fingers tightened around her mug. "You did?"

"Same look in his eyes as when you two were kids." Leo's face creased with a knowing smile.

A warm blush crept across Elizabeth's face. She took a long sip of tea to hide her reaction.

"Thing about roots," Leo said, "is they run deeper than we think. Even when we try to pull them up, part stays behind."

"Noah and I were never..." She paused, searching for the right words. "It was just a teenage crush."

"Mmhmm." Leo's tone carried years of quiet observation. "And Vincent?"

The question caught her off guard. She stared into her tea, watching the steam curl into the night air. "It's just a work arrangement. That's different. It's ... complicated."

"Love usually is." Leo's voice softened. "You know what I've learned? People spend so much time running from hurt, they forget to run toward something."

Elizabeth's chest tightened. She thought of all the assignments she'd taken, the events she'd pursued across continents. And the relationships she'd kept were casual, temporary, simple.

"I'm not running," she protested weakly.

"No?" Leo raised an eyebrow. "Then why haven't you let anyone close enough to matter since your parents died?"

His words cut through her like a knife, and she felt the truth of them in her very bones. She blinked back sudden tears. "Being alone is safer," she whispered. "I don't believe you should give people the power to hurt you by placing your happiness in their hands."

"You know, mijita, a cactus grows thorns to protect itself in the desert, but it still has to open its flowers to survive," Leo said softly, his hands busy with the sage he was bundling. "The heart is the same way -you can guard it, but if you never let it bloom, you'll never know what kind of beauty you might've missed."

Leo's words hung in the night air, striking too close to home. He had deciphered her completely. Had scrutinized her life, her stories, her experiences, and her personality as thoroughly as someone reading the pages of an old, well-worn book. She set her mug on the wooden railing, the ceramic clinking against the warped surface. Her throat tightened as memories of her parents' funeral crashed through her carefully guarded emotions.

"You sound like Vincent." She forced a weak laugh. "With your honesty and x-ray vision."

"That boy learned something from me after all." Leo's chair creaked as he leaned forward. "You know what else he learned? How to recognize when something's worth fighting for."

Elizabeth's phone buzzed in her pocket - Vincent's name flashed across the screen. She silenced it, guilt twisting in her stomach.

"I've built a life around my career," she said. "Being where the action is. Making a difference. That's my life. I chose it. It's what I do, who I am."

"And now the story's here." Leo gestured toward the distant lights of Sweetwater Springs. "Along with a man who can see past those walls you've built around that life you chose."

Elizabeth felt her cheeks burn. "Pretty sure Noah's involved with someone else. Plenty of women around here better suited for the small town way of —."

"That what you're telling yourself?" Leo's dark eyes fixed on hers. "Or is it easier than admitting you're scared of what might happen if you let your walls down? You deserve a life that's stable, rooted. One day, you're going to have to stop running. Time will decide when, but know that day will come."

Elizabeth stood abruptly, pacing the small porch. The boards groaned beneath her feet. Her hands trembled as she ran them through her hair.

"I watched my parents die because people in power decided their lives didn't matter." Her voice cracked. "The same thing's happening now - corporations deciding they can destroy whatever they want. How can I think about relationships when-"

"When what?" Leo's quiet question stopped her mid-stride. "When there's always another flight? Another story? Another reason to keep everyone at arm's length?"

Elizabeth gripped the porch railing, the rough wood grounding her as stars blurred above. She'd spent years building armor around her heart, telling herself it made her a better journalist. More objective. Less vulnerable. But here, in this small town with its big secrets, that armor was cracking.

She stared into the night, Leo's words echoing in her mind. Her phone felt heavy in her pocket, Vincent's missed call a reminder of the choices ahead of her. The night air carried a chill that made her wrap her arms around herself.

"You're right," she admitted, turning back to Leo. "I have been running. But this story -what's happening here in Sweetwater Springs -it matters."

"And the rest?" Leo's eyes held a knowing look that reminded her so much of Vincent.

Before she could answer, headlights swept across the trailer park. A black SUV crawled past Leo's property, moving slower than normal traffic would. Elizabeth's survival instincts kicked in as she noticed the tinted windows and out-of-state plates.

"That's the third time tonight," Leo muttered, setting down his mug. "Been happening more since the town hall meeting."

Elizabeth pulled out her phone and snapped a quick photo of the vehicle as it disappeared around the corner. "They're looking for the activists."

"Looking for something." Leo's voice carried an edge she hadn't heard before. "Question is, what are they afraid we'll see?"

The crickets fell silent. In that moment, Elizabeth felt the weight of everything converging -her personal conflicts, the town's struggle, and whatever secrets lay buried beneath the surface of Ohio Valley Aggregates.

"I should check my messages," she said, pulling out her phone. Three texts from Vincent, one from Noah, and several from her student journalist contacts about tomorrow's protest coverage.

Leo pushed himself up from his chair. "Don't stay up too late. Morning comes early out here."

Elizabeth nodded, but her mind was already racing with possibilities. Whatever was happening in Sweetwater Springs went deeper than a concrete plant. She could feel it in her gut -the same instinct that had served her well at checkpoints and night raids.

She tested the locks on the trailer's doors one final time, her mind still on the mysterious SUV. The kitchen needed attention - dishes from their evening tea cluttered the sink, and Leo's collection of newspaper clippings scattered across the counter begged for organization.

She filled the sink with hot water and dish soap, letting the familiar task calm her racing thoughts. The old porcelain cups clinked against each other as she washed them, careful not to chip their already worn edges. Leo kept his glass jars and bottles, oils and infusers with such care, despite the trailer's age and condition. The kitchen counter revealed its original pale yellow surface as she wiped away decades of accumulated paper and dust. She stacked Leo's newspaper clippings in neat piles -environmental reports, town council meeting minutes, property records. His research was methodical, thorough. Just like Vincent's.

In the small bathroom, she found fresh towels in the cabinet under the sink and laid them out. The mirror needed cleaning, and she spent a few minutes scrubbing away water spots until her reflection shone clear in the glass. The pull-out couch in the living room creaked as she unfolded it. Leo had insisted she take his room, but she'd refused to displace him. The sheets smelled of lavender fabric softener, and the pillow was soft beneath her head as she settled in.

Through the thin walls, she heard Leo's quiet movements in his bedroom -the shuffle of slippers, the soft click of a lamp being turned off. The trailer fell silent except for the distant hum of crickets and the occasional passing car. She pulled the blanket up to her chin, letting out a long breath. Tomorrow would bring new challenges -more protests to cover, more mysteries to unravel. But for now, in this quiet moment, she felt strangely at peace. Her thoughts wandered to Vincent. She grabbed her phone and sent a text.

Hey, where are you?

Seconds later, the same notification appeared again.

Message Not Delivered.

"What the hell, Vin?" She whispered and set her phone aside. *You're definitely blocking my calls now. Got it.* She pushed down the frustration that was morphing into anger and dejection, the knot in her stomach tightening with each suppressed emotion. Well, what did she expect? They knew that things between them were bound to change, but she had pushed the thought away. Now she lay back on the bed, accepting the inevitable. Her eyes grew heavy as exhaustion finally caught up with her. The last thing she saw before drifting off was moonlight filtering through the window, casting soft shadows on Leo's carefully tended houseplants.

* * *

Elizabeth's phone buzzed on the makeshift nightstand, the vibration jolting her awake. She squinted at the bright screen - 2:13 AM. A new text from Noah glowed in the darkness.

Are you up?

She rubbed the sleep from her eyes, considering how to respond. Her fingers hesitated over the keyboard before typing out a reply.

I am now. What's going on?

The little typing bubbles appeared almost instantly.

Can't sleep. Thinking about you.

A small smile tugged at the corner of her mouth as she read his words. She could practically hear the low, suggestive rumble of his voice.

> **Oh yeah? What about me exactly?**

She held her breath, anticipating his response.

> **Your eyes. Your smile. The way you laughed at the rehearsal dinner. How you felt in my arms ...**

The typing bubbles kept pulsing.

> **I missed you, Bet**

There it was -that old nickname that used to make her heart flutter. She bit her lip, feeling that familiar ache stir deep within her. She typed back, using his high school moniker.

> **I missed you too, Monty. Meet me at the stadium in 20?**

She waited, the seconds ticking by with agonizing slowness. Finally, his reply appeared.

> **Already on my way**

Elizabeth slipped quietly out of the trailer, careful not to wake Leo, and walked toward the access road. The cool night air prickled her skin as she hurried down the dirt path toward Main Street. The old high school stadium loomed ahead, the faded green bleachers and towering light posts casting long shadows in the moonlight.

She made her way to the gate, finding it unlocked as always.

Rounding the corner to the field, she spotted Noah's SUV parked on the sidelines. He was leaning against the hood, hands shoved in his pockets as he gazed up at the stars. The crunch of the artificial turf under her feet made him turn. Their eyes met, and suddenly the years seemed to fade away... Memories of Friday night games and stolen glances flooded back as Elizabeth's heart raced as she approached Noah. The stadium felt smaller now, the metal bleachers weathered by time and elements.

"Remember when you used to sit right there?" Noah pointed to a spot in the middle of the bleachers. "Front row of the student section."

"Where I could watch you throw those perfect passes?" Elizabeth traced her fingers along the cold metal railing as they climbed the steps.

"I noticed." Noah's smile caught the moonlight. "Used to make me nervous, having you watch so intently. I would've rather spent more time watching you on the sidelines than actually playing."

They reached the top of the bleachers, where the whole town spread out before them in a blanket of twinkling lights. The night chill bit into Elizabeth, and she pulled her arms tightly around herself for warmth.

"All those times I wanted to ask you out," Noah said, his voice soft. "But I never had the courage."

"The star quarterback, afraid to talk to the awkward newspaper girl?"

"You were never awkward. Just... intense. Like you could see right through people."

Elizabeth turned to face him, their shoulders nearly touching. "And what do you think I see now?"

Noah moved closer, narrowing the gap between them. The touch of his hand on her back sent a spark of warmth through her, electrifying her skin. Her breath caught as he pulled her against him, their bodies fitting together like they were meant to. His other hand cupped her face, thumb brushing her cheek.

"The same thing I hope you've always seen," he whispered. "Someone who could never stop thinking about you."

Elizabeth pulled away from Noah's embrace, her heart hammering against her ribs. The night air felt colder now as she descended the bleacher steps ahead of him, her boots clanking against the metal.

Back in the parking lot, Noah's truck gleamed under the stadium lights. He leaned against the driver's door, arms crossed as they faced off.

"So, what's the deal with you staying out at Echo Ridge? That old trailer park's not exactly five-star accommodation."

Elizabeth kicked at a loose piece of gravel. "It's complicated."

"Come on, Lizzy. There are plenty of nice places in town. I could help you find —"

"I have my reasons." She shifted her weight, avoiding his gaze. "How's the concrete plant expansion proposal coming along?"

Noah stepped forward. "Don't change the subject. I worry about you out there alone."

"I'm not alone. Uncle Leo's there."

"Leonard Montoya? That old man's not —"

"He's been nothing but kind to me." Elizabeth's voice hardened. "And I feel safe there."

Noah reached for her hand, his fingers warm against her skin. "I just want what's best for you."

"I know what's best for me."

He moved closer, backing her against the SUV. His hand came up to cup her face, thumb tracing her bottom lip. Elizabeth's breath caught in her throat, the heat of his gaze making her skin tingle, his intention unmistakable.

"Noah," she said softly, as he leaned in. His lips brushed against hers, soft and inviting. She yielded to his kiss, the warmth surging through her as his tongue teased the line of her lips, urging her to open for him. A sigh escaped her as she parted them willingly, allowing him to deepen the embrace. His arms wrapped around her waist, pulling her flush against him. The cool metal of the SUV pressed into her back as she arched into his touch, craving more of him. Her hands slid up his chest, fingers curling in the fabric of his shirt. She inhaled the intoxicating scent of his cologne, a heady fragrance that blended with the crisp, cool air of the night, leaving Elizabeth breathless. As he nipped at her bottom lip gently before soothing it with his tongue, she couldn't help but press closer, losing herself in a tangle of sensations and memories long buried since high school days spent dreaming of this very moment with Noah Montgomery.

Elizabeth broke the kiss, her breath coming in short pants. Noah's eyes were dark with desire, his pupils dilated as he gazed down at her. She reached for the door handle, tugging it open.

"In here," she breathed against his mouth.

Noah didn't hesitate. He followed as Elizabeth climbed into the vehicle, his larger frame crowding the backseat. She straddled his hips, feeling evidence of his arousal through their clothes, a rush of heat coursing through her at the intimate contact. The SUV's confines amplified every sensation - Noah's warm breath on her neck, the firm muscles of his thighs beneath her, the way he gripped her waist. Teenage dreams and late-night musings flooded back as she found herself lost in Noah's presence once more.

"I've thought about this for so long," Noah murmured, fingers tangling in her hair.

"Me too." She rocked against him, reveling in the delicious friction. Her hands moved to his chest, pushing at the fabric of his shirt. Noah helped her remove it before reaching for hers in turn. The cotton slid up over her head and disappeared onto the floorboard. He cupped her breasts in his hot palms, his thumbs brushing over nipples already hard with anticipation. The rough texture of his skin sent shivers down her back as she gasped at the sensation. She pressed against him, savoring the heat of his hands against her skin, a silent plea for more.

"You're gorgeous, Bet." Noah breathed before lowering his head to take one dark rosy peak into his mouth.

Elizabeth bucked beneath him at the feel of his hot tongue on her sensitive skin, a low moan escaping her lips. Her own hands went to work on his belt buckle, fingers trembling slightly as she sought to free him from the confines of his pants. The urgency in her movements betrayed her desire, years of pent-up longing finally finding its release in this moment with Noah. As she undid the last button and zipper, she marveled at how different it felt from her usual casual encounters—this was Noah, the boy who had captured her heart so long ago.

"Wait—" Noah caught her wrists in one large hand. "Slow down."

Elizabeth nipped at his neck in response. "I want you so bad."

His hold tightened. "But I want to make this good for you."

A small smile curved her lips. "You will."

With nimble fingers, Elizabeth worked open buttons and zippers until Noah sprang free from the confines of cloth and denim. A shudder ran over him as she wrapped her slender fingers around his hot hardness, marveling at the contrast between the softness of his skin and the rigidity of his arousal. She reveled in the power that coursed through her, knowing she had elicited such an intense response from him. As she began to stroke him gently, savoring every twitch and groan that escaped his lips, Elizabeth felt a rush of desire stream through her own body, igniting a fire deep within.

"Oh my god, Lizzy..." The plea was almost a prayer.

As Elizabeth stroked his length, her mind reeled with the electrifying sensation of Noah's bare skin pressed against her own. The heat radiating from him seeped into her fingertips, igniting a fire that threatened to consume her entire being. She could feel every tremble and jolt of tension rippling through his body. Time seemed to slow as she savored the moment, drinking in the sight of him laid out before her like a god. Suddenly, reality snapped back into focus with the crinkle of a foil packet that she retrieved from her jeans pocket, its mundane sound jarringly at odds with the primal urges that had taken hold of her.

"I'm clean," Noah whispered, his breath hot against her ear.

Elizabeth's hand stilled, her eyes locked on his. She waved the condom in front of him, a slight smile playing on her lips. "I'm sure you are, Monty," she whispered back, her voice husky with intent. "But do this for me."

Without waiting for a response, Elizabeth expertly rolled the condom down his length. Noah's eyes fluttered closed, his chest heaving as he let out a low groan. The sound sent a shiver through her, igniting the desperate urges that had been building all night. She marveled at how familiar it felt to be in this moment with him, despite the years that had passed.

Her hands fumbled with the button of her jeans, anticipation thrumming through every nerve in her body. She couldn't remember the last time she'd wanted someone this badly, and Noah Montgomery was far from just anyone. He was the boy who had stolen her heart long ago, only to vanish from her life like sand slipping through her fingers.

As she worked open the fastening of her pants, Noah's eyes roamed over her face hungrily. His own were darkened with lust, pupils blown wide as he watched her disrobe for him. Elizabeth quivered under his heated stare, feeling a rush of power flow through her at the knowledge that she could reduce him to this state so easily.

She shrugged out of her jeans and panties in one smooth motion, leaving herself bare before him. A small thrill ran through her at the sight of Noah's parted lips and slightly glazed eyes as he drank in the sight of her nakedness. Her skin prickled with goosebumps as his hot gaze roved over every dip and swell of flesh.

"You're beautiful," he breathed, his voice rough with want.

Elizabeth smiled to herself at his reverence, a sense of satisfaction curling low in her belly at his reaction to seeing her bared before him like an offering. She knew years spent honing a physique capable of conquering treacherous terrain had toned lean muscle onto once soft curves -but nothing compared to the rush she felt seeing Noah drink in the sight with such blatant hunger.

Arousal coiled tight within her core as his eyes lingered on every inch of exposed skin - tracing down over her collarbones sharpened by frequent fasting on long assignments overseas; skimming across breasts freed from constrictive bras that could never quite contain their fullness; following valleys formed by jutting hipbones into deep indents where her waist narrowed dramatically against the flare of her wide hips; drinking in the taut stomach etched with hard planes from months spent running for survival rather than pleasure. Finally trailing down strong thighs thickly muscled from climbing steep peaks for stories untold by others less determined than she.

"Touch me," Elizabeth breathed, barely recognizing the needy sound issuing from between her suddenly dry lips.

Noah moved immediately. His large hands skimmed up from her knees along her quivering inner thighs until he reached the apex where they widened into hips. His strong fingers curled possessively around the flared bones even as his thumbs brushed teasing touches against her folds glistening slick with desire already. A broken moan tore past Elizabeth's clenched teeth at the electric contact igniting sparks under a touch so light it bordered on torture.

"I've thought about this for so long..." The words tumbled out unbidden from her throat gone tight with want.

"Me too," Noah rumbled back. "It's gonna be worth the wait." The promise hung heavy between them laden with implication.

Elizabeth rocked into Noah's touch seeking more contact as it became clear that years of dreaming hadn't imagined how right it would feel having those hands on her body. It was a feeling she didn't understand, yet it felt strangely familiar, like a lost piece of herself finally found.

She straddled him again, her body aligning perfectly with his as she slowly, deliberately sank down onto him. The sensation of their bodies connecting sent a tremor through her, igniting a blaze across her skin. She closed her eyes briefly, savoring the feeling of him filling her, stretching her in ways both familiar and new. As she began to move, her hips rolling against his, everything melted away, and it was like no time had passed at all. Yet there was something different too -a deeper intensity, a heightened awareness that came from knowing each other so intimately after all these years. Elizabeth gasped as their eyes met, recognizing the raw desire burning in Noah's gaze, and felt herself drawn into the depths of his soulful stare. Noah's hands grasped her hips, plunging her downward as he let out a hoarse whisper.

"So good..."

She guided him home with a throaty moan, reveling in the exquisite sensation as he filled her completely. The sensation was so powerful, her body yielding to the delicious pressure as she savored each moment of their connection. Noah dropped back against the leather seats, closing his eyes rapturously. "Fuck, you feel amazing..."

Elizabeth rolled her hips, eliciting a strangled groan from him that made heat pool low in her belly. The sound sent a shiver down her spine. With a quickening pace, she rocked him, relishing the sensation of his length moving inside her. She was drunk in the power she held over him, the way his body responded so readily to her touch.

"Easy," he whispered, his hands tightening on her waist. "I don't want to come too fast..."

But Elizabeth lifted herself up until just the tip remained inside before sinking back down, taking him deep once more. This time, his voice was raw and guttural, a sound that seemed to come straight from the depths of his being.

That sound he just made... holy hell. I could listen to that all night. Give it to me, come on Noah.

Determined to break his control, she set a relentless pace, her hips moving up and down over his thick length with each powerful thrust. Her nails dug into his shoulders as she rode him hard and fast, chasing her own release. The friction between them was incredible, stoking the fire that burned within her. Her hands slid along his back, feeling the muscles bunch under her touch as he tried to hold her back, his grip on her hips tightening, but she surged forward, ignoring his desperate attempts to slow her down.

Don't slow down now, keep going. Fuck, his hands on my hips trying to guide me. Why isn't he moving?

With a wicked grin, she leaned forward, her long dark hair cascading over them like a curtain of silk. "Give it to me," she whispered against his lips, her voice husky with want. She needed to feel him surrender completely.

Noah met every downward motion with a sharp upward snap of his hips, driving into her again and again, his muscular body taut and straining with effort. Elizabeth delighted in their rhythm, feeling herself grow slicker with each powerful stroke. She leaned back slightly, changing the angle, and gasped as he hit a spot deep within her that sent spasms of ecstasy coursing through her. Her head tilted back against the cool headrest of the passenger seat as another wave built at the base of her spine, radiating outward and igniting every nerve. Noah's hand slid between their sweat-slicked bodies, his fingers finding that sensitive bundle of nerves and rubbing tight, focused circles over her clit. The combination of his deep penetration and touch pushed her closer to the precipice, each movement sending sparks dancing across her vision. She bit down hard on her lip, stifling the moan that threatened to escape as he brought her closer to release with every expert stroke.

"Oh god…" The words fell from her numb lips as she teetered on the brink. *I'm close, so close. Just a little more…*

"You're … so … tight." Each word rasped from his throat. "Come for me, Bet."

The husky timbre of Noah's words ignited the embers of desire within her beyond anything she had imagined it would be with him. Elizabeth arched her back, pressing herself closer to him as she felt his hardness pulse inside her, stoking the fire that had been smoldering low in her belly since they first kissed.

The more Noah demanded that she climax for him, the more Elizabeth held back, drawing out his pleasure and her own, not willing to surrender to the mounting pressure just yet. His hips bucked against hers, seeking release, but she remained in control.

"Come on," he groaned, his voice strained with effort. "Come on, damn it… Lizzy."

But Elizabeth only smiled wickedly and increased her pace just enough to keep herself on the brink without tipping over the edge. She wanted to savor this moment, to draw it out as long as possible. After all these years apart, she wasn't ready for it to end so soon.

Noah's hands gripped the leather seats tightly as he fought for control. His breath came in ragged gasps that mingled with hers in the confined space of the SUV. Sweat beaded on their foreheads and bodies as their passionate dance continued unabated. The scent of their arousal filled the air, intoxicating them both and spurring them onward.

"Damn it," Noah cursed under his breath before surging upward one last time, burying himself deep inside her. "I can't... I can't hold it..."

The anguish in his voice only spurred Elizabeth on further; she wanted him to beg for release. She leaned forward again, her lips brushing against his ear as she whispered seductively: "Then don't."

Her heart raced as she felt Noah's body tense beneath her, his grip on her hips tightening as he neared the edge. The raw desperation in his every movement, the frantic rise and fall of his breath against her ear. The power she held over him, the ability to reduce him to this, sent a thrill through her.

"That's it," she purred, running her nails lightly down his back. "Give it to me." She had done this. Noah's only response was a strangled groan as he arched his back, driving himself harder inside her. "You're so deep," she managed to gasp out between ragged breaths, her nails digging into the slick skin of his back. "I'm... "

The intensity of Noah's groan caused Elizabeth's control to crumble. She came apart with a cry as white-hot ecstasy radiated through her. Pleasure consumed every thought until she collapsed forward against Noah's sweat-slick chest.

His arms wrapped around her trembling body even as he continued his rhythm. Three more thrusts and Noah stiffened beneath her with a hoarse grunt of completion. She felt the powerful muscles in his back bunching as he reached his peak, his body trembling against hers. *Oh god, he feels so good. I did that to him.* A wave of satisfaction washed over her as he collapsed forward onto her dampened skin. She wrapped her arms around him, holding him close and savoring the weight and warmth of his body.

Minutes later found them tangled together on the cramped leather seats, harsh breaths evening out into comfortable silence. Elizabeth's heart still fluttered in her chest as she nestled against Noah's warm skin, their limbs intertwined in the confined space. The leather beneath them creaked softly with each subtle movement, and a thin sheen of sweat cooled on their bodies in the night air. She felt deliciously sated, her muscles pleasantly loose as the last remnants of tension melted away into peaceful contentment.

"You're incredible," Noah breathed against the damp tangles of Elizabeth's hair.

"Mmm-hmm." Elizabeth traced idle patterns on his radiant brown skin.

"So, what now?"

A soft laugh escaped her parted lips at the question. "Now I think we need to get some sleep."

The rumble of agreement vibrated through his strong shoulders before he asked: "My place?"

"Can't we sneak in past Stacy?"

"My car would be there. She'd figure things out."

"Uncle Leo will know I'm not there and be watching out. Can't invite you in—"

"He doesn't like me much, anyway."

"That's not true!" Elizabeth pulled away enough to meet his dark eyes still heavy-lidded.

"Bullshit it isn't," Noah grumbled.

"Well maybe I should just go home alone then..." She started untangling their limbs only for a hand to clamp down on hers.

"No way—"

She jerked free with an eye roll and pulled on her clothing. "The trailer park isn't far."

"You can't walk home alone at 4 am!"

She opened the SUV door before he could protest further. "I feel perfectly safe walking around Sweetwater Springs at any hour."

With that declaration ringing in the night air, Elizabeth slipped out into the cool darkness before starting along the dusty road toward Echo Ridge.

9

Whispers and Warnings

Elizabeth sat at the crowded table in Sweetwater's only coffee shop, watching steam rise from her untouched latte while Stacy and her friends erupted in laughter over some shared memory.

"Remember when Danny crashed his dad's tractor into the Thompson's fence?" Sarah wiped tears from her eyes. "Poor Mr. Thompson nearly had a heart attack!"

"Oh my god, and then Jenny had to help him fix it before his parents got home!" Stacy clutched her sides.

Elizabeth forced a smile, fingers tracing the rim of her cup. These stories belonged to a time when she'd already left town, pursuing her journalism career while they'd stayed behind building lives and connections she couldn't relate to.

"What about you, Elizabeth? You must have some wild stories from your travels," Sarah asked.

"I..." Elizabeth's throat tightened. Her stories of dodging bullets in militia roundups and exposing corruption didn't fit here between tales of small-town mishaps and high school pranks. "Nothing very interesting."

"Oh, come on, you're always posting these amazing photos from around the world," Rachel chimed in.

Elizabeth shifted in her seat. "It's just work stuff, really."

The conversation drifted back to local matters -whose kids were starting kindergarten, the new assistant principal at the high school, drama at the PTA meetings. Elizabeth's mind wandered to her laptop waiting back at Leo's trailer, filled with half-written articles about protests and concrete plants. She felt the familiar itch to be doing something that mattered, something bigger than gossip over coffee.

"Elizabeth?" Stacy's voice snapped her back. "You okay? You seem miles away."

"Yeah, just..." Elizabeth pushed her cold coffee aside. "I guess I've missed a lot while I was gone."

The significance of those missing years taunted her. These women shared a language of inside jokes and mutual history that she couldn't speak. Even Stacy, her oldest friend, had built a life here that she struggled to understand.

Elizabeth grabbed her phone and slipped away from the table, muttering an excuse about work calls. Her fingers hovered over the screen before typing:

Need a friendly face. Free for coffee?

Noah's response came seconds later:

Always got time for you, Lizzy. Come by the office?

Relief washed over her as she waved goodbye to the group. "Sorry, got to make a deadline. We'll catch up again soon."

The fresh air, cool and crisp, hit her face as she stepped onto Main Street, a gentle breeze ruffling her hair as she walked the three blocks south along the pawpaw trees. Noah's community ward office sat above the hardware store, its brass nameplate catching the afternoon sun. She climbed the narrow stairs, each step taking her further from the feeling of being an outsider.

Noah looked up from his desk when she entered, his warm smile reaching his eyes. "Rough morning?"

"That obvious?" Elizabeth sank into the leather chair across from him. The office smelled of coffee and old books, a comforting mix that reminded her of late-night study sessions in college.

"You've got that same look you used to get before big tests." He leaned back, loosening his tie. "The one that says you're overthinking everything."

"Old friends. They're all so… settled." Elizabeth stared at her hands. "They have this whole life here, all these shared experiences. And I'm just…"

"The girl who flew away to chase the bad guys?" Noah's voice held no judgment. "That's not a bad thing, Lizzy."

"Sometimes I wonder." The words slipped out before she could catch them. Here in this quiet office, with Noah's steady presence across the desk, the walls she'd built started to weaken.

"Come here." Noah stepped away from his desk and patted the couch by the window. Elizabeth moved over, letting herself sink into the comfort of his presence as he sat beside her. His shoulder brushed against hers as he settled onto the couch.

Noah cradled her face in his hands, his lips finding hers in a gentle, lingering kiss that transformed into that familiar sensual ache between them. "You know what makes you different from everyone else in this town?"

Elizabeth tensed, years of childhood insecurities flooding back.

"That brilliant mind of yours." His fingers traced lazy circles up and down her arms. "While they were planning bake sales, you were planning how to change the world."

Heat crept up her neck. "Not everyone sees it that way."

"Because they don't understand ambition. But I do." Noah's dark eyes met hers. "You've got more strength in your little finger than half this town combined. The way you track down things, fight for the truth -that's something special."

Elizabeth's heart quickened. "You sound pretty sure about that."

"Think about it - your communication skills, my connections in local government. We could really make things happen here." His voice dropped lower. "Your big brain, my big ideas? Sweetwater wouldn't know what hit it."

"What are you —?"

"These people have no clue what kind of impact we could have as a team." Noah's hand found hers. "All those skills you learned out there in the world? They're exactly what this town needs."

Elizabeth's skin tingled where their fingers touched. She studied his expression. The afternoon sun painted golden stripes across his face, highlighting the earnest look she remembered from their youth. Her breath caught as Noah's fingers intertwined tightly around hers.

"There's a presentation at the Chamber of Commerce tomorrow night about economic development." Noah's thumb pressed gently into her palm. "Come with me."

Elizabeth pulled back slightly. "Are you sure that's a good idea? People talk in this town."

"Let them." As Noah leaned closer, the rich aroma of freshly brewed coffee and leather mingled with the intoxicating scent of his cologne, creating a heady mix. "I've spent too many years caring what others think. Playing it safe."

"Noah, I'm not sure they're ready for—"

"I have dreams, Lizzy." His voice dropped to almost a whisper. "Dreams of us building something real here. Making this town better together." He squeezed her hand. "It's time everyone knew how I feel about you."

Elizabeth's heart hammered against her ribs. The certainty in his voice, the intensity in his dark eyes -it was everything teenage Elizabeth had fantasized about. But now it twisted in her chest, tangling with thoughts of Vincent and her life beyond her hometown's borders.

"The city council, the chamber members —they all respect you." Noah's free hand brushed a strand of hair from her face. "And they'll respect us. Together."

The word 'together' hung between them, heavy with promise and possibility. Elizabeth found herself nodding before she could process all the implications.

"Good." Noah's smile brightened the room. "Pick you up at seven?"

The wooden floorboards creaked as Frank Morrison, the city's finance director, appeared in the doorway clutching a stack of papers. Elizabeth rose from the couch, smoothing her jeans.

"Noah, got those budget numbers you wanted—" Frank's eyes darted between them. "Oh, sorry to interrupt."

"Not at all." Noah stood, his hand finding the small of Elizabeth's back. "Ms. Nelson was just leaving."

Heat crept up her neck as Noah leaned in, his lips brushing her cheek. The gesture felt bold, almost possessive -so different from their careful distance in high school and since her return. Frank's presence made the moment feel real, public, like crossing a line they couldn't uncross.

"See you tomorrow night?" Noah's voice carried a hint of seduction.

Elizabeth nodded, slipping past Frank who gave her a knowing smile. In the stairwell, she pressed cool fingers to her warming cheek. The thought of being seen with Noah, of people knowing about them, sent a flutter through her stomach. No need to sneak glances across crowded rooms or pretend not to notice each other at town events.

Maybe it was time to stop running from connections, from putting down roots. Noah's certainty about them, his willingness to claim their relationship openly, felt both terrifying and thrilling.

She stepped onto Main Street, the sunlight warming her face. Behind her, the low murmur of Noah's voice drifted down through the open window as he discussed budget items with Frank. The normalcy of it, the way their private moment had merged so seamlessly into his public life, settled something inside her. This was what staying looked like -being part of the fabric of this place, not just passing through. And maybe, somehow, she could make it work.

* * *

The next day, Elizabeth's boots crunched through fallen leaves as she wandered the winding paths of Memorial Park. The old playground equipment creaked in the breeze, reminding her of lonely recesses spent with her nose buried in books while other kids played. She paused by the rusty swing set, running her hand along the chain. The metal was cool against her palm, familiar yet distant. How many afternoons had she sat here, watching popular girls like Rachel and Sarah giggle together, dreaming of the day she'd finally leave this place?

"Elizabeth Nelson? Is that you?"

She turned to find Mrs. Harrison, her former English teacher, walking her golden retriever. The older woman's silver hair caught the afternoon light, her kind eyes crinkling behind wire-rimmed glasses.

"Mrs. Harrison." Elizabeth smiled, genuinely happy to see the woman who'd encouraged her writing when everyone else dismissed it as impractical dreams.

"I've been following your work." Mrs. Harrison stopped beside her. "That piece you wrote about the refugee crisis in Syria? Powerful, very inspiring."

Elizabeth blinked in surprise. "You read that?"

"Of course! I always knew you'd do great things." Mrs. Harrison's voice softened. "Even when you were that quiet girl in the back of my class, I could see the fire in you. The determination to tell stories that mattered."

"I wasn't exactly Miss Popularity back then." Elizabeth's fingers twisted the hem of her jacket.

"No, but you were something better -you were authentic. While everyone else was trying to fit in, you were planning your escape to see the world." Mrs. Harrison touched her arm. "That takes courage and it's worth more than any amount of social status."

The words settled into Elizabeth's chest, easing some of the tension she'd carried since returning home. Maybe she hadn't failed at being a small-town girl. Maybe she'd just been becoming who she was meant to be all along.

Hopeful that some local flavor would seep into her writing, she decided to hit the Sweetwater Springs Library. She preferred the quiet solitude of local archives to the rabbit hole of online databases. The scent of old paper felt comforting, a tangible link to the past.

She browsed the local history section, skimming through yearbooks and town chronicles. Most of it was dry accounts of parades and bake sales, the kind of stuff that barely registered on her radar. As she sifted through stacks of faded newsprint, a headline snagged her attention: "Local Architect Pioneering Sustainable Designs: An Interview with Henry Nelson."

A surge of emotion washed over her -confusion, a sting of sadness, and a flicker of pride. Her father.

Cautiously, she pulled out the dated article. It was from shortly before the train derailment, a time when Henry had been lauded for his innovative work on a community center design that incorporated solar panels and rainwater harvesting. His vision, the article proclaimed, was "a testament to his commitment to environmental stewardship and a blueprint for a sustainable future." The county board never approved the plan, and his dream never came to fruition.

Elizabeth scrolled through the interview, her gaze lingering on her father's smiling face. He looked so full of life, his eyes bright with passion for his work. It was a stark contrast to the image she clung to—his hollow eyes staring blankly from her last photograph before the accident.

Memories of his workshops, his tireless dedication to civic projects, flooded back. He'd instilled in her a deep curiosity about the world, a desire to understand the complexities of urban planning and social responsibility. Reading about his accomplishments, Elizabeth felt a bittersweet mix of loss and admiration. He'd been more than just her father; he'd been a champion for his community, a man determined to leave a better world behind.

"You know, I thought my dad was just a boring gardener. But he..."

A quiet voice broke the silence. Pressing her back against the shelf, Elizabeth barely registered the presence of another woman. A graying auburn bob and kind eyes peered at her.

"My father," the woman continued, oblivious to Elizabeth's surprise, "was a tree surgeon. Not as fancy as an architect, I guess." She chuckled softly. "But he believed in taking care of things," the woman finished, leaning against the shelf beside Elizabeth. Her gaze swept over the stacks of old papers. "Leaving things better than you found them."

Elizabeth felt a wave of compassion come over her. The woman's gentle words echoed the sentiment buried deep within her—the echoes of her father's tireless work.

"That sounds like a pretty good life, you know?" Elizabeth offered, surprised by the sincerity in her own voice.

The woman smiled, a faint web of lines crinkling around her eyes. "It was."

She hesitated, her gaze flickering toward the article Elizabeth still clutched in her hand. "Are you looking for something specific?"

Elizabeth looked up, meeting the woman's kind eyes. "Actually, yes. This article... it's about my father."

"Yes, I know. And I remember your father." A flicker of understanding crossed the woman's face. "An architect's work, it has a way of lasting," she said softly, as if sharing a secret. "Even when the people who crafted it..." her voice trailed off.

Elizabeth swallowed the lump in her throat. "Gone before their time."

"That's one way to put it," the woman murmured, a shadow passing over her features.

Silence stretched between them, heavy with unspoken grief. Finally, the woman redirected the conversation, her voice regaining its earlier cheer.

"So, tell me," she said, her eyes twinkling. "What brought you back to Sweetwater Springs after all these years?"

Elizabeth hesitated. "Work." The word felt inadequate, hollow. It didn't encapsulate the tangled knot of emotions pulling her back to this town.

The woman understood. "I get it," she said, her voice low. "Sometimes the past... it has a way of calling you back, yeah?"

Elizabeth nodded, a lump forming in her throat. "A story my dad... a story he never got to finish." She gestured vaguely toward the article again, her voice quickening with anxiety. "There were rumors about the derailment. Government cover-up, something about negligence. Nobody ever wanted to talk about it."

The woman raised her eyebrows in surprise. "Cover-up? That's a serious accusation."

"I know," Elizabeth said, gripping the article tighter. "But the more I think about it, the more it feels like there's something they're not telling us."

"Sweetwater Springs isn't exactly known for its dark secrets," the woman replied, a hint of amusement in her voice. "It's more of a sleepy little town, you know? Bingo halls, community potlucks, that kinda thing."

"Exactly," Elizabeth said, her voice hardening. "That's what makes it so suspicious. It's like they're trying to bury it all under a layer of apple pie and volunteer work." Her grip on the article tightened. "I need to find out the truth."

The woman's gaze drifted to the numerous stacks of old papers scattered around them.

"I'm not so sure you're gonna find it in here."

"It's a start," Elizabeth said, and checked her watch. 5:37. She needed to get back to the trailer with Uncle Leo for dinner before her meet up with Noah for the Chamber of Commerce meeting at seven.

"Thanks for the chat," she said, rising from her seat.

The woman smiled, a warmth radiating from her despite the dust motes dancing in the sunlight filtering through the window.

"Anytime, dear. If you find any… interesting tidbits about the town's old architecture, let me know. Saying that," she smiled, "it might be hard to top the ghost stories I heard growing up."

Elizabeth chuckled, wondering if the woman knew more than she was letting on. But she had to prioritize. "I will," she promised, tucking her notes into her messenger bag, a thrill shooting through her despite the tight knot of worry in her stomach. As she descended the library stairs, the weight of the past felt heavier. The scent of cedar and dust clung to her like a familiar embrace. Sweetwater Springs carried its history like a shroud, its secrets whispered in the wind rustling through the old oaks that lined the town square.

* * *

Elizabeth walked through the dusty streets, her mind flooded with thoughts of the article and the potential cover-up. With each step, the buried trauma felt heavier on her shoulders, like an oppressive weight she couldn't escape. As she approached the outskirts of town, she remembered a remote overlook that offered a stunning view of the valley below, Togan's Bluff. It was a place she had visited many times before, and she knew it would be perfect for capturing some photos to accompany her story.

She turned onto a narrow dirt road that wound its way up the hillside, her heart pounding in her chest as she climbed higher and higher. The air grew cooler, the valley spread out before her like a painting. But as she reached the top of the hill, her heart lurched as she saw two men in dark suits, their eyes like icy pools staring back at her. They blocked her path, their eyes narrowed and their hands hovering near their weapons.

"Let me pass." Elizabeth demanded, her voice steady despite her rising fear.

The taller of the two men stepped forward, his voice low and menacing. "You shouldn't be here," he said. "This is private property."

Togan's Bluff had always been on public land. The idea of some corporate entity blocking the right of way to prevent access to it was… Elizabeth's anger surged through her, a fiery wave of indignation. She had every right to be there, to gather information for her story. But these men clearly didn't care about journalistic integrity or freedom of speech. They were there to protect whatever secrets lay hidden on the other side of the ridge.

Before she could react, one of the men grabbed her arm. Elizabeth struggled against him, but he was too strong for her small frame. She kicked out at him with all her might, connecting solidly with his shin and causing him to stumble back slightly. But it was too late—the other man had already pulled out a gun and aimed it directly at her head. She froze in terror, knowing that any wrong move could cost her everything. She straightened her spine, forcing her trembling legs to steady. They expected her to plead, to freeze. But they didn't know her. *You're smarter. You're faster. You have nothing left to lose.*

In a sudden burst of adrenaline-fueled courage, Elizabeth lunged forward and tackled the man with the gun to the ground, knocking it out of his hand in the process. The two men scrambled to regain their footing as she sprinted back down the hillside toward town, the wind whipping at her hair as she raced along the hidden paths Uncle Leo had shown her. Her heart pounded in her chest as she tried to put as much distance between herself and them as possible.

She made it back into town just as evening was falling and headed straight for the police station to file a report about the altercation at the overlook. But when she arrived at the station, she faced an indifferent officer who refused to take her seriously because she had been trespassing on private property—even though it was clear that these men were trying to intimidate and possibly harm her in order to keep their secrets hidden from prying eyes like hers.

The police station doors swung shut behind Elizabeth with a hollow clang. Frustration coiled in her stomach, a bitter taste that lingered on her tongue. The officer's dismissive words echoed in her ears: "Trespassing, miss. Stay out of trouble."

She hadn't even gotten to mention the rough handling, the gun, the threat.

Elizabeth shoved her hands into the pockets of her worn leather jacket, her gaze fixed on the dusty street beyond. The setting sun cast strange shadows across the town, turning the regular storefronts into something alien and menacing. She had two options: slam the door open, yell about injustice until someone listened, or swallow her pride and accept defeat. Neither felt right.

A glimmer of defiance sparked in her eyes. Uncle Leo would understand. He'd seen his fair share of small-town corruption. He'd scrape by on his Social Security and whatever odd jobs he could find, but he never backed down from a fight. Elizabeth started walking back to Echo Ridge, her footsteps echoing on the empty sidewalk.

Uncle Leo's trailer, bathed in the amber glow of the fading light, came into view. The smell of fried fish hung in the air, a familiar comfort that momentarily eased the knot of anxiety in her chest.

"Elizabeth! You're late," Uncle Leo said, his voice booming across the porch as she climbed the rickety steps. He wiped his hands on a stained rag and gestured for her to come inside and take a seat at their wobbly table.

Elizabeth took a deep breath and forced a smile. "Sorry, Uncle Leo. Had a little… run-in with some folks."

He raised an eyebrow, his gaze sharp and inquisitive.

"Nothing really," she said, her voice barely a whisper, "just stay away from the overlook by Route 10. Togan's Bluff is … off limits."

She gulped down her food, her appetite replaced by a gnawing anxiety. She couldn't shake the feeling of dread that had settled upon her after her encounter at the overlook. Those men were dangerous, their eyes hard and calculating, filled with a ruthlessness that chilled her to the bone.

She hurried to shower and get dressed, throwing on a simple black sundress. She didn't bother with much jewelry—just a pair of small silver earrings that she had purchased at a market in Marrakesh. Her phone buzzed on the counter, a text from Noah.

Running a few minutes late, heading over now

She sighed, smoothing down the wrinkles on her dress one last time. Meeting Noah felt both comforting and disturbing. He represented a semblance of normalcy in her chaotic life, a connection to a past she wasn't sure she wanted to hold on to. But inviting Noah into her world felt like inviting danger, like dropping a delicate wildflower into a swirling storm.

Noah's gleaming black SUV pulled up in front of the trailer, its headlights momentarily blinding her. She took a deep breath and stepped outside. He rolled down the window, his face breaking into a relieved smile. "Hey Lizzy, sorry I'm late."

She slid into the passenger seat, the warm scent of leather and vanilla musk enveloping her.

"No problem," she said, her voice catching slightly.

His gaze met hers, a hint of concern in his dark brown eyes. "Are you okay?"

"Just a long day," she said, forcing a smile.

"You were busy researching something, weren't you?"

She shrugged, trying to deflect. "Maybe a little."

Noah knew her well enough to see right through the flimsy excuse. His gaze lingered on her face, searching for something she couldn't quite put her finger on.

"You're not hiding anything from me, are you?"

Her breath caught in her throat. Then she thought of Uncle Leo's whispered warnings, the grim look on the officer's face. It seemed none of it was her story to tell -not yet.

"No," she said, her voice firm despite the tremor running through her. "Just nothing important."

The air in the car thickened, laden with unspoken words and a mutual sense of unease. Noah reached out and gently clasped her hand. She avoided his gaze.

"Is that so?" he murmured, his thumb stroking her skin in a light, comforting gesture. "Tell you what, we'll talk about it later. Let's head down to the Chamber of Commerce meeting. I know Stacy's been urging you to get reconnected with the town. Ready?"

The Chamber of Commerce. The very thought made Elizabeth roll her eyes internally. Networking, public appearances, mindless pleasantries—she'd much rather be chasing down leads and identifying those guys that stopped her at the overlook.

"FINE," she conceded, letting out a puff of air she hadn't realized she'd been holding. "But just this once."

Noah smiled, the relief apparent in the way his face softened and his eyes crinkled at the corners. He squeezed her hand. "You look amazing, by the way. It won't be so bad, trust me."

He steered the SUV away from the trailer, back onto the dusty road that wound through the heart of Sweetwater Springs. As they drove, he kept up a steady stream of conversation, navigating effortlessly through the vast chasm of unspoken tension.

They pulled up to a brick building with a welcoming facade, the Chamber of Commerce logo emblazoned above the entrance. Noah barely had the car stopped before a flurry of handshakes and greetings descended upon him. "Noah! Wonderful to see you!" boomed a portly man in a tailored suit, engulfing Noah in a bear hug. A gaggle of men and women in various degrees of colorful attire quickly followed suit, peppering Noah with questions about his family and their business.

He seemed perfectly at home in this whirlwind of local politics, his easy charm and handsome frame weaving through the crowd with practiced grace. Elizabeth, however, felt a pang of apprehension.

This world of fake pleasantries and backroom deals felt alien to her, a landscape she'd never quite understood nor cared to.

Impulsively, she slipped away from the clamor, moving toward the portico that shaded the entrance. Cool air drifted through the gaps in the brickwork, carrying the scent of pine mulch and freshly cut grass. The Chamber of Commerce event was in full swing, but on the quiet edge of things, surrounded by the wrought iron details and dried flower arrangements, she found a moment of peace. The porch floor was uneven, worn smooth by years of footsteps. Elizabeth paced, her phone clammy in her hand. She felt like an intruder, an outsider observing a ritual she didn't understand.

A commotion from inside drew her back into the hall. Music pulsed through the open doorway, mingling with the clinking of glasses and snippets of conversation. She saw Noah through the throng, his booming laughter bouncing off the walls. Even from this distance, her heart ached for him. The life he'd built here, the routine life he'd carved out of Sweetwater Springs, contrasted starkly with her nomadic existence. She was eager to be there for him.

And yet, she couldn't bring herself to stay.

Elizabeth pressed her back against the cool brick wall, her heart thumping a frantic rhythm against her ribs. She didn't need to see Noah to know he was headed toward her. She could feel his presence like a shift in the air, his energy cutting through the crowd. The murmur of conversations faded as Noah approached. He stopped a foot away, his brow furrowed, his gaze steady.

"Elizabeth," he said, his voice low and laced with a controlled frustration that sent a shiver through her. "I just heard about you and the trespassing incident. And the police report you requested be filed." He leaned against the wall beside her, taking up space, his presence a tangible barrier to escape.

"It wasn't..."

"Why didn't you tell me?" Noah's voice tightened, the question barely a whisper. He glanced over his shoulder toward the crowd, then turned to face her again, his eyes searching hers. The warmth that usually shimmered in their depths was extinguished, replaced by a cool, hard glare. "Why didn't you tell me you were out there snooping around? What were you looking for?"

"It wasn't... it wasn't my story to tell, Noah. I was following a lead. One that didn't need to involve you."

The lie tasted bitter on her tongue. She averted her gaze from him.

"In Sweetwater, it always involves me. Remember that, okay?" Noah's voice was low, a serious murmur that sent a tremor through her. He sounded hurt, his words dripping with a wounded resentment that she couldn't stomach. He didn't need to say more. There was a crackle in the atmosphere, a tension that had been building since the moment he'd picked her up at the trailer.

"I just... I just..." Elizabeth swallowed, the words catching in her throat. She couldn't bring herself to make eye contact with him. She had seen the hurt in his eyes, a reflection of her guilt for not being able to shield him from what drove her to press into places he considered forbidden. She had to get away, to escape the suffocating intensity of his disappointment. "I should probably go, Noah," she said, backing away. "It's getting late."

He just stood there, like a brick wall blocking her way out.

Elizabeth continued to edge backward. "I'll see you around," she said, her voice a hollow tone that betrayed her fear.

"Lizzy," Noah said, his voice rough, laced with a desperate plea.

The sound of her name on his lips, so close, so intimate, sent a jolt of longing through her. She wanted to turn, to reach out, to tell him she hadn't meant to mislead him. But she couldn't. She forced herself to keep walking, pushing past the insistent pull of his gaze. She reached the double doors leading out of the ballroom and practically flew through them, the cool night air a welcome wash against her skin.

Elizabeth didn't stop running until she reached the parking lot. The moon hung low in the sky, casting elongated shadows across the asphalt. She leaned against a car, catching her breath, her lungs burning. She hadn't heard footsteps. Maybe he wouldn't follow. The rapid beat of her heart echoed in her ears. She squeezed her eyes shut, willing her heart to calm.

A low chuckle cut through. When Elizabeth opened her eyes, Noah stood a few feet away, his silhouette stark against the pale moonlight. He didn't look angry, just resigned, his expression a mixture of hurt and exhaustion.

"So," Noah drawled, amusement dancing in his eyes. "This is how we're going to handle things now? Sneak around like a covert operative?"

Elizabeth wanted to scoff. Noah was acting as if being a journalist in Sweetwater Springs wasn't the equivalent of working undercover in a hornet's nest. But she just sighed, slumping against the car. His presence was both reassuring and unnerving, his warm energy a paradox to the cool detachment she'd built around herself.

"It's not like that," she mumbled, hating the way her voice trembled. "It just..."

"Matters," Noah finished for her, stepping closer, but not too close. "To me, that is." He waited a beat. "You can trust me," he said, his voice low. "You know that you can."

"I know," she whispered, the words ripped from her, unplanned.

"Then tell me what you're working on." The request hung in the air. "I'll help you."

Elizabeth swallowed, her mind replaying his words. Her lips parted, but before a syllable escaped, he reached out, his touch featherlight on her cheek. His thumb brushed a stray strand of hair away from her face. "And you'll help me."

The moment faded away, and she felt like a sixteen-year-old again, the girl who sat across from him in the library, butterflies doing backflips in her stomach. Her breath hitched as he leaned closer. "Tell me, Bet." he breathed, the teenage nickname a balm to her raw emotions.

Her eyelids fluttered shut, a helpless sigh escaping her lips. This was a mistake. A dangerous mistake. But the guarded nature she wrestled with felt insignificant compared to the yearning strumming through her body.

Noah's lips found hers, his kiss tentative at first, then deepening, urgent, needing. Her body softened against him, her fingers searching the expanse of his chest. He gently held her face, his thumb brushing her cheek with a disarming tenderness, showing he understood how vulnerable she felt.

The kiss broke and Noah gazed at her, his eyes dark and intense. "Don't push me away. Not now," he whispered. "We're so damn close to it, Lizzy. Promise me."

Elizabeth nodded, unable to speak, unable to resist the pull of him. He was a beacon in the storm of her secrets, his power a promise of shelter. His hand slid down her arm, his touch making sparks fly under her skin. "Come on," he said, "Let's get out of here."

He led her through the deserted parking lot, his hand warm and possessive on the small of her back. They walked in silence, the city sprawling around them, a tapestry of dark lights and hushed breezes through the trees. She didn't mind the silence. In Noah's presence, words felt unnecessary. Their unspoken understanding was enough.

When they reached the brick facade of City Hall, Noah swiped his key card, the door unlocking with a soft whoosh. "My office," he said, looking at her expectantly. His smile was the brightest star in the night. The allure of his office, the secrecy it promised, was intoxicating.

Noah led her inside, closing the door behind them. He flipped the switch, bathing the room in warm light. It was a space he kept meticulously organized, a stark contrast to the clutter of the ward office above the hardware store and the chaos of her space at Uncle Leo's trailer. He would be expecting her back soon.

"It's late," she said, trying to break the hypnotic mood that was closing around them.

He crossed the room, his eyes intense on hers. "Not too late," he said, his voice huskier than usual.

Her gaze dropped to his lips. "Noah," she breathed. Saying his name left a lingering taste of desire on her tongue. Suddenly, all thoughts of their outing, her investigation, the baggage she carried, faded into oblivion. The only thing she could focus on was the warmth of his eyes, the intensity of his desire burning through her.

He draped his palm at the nape of her neck, drawing her face close to his. "Lizzy, I've waited so long for this. I'm not about to drop the ball now." His voice cracked, raw with emotion.

The touch of his hand ignited a heat within her, a wildfire that swept through her body, and his eyes, focused and unyielding, locked her in his gaze, her will melted away. Noah's lips met hers in a slow, possessive kiss, his touch sending a spark of desire that rippled across her skin. Their embrace was electric, her entire being aching for more. His hands slipped down her arms, his fingers tracing the curve of her waist. Pressed against him, she was surrounded by the alluring scent and sensation of his warm skin against hers. Time ceased to exist. The only thing that mattered was the taste of his kiss, the feel of his hands on her body, the surge of longing that coursed through her veins. They moved together, each touch prompting a fire within her.

Their clothes came off in a frenzy, their desire spilling out in a torrent of kisses and touches, whispers against skin, and the desperate need to forget, to erase the world outside this makeshift haven. Their bodies in motion, a symphony of scent and sound, fueled by a shared hunger that had simmered for years, unspoken but undeniable.

A sharp rapping on the door startled them.

Noah pulled away, his eyes troubled, Elizabeth's heart pounding erratically. He offered her a strained smile.

"Don't move," he muttered, his voice strained, as he got dressed in haste.

Elizabeth instantly flushed, tugging at her dress that had spilled across his desk. As Noah headed for the door, she fumbled with her bra, thinking they should have never come here, wishing she could erase this moment before it could reach a messy end.

Noah stopped momentarily, glancing back at her with a mixture of amusement and concern. "It's probably just the building superintendent," he said, though the uncertainty clouding his voice betrayed his calm.

"Uh-huh," Elizabeth mumbled, her eyes only half-lidded, fixed on the patterned tiles on the floor.

Noah clicked the door lock and turned the handle. "Who is it?"

A professional voice, crisp and clear, cut off his question. "Police. Open up."

Elizabeth's breath caught in her throat. She risked a glance at Noah. The vibrant energy she'd felt moments ago had drained away, replaced by a rigid tension that spoke volumes. He'd stepped away from the door, his back turned, a stance taken somewhere between defiance and a desperate attempt to shield her.

"What is this about?" Noah asked, his voice deceptively calm. Elizabeth could feel the tremor in his hands as he laced theirs together.

A gruff voice, spiked with authority, responded from beyond the door. "Good evening, Councilman. We're looking for Miss Elizabeth Nelson."

Noah turned back, giving her a worried look that ripped through her carefully constructed facade of composure. He offered her a slight smile, a feeble attempt at reassurance. "Whatever they have to say," he said, his voice tight, "they can say it in front of me."

He pressed against the door, his weight a physical barrier. Elizabeth wanted to lunge for the window, to disappear. Her mind darted, frantic scenarios flashing before her eyes: a raid gone wrong, someone realizing she was in the wrong place at the wrong time, the investigation gone south.

"Stand aside, sir," the officer's voice was unyielding, "We need to speak with Miss Nelson privately."

Police presence always made Elizabeth uneasy -a lingering anxiety stemming from the investigation into her parents' deaths. She'd become intimately acquainted with the aura of authority, the unspoken expectation of compliance. But she wasn't sure if she could simply stand there, let them take her, let them drag her out of this haven, this fragile moment of intimacy, into whatever storm awaited beyond the door.

The officer repeated his demand, louder this time.

Elizabeth's eyes flicked back and forth between Noah and the door, her mind reeling. "Noah," she whispered, her voice catching in her throat. He squeezed her hand, his touch the jolt of reassurance that she needed.

"Lizzy," he whispered, "It's going to be okay." But the tremor in his voice belied his words.

She swallowed hard, forcing her fear down as Noah opened the door and allowed the officer access. Elizabeth's world tilted sideways as the officer's words cut through the air.

"We found Leonard Montoya's body near the levee about an hour ago. Initial evidence suggests he took his own life."

The room spun. Her knees buckled. Noah's arm shot out to steady her.

Just this morning, she'd been in Leo's garden, listening to his stories about Vincent's childhood while they planted the cauliflower and Swiss chard. He'd seemed troubled, yes, but definitely not sui—

"That's impossible," Elizabeth said, her voice cracking. "I was just with him. He wouldn't..."

Her stomach lurched. The walls of Noah's office seemed to close in, smothering her. She'd promised Vincent she'd watch after his uncle. She'd promised to keep him away from trouble.

"I need to see him," Elizabeth said, pushing past Noah toward the door. Her legs felt like lead, each step a monumental effort. "I don't believe you."

"The body's been taken to the county morgue, Miss." the officer said. "We'll need you to come down to the station to collect his personal effects."

Elizabeth's hands flew to her mouth, bile rising in her throat. Personal effects? Suicide. What had he discovered? What had driven him to such desperation?

"I'll drive you," Noah said, his hand finding the familiar spot on the small of her back.

But Elizabeth barely heard him. All she could think about was Leo's face, his careful words about the strange trucks, his suspicions about the OVAC plant and politicians. She had to tell Vincent. She had to tell him she'd failed to protect the only family he had left.

Elizabeth's trembling fingers fumbled for her phone, her vision blurring with unshed tears. She pulled up Vincent's number, but her thumb hovered over the screen. The stark reality hit her –none of her messages were reaching him. Maybe he'd switched to burner phones, paranoid about being tracked. Or he might have had other motives for going silent and leaving her out in the cold. Whatever the reason, she had decided to move past it and had pushed that out of her mind. But right now, she needed to reach him immediately to tell him about his uncle's death. The gravity of the situation weighed down on her. Her hand grasped her stomach as a crushing weight settled in her chest, and she felt as if she were about to be sick. *I can't let Vincent find out about his uncle's death from a stranger, or worse, from the news.*

The officer cleared his throat, impatiently waiting for them to follow him back to the station. Elizabeth gathered her things and started toward the door. Her knees gave out. Noah caught her before she hit the floor, his arms wrapping around her like a vice. She pressed her face into his chest, his heartbeat thundered against her ear as he held her close.

"I have to find Vincent," she whispered into Noah's shirt. "He needs to know, but I can't..." Her voice cracked, the words dissolving into quiet sobs.

Noah's hand, warm and comforting, moved slowly on her back, soothing her with every stroke. He didn't offer empty platitudes or false promises. He just held her, letting her grief pour out in the safety of his embrace. She clutched at his shirt, anchoring herself to his solid presence as her world spun out of control. The police officer's words, sharp and cold, reverberated in her mind -"Leonard Montoya's body near the levee..." None of it made sense. Leo had been fine at breakfast, suspicious and worried maybe, but not... She couldn't finish the thought. Instead, she let Noah's strength hold her together as she watched her world fall apart.

10

Conflict and Chemistry

Elizabeth stirred, her head pounding from last night's tears. A soothing warmth enveloped her -Noah's arms wrapped around her waist, his steady breath tickling her neck. Fragments of the previous evening filtered back: the devastating news about Leo, breaking down in Noah's office, him refusing to leave her alone in her grief.

The morning sun filtered through unfamiliar curtains. Noah's townhouse. She'd never been in his bedroom before; the furnishings were minimal yet the space felt intimate, lived-in. Family photos lined the walls, degrees hung in simple frames, a forgotten coffee mug sat on the bedside table.

Noah shifted behind her, his muscles tensing as he woke. With a light touch, his fingers traced across her arm, before he pressed a soft kiss on her shoulder. "Good morning, how are you feeling?" he whispered, his lips brushing her cheek. He reached for his phone and checked the time. "Dammit, I'm late. I've got to get cleaned up, Have to vote on a piece of legislation first thing today."

Elizabeth shifted to look at him, studying his face in the dawn's glow. Time had etched new creases near his eyes since their teenage years, but that smile was exactly as she remembered -sincere, comforting, lighting up those chocolate-brown eyes.

"Big decision?" She heard the raspiness in her own voice, raw from the night's watershed of emotions.

"Mmhmm." He eased himself away with gentle care. "But I'll head straight back afterward, I swear." His palm rested against her face, his thumb wiping away a tear she hadn't felt escape. "Get some more sleep. Make yourself at home."

The bed felt colder without him, but Elizabeth nodded. Sleep pulled at her edges, her body and mind exhausted from the emotional toll of Leo's death. She watched Noah gather his clothes, and methodically fold them, the sharp creases a testament to years of routine, before he disappeared into the bathroom. She pressed the pillow to her cheek, inhaling his scent, grateful for him being in her life right now.

She wanted desperately to return to the trailer, expecting Leo to be there. She could not bear to read the note in the packet of his items the police had given her. Not yet. The envelope sat in her purse, Leo's shaky handwriting spelling out her name. The coroner had handed it to her last night, along with other personal effects - a worn leather wallet, a silver watch that probably hadn't kept proper time in years, and a small wooden box she recognized from Vincent's childhood photos. Her phone buzzed on the nightstand. An Unknown Number lit up the screen, but she let it go to voicemail. *Oh, wait.* Could it have been Vincent? How could she tell him? The words stuck in her throat every time she tried to form them.

The shower stopped running. Noah's footsteps padded across the hardwood floor, followed by the soft rustle of clothing. She closed her eyes, pretending to drift back to sleep. She couldn't face another round of concerned looks, of gentle questions about funeral arrangements. How should they handle the remains? *The remains.*

The bed dipped as Noah sat beside her. His fingers brushed her hair back, tucking it behind her ear. "There's food in the kitchen," he whispered. "Stay in bed as long as you need."

The front door clicked shut moments later. Elizabeth rolled onto her back, staring at the ceiling. Morning light stenciled shadows across the crown molding, dancing patterns that reminded her of the way sunlight used to filter through the trailer's dusty windows. Leo had always been up before dawn, coffee brewing, telling stories about the land and its history.

Now the trailer sat empty. All those stories, all that history -gone. The thought of walking through that door, seeing his empty chair, the coffee pot cold and silent... She pulled Noah's pillow closer, letting the familiar scent anchor her to the present moment. The note could wait. Just a little longer.

Elizabeth's trembling fingers lifted her phone from the nightstand. The screen showed three missed calls since yesterday, each one from an Unknown Number. She scrolled past them and found Fred's contact number at the *New York Citizen*. She pressed Call and announced herself on the second ring. Her mouth went dry as his secretary patched her through.

"Nelson? This better be good. We've been catching hell since we ran that Venezuela piece. Fucking assholes threatening to sue me down to my drawers." Fred's gruff voice carried the sounds of the newsroom behind it - phones ringing, keyboards clicking, voices calling across desks. "But listen, it was your best work yet. All this fallout is proof, you did a helluva job getting—"

"Fred, I need to find Vincent." Her voice cracked. "He's not responding on his regular number and..." She swallowed hard. "His uncle passed away."

A pause. Papers shuffled on Fred's end. "Jesus, that's the last thing he needs to—. Hold on."

Elizabeth pushed herself up and pressed her back against the headboard, clutching Noah's pillow to her chest, longing for the comfort of his arms around her.

"Got a number that might work. He's supposed to be dropping in around here, but god only knows." Fred's voice lowered. "You sure you want to be the one to tell him?"

"Yeah, it has to be. Uncle Leo was like a father to me..." She squeezed her eyes closed. "I meant to him."

Fred read off the number. She scribbled it on her palm with a pen from Noah's planner sitting on the nightstand, the ink bleeding into the creases of her skin.

"Listen, kid." Fred cleared his throat. "He's been asking about you. Says you've gone dark on some story out there. Thought I might know something about it. What are you working on?"

"I can't ... it's complicated."

"With you two, it always is." More sounds of papers rustling and Fred jostling the phone. A door slammed and footsteps pounded, then fell silent as his voice dropped lower. "Just... be careful with him right now. He's not in a good headspace. The stubborn jackass self-discharged from the hospital and got into some trouble. They left him in pretty rough shape. We picked him up just outside of Laredo."

Damn it, Vin. Elizabeth stared at the number on her hand, her vision blurring. "Thanks, Fred." She ended the call. The morning light caught the ink stains on her palm where she'd written it down. Her thumb hovered over the keypad, Vincent's new number staring back at her. Just the thought of the conversation, of having to deliver the news that would devastate him, made her chest ache.

She pressed the first digit, then stopped. The screen blurred as tears threatened again. How could she tell him over the phone? Leo deserved more than that. Vincent deserved more than that. The messaging app opened with a soft click. Elizabeth started typing, deleted it, started again. Each attempt felt hollow, inadequate. Nothing captured the weight of what she needed to say. Finally, she stripped it down to the bare essence:

Trying to reach Vincent Rivera. Important.

Her thumb pressed Send before she could second-guess herself. The message showed as delivered immediately -he had signal wherever he was. The typing indicator appeared, disappeared, appeared again. She clutched the phone tighter, her breath caught in her throat. But no response came. The typing indicator vanished one final time, leaving her message floating alone in the chat window.

She let out a sigh and dragged herself from Noah's bed, her limbs heavy with grief. The hardwood floor felt cold against her bare feet as she padded to his bathroom. Her reflection caught her off guard - puffy eyes, mascara streaks, her usually sleek hair a tangled mess.

The shower's hot water pelted her skin, but she barely felt it. Her mind kept drifting to Leo's empty trailer, to the unopened letter in her purse, to Vincent's unanswered message. She mechanically went through the motions of washing her hair with Noah's shampoo, the unfamiliar scent of sandalwood surrounding her.

In the kitchen, she found a carton of eggs and bread. The routine of cooking grounded her -cracking eggs into the sizzling pan, dropping bread into the toaster. Her hands shook as she ground fresh black pepper over the sunny yellow yolks, watching them quiver with each turn of the grinder.

The TV remote sat on the granite countertop. She clicked it on, needing background noise to fill the silence. The local news channel flickered to life on the wide screen TV mounted on the wall, and her breath caught. There they were -the same group of protesters she'd been working with, their signs bobbing above the crowd outside City Hall. She recognized Maya, the student journalist, holding her microphone high as she interviewed participants. The camera panned across angry faces, determination outlined in their features as they chanted about environmental justice and corporate greed.

The eggs cooled on her plate as she watched, transfixed by the growing crowd on the screen. These were Leo's people, fighting for the cause he'd died believing in. Her throat tightened at the thought. She reached for the coffee pot, Noah's morning brew still warm to the touch, and started to pour a cup, but her hand froze mid-air. The TV anchor's voice cut through her thoughts.

"Breaking news from City Hall, where protesters have gathered in unprecedented numbers following the death of local activist Leonard Montoya."

The coffee pot clattered back onto its base. Elizabeth grabbed her towel, wringing the moisture from her hair as she cranked up the volume. The camera panned across the crowd -twice the size of the previous gatherings. Signs bearing Leo's name bobbed above the sea of faces.

"Mr. Montoya was found deceased late last night," the anchor continued. "Sources say he left behind evidence of alleged corporate misconduct related to the proposed OVAC concrete plant expansion. Protesters are demanding…"

Elizabeth's fingers tightened around the towel. She could feel her heart hammering against her ribs, the adrenaline pumping through her veins. Leo's warnings about strangers and trucks, his suspicious glances toward the construction site, the way he'd clutched that wooden box to his chest the last time she'd visited - it all clicked into place. The unidentified guards that roughed her up when she tried to get a closer look.

The camera cut to Maya, her face flushed with emotion, but her voice was drowned out by the shouts from the angry crowd.

"Leonard Montoya spent his life protecting this land! We won't let his death be in vain!"

Water dripped from Elizabeth's hair onto Noah's pristine kitchen floor as she stood transfixed. The wooden box from Leo's effects sat in her purse, still unopened. What evidence had he found? What had he known?

She raced back to the bedroom, her wet feet leaving damp prints on the living room carpet. Her hands trembled as she dug through her purse, fingers closing around the envelope with Leo's familiar scrawl. The TV's volume carried from the kitchen. She perched on the edge of the bed, sliding her thumb under the envelope's seal.

"Councilman Montgomery!" Maya's voice cut through the air. Elizabeth's head snapped up. "Can you comment on today's vote?"

The room was filled with the sound of Noah's polished tone, a voice that seemed to glide through the rooms. "The council has approved the demolition of the Centennial Community Center with a vote of seven to two. While we understand this decision may upset some residents, the economic benefits of the Ohio Valley Aggregates expansion cannot be ignored."

The envelope slipped from Elizabeth's fingers. She pressed her palm against her chest, trying to steady her breathing. The Centennial Community Center -where she'd attended her first dance, where her mother had taught art classes, where Uncle Leo had spoken at countless town halls fighting to protect the ecosystems and the tributaries that flowed into —.

"But sir, what about the environmental impact studies that Leonard Montoya presented?" Maya pressed.

"Those studies were inconclusive." Noah's voice carried that calculated diplomatic smoothness that made Elizabeth's stomach churn. "The council has reviewed all relevant documentation and determined that OVAC's proposal meets our community's standards."

Elizabeth's legs carried her back to the kitchen. On screen, Noah stood on the City Hall steps in his crisp tailored suit, that winning smile in place as he fielded questions. Just hours ago, he'd held her while she grieved. Now he stood there, dismantling everything Leo had fought to protect. The wooden box in her purse seemed to burn through the leather. What evidence had Leo discovered? What had he left behind?

Noah's voice continued from the TV: "Change is necessary for progress. This vote represents a step forward for Sweetwater Springs."

Elizabeth's throat tightened. The man on TV wasn't the same one who'd comforted her all night. This was *Councilman* Montgomery, doing exactly what Uncle Leo had feared -selling out their town piece by piece.

She hurled curses at Noah's image on the screen. "You two-faced bastard!" Her fist slammed against the granite countertop. "Lying piece of shit!" The smile that had comforted her hours ago now made her blood boil. She stormed back to the bedroom, snatching up Leo's envelope from where it had fallen. Her fingers trembled as she tore it open, desperate for answers, for something to make sense of this betrayal.

But the pages inside stopped her cold. Instead of Leo's regular penmanship, strange symbols and characters covered the paper - curves and lines that looked vaguely hieroglyphic, but unlike any language she recognized. Intricate geometric patterns filled the margins, circles intersecting with triangles, spirals weaving through straight lines.

"What the hell?" Elizabeth flipped through the pages, her heart sinking with each incomprehensible sheet. Drawings of what might have been maps or blueprints covered the last page, but they were marked with more of the mysterious symbols instead of labels.

She slumped onto Noah's bed, the papers scattered across her lap. Why would Leo leave her a message she couldn't read? He'd known she was investigating, had trusted her with his suspicions. This felt like a cruel joke -another dead end when she needed answers most.

Tears of frustration burned her eyes as she gathered the strange pages. As the morning sun's rays fell across the page, the symbols seemed to flicker and glow, their ink catching the light and creating a shimmering effect. She'd seen Leo's handwriting countless times over the past weeks -grocery lists, garden notes, old letters to Vincent. This was nothing like his usual style.

Elizabeth yanked the black cocktail dress over her head, not caring that it was wrinkled and disheveled. Her fingers fumbled with the zipper, catching strands of her hair in their rush. The silk that had felt so elegant against her skin last night now seemed to mock her, a reminder of Noah's treachery.

She stuffed Leo's cryptic papers into her purse along with the wooden box, scanning Noah's bedroom for anything she might have left behind. Her reflection in his mirror caught her eye–lids red-rimmed and swollen, hair still damp and tangled from the shower. She looked as wrecked on the outside as she felt within.

The TV still blared from the kitchen, Noah's voice carrying up the stairs as he continued his press conference. Elizabeth couldn't bear to hear another word. She had to get out before he returned, before she had to face those lying eyes and that disingenuous smile.

Her heels clicked against the hardwood as she fled down the stairs and out the front door. The direct sunlight beat down on her face, too bright, too cheerful for the storm in her chest. She ran, her dress hiking up with each stride, purse bouncing against her hip.

Past the manicured lawns of Noah's neighborhood, past the historic homes with their wraparound porches, she ran until her lungs were flames. The fancy heels she'd worn to impress Noah's colleagues last night bit into her feet, but she pushed on.

Finally, her legs gave out. And she doubled over at the corner of Maple and Third, coughing as she tried to catch her breath. Her hair fell in a curtain around her face as she braced her hands on her knees, each gasp tasting of betrayal and grief.

A fresh reggae ringtone jingled in her pocket. It was Harper. She didn't pick up but instead listened through the speaker as Harper recorded her voicemail message.

"I'm watching the live stream from city hall. Oh my God! That town is going to explode. If you need a neutral space, come stay at my place. There's plenty of room and I'm hardly ever home, anyway. I'll text you the address and where I stash the spare key. Stay safe, girlfriend."

Elizabeth's lungs burned as she tried to steady her breathing, the morning sun beating down on her tear-stained face. A car engine rumbled behind her, slowing as it approached. She glanced over her shoulder, recognizing Jimmy's beat-up Chevy with its mismatched door. He was the trailer park neighbor who sold her the janky Subaru.

He leaned across the passenger seat, cranking down the manual window. His work uniform was covered in grease stains, and dark circles under his eyes suggested he'd just finished the night shift at the plant.

"Need a ride?" He pushed open the passenger door.

Elizabeth slid into the worn seat, the smell of motor oil and cigarettes filling her nostrils. Her legs ached from running in heels, and the dress clung uncomfortably to her skin.

"Take me home," she said, pulling the door shut.

Without a word, Jimmy made the turn toward the road leading north. The ancient suspension creaked as they hit every pothole on the way back to Echo Ridge.

CONFLICT AND CHEMISTRY

* * *

The Chevy's engine died with a sputter, leaving only the tick of cooling metal in the morning air. Elizabeth stared at Leo's front door, her legs too heavy to climb the worn wooden steps. The familiar wind chimes Leo had hung last spring tinkled softly, their melody hollow without his presence.

She sank onto the bottom step, her black dress gathering dust. The wooden box and cryptic papers pressed against her side through her purse, a physical reminder of all the questions Leo had left behind. Her fingers traced the weathered grain of the step where he used to sit in the evenings, watching the sunset while sharing stories about Vincent's childhood.

Elizabeth didn't turn around, but she heard a car door open and close, followed by slow footsteps. Gravel crunched behind her. She looked up to see Jimmy had paused a few feet away, shifting his weight from one foot to the other. The silence stretched between them, thick with unspoken grief.

"I can't believe he's dead." Jimmy's voice cracked on the last word.

Elizabeth felt a lump in her throat when she looked up at him. Jimmy's usual easy smile was gone, replaced by sunken eyes and deep worry lines around his mouth. He'd known Leo longer than she had - helped him with trailer repairs, shared meals, listened to his stories about the old days. Now they were both sitting with the weight of his absence, neither knowing quite what to say.

Elizabeth pulled the strange papers from her purse, tilting the sheets toward the sunlight, catching the intricate symbols.

O~ᏋᏗ EGVꚙ Dꚙ ᎷᎸ SႦ DꚙᏆh.

Her fingers trembled as she smoothed the crinkled edges.

"What's that?" Jimmy leaned closer, squinting at the pages.

"Uncle Leo left this for me, but..." She shook her head, frustration tightening her chest. "I can't make sense of it. It's not like any writing I've seen before."

Jimmy's eyes widened as he studied the geometric patterns and flowing characters. He reached for the paper with oil-stained hands, then caught himself and wiped them on his coveralls first.

"I know what this is." He pointed to a series of curved letters. "It's a type of Cherokee writing - well, sort of. Not the modern kind you see today, but an older style. My grandfather used to show me similar markings when I was a kid."

Elizabeth's heart skipped. "You can read this?"

"Nah, our people's tradition was mostly oral. But these symbols..." Jimmy traced the intricate patterns with a careful finger. "They were used to pass on important information, especially about the land. My grandfather said they contained ancient knowledge that needed protecting. Not sure about all that, but..." He shrugged.

Elizabeth stared at the mysterious characters with new understanding. Of course, Leo would use this writing -he'd always spoken proudly of his heritage. He must have known these pages would mean something to the right person.

She clutched the papers, her heart racing. "Jimmy, could you -would you be able to translate these?"

He shook his head, rubbing his chin. "Not me personally. But my aunt on the reservation -she studied the old writings. Been teaching it to the younger generation too." He paused, considering. "I think she could help us understand what Uncle Leo was saying with these."

Elizabeth's fingers tightened on the pages. Part of her wanted to keep Leo's last messages close, protected. But what good were they if she couldn't read them? She smoothed the crinkled edges one last time, memorizing the intricate patterns before holding them out to Jimmy.

"Take them. Find out what they mean." She swallowed hard. "Uncle Leo trusted me with this. I need to know why."

Jimmy carefully folded the papers, tucking them into his breast pocket. He patted the spot over his heart. "I'll guard these with my life, Elizabeth. Uncle Leo was family to all of us here."

As his truck rumbled away, Elizabeth watched the dust settle on the gravel road. Leo's wind chimes sang their lonely melody above her, and she remembered something he'd told her while they worked in his garden:

"The earth remembers every secret we bury, every truth we try to hide. Sometimes you just need to know where to dig."

* * *

Elizabeth sat on the trailer steps, her shoulders slumped, the morning's betrayal a heavy weight on her chest, leaving her feeling hollow. The crunch of tires on gravel made her look up. Noah arrived in a new black Mercedes. It rolled to a stop, looking out of place among the modest homes.

"I knew you'd be here." He stepped out, his suit jacket slung over one arm.

Her stomach clenched. "How could you? I saw the press conference."

"Listen, the decision had already been made. I was going to tell you later. The vote was nothing more than a formality. Someone had to make the statement to the media. They asked me to do it—"

"Asked or commanded?" The words shot from her mouth like bullets.

"Babe, be fair. You of all people know how this works." Noah's perfectly crafted smile slipped.

"What are you saying?"

"Everyone knows this is an unpopular issue. Somebody had to be the sacrificial lamb and face the public. I'm the newest guy in the ranks. It fell to me. C'mon, I don't have to spell this out for you. You're smarter than that, Lizzy."

Elizabeth's chest tightened. She understood the game all too well - had covered enough stories to recognize when someone was being used as a pawn. The realization both softened her anger toward Noah and intensified her disgust at the whole situation.

"Elizabeth, don't let this get between us. You know this has nothing to do with me and you. I would never do anything to harm our relationship. After I've finally got you back, do you think I'd risk losing you again? Babe, we've got a second chance to make our lives everything we dreamed about as kids. And for our kids someday."

Elizabeth's stomach flinched at Noah's mention of children and dreams. His words painted a picture of the life she'd once imagined as a little girl - the perfect house, the white picket fence, the family she craved before leaving Sweetwater. But Uncle Leo's warnings, as haunting as the silence of his abandoned trailer, echoed in her mind.

"Noah, I—" She swallowed hard. "Uncle Leo is gone. And now this announcement about the plant expansion… What am I supposed to think?"

Noah's face fell. "I'm sorry about Mr. Montoya but—"

Elizabeth wrapped her arms around herself. "The timing feels wrong. All of it."

Noah drew nearer. "Let me help you. I'll take care of—"

"No." Elizabeth stood up. "I need to handle this myself."

"You don't have to do everything alone." Noah reached for her hand. "That's what I'm trying to tell you. We're a team now."

His touch was warm, familiar. For a moment, Elizabeth let herself lean into it, remembering the comfort she'd felt in his arms at the wedding reception. But Vincent's face flashed through her mind - his crooked smile, the way he'd trusted her with his camera while filming the Kīlauea volcano eruption on the Big Island while he carried her across the steaming rocks, how he'd never asked her to step into the lion's den without being by her side.

She pulled away from Noah. The loss of Leo and this apparent betrayal had shaken her more than she cared to admit. Vincent was out there somewhere, probably still healing, possibly in danger. The thought of facing him, of explaining how she'd lost track of his uncle while chasing her own demons in Sweetwater Springs, made her heart ache. She turned her back.

"I need time," she whispered, more to herself than to Noah.

Noah's footsteps crunched across the gravel, each step widening the gulf between them. Elizabeth watched his Mercedes pull away, leaving only dust and the hollow echo of their conversation.

The garden beckoned her. She sank to her knees beside the cabbage plants she and Leo had tended together just days ago. Her fingers traced the leaves, remembering how his expert hands had shown her the gentle way to handle intrusive insects and ….

"Suicide?" The word was like a shard of glass on her tongue. The police report lay crumpled in her purse, its clinical language failing to capture the man she'd known. Leo had been cautious, deliberate in every action.

She plucked a weed from between the plants, her mind in motion. Leo had been gathering evidence - documentation of illegal land deals, environmental reports that contradicted official statements. He wouldn't have abandoned that fight. Not willingly. The timing was too convenient. His disappearance coincided perfectly with the plant announcement, erasing the strongest voice of opposition. She'd seen similar patterns in her investigative work - whistleblowers silenced, evidence vanishing, truth buried beneath carefully constructed narratives.

Her gaze drifted to the empty trailer. Leo's photographs lined the walls, but she remembered each one -especially the shot of young Vincent proudly holding up his first camera. Those weren't the belongings a man would leave behind if he planned to die. They were the treasures someone would protect, preserve, pass down.

The garden's rich soil crumbled between her fingers as she remembered Leo's last words to her:

"Trust your instincts, Elizabeth. They'll lead you to the truth."

Her mind began connecting the dots, formulating questions. Who benefited most from Leo's silence? And most importantly - where would he have hidden the evidence that cost him his life?

11

Digging Deeper

Elizabeth's fingers flew across her laptop keyboard, her heart racing as each new piece of information fell into place. The dim light of Leo's trailer cast long shadows across the scattered papers and empty coffee cups surrounding her makeshift workstation.

"Three violations in Michigan... water contamination in Pennsylvania..." She muttered, scanning through environmental reports. Her stomach twisted as she pulled up satellite images showing the devastating impact of similar concrete batch plants on neighboring communities.

The documents from public records revealed a pattern -OVAC Industrial Operations consistently opened plants near small towns, promised jobs and economic growth, then left behind contaminated groundwater and respiratory illness clusters. Her hands trembled as she opened another file showing cancer rates skyrocketing in communities downwind of their facilities. Her phone buzzed. A text from Stacy lit up the screen:

Pierson's had another asthma attack. At the ER again.

She released a heavy sigh. The proposed plant expansion site sat less than a mile from Stacy's house. She pulled up a wind pattern analysis, overlaying it with the town map. The prevailing winds would carry particulate matter directly over the elementary school.

A knock at the trailer door made her jump. Through the window, she spotted Noah's silhouette. She quickly minimized her browser windows and shoved the papers under a cushion.

"Come in," she called, her voice steadier than she felt.

Noah stepped inside, his presence filling the small space. "Working late?" He moved behind her, hands resting on her shoulders.

She fought the urge to pull away, hyper-aware of the damning evidence hidden beneath her. "Just following up on some leads."

His fingers tensed slightly. "You know, you could work on this story from my place. It's more comfortable than —"

"I like it here," she cut him off, remembering Leo's warnings about the strangers in trucks. The same company logo she'd just spent hours researching. Could they be linked to the same guys that threatened her at the overlook? She had so much more work to do and zero time for distractions.

Noah's hands slid from Elizabeth's shoulders. A faint, lingering scent of spicy woods and musk, his signature scent, filled the air as he leaned against the kitchen counter.

"The council's voting on the final permits next week," he said.

Elizabeth kept her eyes fixed on her laptop screen, pretending to read while her thoughts whirled. The evidence she'd uncovered painted a clear picture -one that would devastate Noah's political career if it came to light.

"I've been meaning to ask you something." His voice softened. "About us."

A harsh, white beam from the newly installed security flood light at the concrete plant site sliced through the trailer park, casting an unsettling, shifting pattern of shadows through the window. Elizabeth drew in a sharp breath."

"I know things are difficult right now," Noah continued, unaffected by the intrusion. "But I've been thinking about the future. Our future."

Elizabeth's throat tightened. Leo's death, the hidden note, Vincent's silence, and the increasing evidence of corporate negligence all added to the pressure she felt. Noah represented everything she'd convinced herself that she needed - stability, acceptance, a chance to belong. But at what cost?

"Noah, I -" Her phone buzzed again. A message from Jimmy: "Auntie says the note's important. Meeting her tomorrow." She took a deep breath and exhaled slowly.

"Who's that?" Noah asked, too casually.

"Just Stacy," She lied, sliding the phone face-down. "Wedding follow-up stuff."

She felt the pull between truth and protection, journalism and loyalty. Noah stepped closer, and she caught a glimpse of the earnest expression she remembered from high school —resurrecting at each opportune moment. He could discern the tension. And he always found a way to appease everyone, seeing both sides of the issue, and ensuring everything remained as it was. Sweetwater thrived on the familiar, and Noah had honed the art of keeping everyone content with a simple smile. But now that look reminded her of all the questions that still needed answers.

Elizabeth shifted in her chair, the ancient springs creaking beneath her. The evidence on her screen glowed accusingly - a digital trail of OVAC's environmental violations that she couldn't unsee. Noah stood silently, his presence simultaneously reassuring and stifling, expecting a response that she was not yet prepared to give.

"It's getting late," she said, closing her laptop. The snap of the lid echoed in the trailer's cramped space.

"You're avoiding the conversation." Noah's voice carried that usual note of persistence, the same tone he used at council meetings when pushing for a vote.

"I'm not avoiding anything." Elizabeth stood, needing distance between them. "I just have an early call tomorrow."

"Is that so? " One eyebrow arched, he asked, "With who?" His voice was flat, but his eyes betrayed his curiosity.

The question hung sharp in the air. Elizabeth's phone pressed against her leg, a tangible reminder of Jimmy's text about Uncle Leo's note, the words scorching through her like fire. She moved to the kitchenette, busying herself with rinsing out her coffee mug.

"Just following up on some local stories," she said, the lie bitter on her tongue. The water splashed over her hands, too hot, but she welcomed the distraction of the sting.

Noah stood behind her, his reflection appearing in the window above the sink. "I meant what I said about us having a future, Lizzy. Once this plant expansion deal goes through, things will settle down. The town will see the benefits."

Elizabeth's hands tightened on the mug. Benefits like increased asthma rates? Like contaminated groundwater? Like whatever had driven Uncle Leo to his death? But she couldn't voice these thoughts, not yet. Not until she had all the pieces.

"I need time," she said, setting the mug in the drain rack with deliberate care. "Everything's happening so fast."

Noah's hands slipped around her waist, and she tensed at his touch. The sensation, which used to excite her, now felt oppressive in the tight space of the trailer.

"I should get some sleep," she said, stepping away from his embrace. She moved toward the door, making her intention clear.

Noah's shoulders dropped, but he nodded. "Alright. Just... think about what I said?" He reached for the door handle, pausing. "About our future."

"I will." The words felt hollow in her throat.

She watched through the window as Noah's luxury car kicked up dust on the gravel road. Only when his taillights disappeared around the bend did she let out the breath she'd been holding. She double-checked the locks, then returned to her laptop.

The evidence glowed on her screen - damning proof of OVAC's environmental violations. She thought of Stacy's son in the ER, of Leo's suspicious death, of Vincent's warnings. The pressure of the situation bore down on her as she backed up her research to an encrypted drive.

Tomorrow she'd call Jimmy for an update about Uncle Leo's notes. For now, she needed rest. She stowed away her laptop and pulled the scattered papers from beneath the cushion, securing them in her locked briefcase. Then she headed to the bathroom for a nice warm shower.

The scent of lavender from her sleep mask mingled with the lingering warmth of the day as she got ready for bed, but Noah's words about their future still repeated in her thoughts. With a sigh, she stretched out under the blanket, hoping that in her dreams she would find a way to hold on to Noah forever and have the bright future he promised. And that he would see the facts objectively and not view her as the source of false or biased information. She understood that Noah saw the expansion project as an economic lifeline for his constituents. But when she closed her eyes, all she could see were the satellite images of devastated communities left in OVAC's wake.

***

The morning sun cast its rays through the dusty windows of the trailer, illuminating Elizabeth's nimble fingers as they moved across the keyboard. Up before dawn, she forged ahead with her work, downloading EPA reports, making calls, and recording witness accounts. The evidence she'd gathered painted a more devastating picture: OVAC's track record of environmental violations, cancer clusters in communities near their other plants, and suspicious deaths of whistleblowers.

She paused, rubbing her tired eyes. The *Sweetwater Springs Independent* had agreed to run her piece -a small weekly paper that still believed in actual journalism. Her article laid out the facts in stark detail: contaminated groundwater in three western New York counties, increased respiratory illnesses in Indiana, and mysteriously dropped investigations in Texas. Her phone buzzed. A text from the paper's editor:

> **It's live on our website. Already getting picked up. Good job, Elizabeth.**

Elizabeth pulled up the newspaper's website. Her headline blazed across the screen:

"Under a Cloud of Dust: Ohio Valley Aggregates' Dark Legacy of Pollution and Corruption."

Below it, satellite images showed the destruction left behind at other OVAC sites. She'd included quotes from former employees, medical reports, and EPA violations.

Within hours, her social media notifications blew up with comments and shares. Local environmental groups shared the article, adding their own stories. Parents posted about their children's unexplained illnesses. Former plant workers confirmed her findings.

"Ohio Valley Aggregates Corporation: A History of Environmental Devastation."

"Toxic Legacy Uncovered: Ohio Valley Aggregates Exposed as Serial Polluter Across Multiple States."

"Ohio Valley Aggregates' Dirty Secrets: A Trail of Pollution and Violations from Coast to Coast."

Then came the pushback. The Chamber of Commerce released a statement dismissing her as an "outsider stirring up trouble." City Council members called it BS and described her as a "talentless hack" and "pathetic attention seeker". But they could not dispute her sources or the documented evidence. The mayor's office demanded a retraction. Elizabeth smiled grimly as she read their email, remembering the boxes of evidence stored safely away. She'd anticipated this reaction and had protected her sources.

Her phone rang -Noah's number. Elizabeth let it go to voicemail. She had more important things to focus on, like the follow-up piece she was writing about the suspicious timing of Leo Montoya's death and the community center's rushed demolition approval. The truth was finally coming to light in Sweetwater Springs, and she wasn't about to stop now.

She stared at her phone, the message she had sent to the number Fred had given her still showing no response. A week had passed since that first attempt. She'd called twice, left voicemails that felt hollow and inadequate. How could she tell him his uncle was deceased through a text message? Circumstances left her no choice but to...

Vincent, if this reaches you, I'm sorry but your uncle has passed away. I'm here at the trailer in Echo Ridge. Please call me when you can.

The funeral home had contacted her the previous day about the remains. The image of his body, shrouded in white, lying in the cold, sterile basement of the funeral home, made her sick. With no word from Vincent and no other family to consult, Elizabeth had made the decision herself. Leo had once mentioned to her that when his day came, he wanted his ashes scattered on the ridge overlooking the valley. She'd signed the cremation papers with trembling hands. The director had been kind, explaining the process, asking if she wanted to keep some ashes in an urn. Elizabeth chose a simple wooden box, something that matched Leo's modest nature. She tried Vincent's number again. Straight to voicemail.

"Vin, it's me again. I had to make some decisions about Uncle Leo's arrangements. I… I had him cremated. I remember him saying he wanted his ashes scattered on the ridge. But I'm waiting for you before doing anything else. Please call me back. I'm worried about you."

She ended the call and set the phone down next to the wooden box on Leo's kitchen table. The trailer felt emptier now, Leo's absence like a physical weight in the air. His coffee mug still sat unwashed by the sink where he'd left it that last morning. She couldn't bring herself to move it.

Her phone buzzed against the wooden table, Noah's name flashing on the screen. Her stomach tightened as she answered.

"My god, Elizabeth!" Noah's voice crackled through the speaker, sharp and strained. "Do you have any idea what kind of damage your article is doing? What were you thinking?"

"I was thinking of telling the truth." Elizabeth kept her voice steady despite her racing pulse. "Everything in that piece is documented,

Noah. Environmental reports, health statistics, witness statements —"

"Those reports are outdated. OVAC has new safety protocols now. You're scaring people for no reason."

"Really? Then explain Uncle Leo's death. Explain why he died right after warning everyone about the dangers of this plant expansion."

A pause. Elizabeth heard Noah's heavy exhale. "Don't turn Montoya's suicide into some conspiracy theory. He was an eccentric old man, Bet."

"Stop calling me that." The childhood nickname felt wrong now, tainted. "And Uncle Leo didn't kill himself. You know it, I know it, and soon everyone else will too."

"Is that what this is about? Revenge?" Noah's tone softened, taking on that persuasive quality she'd heard him use in public. "Look, I care about you, deeply. We can work this out. Once you issue a retraction, there shouldn't be any —"

"A retraction?" Elizabeth stood up, pacing the trailer's narrow kitchen. "People deserve to know what they're dealing with regarding OVAC and what they have planned for Sweetwater. This isn't about us, Noah. It's about doing what's right."

"You're going to regret this, Elizabeth. Some stories aren't worth the cost."

The threat in his words hung in the air between them. She ended the call without responding, her hands shaking as she set the phone down. She glanced at Leo's coffee mug by the sink, remembering his warnings about the plant, about the politicians, about the changes coming to her hometown. She wouldn't back down. Not now. Not when she was finally uncovering the truth.

She stepped onto the trailer's rickety porch, the evening air cooling her flushed cheeks. Her confrontation with Noah had left her rattled, but the sight before her stopped her short.

Scattered across Leo's small yard stood dozens of candles flickering in mason jars, their warm light pushing back the gathering darkness. Behind them, familiar faces from the trailer park community emerged from the shadows - Mrs. Rodriguez from three trailers down, the Perkins family, old Mr. Cooper with his worn baseball cap.

"We read your article," Mrs. Rodriguez said, stepping forward. "Leo tried to warn us for years. We should have listened sooner."

Elizabeth's heart ached with emotion as she listened to others recounting Leo's apprehensions about the plant. A young mother clutched her infant closer, describing her worry about the increased respiratory problems in the neighborhood. Elizabeth went back inside to grab her phone to record their remarks. The sound of someone rummaging through the trailer caught her by surprise. She turned, expecting to see another supporter, but instead faced a masked figure emerging from the room. The glint of metal in their hand sent ice through her veins.

Without thinking, she grabbed Leo's old walking stick from beside the door. The intruder lunged forward, but years of covering front line protests had honed her reflexes. She swung hard, connecting with their arm. The weapon - a knife - clattered to the floor, and the attacker fled out the door. The community members surged forward, Mr. Perkins and his sons leading the charge. The intruder stumbled backward, clearly not expecting such resistance. They scrambled away into the darkness, leaving only disturbed gravel and shaken nerves behind.

Mrs. Rodriguez wrapped Elizabeth in a tight embrace. "You're not alone in this fight, mija. Leo would be proud."

Elizabeth nodded, her hands still wrapped tightly around the stick. The scattered candles continued to flicker and glow against faces now marked with determination rather than fear. This was what Leo had tried to protect -not just the land, but the people who called it home.

She stepped back inside the trailer. Her hand shook as she filled the kettle, still gripping Leo's walking stick with her other hand. The familiar motions of making tea helped steady her nerves -filling the kettle, setting it on the old stove, pulling Leo's chipped mug from the cabinet. She couldn't bring herself to use his coffee mug by the sink, but this one felt right.

Through the kitchen window, orange light flickered across the trailer's thin walls. She peered out, her heart skipped before she recognized the source -a bonfire had sprung up in the clearing where Uncle Leo used to host community barbecues. The Perkins brothers and Mr. Cooper stood guard around it, joined by other men from the community. They'd positioned themselves in a loose circle, some holding makeshift weapons - baseball bats, tire irons, pieces of pipe.

The kettle whistled, making her jump. She poured the hot water over the mesh ball filled with a cluster of loose leaves, watching the liquid turn amber. Steam rose from the cup, carrying the soothing scent of chamomile and lemongrass. She wrapped her hands around the warm ceramic, drawing comfort from its heat.

Elizabeth spotted more silhouettes moving outside as additional neighbors joined the gathering. She recognized Jimmy's tall frame among them, his stance protective as he scanned the darkness beyond the fire's reach. The flames cast their faces in sharp relief, determination etched in every line. They were standing watch, she realized. Protecting her. Protecting each other. The fear was still there, but her certainty was like a powerful current, pulling her forward.

12

Protest and Passion

Elizabeth's palms tingled as she gripped the makeshift protest sign. The late afternoon sun beat down on the crowd gathered outside City Hall, their voices rising in unified chants against the OVAC expansion project. Her throat felt raw from shouting, but she couldn't stop - not after Leo's death, not after everything she'd uncovered.

"Say No to OVAC, save our home!" The chant rippled through the crowd. Neighbors from the trailer park stood shoulder to shoulder with environmental activists and concerned citizens. Their determination fueled her own.

Sweat trickled down her neck as she pushed forward through the mass of bodies. Jimmy appeared at her side, his own sign held high above his head. The steps of City Hall loomed before them, blocked by a line of stern-faced police officers.

"Leo Montoya knew. He tried to warn us all." Elizabeth's voice cracked. The old man's absence felt like a physical wound, each breath a reminder that he'd never share another cup of tea with her on that old porch and watch the fireflies sparks over the garden.

A news crew arrived, cameras swinging toward the crowd. Elizabeth ducked her head, muscle memory from years of being behind the lens instead of in front of it. But Leo's voice haunted her mind -some stories needed to be told, no matter the cost. She straightened her spine and lifted her sign higher. She steeled herself knowing the repercussions in store for her by taking a stand. Elizabeth didn't care if she never sold another story, or if her name was blacklisted. She had a voice, and she was going to use it. *I can say whatever the hell I want.* The message was clear: "Justice for Leo Montoya - Stop OVAC Now!"

"They think they can silence us," Jimmy said, his jaw set. "But Leo's death only made more people listen."

Elizabeth nodded, scanning the growing crowd. Each face held a story -families worried about contaminated water, workers fearing for their health, elderly residents who'd spent their entire lives in homes now threatened by corporate greed. Leo had seen it coming, had tried to protect them all. The responsibility now rested on her shoulders.

The protest swelled, voices rising in memory of a man who'd loved this land enough to die for it. Elizabeth thought of the note he had left behind, its untranslated message burning like a brand in her mind. She might not understand the words yet, but she understood their cost.

* * *

Elizabeth clutched her folder of evidence as she approached the podium. The fluorescent lights of the county courthouse buzzed overhead, casting stark, unflattering shadows across the faces of the board members. Victoria Caldwell sat among them, her honey-blonde hair gleaming, perfect posture radiating authority.

"The environmental impact reports clearly show elevated toxicity levels at similar facilities," Elizabeth said, her voice steady despite her racing heart. She pulled out satellite images and soil samples data from various independent sites. "These corporations have a history of violations-"

"Ms. Nelson." Victoria's lips curved into a practiced smile. "While your concern for the community is admirable, these examples are from unrelated facilities in different jurisdictions. OVAC has provided comprehensive environmental assessments that meet all state requirements."

"Requirements they helped write through lobbying." Elizabeth's fingers tightened on the podium. "I have documentation of-"

"Speculation and hearsay." Victoria's voice cut through the murmurs of the crowd. "The county has thoroughly reviewed OVAC's proposal. Their containment systems exceed current environmental standards."

"The same standards that failed to protect communities in Texas and Oklahoma?" Elizabeth pulled out more photos. "These families lost everything when-"

"We're discussing Sweetwater Springs, Ms. Nelson, not other states." Victoria's green eyes flashed. "Unless you have evidence specific to this project, I suggest we move on to speakers with relevant concerns."

Heat rushed to Elizabeth's cheeks. She recognized Victoria's tactics -the subtle dismissal, the way she'd framed her research as emotional rather than factual. But beneath Victoria's polished exterior, Elizabeth caught a glimpse of something personal in her opponent's gaze. This wasn't just about the plant anymore.

"The evidence is relevant because it shows a pattern," Elizabeth pressed. "One that's already started here with Leo Montoya's death."

Victoria's composure cracked for just a moment. "That's speculation and you know it. This board won't entertain unfounded accusations."

Elizabeth gathered her papers with shaking hands, refusing to break eye contact with Victoria. The meeting room's tension crackled like static electricity. She'd expected resistance, but Victoria's dismissive tone felt personal, calculated to undermine her credibility.

"The chair recognizes Jimmy Whitecloud," Victoria announced, already turning away from her.

Elizabeth slid back into her seat as Jimmy approached the podium. Her chest tightened with frustration. She'd spent weeks compiling this evidence, connecting the dots between similar facilities and their devastating impact on other communities. But Victoria had dismissed it all with a few carefully chosen words.

Her phone buzzed in her pocket -another missed call from Noah. She ignored it, focusing instead on Jimmy's presentation about the cultural significance of the land OVAC planned to develop. His voice carried the weight of generations, speaking of sacred spaces and broken promises.

Victoria's impeccably manicured nails rapped on the wooden desk, clearly showing her impatience, even from Elizabeth's vantage point. The contrast between Victoria's designer blazer and Jimmy's worn flannel shirt highlighted the divide in their community - those who saw progress in concrete and steel, and those who understood the true cost of that progress.

Uncle Leo's notes filled her thoughts, picturing Jimmy's aunt painstakingly translating them word by word. The symbols remained a mystery as yet, but she felt their importance growing with each passing day. Whatever message he'd left behind, she knew it was worth fighting for. Worth dying for, in Leo's case.

The thought sent a chill down her spine. Suicide, they'd said. But Elizabeth had seen the fear in Leo's eyes during their last conversation, heard the urgency in his warnings about strangers watching the trailer park. He'd known something - something important enough to get him killed.

She slipped away from the county board meeting, her heart still pounding from the confrontation with Victoria. The evening air, cool and crisp, brushed against her cheeks as she pushed through the heavy courthouse doors. She needed space to think, to process the calculated way Victoria had dismantled her evidence.

Her phone buzzed again -Noah. She silenced it and headed toward her car, heels clicking against the pavement. The parking lot had emptied except for a few vehicles, their shapes dark against the setting sun. A figure stepped out from behind a truck. Elizabeth's muscles tensed, ready to run, until she recognized Jimmy's familiar outline.

"Your aunt send a translation of the notes yet?" Elizabeth asked, keeping her voice low.

Jimmy shook his head. "She's working on it. Says some of the symbols are old, real old. Not the kind of language most folks know nowadays."

Elizabeth leaned against her car, exhaustion seeping into her bones. "Victoria shut us down in there. Like none of it mattered - the research, the violations, Uncle Leo's death."

"That's because we're getting close." Jimmy's eyes darted around the empty lot. "My aunt, she mentioned something else. Said these symbols, they're not just words. They're coordinates. Like locations."

Elizabeth's breath caught. "Coordinates? To what?"

"Don't know yet. But whatever Leo was trying to tell us —" Jimmy stopped abruptly as headlights swept across them. A black SUV crawled past, its windows tinted dark.

Elizabeth watched it disappear around the corner, her skin prickling. "We need that translation, Jimmy. Soon."

She slid into her car, hands still shaking from the confrontation with Victoria. The parking lot's shadows stretched longer as the sun dipped behind the courthouse, casting an eerie glow across the empty spaces. She gripped the steering wheel, trying to steady her breathing. Her phone buzzed again -Noah's face lighting up the screen. She let it ring, unable to deal with his attempts to justify the project right now. Not after Victoria's calculated dismissal of her evidence.

She couldn't get Jimmy's words out of her head. Coordinates? Leo hadn't just left a message -he'd left directions. But to what? The old man had been paranoid in those final days, muttering about strangers watching the trailer park, about things hidden in plain sight.

A sudden movement caught her eye in the rearview mirror. The black SUV had circled back, crawling past her parking spot at a snail's pace. Elizabeth felt her heart thumping in her chest. She couldn't make out any faces behind the tinted windows, but she felt their eyes on her.

She turned the key in the ignition, the car's engine roaring to life. The SUV lingered at the corner, its brake lights glowing red in the gathering dusk. Elizabeth pulled out of her spot, hands clenched tight around the wheel. As she turned onto Main Street, the other vehicle pulled away from the curb, keeping pace three cars behind. She took a sharp right at the next intersection, then another, her pulse quickening as the SUV matched her turns. Leo's warnings didn't seem so paranoid now. She pressed the accelerator, weaving through the quiet streets of Sweetwater Springs, looking for a way to lose her tail. Her hands trembled as she checked her phone again. Even though she'd lost sight of the black SUV after a winding path through the residential streets, her unease lingered, her nerves still taut. Noah's text glowed on the screen:

Meet me at O'Malley's for drinks? Need to talk.

She hesitated. After their fight about the community center and her article, after Victoria's dismissal of her evidence, drinks with Noah felt like a step up for another confrontation. But something in his message carried an urgency she couldn't ignore.

The drive to O'Malley's took her past the Centennial Community Center. Even in the growing darkness, she could make out the protest signs still taped to its windows. She felt a lump form in her throat at the sight. She pulled into the bar's parking lot, scanning it for the black SUV before cutting the engine. O'Malley's neon sign flashed a red-orange glow across her dashboard. Through the windows, she saw the usual crowd of locals unwinding after work, their laughter muffled by the thick glass. Her phone buzzed again.

Inside at the corner booth.

Elizabeth grabbed her purse, making sure the index card with her talking points was still tucked safely inside. Whatever Noah wanted to discuss, she wouldn't let him dismiss her concerns like Victoria had. Not this time.

Dim amber lights flickered above the long mahogany bar, casting a devilish hue across Noah's face as she slid into the corner booth next to him. The bar's usual late-night crowd had thinned to a handful of regulars, leaving them in relative privacy. A jukebox in the corner hummed soft blues, its worn-out speakers adding a crackle to the melancholy tune. The low murmur of conversations blended with the occasional clink of ice against glass, and the sharp hiss of a soda gun. The air was thick with the scent of aged whiskey, stale beer, and a faint trace of wood polish. There was a smoky undertone, even though no one had smoked there in years—just the lingering ghost of old habits. It was the kind of place where secrets were whispered, where tension hung in the air like a storm waiting to break.

"I ordered you a whiskey sour." Noah pushed the drink toward her.

Elizabeth wrapped her fingers around the cold glass. "Thanks. I needed this after today."

"About that." Noah leaned forward, his shoulders tensing. "These protests are getting dangerous. That crowd outside city hall this morning? Someone could've gotten hurt."

"People are passionate about protecting their families."

"I get it, but throwing rocks at windows isn't the answer." Noah's hand found hers across the table. "I worry about you being out there in the middle of it all."

She pulled her hand back and took a long sip of her drink. "I can handle myself."

"I know you can. But with everything that's happened..." His voice softened. "Maybe you should stay somewhere else for a while. Not at Leo Montoya's trailer in Echo Ridge."

"Harper offered me her spare room in Clover City."

Noah's expression brightened. "That would be perfect. Just until things settle down."

"Every storm has to end eventually, right?" Elizabeth traced the rim of her glass. "And it would probably look better for you if I wasn't so... visible right now."

"That's not what I meant—"

"No, you're right. More like, these protests won't last forever. And then we can focus on rebuilding, on the future. That's what you meant. Right?" The words felt strange in her mouth, like promises she wasn't sure she could keep.

Noah reached for her hand again, and this time she let him take it. "That's all I want."

She studied his face in the dim bar light, remembering how his smile had once made her weak in the knees back in high school. That hadn't changed. His thumb traced circles on her palm, sending tingles up her arm.

"Remember that time behind the bleachers?" Noah's eyes sparkled with mischief. "When Coach Peters almost caught us?"

Heat crept up her neck. "You mean when you convinced me to skip track practice?"

"I was very persuasive back then." Suddenly, his gaze held a hint of sadness. "I wish I had taken the chance and asked you out. Our lives would have taken a completely different path." He lifted her hand and pressed a tender kiss to her fingers. "But we still have time."

Elizabeth's breath caught as she looked into his eyes. His subtle touch, soft as a whisper, filled her senses and brought a fleeting moment of peace, a brief respite from their conflict. She needed to compartmentalize - to separate the man across from her from the politician signing demolition orders.

"Noah..." She slipped her hand free and wrapped both palms around her glass. "We can't mix this with what's happening in town."

"Why not?" His fingers brushed her wrist. "You have a right to your beliefs. And I accept that we see things differently. Simple. All the fighting? What we have is separate from all that."

"Is it?" Elizabeth took another sip of whiskey, letting the burn ground her. "Because right now, everything feels tangled up."

"Then let's untangle it." Noah slid closer, his knee pressing against hers under the table. "Right here, right now - it's just us. No protests, no politics. Just Elizabeth and Noah."

The warmth in his eyes pulled at something deep in her belly. For a moment, she wanted to believe it could be that simple - that they could exist in this bubble where their opposing sides didn't matter.

She lifted her glass and gave the ice a gentle swirl with the tip of her finger, watching the pale amber liquid catch the light. The familiar odor of stale beer and worn leather seats at O'Malley's brought back memories of simpler times of college homecoming and graduation parties, before protests and politics had drawn their battle lines.

"Listen," she started, her voice soft but steady, "I know we're on opposite sides of this fight, and I hate that it's come between us like this. When I came back to Sweetwater, I never expected to find myself caring so much about this place again—or about you." She met his eyes across the table, noting how his carefully perfect persona seemed to slip just a bit more as he let his guard down, revealing something genuinely humble beneath. She reached out and touched his hand. "Maybe we could find some middle ground? There has to be a way to protect both the town's future and its soul."

Her thoughts raced as she studied his expression, comparing the boy who'd been her first crush and the man who'd rekindled those feelings. *I want to believe in you.*

She wanted to believe they could bridge this gap between his ambitions and her principles. But every time she reached for that belief, she heard Uncle Leo's voice warning her about the price of compromise. The thought of her journalist's notebook in her bag felt like a reminder of all the questions she still couldn't bring herself to ask him, all the truths she feared might shatter whatever fragile peace they could build.

"We start by listening," Noah said quietly, his voice low and husky. "I don't have to agree with you every time, and you don't have to agree with me. But if we can respect why the other feels the way they do—what they've seen, what they've lived through—maybe that's enough."

He withdrew his hand from hers, the gentle smile fading from his face as a serious expression replaced it. "It won't be easy, but nothing worth holding on to ever is. We fight the world out there, but in here"—he gestured between them— "we fight for each other."

Noah stood up and helped Elizabeth from her seat, then led her out of O'Malley's, his hand resting reassuringly on her back. The night air stroked her face, crisp and clean after the smoky bar atmosphere. Main Street stretched before them, storefront windows dark except for the soft glow of security lights.

"Remember when this place used to roll up the sidewalks at eight?" Noah's shoulder bumped against hers as they walked.

"Now it's nine." Elizabeth giggled despite herself. Their footsteps echoed off the brick buildings, synchronized in the quiet night.

They passed the old movie theater where they'd shared their first almost-kiss sophomore year. The marquee still needed fixing, letters missing from last week's showing. Noah's fingers brushed against hers, then interlaced. She didn't pull away.

"I used to walk this route home from football practice," Noah said. "Always hoped I'd run into you coming back from the library."

"Did you know I actually took the long way sometimes?" Elizabeth felt the memory's warmth spreading through her chest. "Past the field, just to watch you practice."

Noah stopped walking, turned to face her under the glow of a streetlamp. His eyes searched hers. "We were both so shy back then."

The distant sound of a train whistle floated through the night air. Elizabeth closed her eyes for a moment, allowing the familiar sound to soothe her. As if she could hop into one of the cars, whoosh back in time. and say all the things that had been bottled up in her young heart. When she opened her eyes again, Noah had stepped closer.

"Dance with me?" He pulled her into the circle of light.

"There's no music."

"Are you sure? Listen closer." He wrapped his arms around her waist, drawing her near. Elizabeth found herself swaying with him on the empty sidewalk, the ghost of their teenage selves dancing in their shadows.

She leaned into Noah's embrace, letting the rhythm of their slow dance carry her thoughts away. His chest was solid and warm against her cheek, his heartbeat steady beneath her ear. The streetlamp cast their merged shadow across the empty sidewalk, stretching it long and dark against the brick storefront.

"Remember our last homecoming dance?" Noah's voice rumbled in his chest. "When you wore that blue dress with the slit up to your thigh? Hot."

"And you stepped on my toes during every slow song." Elizabeth smiled against his shirt. The memory was bittersweet - she'd spent weeks practicing dance steps in her bedroom, hoping to impress him.

Noah's hand slid lower on her back, pulling her closer. "I've gotten better since then."

The distant train whistle faded, leaving only the sound of their breathing and the soft scuff of shoes on concrete. Elizabeth closed her eyes again, drawing in a deep breath, the captivating scent of his skin mixed with the cool, earthy smell of the night. For a moment, she could pretend they were those same teenagers, full of hope and uncomplicated dreams.

His fingers traced tantalizing patterns against her lower back, each touch sending sparks through her body. When she tilted her head up to look at him, his eyes were dark with desire. He dipped his head, his lips brushing against hers with a gentleness that made her ache.

"Come home with me," he whispered against her mouth.

Her heart was pounding as she nodded and let him lead her to his car parked down the block. The practical part of her brain tried to sound warnings about mixing pleasure with politics, but the heat of Noah's hand in hers drowned out everything else.

She settled into the passenger seat of Noah's car, the leather cool against her bare legs. As he drove through the quiet streets, his hand gripped hers across the center console. The flickering beams of the streetlights painted his face in shifting shadows, drawing attention to the strong line of his jaw and the subtle curve of his lips. She studied his profile, remembering all the reasons she'd fallen for him back then.

Sure, they disagreed about OVAC. He couldn't see past the promise of economic growth, couldn't accept her data about the environmental impact that worried her so deeply. But looking at him now, she realized that didn't have to define everything between them. People could disagree and still care for each other. Still want each other. Noah might be naïve about the company's true intentions, but his heart was in the right place. He genuinely believed he was doing what was best for the people of Sweetwater Springs.

And tonight, none of that had to matter. Tonight, could just be about two people who'd always been drawn to each other, finding comfort in familiar arms. They were both single, both consenting adults. There was nothing wrong with seeking shelter from their complicated lives in each other's company. She squeezed his hand, earning a warm smile that made her heart flutter. Sometimes the simplest truth was the best - they didn't have to agree on everything to still enjoy what they had together.

Elizabeth followed Noah into his townhouse, her pulse quickening as he flipped on a single lamp. Warm light spilled across the mid-century modern furniture and hardwood floors. The space felt both foreign and familiar - like Noah himself.

He turned to her, his eyes smoldering with passion. "Can I get you anything?"

Elizabeth shook her head, closing the distance between them. Her fingers found the buttons of his dress shirt while his hands, rough and warm, explored the curves of her back beneath the silken fabric of her blouse. Their lips met in a hungry kiss, years of unspoken longing pouring out. Noah walked her backward until her legs hit the couch. She pulled him down with her, their bodies fitting together like puzzle pieces.

"You're sure about this?" Noah breathed against her neck.

"Yes," Elizabeth whispered, her entire body responding to his touch.

All thoughts of protests and politics melted away under his hands, replaced by pure sensation. Right now, they were just Elizabeth and Noah, two people who'd always wanted this.

Their clothes formed a trail to his bedroom, the sheets were cool against her skin as he joined her, their bodies moving in a heated rhythm. She surrendered to his control as the moonlight painted silver patterns across their bodies. The gentle caress of his hands on her skin awakened a longing, one she had carried with her since her high school days when thoughts of him consumed her nights. As her fingers explored the contours and strength of his arms, each touch ignited an overwhelming desire to memorize every detail of this moment, savoring the intimacy they now shared.

Their kisses deepened as they moved together, breaths mingling in the quiet darkness. Noah whispered her name against her neck, his voice rough with emotion. Time seemed to slow, stretching like honey as they rediscovered each other. The world beyond his bedroom faded away - Noah's weight above her felt right, grounding her in the moment as pleasure built between them. With each brush of skin against skin, each deepening kiss, Elizabeth felt herself drawn into him, pleasure building at the center of her being like a slow-burning fire.

In this moment, there were no conflicting loyalties to navigate or choices to make. There was only the here and now - Noah's hands mapping her curves with a burning lust, his breath hot against her neck as he murmured words she couldn't quite make out but understood perfectly. The restlessness that had driven her for years fell away as she yielded to his touch, letting him claim her entirely.

Noah shifted and settled more fully between her thighs. She could feel every hard line of him pressing against where she was already hot and ready for him. She rocked against him instinctively seeking more friction and Noah groaned low in his throat even as he continued kissing a path down the column of her neck to where he closed his lips around one sensitive nipple.

The sensation zinged through her straight to where their hips were now aligned so perfectly and she gasped at how close he was to where she needed him most. Her hands drifted lower to grasp his hips urging him on without breaking stride even as Noah lavished attention on first one breast then switching his attentions fully to its neglected twin while Elizabeth arched beneath him lost completely to the sensation.

It wasn't until Noah finally sheathed himself fully inside her, filling and stretching her in a delicious drag that Elizabeth realized how much she'd been holding herself back all these years. A sharp intake of breath hissed between her teeth at the suddenness of his entry even as her body welcomed him greedily, clenching around the hard length of him. Noah stilled for a moment giving her time to adjust to his presence before beginning a slow grind. A guttural groan escaped his throat as he rolled his hips, pulling himself nearly free, then pushed forward with a raw force, leaving no doubt about the intense connection between them -a bond that was undeniable. The world narrowed down until all that existed was that connection. As they began moving together, it felt almost inevitable -like two pieces coming home after being apart too long.

He set a steady rhythm, his hips rolling against Elizabeth's in a slow grind that built tension with each measured thrust. The room was filled with the sounds of their labored breathing and the slap of skin on skin as they moved together.

"Noah," she breathed on a gasping sigh as he shifted and changed his angle just so, stroking over that spot within her that sent jolts of pleasure straight up her spine.

The bed creaked in time with their movements as Elizabeth rocked beneath him, urging him deeper, harder. One hand fisted in her hair angling her head just so while he ravaged her neck with hot open-mouthed kisses and sharp nips at the sensitive skin there. The sting only added to the overwhelming sensations building inside her.

"Noah. Oh my God!" The cry broke free out of a sobbing moan after his fingers slipped down between them and seized that perfect spot before starting to rub tight circles over where she was most sensitive.

"Come on baby," Noah urged against her ear, his breath hot and ragged. "Come on."

She curved into each thrust, angling to take him deeper as need coiled tighter in her belly. One hand gripped the sheets beside her head while the other raked down his back, tracing every flexed muscle and dip between them. Her legs wrapped around his waist clinging tightly even as Noah continued his relentless rhythm driving them both ever closer to the edge.

"Noah," she breathed his name again as a plea for more even as her free hand drifted down to clutch at his hip urging him deeper. "Please…"

"Tell me what you want," Noah gritted out through clenched teeth not breaking stride in his persistent pace. He shifted changing the angle until he ground against that secret spot inside her with each press forward.

A groan escaped her throat as pleasure flowed down her thighs and she dug her nails into the hard curve of Noah's rear pushing him deeper still. "More," she gasped out before words became impossible.

Noah obliged increasing his tempo driving into her now with long hard thrusts. His mouth crashed over hers capturing any further cries as they chased completion together lost in this dance of give and take.

It wasn't until Elizabeth began trembling around him, pulsing with the first waves of release that Noah allowed himself to let go completely, chasing after his own with wild abandon until he crested tumbling over that edge entwined both body and soul.

When they finally stilled, wrapped in tangled sheets and each other's arms, Elizabeth rested her hand on Noah's chest. His heartbeat thundered beneath her palm, gradually slowing to match the peaceful rhythm of the night.

"Stay," Noah murmured into her hair, pulling her tight against his chest. Elizabeth nodded, letting her eyes drift closed as exhaustion swept over her.

As she lay curled against him, her head resting on his chest, she listened to the steady cadence of his heartbeat. It was a sound she could lose herself in, a quiet reassurance that, for this moment, everything was exactly as it should be. His arm draped over her, holding her close as though he feared she might slip away. Could this be real? Could they really hold on to this fragile peace, this happiness, and make it last? She wanted to believe that the world beyond this room couldn't touch them, that the strength of their connection could outlast the storms waiting outside. If she could bottle this feeling —the safety, the intimacy, the quiet certainty of being exactly where she belonged —she would never let it go.

For now, she let herself believe that this moment, this peace between them, could stretch on forever.

* * *

Elizabeth woke to early morning sunlight streaming through Noah's bedroom windows. Her head rested on his chest, rising and falling with each steady breath. Last night flooded back -their dance on Main Street, the desperate kisses, clothes scattered across his townhouse floor.

She carefully extracted herself from his arms, gathering her clothes quietly. Noah stirred but didn't wake as she slipped into his bathroom.

Her reflection revealed raccoon eyes from the smeared mascara and her hair a tangled mess. She splashed cold water on her face, trying to clear her thoughts. Her phone showed three missed calls from Jimmy. A text message followed:

My aunt translated the notes. Call me ASAP.

Elizabeth could feel her heart pounding in her chest. Uncle Leo's final message -what secrets had he left behind? She quickly finished dressing, scrawling a note to Noah on his kitchen counter:

Had to run. Talk later.

Stepping outside, she was greeted by the crisp morning air, her hand instantly reaching for her phone to call Jimmy. Behind her, Noah's townhouse stood quiet in the dawn light. For a moment, she allowed herself to imagine a simpler life -one where she could wake up next to him without the weight of investigations and environmental protests hanging over them.

But Leo's note waited, and with it, possibly the truth about what was really happening in Sweetwater Springs. Elizabeth squared her shoulders and walked away from Noah's door, leaving last night's temporary escape behind.

13

Vincent's Return

The evening sun, a fiery ball sinking below the horizon, cast long shadows across the protest line, painting the faces of the demonstrators in a soft, orange light. Elizabeth, her arms heavy with fatigue, held her sign high, her voice hoarse from chanting slogans. *This is for Uncle Leo*, her journalistic ethics contending with the grief that had driven her to join the crowd. She remembered her old professor's charge: "Observe, document, remain objective." But Uncle Leo's garden flashed in her memory - the careful rows of medicinal plants now withering, his meticulous notes about soil contamination left unfinished. As a reporter, she knew she should be on the sidelines, notebook in hand, documenting the growing unrest with professional detachment.

She'd write her article later, she promised herself, with all the objectivity she could muster. But for now, in this moment, she needed to be more than just a witness. She justified it to herself as deep immersive journalism - after all, how could she truly understand the protesters' fury without standing among them? But the truth was simpler and messier: Uncle Leo's death had crossed the line between subject and personal crusade. She could almost hear Vincent's voice in her head, that mix of sarcasm and wisdom: "Sometimes the only way to tell the real story is to become part of it." So she compromised, her phone recording in one hand while the other held her sign, straddling the line between journalist and activist. She would write about this protest with the detachment her profession demanded, but for now, in this moment, she allowed herself to be what Leo had asked of her in those final days -a voice for those who could no longer speak. Her ethical wrestling match dissolved into shock as a familiar silhouette emerged from the sea of protesters. Her heart skipped. Vincent.

He looked thinner, his usual confident stride hampered by a slight limp as he approached. Fresh scars marked his forearms, visible where he'd rolled up his sleeves, and a partially healed cut ran along his jawline. His eyes held a haunted weariness she'd never seen before, and the shadow of a bruise still colored his left temple. His camera, usually an extension of his body, was conspicuously absent. Their eyes locked across the distance.

"Liz." His voice carried over the noise, rougher than she remembered. "I knew I'd find you here causing trouble."

Her throat tightened, questions about his condition fighting to break free. "Your uncle -"

"I know." Vincent's jaw clenched, the movement highlighting the fresh scar tissue. "We'll talk about it later." His hand brushed her arm, the touch electric through her sleeve, and she noticed fresh burn marks across his knuckles.

"Elizabeth." Noah's voice cut through their moment. He appeared beside them in an impeccable suit, his presence commanding attention. "Ready for dinner?"

Vincent's expression darkened as Noah slipped an arm around Elizabeth's waist, pulling her close.

"I made reservations at Marcello's." Noah's lips grazed her temple. "That little corner table you love."

Elizabeth's muscles tensed, caught between Vincent's intense stare and Noah's possessive embrace. The protest signs around them lowered as people turned to watch the scene unfold.

"We need to talk," Vincent said, his voice grave and urgent.

"She's busy tonight." Noah's smile didn't reach his eyes. "Maybe another time."

Elizabeth felt the tension radiating between the two men. Noah's grip on her waist tightened as Vincent stepped closer, his presence drawing stares from the protesters around them.

"Hey man, sorry about your uncle." Noah's voice carried that practiced political tone she'd grown to recognize. "He was always at our games back in high school. Even after you transferred senior year, he still showed up."

Vincent's eyes narrowed. "Yeah, watching you take my quarterback spot after Coach benched me for that knee injury."

"Ancient history." Noah pulled Elizabeth closer. "We've all moved on. Speaking of which, we've gotta run. Lizzy and I have dinner plans to discuss our future together."

Elizabeth's chest tightened at Noah's words. She caught the flash of pain across Vincent's face before he masked it.

"*Our future?*" Vincent's eyes, like lightning strikes, met Elizabeth's in a riveting stare.

"That's right." Noah's smile held a hint of triumph. "Sometimes you have to know when to let the past stay in the past. Elizabeth is home now, where she belongs."

Elizabeth wanted to speak up, to say something -anything -but the words stuck in her throat. Vincent's appearance was so startling that she had to consciously remind herself to breathe.

"I didn't come back to rehash high school football rivalries," Vincent said, his voice clipped and cold. "This is about more than your political games, Montgomery."

Elizabeth's stomach churned as Noah's arm tightened around her waist. His usual charm vanished, replaced by a coldness she'd never seen before.

"Listen," Noah's voice cut like steel, "I've been polite, but let me be clear. You're not welcome here. This isn't Venezuela where you can stir up trouble and disappear. Sweetwater Springs has rules, order. People respect that." He cocked his jaw, a glint of defiance in his eyes, and took a step forward. "And if you're thinking about causing problems over your uncle's death, remember - the police ruled it suicide. Don't make this harder than it needs to be."

Elizabeth sensed Noah's fingers dig into her side, but she barely registered the pressure. Her mind was reeling, still trying to process Vincent's sudden appearance. For weeks she'd jumped at every phone notification. The silence had been deafening. No texts, no calls, nothing but the gnawing fear that something had happened to him after El Paso. Now here he stood, bearing the evidence of whatever violence he'd endured, and she couldn't find the words to bridge the gap between them.

Vincent's features hardened; his face flushed, a stark warning to anyone foolish enough to stand in his way. Elizabeth watched his hands clench into fists, knuckles stretched taut with restraint. The surrounding protesters had gone quiet, their signs forgotten as they watched the confrontation. She wanted to reach out, to demand answers about where he'd been, what had happened to him. The words stuck in her throat as memories flooded back - the easy rhythm they'd shared in the field, the silent communication that had kept them alive in countless dangerous situations, the trust that had always been unshakeable between them.

"You always were good at playing both sides, Montgomery." Vincent's voice, tight with barely suppressed rage, was a strained whisper. "Still hiding behind that all-star smile while you sell out your own hometown."

Noah's laugh held no warmth. "I think we're done here. Come on, babe. Our reservation's waiting."

Elizabeth felt herself being steered away from the crowd, Noah's hand firmly against her back, her feet moving automatically though her mind screamed to stay. She glanced over her shoulder and caught one last glimpse of Vincent standing alone, his expression unreadable in the fading light. The guilt hit her like a physical blow - walking away from him now, after everything they'd been through together, felt like a betrayal of something fundamental between them. She was choosing the safety of Noah's world over the complicated truths Vincent represented, and the weight of that choice settled in her chest like lead.

The scene fell silent, as the protesters watched her leave with Noah. Elizabeth felt the distance growing with each step - not just the physical space between her and Vincent, but the widening gulf between who she'd been with him and who she was becoming in Sweetwater Springs. The worst part was knowing that Vincent would understand completely. He'd seen her make this choice before, always putting the story first. But this time, she was walking away from him - her partner, her confidant, the one person who had always understood her drive to uncover the truth no matter the cost. She was choosing the comfort of Noah's ordered world over the raw honesty that had always existed between her and Vincent, and that choice felt like a fracture in her own identity.

※

In the car ride to Marcello's, Elizabeth stared out the window as Noah talked about dinner specials and wine pairings. His words washed over her in a meaningless stream while her mind replayed years of shared moments with Vincent - huddling together in a bombed-out building in Syria, his steady hands holding the camera while she reported; sharing stale coffee and gallows humor in countless hotel rooms; the way he could read her silences and know exactly when to push and when to let her process. With Vincent, she had been fearless, relentless in her pursuit of the next lead story. She hadn't worried about fitting in or playing a role or smoothing her rough edges to match someone else's expectations.

Who was she becoming in Sweetwater Springs? The woman who let Noah guide her away from uncomfortable confrontations? The politician's partner, more concerned with appearances than truth? She barely recognized herself anymore - this version of Elizabeth who wore designer dresses to charity functions and smiled politely at community meetings. The sharp-edged journalist who had faced down warlords and corrupt officials seemed to be fading like an old photograph, replaced by someone softer, more palatable to small-town sensibilities.

Vincent's appearance had shattered that careful illusion. One look at his battle-worn face had awakened something she'd been trying to suppress -that fierce hunger for the facts that had always driven her forward. The Elizabeth who had traveled the world with Vincent would never have walked away from those fresh scars and haunted eyes without demanding answers. She would have pursued the story of his disappearance, of Uncle Leo's death, of the protests rocking her hometown, with single-minded determination.

"Everything okay?" Noah said, reaching for her hand across the table at Marcello's. She simply nodded, barely registering his words. His touch was gentle, possessive, everything she thought she wanted. But all she could feel was Vincent's calloused fingers brushing her arm at the protest, and the electric current of shared history that had passed between them.

She took a long sip of wine, letting the rich flavor ground her in the present moment. She was trying to belong here, to fit into this life Noah offered. But Vincent's return had revealed the truth she'd been avoiding -she was playing a part, reading from a script written by someone else's expectations. And somewhere between Venezuela and Sweetwater Springs, she'd lost sight of who she really was.

Elizabeth pushed her half-eaten pasta around the plate, Vincent's appearance at the protest replaying in her mind. The candlelight at Marcello's cast shadows across Noah's face as he reached for her hand across the white tablecloth.

"You're quiet tonight." His thumb, warm against her skin, traced circles on her palm, his touch a silent message. "The protests are getting more dangerous. I don't want you mixed up in this anymore."

"I'm a journalist, Noah. It's my job." She pulled her hand back, taking another sip of wine to avoid his gaze.

"Stay with me tonight." His voice dropped lower. "It's where you belong. Let me take care of you. Okay?"

Elizabeth pushed her wine glass away, studying Noah across the candlelit table. The old her would have been halfway around the world by now, chasing another story, another flight, with Vincent at her side. But Uncle Leo's words echoed in her mind - about roots growing deep, about finding strength in staying still. What had all those years of running given her, really? A collection of press badges, hotel key cards, and battle scars that never quite healed.

Maybe this was what growing up meant -learning to find adventure in stability, truth in the quiet moments. She'd spent so long defining herself by deadlines and datelines that she'd forgotten there were other ways to make a difference, other ways to live. Noah reached across the table, his fingers intertwining with hers, and she felt the steady warmth of his touch anchor her to this moment, to this choice.

"Yes, let's go home," she said softly, surprising herself with how much she meant it. The word "home" no longer felt like a betrayal of who she used to be, but rather a permission slip to become someone new. Someone who could balance passion with peace, someone who could put down roots without losing herself entirely. Was that even possible?

Elizabeth nodded, knowing what would follow -the familiar dance they'd perfected since her return to Sweetwater. She let Noah guide her from the restaurant, her mind a fog of wine and warring emotions. The drive to his townhouse passed in silence, streetlights flashing across his determined profile. Her body felt heavy with resignation, accepting what seemed inevitable.

The moment they stepped through his door, Noah's mouth crashed against hers. His kiss held none of the tenderness of their previous encounters -this was raw possession, marking territory. Elizabeth yielded, allowing him to press her against the wall, his hands already working at the buttons of her blouse. She didn't resist as he lifted her, carrying her to the bedroom. This was her fate now, tied to Noah and all he represented in Sweetwater Springs. His touch commanding her to erase thoughts of Vincent, of protests, of Uncle Leo's mysterious death.

She arched into his demanding caresses, surrendering to the seductive rhythm they'd established since their reunion. Their clothes fell away, and she lost herself in sensation, letting physical pleasure drown out the whispers of doubt in her mind.

Noah's fingers tangled in her hair, tilting her face to his. His eyes held a fierce triumph as he positioned himself above her. She closed her eyes, ready to accept his possession of her body even as her heart remained conflicted. This was her place now -in Noah's bed, in his life, in the carefully ordered world he'd created in Sweetwater Springs.

"Where are you?" Noah drew back, his breath warm against her cheek. When she didn't answer, he propped himself up on his elbows, studying her face in the dim light filtering through his bedroom window. "You've been somewhere else all night."

"I'm sorry," she whispered, pushing gently against his chest. "I can't... not tonight." Elizabeth turned her head away, unable to meet his searching gaze. How could she explain that she was lost between two versions of herself -the woman who belonged in his carefully structured world and the one who had spent years chasing stories across war-torn countries with Vincent at her side? The weight of Noah's body above her suddenly felt suffocating, a physical reminder of the role she was trying to play.

"I should go." She gathered her clothes in the soft light. "Harper's expecting me."

"You don't have to leave." Noah propped himself up on an elbow. "Your things are already here. Stay."

"I need space while I cover these protests." Elizabeth slipped on her undergarments. "It's better this way -for both of us."

"My place is closer to City Hall than Harper's condo."

"Noah." She touched his cheek. "You know why I can't stay. Your position on the council, my articles -we need boundaries."

"Is this about him?" Noah's voice held an edge she rarely heard, sharp enough to make her pause in the act of buttoning her blouse. "About Rivera showing up today?"

"I have an early meeting with some of the protesters tomorrow. I should sleep at Harper's." Elizabeth stepped into her heels, avoiding the question and his eyes.

"Lizzy" Noah sat up in bed, sheets pooled around his waist. In the half-light, he looked like everything she should want -successful, stable, safe. "Don't let him get in your head. Whatever you had with him... that's not real life. This is real life."

Elizabeth's hand froze on the doorknob. Real life. As if the years she'd spent documenting conflicts and uncovering corruption were somehow less real than council meetings and charity galas. As if the career she'd built with Vincent through countless dangerous situations was less substantial than Noah's carefully planned future.

"I'll call you tomorrow," she said quietly, stepping into the hallway before he could respond. She grabbed her purse and phone, leaving Noah alone in the darkness of his townhouse. The night air felt clean against her skin as she walked to her car parked at the protest site, like washing away the remnants of choices made for the wrong reasons. The click of her heels on the empty sidewalk echoed through the quiet streets of Sweetwater Springs, each step forcing her to confront an uncomfortable truth -somewhere along the way, she'd started mistaking safety for happiness.

* * *

Elizabeth's headlights cut through the darkness as she navigated the winding road from Noah's townhouse to Harper's condo. Her lips still tingled from his kisses, but her mind wandered to Vincent's appearance at the protest. A flash of light caught her attention - industrial floodlights blazing across the ridge where she'd spotted those shipping containers weeks ago.

She pulled her car onto a gravel turnout, killing the engine and lights. The rough ground crunched under her heels as she climbed out. She switched to the hiking boots she kept in her trunk - old habits from her field reporting days.

The familiar trail stretched before her, the one where Uncle Leo had taught her to identify edible mushrooms and wild berries. Her phone's dim light illuminated the path just enough to avoid roots and rocks. The sounds of heavy machinery grew louder - excavators and dump trucks working well past normal hours.

Elizabeth crouched low as she approached the ridge's edge. The security fence gleamed under harsh floodlights, but she noticed a gap in the patrol pattern. Two guards made their rounds, their flashlight beams sweeping in predictable arcs. She pressed herself against a tree trunk, counting the seconds between passes. The guards' voices carried on the night air.

"Another shipment coming in at midnight."

"Better than doing this during the day with all those protesters watching."

Elizabeth's pulse quickened. She inched closer, using the shadows between floodlights. The sharp scent of diesel fuel and freshly turned earth filled her nostrils. Through the fence, she could make out rows of concrete barriers being positioned around massive holding tanks.

A twig snapped behind her. Elizabeth froze, her breath catching in her throat. Heavy footsteps approached through the underbrush. She pressed deeper into the shadows, remembering her last encounter with OVAC's security. The footsteps grew closer.

"Liz?" Vincent's voice was a low murmur, barely audible above the drone of machinery.

"What are *you* doing here?" Elizabeth whispered, heart hammering against her ribs.

"Hunting for Sasquatch. What do you think?" His eyes scanned the scene, taking in the activity within the compound.

"Uncle Leo was right. Something's going on here. He kept talking about...chemicals, something about the water... But he didn't know what they were shipping in," Elizabeth said, remembering Leo's constant worried frown. "He just knew it wasn't right."

Vincent finished attaching the infrared lens to his camera and reached for his backpack. "Yeah, but you shouldn't be –" Suddenly, he froze. Elizabeth looked down, following his line of sight. A pinpoint of red light danced across her torso.

"Fuck." In a split second, Vincent launched forward and tackled her to the ground, the impact sending them crashing into the damp earth, their limbs entangled in the thorny brush. The air cracked with the sound of splintering wood as bullets pierced the tree trunk above them, where Elizabeth's head had been a moment before.

"Run," Vincent hissed, shoving her forward. "Don't wait for me. *Go!*" He scrambled back, reaching for his camera bag.

Elizabeth hesitated, adrenaline coursing through her body. Then, she ran. The darkness swallowed her whole as she stumbled down the uneven trail, the floodlights disappearing behind the trees. Disoriented, she tripped over a root, sprawling onto the forest floor. She scrambled back to her feet. Panic threatened to overwhelm her. But she kept running. Each gasp of air felt like fire in her lungs, and her legs ached with the strain of pushing forward, her breath coming in ragged bursts. She froze in her tracks, searching the darkness. Fumbling for her phone, she activated the night mode setting. Her trembling fingers typed a message to Vincent.

I'm lost

A reply blinked back almost instantly.

Earbud

She quickly retrieved her earbuds from her pocket and inserted them. His voice filled her ears. "I've got you in my site. I'll guide you."

Elizabeth's heart pounded as she followed Vincent's calm tone through her earbuds. His steady instructions guided her through the darkness, away from the industrial compound's perimeter.

"Take ten paces left. There's a fallen log - step over it."

She obeyed, her boots finding solid ground. The scent of pine needles replaced the acrid industrial smells.

"You're doing great, Liz. Another seven yards straight ahead."

Finally, her car emerged from the darkness like a sanctuary. Vincent materialized from the shadows, his camera bag slung across his chest. Just as she was about to speak, he grabbed her, taking her shoulders in a firm grip and pulling her into a fierce embrace.

"Damn it, Liz. What the hell were you thinking roaming around out here by yourself?" His voice cracked. "I mean, what the fuck, woman? You could've been killed."

Elizabeth felt his heart racing against her cheek. "Uncle Leo knew something was wrong. I had to —"

"Yeah, yeah. I get it." Vincent's arms tightened. "But not alone. Not anymore."

She pulled back, studying his face in the moonlight. "You're staying at the trailer?"

"Where else would I be?" His thumb brushed her cheek. "Someone's got to watch your back while you chase this story."

Elizabeth stepped away, missing his warmth immediately. "I'm going to stay at my friend Harper's condo in Clover City."

"Liz —"

"It's safer this way. For both of us." She fished her keys from her pocket. "Whatever's happening here, it got Uncle Leo killed."

Vincent's jaw clenched. "I've spent my whole life documenting war crimes and corruption. You think I can't handle some bullshit in Sweet—"

"This isn't about handling anything." She touched his arm. "We need to be smart. Work different angles. I'll be thirty minutes away, not across the world."

He caught her hand, his fingers intertwining with hers. "Promise me you'll be careful."

"Always am."

"That's not what I've seen." A ghost of a smile crossed his face. "But I'll take it."

Vincent's palm cupped Elizabeth's cheek, his touch sending sparks through her body. She forced herself to break away, the warmth of his touch lingered on her skin, a phantom sensation threatening to unravel her resolve.

"I missed you." His voice was rough with emotion. "These past weeks, not knowing if you were safe..." He shook his head. "Being apart was harder than I expected."

Elizabeth wrapped her arms around herself, as she fought the urge to reach for him. "Vin, I —"

"Meet me tomorrow. The town's having their Strawberry Festival." His eyes held hers. "We need to talk about what's really happening around here."

"Noon?" Elizabeth asked, already knowing she'd agree. She'd never been able to refuse him when it mattered.

"I'll find you." He stepped back, melting into the shadows like he'd never been there.

Elizabeth's hands shook slightly as she climbed into her car. Her phone buzzed just as she pulled out of the parking spot. Noah's text lit up her screen:

Whatever comes out about the OVAC plant, whatever people say - I'm choosing you, Lizzy. No matter what happens, we're in this together.

Elizabeth's stomach twisted. There was something in those words - "no matter what happens" - that felt less like reassurance and more like a warning.

The drive to Harper's condo in Clover City passed in a blur of streetlights and scattered memories. Noah's message kept floating back to the surface of her thoughts. Her finger hovered over the reply button, but she couldn't find the right words. Instead, she grabbed her overnight bag and headed for the condo door, leaving Noah's message unanswered.

What did he know that she didn't? And why did his promise of loyalty feel more like a cage than comfort?

14

Swept Away

The annual Sweetwater Springs Strawberry Festival was in full swing, the historic district's cobblestone streets were lined with colorful booths, and the air sweet with the scent of ripe berries. Elizabeth, her camera hanging around her neck, wove through the cheerful crowd, capturing snapshots of smiling faces and children with strawberry-stained cheeks.

"Liz! Over here!" Stacy's voice carried over the festive chatter. Elizabeth turned to see her friend waving from a pie-eating contest booth, little Pierson perched on her hip, his face a mess of red juice and crumbs.

As Elizabeth approached, she felt a presence at her back. Noah's warm breath tickled her ear as he leaned in close. "Quite a turnout this year," he said, his hand brushed across her lower back, then slid down and gently caressed her hip. His grip tightened for a moment, then released. The touch sent a shiver through her, despite the humid air.

"Noah," she said, turning to face him. His charming smile faltered slightly as their eyes met.

Stacy's laugh broke the moment. "You two, I swear. Come on,

Pierson wants to try the strawberry bounce house."

As they made their way through the thickening crowd, Elizabeth couldn't shake a growing sense of unease. The sky, once a cheerful blue, had darkened ominously, heavy with the threat of a downpour. A damp breeze, carrying the scent of rain and dank earth, swirled around her, raising goosebumps on her arms despite the earlier humidity. She glanced nervously toward the river, barely visible beyond the brightly colored tents and bustling stalls at the town's edge. Its waters, she noted with apprehension, were swollen and muddy, a testament to the days of relentless rainfall folks living along the Alleghany and Monongahela rivers had endured. The normally gentle current seemed agitated, almost angry.

A low rumble of thunder echoed in the distance, vibrating through the ground beneath her feet as they finally reached the brightly colored strawberry bounce house. Pierson, thankfully oblivious to the changing weather and the tension radiating from Elizabeth, clapped his hands excitedly, small squeals of delight escaping his lips.

"I've got him," Noah offered, his voice a reassuring presence in the gathering gloom. He effortlessly lifted Pierson, his smile warm and genuine as he helped the boy navigate the inflatable entrance. Elizabeth watched them, a pang of something bittersweet—envy?—twisting in her chest. The easy familiarity between Noah and Pierson, the way Noah's face softened when he looked at the boy, stirred something deep within her.

She scanned the festival crowd, looking for Vincent. They'd agreed to meet here, but the sea of faces offered no glimpse of him.

"Want some strawberry lemonade?" Stacy offered, juggling Pierson's toys in her arms while trying to fish out her wallet.

"Let me," Elizabeth said, grateful for the distraction. She paid the vendor and handed a cup to Stacy, who was attempting to wrangle Pierson away from the bounce house entrance.

The humidity surrounded them like a wet blanket, making Elizabeth's hair stick to the back of her neck. Another rumble of thunder rolled across the sky, closer this time. Festival-goers glanced upward nervously, some already packing up their lawn chairs and picnic blankets.

Movement caught her eye - a flash of a camera lens near the river's edge. Elizabeth's heart quickened. Vincent. He was doing exactly what she should have expected, documenting the swollen waters rather than enjoying the festival. She watched him work for a moment, admiring his focus even as anxiety gnawed at her gut.

"Earth to Liz," Stacy waved a hand in front of her face. "You okay? You seem distracted."

"Yeah, just..." She trailed off as she spotted Noah making his way toward them through the crowd, his public official smile fixed firmly in place. Her stomach twisted. Between Noah's text about being together 'no matter what happens' and Vincent's return, she felt pulled in too many directions.

"Ladies," Noah greeted them, his hand finding its way to Elizabeth's lower back again. She stepped away, pretending to adjust her camera strap. When she looked up again, Vincent had vanished from his spot by the river.

That's when they heard it—a deep, resonating explosion, a sound so powerful it felt like the earth itself was splitting apart. It pierced the air, leaving them frozen in place. For a heartbeat, everything went silent.

Then chaos erupted.

A wall of water had burst through the old levee, surging into the historic district with terrifying speed. Screams pierced the air as festival-goers scrambled for safety. Booths toppled like dominots, the once-cheerful decorations now debris in the muddy torrent.

The world turned into a swirling vortex of brown water and

panicked shouts. Elizabeth's breath hitched, a cold dread gripping her as she watched the wave engulf the bounce house where she had seen Noah and Pierson just minutes before. Her camera slipped from her numb fingers, clattering against the cobblestones, now submerged under a foot of churning water. Terror gripped her, sending a wave of panic through her body as her heart pounded in her chest.

"Noah!" she screamed, her voice swallowed by the deafening roar of the rushing water.

The current tugged at her legs, threatening to sweep her away. She stumbled, grabbing onto a lamppost, the metal cold and slick against her palms. Debris swirled around her—a splintered picnic table, a vendor's overturned cart, a child's lost balloon bobbing pathetically on the surface. The festive music, moments ago cheerful and bright, was now a distorted, gurgling echo beneath the water's surface. The air, thick with the scent of strawberries just moments before, now carried the metallic tang and the earthy smell of displaced soil.

She scanned the churning water frantically, searching for her friends. Where were they? Had the current already dragged them away? A flash of red caught her eye—Pierson's shirt. He was clinging to a piece of the collapsed bounce house, Noah fighting to keep him above the surging water. They were being swept toward the river, the current gaining strength with every passing second.

Elizabeth didn't hesitate. She pushed off the lamppost, fighting against the rushing water, her lungs burning. Each breath was a struggle, each movement a desperate effort against the relentless force of the flood. She had to reach them. She had to.

"Pierson!" Stacy's scream cut through the pandemonium. Elizabeth whirled around to see the bounce house, with Pierson still holding on, lifted by the rising water and carried away.

Noah was already moving, plunging into the water without hesitation. The deafening roar of the water filled her ears, the spray of the waves stinging her face as Elizabeth watched him struggle against the ruthless current, reaching for the bounce house as it bobbed in the roiling water.

"Noah!" she cried out, but his name was lost in the deafening sound of the chaos surrounding her. She grabbed Stacy's arm, pulling her toward higher ground as the water lapped at their chests. The last thing Elizabeth saw before they rounded a corner was Noah's outstretched hand, inches from the bounce house, and Pierson's terrified face pressed against the plastic window. Then they disappeared from view, swallowed by the merciless flood that was quickly engulfing the heart of Sweetwater Springs.

Elizabeth's heart pounded a frantic rhythm in her chest as she battled against the raging current, her eyes frantically examining the murky, swirling water for any sign of Pierson or Noah. The flood had transformed the once-charming streets into a treacherous river, carrying debris and memories alike in its ruthless path.

She pushed forward, her clothes clinging to her body, weighing her down. The water level rose rapidly, already chest-deep in some areas. Panic clawed at her throat as she realized the danger she was in, but the thought of Pierson alone and terrified drove her on.

A familiar structure loomed ahead—the Centennial Community Center. Its red brick walls, usually so sturdy and comforting, now stood as a crumbling testament to the flood's destructive power. The white columns that had graced its entrance for generations were nowhere to be seen, likely swept away in the initial surge.

"Pierson!" Elizabeth's voice, hoarse and strained, was barely audible over the thundering roar of the waves. She struggled toward the remnant of the building, hoping against hope that the boy had somehow found refuge there.

As she neared the community center, a sudden surge knocked her off her feet. She gasped, swallowing a mouthful of muddy water as she went under. The world became a swirling vortex of brown and green, disorienting her completely. The water pressed down on her, and her lungs screamed for air as she struggled to break free from the relentless motion of the waves.

Just as black spots began to dance at the edges of her vision, Elizabeth's head broke the surface. She coughed violently, spitting out water and gulping in precious air. The building was gone, reduced to a pile of rubble barely visible above the floodwaters.

Exhausted and terrified, Elizabeth realized she was being swept further away from where she'd last seen Pierson. The current was too strong; she couldn't fight it any longer. As her strength waned, she caught sight of something colorful bobbing in the distance—was it part of the bounce house?

With one last swell of desperate energy, Elizabeth struck out toward it, praying she wasn't too late. Her muscles tightened in protest as she battled against the current. Her lungs burned, still recovering from her near-drowning experience. But the flash of color in the distance drove her forward, a beacon of hope in the murky chaos.

As she drew closer, her heart leaped. It was indeed a piece of the bounce house—a torn fragment of plastic, its cheerful strawberry pattern now a stark contrast to the destruction around her. She grabbed onto it, using it as a makeshift flotation device.

"Pierson!" she shouted again, her voice raw. "Noah!"

The flood swept her past what remained of Main Street. Shop fronts she'd known since childhood were now unrecognizable, their windows shattered, awnings torn away. A wave of grief washed over her, as palpable as the muddy water surrounding her.

Suddenly, a sound cut through the din—a child's cry. Elizabeth's head whipped around, searching frantically for the source. There, caught in the branches of a partially submerged tree, were the battered remains of the bounce house. The flood waters were rising swiftly around them.

With revived willpower, Elizabeth kicked her way toward it. As she neared, she could make out Pierson's terrified face pressed against the plastic. Noah was there too, his arms wrapped protectively around the boy, his face a mask of exhaustion and relief as he spotted her.

"Hold on!" she yelled, reaching for them. The current threatened to tear them apart, but Elizabeth refused to let go. With every ounce of strength she had left, she pulled Pierson and Noah free from the tangle of branches.

Together, they clung to the debris, the flood carrying them further from the town they knew. Elizabeth's journalist skills kicked in, cataloging the devastation even as she fought for survival. This was a story that demanded to be told—but first, they had to live through it.

She clung desperately to Pierson. The boy's small body shook with sobs, his face buried against her chest. Noah's strong muscular frame struggled beside them, fighting to keep them all afloat. Through the haze of exhaustion and fear, she spotted something in the distance - a large, partially submerged vehicle. As they drew closer, she realized it was a school bus, its yellow paint barely visible above the muddy flood.

"Noah!" she shouted, her voice hoarse. "The bus!"

Noah's eyes followed her gaze. With renewed determination, he began to swim, pulling Elizabeth and Pierson along with him. The current was a raging river, but Noah's powerful strokes, strong and determined, cut through the water, closing the distance with each stroke.

As they neared the bus, Elizabeth could see that its rear emergency door was open, hanging just above the water line. Noah reached it first, hauling himself up with a grunt of effort. He turned back immediately, extending his arms.

"Give me the boy!" he called out.

Elizabeth lifted Pierson as high as she could while gripping the rear bumper for stability. Noah leaned out, his muscles straining as he grasped Pierson under the arms and pulled him to safety. The moment the child was secure, he reached for Elizabeth. Their eyes met, and in that instant, all the complications of their past and present fell away. There was only this moment, Noah's strong hands gripping her wrists, pulling her from the flood's grasp. With a final burst of strength, Elizabeth scrambled onto the bus, collapsing beside Pierson. She gasped for air, her body trembling with fatigue. Noah kneeled beside them, his hand resting on her shoulder.

"We made it," he said, his voice hoarse, a deep sigh escaping his lips. "You're safe."

Safe. The words echoed in Elizabeth's mind, a fragile shield against the fear swirling around her. She clung to Pierson, his small body trembling against hers, the rhythmic thud of Noah's heart a counterpoint to the boy's ragged breaths. Rain lashed against the shattered windows of the school bus, a relentless reminder of the devastation outside. The bus, miraculously lodged against a sturdy oak, rocked gently with the still-rising floodwaters, creaking ominously with each sway.

Noah paced the aisle, his face a mask of fury. "Damn it!" he exploded, slamming his fist against a seat. "That levee passed inspection just last month. Passed! How the hell...?" He ran a hand across his face, his voice laced with disbelief. "How could this happen?" His eyes darted frantically around the bus, as if searching for answers in the water-stained upholstery and bent metal frames. He stopped abruptly, turning to face Elizabeth, his anger momentarily replaced by a raw vulnerability. "Are you okay? Is Pierson...?" His voice cracked slightly.

Elizabeth nodded, tightening her grip on the boy. "We're okay. Shaken up, but okay." Pierson whimpered, his small hand reaching up to clutch her shirt. She could feel his rapid heartbeat against her chest, a stark reminder of how close they'd come to losing him.

Noah's jaw tightened with anger, a muscle twitching beneath his skin. "I need to get in touch with emergency services. See what's happening, what kind of help we can get." He pulled out his phone, its screen flickering erratically. "No signal. It's dead."

He slammed the phone back into his pocket, frustration radiating off him. He glanced out the window, his eyes scanning the rushing water. Debris swirled past—pieces of houses, uprooted trees, even the red rocking chair from Stacy's porch. Elizabeth's stomach lurched at the sight, her mind filled with thoughts of their neighbors and friends.

"We need to get to higher ground," he said, his voice tight with urgency. "This bus won't hold forever." He looked at Elizabeth, his gaze searching hers. "We'll figure this out. We'll get through this." Despite the resolve in his words, Elizabeth could see the flicker of uncertainty in his eyes, mirroring her own fears about what lay ahead. She watched Noah's face as he moved toward the emergency exit, muscles tensing as he prepared to leave them. She could see the struggle in his eyes, a conflict between his sense of duty and his own survival.

"I'll be back," he said, his voice barely discernible. The words seemed to catch in his throat, as if he wasn't entirely sure he could keep that promise. "Stay here, stay safe. I'll find help." His gaze lingered on her for a moment, conveying a silent plea.

Before Elizabeth could protest, before she could reach out and stop him, Noah plunged back into the menacing waves. She clutched Pierson tighter, her heart aching as Noah's form disappeared beneath the murky surface. Seconds stretched into agonizing minutes as she stared out the bus window, her heart throbbing in her ears, searching for any sign of him. Her breath fogged the glass, and she wiped it away frantically, unwilling to miss even a glimpse of his return.

The bus creaked and groaned, the floodwaters rising steadily.

Elizabeth whispered soothing words to Pierson, trying to calm her own frayed nerves as much as the boy's. The child's warmth against her chest was both a comfort and a reminder of the responsibility weighing on her shoulders. She couldn't shake the image of Noah, battling against the current, risking his life to save them. Her mind filled with every possible scenario, each more terrifying than the last.

Just as despair began to set in, as the cold fingers of fear threatened to close around her heart, a familiar shout cut through the din of the storm. She jerked her head up, her eyes straining to see through the rain-lashed windows. There, in the distance, was Noah, maneuvering a small boat through the debris-filled water. Hope surged within her as Noah guided the boat alongside the bus. He secured it to the emergency exit, his clothes soaked through, and his breathing labored.

"Come on," he called out, reaching for them. His voice was rough but determined. "We need to move fast!" The urgency in his tone spurred Elizabeth into action.

She helped Pierson into Noah's waiting arms, her heart in her throat as she watched the exchange. Then she scrambled into the boat herself, the metal hull slick beneath her feet. As soon as they were aboard, Noah gunned the engine, steering them away from the sinking bus and toward higher ground. The boat rocked beneath them as Elizabeth gripped the side with clenched fingers. They navigated through the flooded streets, her eyes taking in the devastation around them. The town she had known her entire life was now unrecognizable, transformed into a watery wasteland. Familiar landmarks peeked out from beneath the dark water—the top of a stop sign here, the roof of a car there. It was like a nightmare come to life. Elizabeth blinked back tears, overwhelmed by the scope of the destruction.

The boat scraped against the parking lot pavement of Sweetwater Springs High School, now an impromptu rescue station. Elizabeth's legs wobbled as she stepped onto solid ground, Pierson still clinging to her neck. Emergency lights painted everything in harsh reds and blues.

Through the commotion of rescue workers and dazed survivors, a familiar figure caught her eye. Vincent. He was balancing on the edge of a rescue boat, reaching down to help pull an elderly woman to safety, his muscled arms straining against his soaked t-shirt. His movements were precise, calculated - just as they had been in Botswana during that terrifying night in the refugee camp when a dam burst and engulfed their entire encampment in mere minutes. Even from this distance, she could see the determination etched in his expression, that intense focus she'd seen countless times before when lives hung in the balance. The flashing lights of the rescue vehicles glinted off the dampness in his dark hair, creating an otherworldly shimmer that set him apart from the surrounding darkness. Her heart skipped. She took a step forward, but Noah's hand caught her arm.

"You need to get checked out by the medics," Noah said, his grip firm but gentle. "Both of you." He nodded toward Pierson.

"But I can help—" Elizabeth started.

"Ma'am, this way please." A first responder in a reflective orange vest appeared beside them, gesturing toward the school building. "We're moving everyone to higher ground."

Elizabeth hesitated, her eyes drawn back to Vincent. As if sensing her gaze, he looked up. Their eyes met across the crowded lot. His expression shifted, softened for just a moment. She saw his lips part as if to call out to her, but he gestured with a nod for her to go.

"Now, ma'am," the first responder insisted, guiding her toward a waiting pontoon boat.

Elizabeth let herself to be coaxed away, her eyes still locked with Vincent's until the crowd swallowed him from view. The pontoon's engine roared to life, carrying her away from both men and toward the evacuation point. Elizabeth gripped Pierson's small hand, scanning the sea of shocked faces under the harsh emergency lights. Her clothes clung to her skin, heavy and cold, but she barely noticed. The boy's fingers trembled in hers as they snaked through the crowd of survivors huddled outside the high school.

"Pierson! Oh my god, Pierson!"

The raw desperation in Stacy's voice cut through the noise of the rescue operations. Elizabeth turned toward the sound, spotting her friend pushing past a cluster of paramedics. Pierson broke free and ran to his mother. Stacy fell to her knees, wrapping her arms around her son. Her shoulders shook with sobs as she pulled him close, pressing kisses to his wet face. "Baby, I was so scared. So scared."

Elizabeth's hand moved instinctively to her hip where her camera usually hung but found only wet denim. For the first time in years, she hadn't documented a crisis. No photographs of desperate rescues, no interviews with shell-shocked survivors, no footage of nature's fury. She'd been too busy fighting the flood, keeping Pierson's head above water, praying they'd make it out alive.

The realization hit her like a punch in the gut. All those times she'd stuck her camera in people's faces during their worst moments, she'd told herself she was helping by sharing their stories. But she'd always been separated from their pain, protected by the lens between them. Now the barrier was gone. She was one of them -soaked, frightened, grateful just to be alive. She wrapped her arms around herself, shivering as she watched mother and son reunite. Her throat tightened. This time, the story wasn't hers to tell.

Elizabeth watched as paramedics draped blankets over Stacy and Pierson's shoulders. Her own clothes felt like ice against her skin, but she couldn't bring herself to seek warmth yet. The adrenaline that had carried her through the flood waters was fading, leaving exhaustion in its wake.

A commotion near the school entrance drew her attention. Noah emerged from the building, his suit jacket gone, sleeves rolled up as he directed volunteers carrying supplies. His eyes met hers across the parking lot, relief washing over his face. He started toward her, but stopped as Vincent appeared at his side, speaking urgently and pointing toward a map spread across the hood of a police cruiser.

Elizabeth's chest tightened. The two men who had complicated her return to Sweetwater Springs were now working side by side to save it. Vincent's presence wasn't surprising - he had a habit of showing up when disaster struck. But seeing him here, now, after everything that had happened...

"Elizabeth." Stacy's voice pulled her from her thoughts. Her friend stood before her, Pierson still clutched to her side. "Thank you. If you hadn't found him -" Her voice cracked.

Elizabeth pulled them both into a hug, careful not to squeeze too tight. "He's safe now. That's all that matters."

She held them tightly, the weight of the past few weeks settling over her like a thick fog. Uncle Leo's warnings about the concrete plant, the suspicious circumstances of his death, the rising tensions in town -it all seemed distant now, washed away by the flood waters that had nearly claimed them all. But she knew those waters would recede, and when they did, the truth would still be waiting to be uncovered.

For now though, she was content to stand here. Amid the shouts of rescue workers and the drone of helicopters overhead, she took a moment to appreciate this small victory: standing safely with her friend, and with her precious son they'd managed to save from the flood's fury.

15

Beneath the Surface

Elizabeth waded through ankle-deep mud, her boots sinking and slipping with each step as she helped clear debris from what remained of Main Street. The stench of sewage and river muck hung thick in the air. Around her, volunteers formed human chains, passing water-logged furniture and personal belongings from flooded buildings to waiting trucks.

"Over here!" A man's voice called out. "Found another photo album."

Her heart clenched as she watched him add it to a growing pile of water -damaged memories. Family photos, yearbooks, letters -pieces of people's lives scattered by the flood's fury.

Generators hummed in the background while emergency crews pumped water from basements. The once-grand buildings of the historic district were now scarred and broken, creating an eerie and unsettling atmosphere like the set of a dystopian film. Piles of ruined drywall and insulation lined the streets. Shop windows gaped empty, their contents washed away.

"Need some help with this?" A volunteer approached, gesturing to a warped cabinet Elizabeth had been struggling with.

She nodded, grateful for the assistance. Together they hauled it to a growing mountain of destroyed furniture. Her muscles burned from hours of lifting, but she couldn't stop. Not while her hometown lay in ruins. National Guard trucks rumbled past, bringing fresh supplies of bottled water and disinfectant cleaning materials. The sound of chainsaws filled the air as crews worked to clear fallen trees that blocked side streets.

She paused to wipe sweat from her forehead, surveying the devastation. The community center's remains sat like a broken tooth in the landscape -its walls partially collapsed, windows shattered. But amid the destruction, neighbors helped neighbors. Volunteers distributed hot meals from makeshift stations. Children too young to help with heavy lifting passed out water bottles to workers.

The flood had taken so much. But watching her community come together, Elizabeth saw glimpses of the Sweetwater Springs she remembered -before the politics and division, when people still looked out for each other. Her muscles ached as she hauled another load of debris to the growing pile. The physical labor helped quiet her gloomy thoughts, gave her something concrete to focus on besides the overwhelming destruction around her.

"Need a break?" Noah's voice cut through her concentration. He stood a few feet away, sleeves rolled up, designer clothes traded for work boots and jeans caked in mud.

"I'm fine." But her arms trembled as she dropped the sodden carpet.

"Here." He handed her a bottle of water. "You've been at this for hours."

She took a long drink, studying him. His usually flawless appearance was disheveled, face streaked with dirt. This wasn't the slick politician she'd grown used to seeing in public. This was the Noah she remembered from childhood -the one who'd help anyone who needed it, no questions asked.

"The ridge camps are filling up fast," he said. "Vincent's been coordinating supplies up there, making sure everyone has blankets and basic necessities."

Her stomach tightened at the mention of Vincent's name. She hadn't seen him since the rescue boats had separated them.

"The community center's gone. Totally destroyed," Noah continued, his voice heavy. "If I'd known the flood was coming —"

"How could you have known?" Elizabeth cut him off. She didn't want to think about the political affairs right now. Not when their town lay in ruins around them.

They worked side by side, falling into an efficient rhythm. Noah's presence beside her felt steadying, comforting. When he reached to help her with a particularly heavy piece of bedding, their hands brushed. The simple contact sent warmth through her despite her exhaustion.

"We should check on the camps soon," Noah said. "Make sure they have everything they need and the supply chain hasn't gotten bogged down in red tape or a miscommunication."

Elizabeth nodded, trying to ignore the unease in her stomach at the thought of seeing Vincent again. Right now, their town needed them. Everything else they needed to talk about would have to wait.

Noah pulled her aside, away from the other volunteers, his voice a low, urgent whisper. "The levee didn't just fail, Lizzy. Someone tampered with it."

Her heart dropped. "What are you saying?" Her hands stilled on the rubble she was clearing as his words sank in.

"Security cameras picked up suspicious activity near the levee the night before. People wearing dark clothing and face masks, carrying boxes." Noah ran a hand through his mud-caked hair. "The timing's too convenient, right when OVAC's about to break ground on the new expansion."

Elizabeth's jaw clenched. "You think the protesters did this? That's ridiculous. They're trying to protect the town, not destroy it."

"Think about it - who benefits from making OVAC look bad? Those activist groups will do anything to stop the development."

"Or maybe," Elizabeth stepped closer, keeping her voice down, "OVAC orchestrated this to force people out. Clear the way for their expansion plans. Why did they wait to report the "suspicious activity" until after the damage was done? Uncle Leo warned about strangers with equipment in the area."

Noah's expression hardened. "You're letting your personal feelings cloud your judgment. These eco-terrorists —"

"Eco-terrorists?" Elizabeth cut him off. "The only terrorism I've seen is corporate. The threats, the intimidation, Uncle Leo's death —"

"We don't know what happened to Montoya." Noah grabbed her arm, his grip tight. "Don't throw around accusations without proof."

Elizabeth yanked free. "Then maybe we should both look harder for the truth instead of jumping to conclusions that fit our agendas."

They stared at each other, the gulf between them suddenly feeling wider than the flooded river. The same evidence, two completely different interpretations. She wondered if they would ever see eye to eye about anything.

Elizabeth watched Noah's retreating back as he stormed off toward the emergency command center. Her fingers traced the spot on her arm where he'd grabbed her, the skin still stinging from his touch. The accusation in his eyes haunted her - as if she was betraying him by questioning OVAC's role in this disaster.

She turned back to the debris field, mechanically lifting chunks of wood and shattered glass. The physical labor helped calm her nerves, but she couldn't shake the disappointment that Noah was wrong for accusing the protesters of sabotage. She'd spent time with them, seen their commitment to peaceful resistance. Destroying the levee would go against everything they stood for.

The sound of helicopter blades chopped through the air as another National Guard transport passed overhead, heading toward the ridge camps. She paused her work, shielding her eyes against the sun as she tracked its path. Vincent was up there somewhere, helping to coordinate relief efforts. He'd understand her suspicions about OVAC. He would help her investigate. But going to Vincent meant potentially burning bridges with Noah. The thought made her stomach twist. Despite everything, despite their differences, part of her cared deeply for Noah. She still wanted to believe in the man who'd just helped her rescue a child from the flood waters.

A volunteer called out for help nearby, snapping Elizabeth from her feelings. She had to focus on the immediate crisis. The investigation could wait. Right now, the town needed every able body to help with cleanup and recovery. As she joined the human chain passing salvaged items to waiting trucks, she caught snippets of conversation around her. Theories about the flood, whispered accusations, fears about what would happen next. The disaster had cracked open the town's facade, exposing the deep divisions that had been simmering beneath the surface.

Elizabeth knew she'd have to choose a side soon. But in this moment, she lost herself in the rhythm of the work, letting the physical exhaustion drown out the emotional turmoil that filled her soul.

She spotted Maya organizing a group of student activists who had traded their signs for shovels and work gloves. They moved through the debris with purpose, helping families salvage what they could from their abandoned homes. These were the same people Noah had accused of sabotaging the levee.

Maya caught her eye and headed over, wiping mud from her hands onto her already filthy jeans. "We've got teams checking on elderly residents, making sure they have medications and supplies." She gestured to the volunteers behind her. "Everyone's pitching in."

"I saw." Elizabeth's throat tightened. "So much for eco-terrorists, right?"

"What?" Maya's eyes narrowed.

"Nothing. Just something Noah said." She shook her head. "He thinks protesters might have damaged the levee."

Maya's laugh was sharp and bitter. "Right. Because we'd deliberately destroy our own homes and risk people's lives to make a point." She kicked a chunk of broken glass. "Meanwhile, OVAC's equipment was spotted up there the night before. But I'm sure that's just a coincidence."

Elizabeth's instincts perked up. "What kind of equipment?"

"Heavy machinery. My brother works security at the plant. Said they brought in some specialized drilling gear last week. Weird timing, don't you think?"

Before Elizabeth could press further, Maya's walkie-talkie crackled. Another team needed help with moving the fallen trees. Maya squeezed Elizabeth's arm before hurrying off, leaving her with more questions than answers. She watched the students work, their dedication obvious in every action. These weren't the dangerous radicals Noah had described. They were neighbors helping neighbors, proving their commitment to the community through actions rather than words. Elizabeth hefted another waterlogged box onto the pile when a voice called out behind her.

"Miss Nelson? Got a minute?"

She turned to find Officer Cortez shifting his weight between debris piles, wearing a pair of camo hip wader boots. His uniform was splattered with river muck, a far cry from his spotless appearance at the police station weeks ago.

"I'm a bit busy here." Elizabeth wiped sweat from her face, leaving a streak of dirt across her forehead.

"I know. That's actually why I wanted to talk." He removed his cap, running his fingers through his damp hair. "Been watching you work since dawn. You haven't taken a break all day."

Elizabeth's shoulders tensed, remembering his dismissive attitude when she'd tried to report the incident at the overlook. "Did you need to say something specific, Officer?"

"Yeah. An apology." He met her eyes directly. "I was wrong to brush off your concerns that day at the station. Should've taken your report more seriously."

Elizabeth paused, studying his face for any trace of insincerity. Found none.

"Seeing you out here, doing the heavy lifting, getting your hands dirty alongside everyone else..." He shook his head. "Well, it's clear you care about this town. I misjudged you, and I'm sorry for that."

The simple admission caught her off guard. She would have never expected this from the same officer who'd practically laughed her out of the station.

"I appreciate that," she said quietly.

"For what it's worth, I've been keeping an eye on that overlook since you came in. Something's not right up there." He replaced his cap. "If you notice anything else suspicious, my door's open. For real this time." He excused himself and returned to his team helping with safety patrols.

Elizabeth paused in her debris clearing, her attention caught by movement near the emergency command tent. Noah stood close to Victoria Caldwell, their heads bent together in intense discussion. Victoria's hand rested on Noah's forearm, her perfectly manicured nails a stark contrast to his mud-stained skin. The familiar ache of jealousy twisted in Elizabeth's stomach. She'd seen them like this before, back in high school - the golden couple. Victoria leaned in closer, whispering something that made Noah's brow furrow.

Elizabeth gripped the shovel tighter, debating whether to walk over and interrupt. Noah had been clear about wanting a future with her, hinting at marriage even amid the chaos of the flood recovery. But watching him with Victoria now, she wondered if she was fooling herself. Their bodies angled toward each other with the easy familiarity of old lovers, sharing secrets in the midst of the disaster.

Should she confront him about it? Ask what they were discussing so privately? The thought made her chest tight. A knot of fear tightened in her stomach as she considered the answer, unsure if she could handle the truth. Despite Noah's promises, despite the intensity of their recent encounters, something held her back from fully committing to the future he described.

Victoria's laugh carried across the debris field, light and musical even in these circumstances. Elizabeth watched Noah's face soften in response, and that old insecurity from her teenage years crept back. She might have grown into herself since then, but Victoria had always been exactly who she was meant to be - polished, confident, perfectly at home in Sweetwater Springs' upper circles.

Elizabeth turned away, focusing on the work at hand. She'd seen enough. Whether she confronted Noah about this moment or not, it added another layer of doubt to her already complicated feelings about their relationship.

She wiped her grimy hands on her jeans and headed toward the supply trucks, needing distance from the sight of Noah and Victoria. Her muscles ached from hours of hauling rubbish, but the physical pain was easier to deal with than the emotional turmoil churning inside her.

A gust of wind carried the muggy stench of sludge and river water, reminding her of Venezuela. Of Vincent. Though she knew he was busy volunteering in the ridge camps, part of her longed to head up there, to lose herself in the simple comfort of his presence. Vincent never played games or left her guessing where she stood. When she felt empty, he filled her cup. No strings. Simple.

"Elizabeth!" Harper's voice broke through. Her friend jogged over, camera bouncing against her hip. "Just came back from the ridge camps. You need to see these photos."

Harper pulled up several images on her camera display. Elizabeth's breath caught as she saw the drilling equipment Maya had mentioned, partially hidden under tarps near the levee. The timestamp showed the night before the flood.

"This was sent to me," Harper said, her voice low. "That's industrial-grade equipment. The kind used for—"

"Concrete manufacturing," Elizabeth finished, her heart pounding. The pieces were starting to fit together, forming a picture she didn't want to see. She glanced back at Noah and Victoria, still deep in conversation by the command tent. Had Noah known about this? Was that what Victoria was telling him now? The weight of the evidence was so heavy, she felt like it was suffocating her. She couldn't ignore this, no matter what it meant for her relationship with Noah. People had lost everything in this flood. They deserved to know the truth.

She stared at Harper's camera display, her fingers trembling as she zoomed in on the equipment photos. The industrial drilling gear matched what she'd seen during her nighttime encounter with Vincent at the overlook. "We need to get these to a news outlet," Harper said, already typing on her phone. "I've got contacts at—"

"Wait." Elizabeth grabbed Harper's wrist. "Let me handle this. I've got an inside connection at the New York Citizen. High up. They'll want an exclusive." She glanced over her shoulder, making sure no one was within earshot. "Plus, we need more evidence. Photos aren't enough to prove OVAC deliberately sabotaged the levee."

Harper nodded in agreement, then followed Elizabeth's line of sight to where Noah and Victoria were huddled in deep conversation. "Tori Caldwell," she said. "Current Acting District Attorney with her sights on being the first female Law Director in Sweetwater Springs, if whoever becomes the next mayor appoints her. In the meantime, she maneuvers onto every advisory board and committee for exposure and, well…"

"That tracks," Elizabeth said, "She handed me my ass at the last protest meeting after Uncle Leo's death. Shut down any consideration of the facts we had gathered. Maybe she already knew."

Harper's dark eyes narrowed. "What about your boyfriend? Sweetwater's favorite son over there?" She nodded toward Noah. "You really think he didn't know about this?"

Elizabeth's face heated as she watched Noah and Victoria head inside the command tent together. The easy intimacy of their body language made her stomach tight.

"I don't know what he knows," Elizabeth admitted, ignoring the hint of sarcasm in Harper's voice. "Or what Victoria has up her sleeve. But it doesn't matter. I can't let personal relationships interfere with uncovering the truth." The words, sharp and bitter, lingered on her tongue, but she meant every syllable. She'd learned that lesson the hard way.

"Then what's your next move?" Harper tucked her camera away, protecting it from the fine mist that had started falling.

Elizabeth pulled out her new phone, thumbing through her recent messages until she found Vincent's last number. "First, we need someone who knows these hills better than anyone. Someone who can help us track down where that equipment came from and where it went."

Her thumb hovered over the call button as rain began falling harder, drumming against the piles of debris around them. The easy choice would be to walk away, to let someone else expose this story. But she remembered Uncle Leo's warnings, his suspicious death, the anxiety in his eyes when he talked about strangers on the ridge.

She pressed Call.

The connection went straight to voicemail. She ended it without leaving a message and fired off a quick text:

Need your help. Meetup tonight?

"You sure about this?" Harper shifted closer, shielding Elizabeth from the increasing rain. "Vincent had been off-grid for weeks. What if he doesn't show?"

Elizabeth tucked her phone in her pocket, her thoughts swiftly moving to contingency plans. "He'll come. He cares about this town as much as we do." She glanced at the command tent where Noah had disappeared with Victoria. "Maybe more than some people."

The rain picked up, driving most volunteers toward shelter. Elizabeth and Harper joined the exodus, ducking under the awning of a relief station. Water streamed off the canvas in sheets, creating a curtain between them and the rest of the world.

"I should get these photos backed up somewhere safe," Harper said, patting her camera bag. "In case anything happens to the originals."

Elizabeth nodded, remembering the laser site that had targeted her that night on the ridge. Someone had already tried to silence her once. They might try again if they knew what she and Harper had discovered.

Her phone buzzed. A single word response:

Midnight

Elizabeth released a breath she hadn't realized she was holding. First step accomplished. Now she just had to avoid Noah's questions until then - and figure out exactly how much he knew about OVAC's activities the night before the flood.

16

Between Two Worlds

Elizabeth and Stacy sat on the screened-in back porch of her friend's house, feeling the warmth of the late afternoon sun on their skin. The flood's aftermath still lingered - mud-caked debris piled along the streets, the smell of wet wood and mildew hanging in the air.

"You could have a real life here, Liz." Stacy wrapped her hands around her coffee mug. "Noah's changed. He's not that shallow boy from high school anymore."

Elizabeth traced the rim of her teacup. "It's not that simple."

"What's complicated about it? He loves you. Anyone with eyes can see that." Stacy leaned forward. "And after everything and losing Leo, don't you think it's time to put down roots somewhere?"

The mention of Uncle Leo sent a fresh wave of grief through Elizabeth's heart. She looked away, blinking back tears.

"I know you're hurting." Stacy's voice softened. "But running away won't fix that. Noah could give you stability, a home. The kind of life most people dream about."

"The kind of life you have?" Elizabeth met her friend's gaze.

"Yes! Is that so terrible?" Stacy gestured toward her house. "Mark and I don't agree on everything but what we have is good. Better than good. I have love, family, purpose. Noah's offering you the same thing. He wants to build a future with you."

Elizabeth stood, pacing the wooden planks. "While the town falls apart around us? While people suffer?"

"The town will heal. Communities always do." Stacy crossed her arms. "But you need to decide if you're willing to be part of that healing or if you're just passing through again."

"I can't ignore what's happening here just because Noah makes me feel safe." Elizabeth's voice cracked. "Uncle Leo deserved better than that. This town deserves better."

"Maybe making a home here is exactly how you fight for what's right." Stacy reached for her hand. "You're stronger with roots, Liz. And Noah? He'd stand by you through anything."

Elizabeth stood, her jaw clenched. "You really don't see it, do you? The concrete plant expansion isn't just about jobs. Look at what happened to the historic district after the flood. Just because your house survived—"

"Not everything is a conspiracy, Liz." Stacy's tone sharpened. "Sometimes things just happen. The levee was old."

"The levee was deliberately neglected. And OVAC sent in their equipment the night before. Why?" Elizabeth's hands trembled. "People lost everything, Stacy. Your son almost—"

"Don't." Stacy stood, coffee forgotten. "Don't you dare use Pierson to push your agenda."

"My agenda? Uncle Leo tried to warn everyone about OVAC. Now he's dead and you're acting like it's just another tragedy to sweep under the rug."

"Vincent Rivera's uncle was a troubled man who lived in a rundown trailer park. You barely knew him."

The words hit Elizabeth like a slap in the face. She stepped back, heat rising in her cheeks. "That troubled man had more integrity than half this town. At least he wasn't willing to trade safety for a pretty facade."

"You've been gone for years, Liz. You drop in, help stir up trouble, then what? Run off to your next headline?" Stacy's voice cracked. "Some of us have to live here after you're gone."

"And what kind of place will be left to live in?" Elizabeth grabbed her jacket from the chair. "I need some air."

She pushed through the screen door, letting it bang shut behind her. The evening air felt thick, oppressive. Her feet carried her down the porch steps and onto the sidewalk, away from the stifling weight of Stacy's willful blindness.

***

Elizabeth's boots crunched against broken twigs and debris as she walked along the muddy path near the creek. The setting sun painted the sky in shades of amber, but her mind overflowed with darker thoughts. Stacy's words echoed in her head, mixing with memories of desperate faces at town meetings - people pleading for work, for change, for hope.

She paused at a fallen tree, running her hand along its rough bark. The concrete plant expansion would bring jobs - good-paying ones that could put food on tables and keep families from leaving Sweetwater Springs. Her stomach twisted. How many times had she covered stories of towns dying slow deaths when their young people fled for better opportunities?

But then there was Uncle Leo's voice, his warnings about the trucks, the mysterious activities at night. His death still felt wrong, like a splinter under her skin she couldn't quite reach. The environmental reports she'd uncovered painted a grim picture - contaminated groundwater, respiratory issues, property values plummeting in similar communities.

A fish jumped in the creek, breaking the water's surface with a quiet splash. She pulled out her notebook, thumbing through pages of interviews. Mrs. Chen's tearful account of her garden dying after the test drilling began. Mr. Rodriguez's fears about his children's asthma getting worse. The plant workers in Tennessee who'd lost everything when their town became unlivable.

"Some voice for the voiceless I am," she muttered, shoving the notebook back in her pocket. "Can't even figure out which voices matter more."

The truth was, both sides were right in their own way. People needed work - real work that could sustain families. But at what cost? How many generations would pay the price for temporary prosperity?

Elizabeth picked up a smooth stone, turning it over in her palm. This wasn't just about facts and figures anymore. It was about Uncle Leo, about Stacy's son, about a community tearing itself apart trying to survive. She tossed the stone into the creek, watching ripples spread across the murky surface. The water had receded since the flood, leaving behind a thick line of mud and garbage along the banks. Nature's own evidence of destruction, as damning as any of her investigative findings.

Her phone buzzed. Another text from Noah, probably asking about dinner plans or trying to convince her to move in with him. She left it unanswered in her pocket. The weight of his expectations, of Stacy's well-meaning but unwelcome advice, pressed down on her shoulders.

The evening breeze carried the choking odor of diesel fuel from the construction vehicles parked near the old Centennial Community Center site. Even now, they were eager to build on the ruins, like vultures circling fresh carrion. Her throat tightened at the thought of

Leo's suspicious death and Vincent's determination to uncover what really happened.

Vincent. His name alone sent a flutter through her chest - not the comfortable, familiar warmth she felt with Noah, but something wilder, more driven. He understood her need to follow leads, to expose exploitation, to make a difference.

Elizabeth straightened her shoulders and took one last look at the creek. The sun had dipped below the horizon, leaving only purple shadows dancing across the water's surface. She couldn't fix everything wrong with Sweetwater Springs, but she could give voice to those who needed it most. That would have to be enough.

She turned away from the water and headed back toward town, her steps sure and determined despite the muddy ground beneath her feet. Her phone buzzed against her hip as she walked back toward town. Vincent's name flashed across the screen, making her pause mid-step.

> **Ready to light the fuse and blow this place wide open**
> **Midnight at the overlook**
> **Time to expose everything—the money, the flood, all of it**
> **Let's drop the dynamite and get the hell out of here**

Her throat tightened. The anger in his words matched the fury she'd felt discovering the diverted levee funds, the covered-up environmental reports, the incredulous police report about Uncle Leo's death. But something made her hesitate. She thought of Stacy's son Pierson, still having nightmares about being swept away in the flood. Of the elderly couple who'd lost their antique shop -three generations of family history gone in one night. Of Mrs. Chen's trembling hands as she described watching her life's work wash away.

The corporations behind this wouldn't feel the blast -they never did. They'd weather the scandal with PR teams and legal departments, maybe pay some fines. But the people of Sweetwater Springs? They'd be the ones picking up the pieces. Again.

Elizabeth's fingers hovered over the phone. Exposing fraud was supposed to help people, not heap more pain on an already wounded community. She thought of Stacy's wedding day, of the hope in people's faces as they celebrated new beginnings even amid the hard financial times. She typed back...

Can't make it tonight. Need time to think this through. These people here have suffered enough.

She hit Send before she could change her mind. The truth mattered -it always would. But maybe there was a way to expose it without burning down what little these people had left.

* * *

Elizabeth sat at Harper's kitchen island, watching Raphael expertly dice vegetables for dinner. The aroma of garlic and herbs filled the modern condo kitchen. Harper leaned against the counter, her magenta-streaked hair catching the pendant lights as she gazed at her fiancé with pure adoration.

"You should have seen him that first day at my best friend, Amira's party." Harper's eyes sparkled. "I was doing a story on celebrity chefs, and there he was, cooking up a storm in her backyard."

Raphael glanced up from his cutting board. "You mean criticizing my technique the whole time."

"I was not." Harper swatted his arm playfully. "I was admiring your knife skills."

"Among other things," he teased, leaning over to kiss her temple.

Elizabeth's chest warmed at their easy affection. The way they moved around each other in the kitchen spoke of a comfortable intimacy she'd never experienced. "How did you know?" she asked. "That this was real?"

Harper's expression softened. "Because I wasn't looking for it. Amira kept telling me to open my eyes -that sometimes the best things are right in front of us." She accepted a spoonful of sauce Raphael offered her to taste. "It's not about who makes your heart race, Liz. It's about who's already there, showing up every day."

"But what if you're drawn to someone else?" Elizabeth traced patterns in the condensation on her water glass.

"Being drawn to someone isn't the same as building a life with them." Harper reached across the counter to squeeze Elizabeth's hand. "Love isn't always about the chase or the drama. Sometimes it's about recognizing what's been right in your face all along."

Elizabeth watched as Raphael wrapped his arms around Harper's waist, whispering something that made her laugh. The sight made her throat tight with longing -not just for romance, but for that kind of certainty.

She sat on Harper's plush velvet couch, watching them move in perfect sync through their evening routine. Their shared laughter, the casual touches, the way they anticipated each other's needs -it painted a picture of intimacy that made her heart ache.

Harper tossed a cherry tomato into Raphael's mouth from across the kitchen. He caught it with theatrical flair, making her giggle. The sound echoed off the kitchen fixtures, filling the space with joy. Elizabeth's chest tightened. This was what real partnership looked like -something built day by day, choice by choice. Her phone buzzed against her thigh. Noah's name lit up the screen:

Can we talk? I have something important to discuss with you.

A sinking sensation dropped in her stomach that sent her heart pounding. She knew that tone, even through a text. It carried weight, expectations, a future she wasn't sure she was ready to face. Harper glanced over, catching Elizabeth's eye. Her friend's knowing smile spoke volumes - she'd been here before, on the edge of something real, terrified of taking that final step.

She stared at the message, thumb hovering over the Reply button. The warmth of watching Harper and Raphael faded, replaced by a cold knot of anxiety. She'd spent so long running, tracking reports, keeping everyone at arm's length. Was she ready to stop? Could she?

Her gaze drifted back to the couple in the kitchen. They'd found their answer. Maybe it was time she found hers. But was she willing to fight for it?

17

Noah's Dilemma

Elizabeth's heart fluttered as she peered around the heavy velvet curtain, her fingers trembling against the rich fabric. The Hope Rising: Flood Recovery Benefit Auction in the grand ballroom of the Sweetwater Springs Country Club stretched out before her, a glittering sea of wealth and influence. Crystal chandeliers bathed the crowd with a golden yellow cast, their light dancing off sequined gowns and polished cufflinks. She felt painfully out of place in her simple black cocktail dress, a stark contrast to the opulence surrounding her. The scent of expensive perfume mingled with the aroma of gourmet hors d'oeuvres being circulated amidst the guests. Suddenly, Noah's urgent whisper reached her ears, Elizabeth's stomach clenched. She leaned in closer, straining to hear over the muted chatter and soft music filling the ballroom.

"Tori, we need to be careful," Noah's voice was low, tinged with nervousness. "Elizabeth can't find out about this."

Elizabeth's breath caught in her throat. She inched forward, her heart pounding so loudly she feared it might give her away. As she peeked around the curtain, the sight before her sent a jolt of pain through her chest. Noah stood intimately close to Victoria, his hand resting on her bare shoulder. Victoria's fingers curled around Noah's lapel, their faces mere inches apart. The secretive tableau spoke volumes, shattering Elizabeth's fragile optimism.

"Noah?" Stepping into view, she fought to hold back the tears that threatened to spill, her voice catching as she spoke, betraying the torrent of emotions raging within.

They jumped apart, shock flashing across their faces before Noah's mask slipped seamlessly back into place. Elizabeth's heart sank, recognizing the ease with which he switched personas.

"Lizzy! There you are," he said smoothly, stepping toward her with an easy smile. "I was just discussing some sensitive legal matters with Victoria about the flood disaster reports."

Elizabeth's eyes narrowed, her instincts screaming that something was terribly wrong. The closeness she had witnessed went far beyond a professional discussion. Doubt and suspicion warred within her, threatening to shatter the tenuous trust she had placed in Noah. She stared at them, their anxious expressions confirming her worst fears. The glittering ballroom suddenly felt like a cage, the chatter of the crowd fading to a dull roar in her ears.

"Sensitive legal matters?" she repeated, her voice barely hiding her disgust. "Is that what we're calling it now?"

Noah's smile faltered for a moment before he regained his composure. "I can explain—"

"Save it," she cut him off, anger rising to replace the initial shock. "I've seen enough."

Victoria stepped forward, her eyes darting between Noah and Elizabeth. "This isn't what it looks like," she began, but Elizabeth held up a hand to silence her.

"I thought we were working together on the flood recovery," Elizabeth said, her gaze locked on Noah. "But it seems you've been keeping secrets. What else aren't you telling me?"

Noah's facade cracked, a genuine distress showing through. "Lizzy, please. We're all on the same side here."

But Elizabeth wasn't sure she believed that anymore. She felt foolish for having trusted him, for letting her guard down and believing things could be—what? *White picket fence perfect.*

"I need some air," she muttered, turning on her heel and pushing through the crowd. She ignored Noah calling after her, focusing solely on escaping the smothering atmosphere of wealth and deceit.

The cool night air hit her like a wave as she burst through the huge ornate doors, her mind racing with a million thoughts. What had she really seen? What did it mean for her own stalled investigation? And most painfully, what did it mean for her rekindled feelings for Noah?

She leaned against a marble pillar, taking deep breaths to steady herself. The sound of approaching footsteps made her tense, preparing for another confrontation. Her heart fluttered as Noah's arm encircled her waist, his touch evoking conflicting emotions within her. She wanted to sink into the warmth of his embrace and forget what she had seen. But doubt gnawed at her, refusing to be silenced.

"I'm not imagining things, Noah," she said softly, her eyes searching his face for any sign of deception. "I know what I saw... the two of you were practically..."

Noah's chuckle cut her off, his voice smooth as honey. "Lizzy, you know how these things can look. Victoria and I were just discussing some sensitive information about a case that's coming up involving a resident in my ward. She asked my opinion. Strictly confidential. Nothing more."

As he guided her back inside and onto the dance floor, she felt herself being swept up in his charm once again. Her nerves had been worn raw in recent weeks. The sharp, calculated moves she'd perfected in her career had left her ill-equipped for the rollercoaster of emotions that came with the prospect of commitment and the complex web of feelings that came with the possibility of love. The music swelled around them, and for a moment, she wanted nothing more than to lose herself in the fantasy of it all. Noah's hands on her body, his breath warm against her ear—it was intoxicating.

"You know you're the only woman I want." Noah whispered, his lips brushing her earlobe.

She nodded, forcing a smile. Her heart ached with the desperate need to believe him. Yet as they turned, she locked eyes with Victoria's across the room. The other woman's expression was unreadable, but there was something in her eyes that made Elizabeth feel uneasy.

As they continued to dance, her mind wandered. The pieces didn't quite fit, and she knew she shouldn't ignore her instincts. As the music faded, Noah leaned in close, his breath tickling her ear.

"Babe, I can tell you're still upset. This isn't the place for us to have a conversation. Why don't we get out of here?"

She hesitated, torn between her desire for answers and her instinct to guard her heart. Noah must have sensed her reluctance because he quickly added, "We can go back to my place. It's quiet there, and we can talk things through in private without any interruptions."

Elizabeth's gaze flickered across the room, catching Victoria's eyes for a brief moment.

"I... I don't know, Noah..."

"Please," he pressed, his hand gently squeezing hers. "There's a lot that I need to explain. You deserve to know the whole picture, and I want to give it to you. Just between us, away from all of this." He gestured vaguely at the dazzling crowd around them, the facade of wealth and power that suddenly felt threatening to her.

She took a deep breath, weighing her options. Part of her wanted to run, to protect herself from potential heartbreak. But the journalist in her, the part that always sought honesty, couldn't resist the opportunity for answers. "Okay," she finally agreed, her voice steadier than she felt. "Let's go."

Noah's relief was tangible, the tension eased from his arm as he guided her toward the exit, his hand resting lightly around her waist. As they made their way through the crowd, Elizabeth couldn't shake the feeling that she was stepping into something far more complicated than she had imagined.

The drive from the country club had been a blur of green fields and flashing lights. Her head swam with conflicting emotions as she followed Noah into his townhouse. As he flicked on the lights, the cool contemporary interior came into focus—all clean lines and muted colors, a far cry from the bright eclectic atmosphere of Harper's condo.

"Make yourself comfortable," Noah said, his voice soft and intimate. "I'll fix us a drink."

Elizabeth sank onto the leather couch, her fingers tracing the smooth surface as she watched Noah move through the kitchen. The clink of glasses and the soft gurgle of liquid being poured filled the silence between them. Her eyes followed his every movement, taking in the familiar yet somehow different way he carried himself. Her body vibrated with a curious mixture of lingering tension from their confrontation at the country club and a raw, sensual energy that sent shivers through her.

She shifted slightly, trying to find a comfortable position on the couch that felt worlds away from her life of shabby hotel furnishings on long road trips between assignments. The sophisticated decor of Noah's townhouse seemed to emphasize the distance between their lifestyles, and she felt a sudden twinge of unease. As he approached with two glasses in hand, she took a deep breath, steeling herself for whatever conversation lay ahead. Their fingers brushed as she took the glass, sending an unexpected jolt through her. She took a sip, the whiskey burning a path down her throat, warming her from the inside out.

"Lizzy," Noah began, settling beside her on the couch. His thigh pressed against hers, and she felt her resolve wavering. "About what you saw earlier—"

"Noah, please," she interrupted, her shoulders slumped. She exhaled a deep sigh and set her glass down on the sleek coffee table. "I just... I don't want to talk about it anymore." Her mind had been a whirlwind of worries, the recent flood disaster adding to the turmoil, and she felt drained from the constant effort of trying to make sense of it all. Not another conversation that spelled out their conflicting views, her insecurities on full display once again. She was simply... exhausted.

Noah nodded, his gaze never leaving her face as she finished her drink. Elizabeth closed her eyes and inhaled the peace and quiet of the room. The soothing atmosphere and comforts of the space momentarily eased the gnawing uncertainty that plagued her mind. Noah reached out, his fingers gently tucking a strand of hair behind her ear. The tender gesture made her heart ache.

"I've missed this," he murmured, leaning in closer. "Missed us together."

Elizabeth's breath caught in her throat as Noah's lips hovered mere inches from hers. The air between them crackled with tension, a heady mix of desire and uncertainty. Part of her wanted to give in, to lose herself in the security of Noah's arms. But the image of him with Victoria lingered in the back of her mind, a reminder of the secrets that still stood between them. Of course, she had secrets of her own to settle with before opening a channel with Noah about them. Some of them grim and heavy. Would she ever share them? *Just let it go.*

Her resistance crumbled under the intensity of Noah's eyes. The whiskey warmed her blood, dulling her senses and clouding her judgment. As his lips met hers, all thoughts of Victoria and her suspicions melted away, replaced by the heat that had always burned between them.

Noah's touch was slow and deliberate, his hands skimming up her thighs. He tugged on the delicate neckline of her dress, his touch sending shivers through her body as he drew the fabric downward, exposing more of her breasts with each seductive second. His kisses never wavered, lingering on her lips with a fiery intensity that matched the heat emanating from his touch. The sensation consumed her in a wave of desire that threatened to overwhelm her once again. His fingers gently traced the curve of her collarbone, sending goosebumps dancing across her skin.

She moaned into the kiss as Noah's hand cupped her breast through the lace of her bra, teasing the hardened peak through the fabric. She melted into his touch, craving more contact, desperate to feel him against her. His mouth found its way to the swell of her breasts, teasing each nipple through the lace before unhooking it and discarding it on the floor.

"You like this?" he murmured against her skin before taking a taut nipple between his lips.

She gasped when Noah's fingers slipped between her legs, finding the warm wetness that had gathered in anticipation of his touch. His other hand moved to the zipper of her dress, his fingers working it downwards with a slow ease. The fabric draped around her ankles, leaving her clad only in a pair of lacy black panties and heels. He took in the sight of her, his eyes dark with hunger.

"So beautiful," he rasped before leaning in to kiss her neck, trailing hot, open-mouthed kisses down her throat. His warm breath sent shivers down Elizabeth's spine as his hands roamed over her body, over every curve as if it had been years since their last encounter instead of just a few weeks.

His hands moved lower once again, slipping underneath her panties and stroking against the swell of her arousal. Elizabeth couldn't believe how much she had needed this—needed him. Her hands roamed over his muscular back, her nails raking lightly over his shirt, desperate to feel more of him. Noah's lips trailed a path down her stomach, his tongue dipping into her navel and making her gasp with delight. He hooked his fingers in the waistband of her panties, slowly sliding them down her legs and tossing them on the floor with the rest of her discarded clothing.

"This is all I think about... all day," he breathed against her skin, the heat sending a blaze through her core. "About you. My god...."

Elizabeth couldn't find the words to respond as Noah continued his sensual exploration of her body, leaving a trail of hot kisses and bites in his wake. His tongue danced between her thighs, teasingly close to where she needed him most but never quite touching.

"Noah," she whimpered, hips bucking involuntarily against him. "Please..."

He moaned softly against her skin before finally granting her relief, his tongue flicking against her clit in slow circles that made her see stars. Her nails dug into the leather couch as wave after wave of pleasure crashed over her. She needed this release tonight. This shameless escape. "Yes," she breathed, the tension draining from her body. She trembled from the raw intensity of desire for him as it burned within her.

As the last vestiges of pleasure ebbed away, Elizabeth collapsed back onto the couch, spent and breathless. Noah stood up and began undressing himself—shirt discarded carelessly on the floor, followed by trousers and boxers—revealing an erection that left no doubt about his intentions.

The heat of his stare ignited a fire deep inside; her heart pounded like a drum in her ears. The soft lighting cast a warm glow upon his sculpted, muscular physique, highlighting the rich brown tone of his skin. She couldn't tear her eyes away from his erection, which stood proudly between them. Noah reached out and gently caressed her cheek with his fingertips, tracing the slope of her jawline and down her neck. He gently rolled her onto her back and positioned himself above her, his body pressed against hers.

Elizabeth bit her lower lip, trying to regain some semblance of control. "Noah…" she began, but her words trailed off as he captured her lips once more. This time, their kiss was more urgent, more desperate than before. Their tongues danced together as their hands roamed over each other's bodies, reacquainting themselves with every curve and crevice. They melted into a passionate kiss, rediscovering their intense connection.

His hand slipped between her thighs, brushing against her wet, swollen vulva and stroking her slick folds. She moaned into the kiss as he teased her entrance with his fingers, sending another wave of pleasure crashing through her body.

"Yes, that's it," she whimpered into the darkness, hips bucking involuntarily to meet him.

He groaned softly against her hair before finally entering her in one smooth motion—long-awaited relief. As Noah's strokes deepened, Elizabeth's grip on the couch cushions tightened, scarring the leather with her nails. The rhythm of their bodies in syncopation filled the room, their heavy breathing and moans the only soundtrack to their passionate reunion.

"Oh god," Noah exhaled, his breath hot in her ear. His pace quickened, his breathing ragged as they hurtled toward release. "Lizzy," he panted out between strokes. "I… I…" He hesitated for a moment before blurting out, "I love you." His words trailed off into a primal grunt as he came inside her with one final powerful thrust, his body shuddered above her.

The confession caught Elizabeth off guard but deep down she knew it was true; and she had always loved him but was too afraid to admit it out loud until now. As Noah's body tensed above hers, Elizabeth felt an overwhelming wave of emotion fill her being.

"I love you too," she breathed out, hardly able to believe the words were coming from her own mouth. *Did I really mean that?* The words felt foreign on her tongue, a knee-jerk reaction to his vulnerability more than a genuine confession.

She'd spent a lifetime building walls around her heart, protecting herself from exactly this kind of vulnerability. Now, lying here in Noah's arms, she felt exposed and uncertain. The ease with which he proclaimed his love terrified her -his certainty a stark contrast to her own internal chaos. Deep down, maybe there was truth in those three words she'd uttered, but the thought of fully embracing that truth, of letting herself be that vulnerable with Noah, made her chest tighten with anxiety. She was tired of this constant back-and-forth with her feelings, exhausted by the way Noah could make her feel simultaneously safe and unsure.

As their breathing slowly returned to normal, Noah collapsed onto the couch beside her, pulling her close. She snuggled against his chest, enjoying the feel of his bare skin against hers, and the steady rhythm of his heartbeat against her ear brought a sense of calm.

"I'm sorry," Noah said after a long moment of silence. "For everything."

Elizabeth tilted her head up to look at him, her eyes meeting his in the dimly lit room. "What do you mean?"

"For not being honest with myself about how I really feel." He brushed a strand of hair from her cheek. "My focus has been ... scattered."

Elizabeth nodded slowly, as she grasped the meaning of his words. "It's okay," she said softly. "I know you have obligations here ... and that there's a lot at stake for you."

Noah pulled back slightly, holding her gaze intently. "There is," he admitted. "But that doesn't mean I should let fear keep me from being honest about what I want."

"What do you want?" Elizabeth asked hesitantly.

"You," he said simply, no hesitation in his voice this time around. "Us. Don't you think we have something special? Something that could last. I mean, what do you think?"

Elizabeth bit her lower lip as tears pricked at the corners of her eyes. In this after glow, she wanted nothing more than to flow with him, but life had taught her it wasn't so simple. "It's complicated…" Her usual response.

"I know it is," Noah interjected before she could continue. He cupped her face in his hands, thumbs brushing over her cheekbones as he searched her eyes earnestly for understanding and acceptance in this pivotal moment between them.

With Noah's confession hanging in the air, Elizabeth felt a whirlwind of emotions. On one hand, she was overjoyed to hear him finally admit his true feelings for her; on the other, she couldn't help but wonder if it was too little, too late. After all, they had both changed so much since their high school days.

As if he could sense her reluctance, his eyes lingered on her face, full of concern searching for a sign that she was on board. "You're right, it's complicated," he said softly. "But I can't keep denying how I feel about you any longer."

Elizabeth took a deep breath, her heart pounding in her chest as she weighed her options. She knew that if she gave in to her feelings for Noah now, there would be no turning back. But after years of running from her past and pursuing a career that sent her around the world, maybe it was time to face the music and see where this led them.

"I… I don't know what tomorrow will bring," she said at last, her voice shaky with emotion. "But right now… right now I just want to be here with you."

Noah's face broke out into a relieved grin as he leaned in to capture her lips in a searing kiss that left them both breathless once more. Their passion reignited like an inferno rekindled by a stray spark, and before they knew it, they were making love again.

This time around, their movements were slower but no less intense as they savored every touch and caress like it was their first time all over again—or perhaps even their last. Elizabeth wrapped her legs around his waist. As Noah's hips rocked against hers, they lost themselves in each other's heated fury.

Finally, with a shared gasp and shuddering breaths, they reached their peak together this time, clinging to one another in the aftermath of their passion. They lay there for what felt like hours, panting and spent in each other's arms until reality began to seep back in once more. Elizabeth nestled against Noah's warmth, savoring this moment of perfect connection. But even as his steady heartbeat soothed her, she couldn't silence the nagging voice reminding her that beyond these walls, they stood on opposite sides of a battle that threatened to tear their town apart.

* * *

The next morning dawned bright and early despite the late night they had shared together. Rays of morning light filtered into the room, bathing every corner of his spotless dwelling in a warm glow. Elizabeth roused from her peaceful rest, her body still curled against Noah's torso on the sofa. The bedding remained wrapped around their forms, their feet intertwined beneath the cozy duvet that shielded them from the cool air seeping through the space.

She blinked awake, momentarily disoriented. As the fog of sleep cleared, she became acutely aware of Noah's warm body pressed against hers. Memories of the previous night flooded back, sending a rush of heat to her cheeks. She shifted slightly, causing Noah to stir beside her. His eyes fluttered open, a slow smile spreading across his face as he met her gaze.

"Good morning," he murmured, his voice husky with sleep.

Elizabeth felt a flutter in her stomach at the intimacy of the moment. "Morning," she replied softly.

They lay there for a few moments, neither wanting to break the spell. Finally, Noah stretched and sat up, running a hand through his hair. "We should probably get moving," he said, glancing at the clock. "I have a meeting later this morning."

Elizabeth nodded, suddenly feeling self-conscious about her wild appearance. Noah stood and held out his hand to her, helping her up from the couch.

"Care to join me?" he asked with a playful grin, nodding toward the bathroom.

Elizabeth hesitated for a moment before following him. They made their way to the spacious bathroom, hands still intertwined. Noah turned on the shower, adjusting the temperature before stepping under the warm spray. He held out his hand, inviting Elizabeth to step in next to him. He pulled her close, his hands running along her curves. Their lips met in a passionate kiss, reigniting the spark from the night before. The warm water cascaded over them, steam rising around their bodies. His hands slid over her skin, leaving trails of heat in their wake. She leaned into his touch, savoring the intimacy of the moment. She ran her fingers across Noah's wet hair, pulling him into another delicious kiss. They explored each other's bodies with a renewed sense of urgency, the shower providing a sensual backdrop. As they finished washing up, Noah reached for a fluffy towel and wrapped it around Elizabeth, gently patting her dry. She blushed at his tender gesture. So sweet.

Once they were both dried off, Noah slipped on a robe and headed to the kitchen. Elizabeth heard him on the phone, ordering breakfast to be delivered. She made her way back to the living room, searching for her scattered clothing from last night.

Later she watched as Noah accepted the food delivery at the door, thanking the courier with a warm smile, and a hefty tip. She busied herself in the kitchen, locating plates and utensils to set out their breakfast. The aroma of freshly brewed coffee filled the air as she poured two steaming mugs. As she arranged the food on their plates, Elizabeth felt a sense of domesticity that both calmed and unnerved her. It was all too easy to imagine this becoming a regular occurrence -lazy mornings spent together, sharing meals and quiet conversation. But she quickly pushed those thoughts aside, reminding herself of the complicated reality of their situation.

Noah joined her in the kitchen, setting the delivery containers on the counter.

"This smells amazing," he said, inhaling the delicious aroma of the veggie omelets, turkey sausage, and strawberry filled croissants, then turned and placed a quick kiss on her cheek. The casual intimacy of the gesture sent a flutter through her stomach.

They worked in comfortable silence, moving around each other with ease as they finished preparing their meal. Elizabeth was hyper-aware of Noah's presence, the warmth radiating from his body as he brushed past her to grab napkins from a drawer.

Once everything was ready, they settled at the kitchen table. Elizabeth took a sip of her coffee, savoring the rich flavor as she watched Noah dig into his breakfast with enthusiasm. The normalcy of the moment struck her - how easily they had fallen into this pattern. As they ate, they chatted about inconsequential things -

the unseasonably warm weather, a funny story Noah had heard at his office the day before. Elizabeth found herself relaxing, enjoying the simple pleasure of sharing a meal with someone she loved. But beneath the surface, questions and uncertainties still lingered, waiting to be addressed.

She watched as Noah gathered his belongings, her heart heavy with the weight of their shared night and the uncertain future that lay ahead. She could sense his inner turmoil as well, the sudden way his shoulders tensed as he moved about the room. This was the rollercoaster of relationships that always caused her to swear off intricate affairs.

Finally, he turned to face her, his expression a mix of love and anguish. "I need to tell you something," he began, his voice a hushed whisper in the quiet room.

Elizabeth braced herself, her pulse quickening. "What is it?"

Noah took a deep breath. "I'm torn, to be honest. My feelings for you… they're stronger than ever. But my career… my responsibility in the community, their expectations. The pressure is relentless."

She nodded, understanding all too well the complexities of his position.

"The county executive director is pushing hard," Noah continued. "They want us to wrap up the flood investigation and move on with the OVAC plant expansion, in spite of …" He took a deep breath to shore up his courage. "And I… I have plans. Big plans." He paused, meeting her gaze. "I'm going to run for mayor in the next election. It's my time, Lizzy. I can feel it in my bones."

Elizabeth's eyes widened at the news. "Noah, that's… that's huge."

He nodded, a knowing smile lifting the corners of his lips, at the secret shared between them. "I'm asking you to keep it confidential for now."

"Of course," Elizabeth assured him, touched by his trust in her.

NOAH'S DILEMMA

Noah reached out, taking her hands in his. "And I need you to be patient with me, Lizzy. I'm trying to serve my constituents, to do what's best for Sweetwater. But I also want us to have a chance. I don't want you to feel like our relationship is not the most important thing in my life just because my council work takes up most of my time. Do you understand?"

The complications were undeniable, yet Elizabeth couldn't help but feel a surge of warmth at his words, a feeling that spread through her like a comforting embrace. "I understand," she said softly.

"There's one more thing," Noah added, his eyes hopeful. "I could use your help with the campaign. Your support would mean everything to me."

Elizabeth hesitated for a moment, weighing the implications. But as she looked into Noah's eyes, she found herself nodding. "Yes, I'll help you," she agreed, her voice firm with resolve. "Of course, I will."

Noah's face lit up with pure joy, his worried expression dropping away to reveal a genuine emotion. He pulled Elizabeth close, lifting her slightly off her feet in his excitement.

"Lizzy, thank you," he beamed, setting her down but keeping his hands on her waist. "With you by my side, we can make real changes here. You're exactly what this town needs —what I need."

His brown eyes sparkled with enthusiasm as he started outlining his vision. "Just think about it —we can restore the historic district, bring in sustainable businesses, create a future that honors our past while moving forward." He squeezed her hands. "And you'll be there, helping shape that future with me."

Noah's charisma was in full force as he spun her around. "I've been waiting for the right moment to tell you about running for mayor. I knew you'd understand why it's so important." He stopped, his expression growing serious but tender. "You're the only one I trust with this, Lizzy. The only one who really gets it. That sees the potential for this town the way I do."

He pulled her into a deep kiss, then rested his forehead against hers. "Together, we're unstoppable. You and me —we can make Sweetwater Springs everything it should be."

His happiness was infectious, eclipsing any doubts Elizabeth might have had. In that moment, caught up in Noah's enthusiasm and charm, it was easy to believe in his vision of their future together.

"Let's celebrate," he grinned, already reaching for his phone. "I'll make reservations at La Maison. Just us, champagne, and the start of our next chapter."

She watched as Noah got dressed, her eyes tracing the contours of his athletic frame. His deep mahogany skin seemed to glow in the morning light, accentuating the strong lines of his shoulders and back. She admired the way his crisp white shirt contrasted beautifully against his rich complexion, highlighting the sharp angles of his jawline and the warm depths of his dark brown eyes.

As he adjusted his tie, Elizabeth was captivated by his graceful movements. With both strength and gentleness, Noah's hands moved fluidly as he buttoned his suit jacket. The tailored fabric hugged his broad shoulders and trim waist, creating a silhouette that exuded confidence and power. He caught her gaze in the mirror and flashed a warm smile that made Elizabeth's heart skip a beat.

"Can I drop you somewhere?" Noah asked, his voice a low rumble that sent a sweet longing through her once again.

She hesitated, torn between the desire to spend more time with him and the need to process everything that had just happened. "I'd like to hang back for a while and make a few calls and check emails," she said. "I'll call for a ride later, if that's okay."

Noah paused, his brow furrowing slightly as he considered her request. After a moment, he nodded. "Sure, that's fine," he said, though Elizabeth could sense a hint of reluctance in his tone. "Make yourself comfortable. There's plenty of coffee in the kitchen if you need it."

He moved in closer, his aftershave hovering around her in a warm, spicy fragrance. Elizabeth's breath caught in her throat as he leaned in, placing a gentle kiss on her cheek. "I'll see you later?" he murmured, his lips brushing against her skin.

"Definitely," Elizabeth said, wanting him to linger for a few more hours with her. She watched as Noah left for his meeting, her mind captured by a mix of emotions. As the door closed behind him, she sank onto the couch. The events of the past few hours replayed in her mind, each moment sending a flutter through her stomach.

For the first time in years, Elizabeth felt a sense of belonging that had eluded her since leaving Sweetwater Springs. Noah's confession of love and his request for her support in his mayoral campaign had shifted something fundamental within her. She realized that her feelings for him were taking precedence over everything else in her life - her career, her investigation, even her concerns about the OVAC plant expansion.

A small smile played at her lips as she thought about the possibility of a future with Noah. It was a stark contrast to the nomadic lifestyle she had embraced for so long. The idea of putting down roots, of being part of something bigger than herself, was both thrilling and terrifying.

Elizabeth's thoughts drifted to her work, and the incredible events she had witnessed around the world. While they had given her purpose, they had also kept her at arm's length from forming lasting connections. Now, with Noah, she felt anchored in a way she had never experienced before. As she sat there, surrounded by the warmth of his home, she accepted the fact that her priorities were shifting. The urgency of her investigation seemed to fade in comparison to the potential of building a life with councilman and future mayor, Noah

Montgomery. She found herself imagining a future where she could use her skills to support his political aspirations while still making a difference in their community in her own way.

For the first time in years, Elizabeth felt like she truly belonged somewhere. Sweetwater Springs, once a source of painful memories, now held the promise of a bright new chapter in her life. With Noah by her side, she could envision herself becoming an integral part of the town's future, no longer an outsider looking in.

18

Fault Lines

Elizabeth sat across from Jimmy, her hands wrapped around a coffee mug more for comfort than warmth. His dark brown eyes were focused on the folder in front of them, his copper skin weathered from years working construction sites. His black hair, streaked with early gray at the temples, was pulled back in a neat braid that hung past his shoulders. Their rendezvous had been delayed at every turn due to schedule conflicts with the activist's protest meetings, Jimmy's work schedule, and the flood recovery efforts. She could barely contain her excitement now that they were seated across from each other. The planning of Noah's mayoral campaign took a backseat to the possibility of finally understanding what Uncle Leo had left behind for them.

"My aunt Running Deer lives out on the Eastern Cherokee reservation in North Carolina. She said it took her days to read these," Jimmy said, his voice low and reverent. "She hadn't seen something like this since she was a girl."

Elizabeth leaned forward. "Your aunt translated all of this?"

Jimmy opened the folder, revealing the pages of Leo's precise drawings of plants alongside the words. "It's more than just a record of dying plants. He was documenting everything—soil changes, water quality, wildlife patterns. Leo knew something was wrong months before anyone else noticed."

He pulled out one of the translated pages. "Look here. He wrote: 'The yarrow doesn't bloom anymore where the morning mist settles. The soil turns gray, like ash, and nothing grows. Our medicines are dying, and with them, our connection to this land.'"

Elizabeth's throat tightened with emotion as she whispered, "He was building evidence."

"And here." Jimmy's finger traced a particular entry. "Leo tracked the deer population dropping off years ago. Said they wouldn't drink from certain streams anymore. Then the fish started dying."

A chill ran through Elizabeth's body despite the warm coffee in her hands. "He was documenting environmental changes?"

"More than that. He mapped out truck routes, recorded late-night activity. The words get more urgent toward the end - like he knew something bad was coming."

The diner's fluorescent lights buzzed overhead as Elizabeth studied the translations. She recognized dates that lined up with her own observations. Leo hadn't been paranoid - he'd been methodically building a case.

"Did he say anything about being threatened?" Elizabeth asked, thinking about the circumstances of his death.

Jimmy's jaw clenched. "Last entry, a day before he died. 'They offered money for silence. They don't understand—our healing plants are worth more than their gold. A man in a fancy suit says progress demands sacrifice. I say one child's health is not a fair trade.'"

Elizabeth noticed the fresh ink on Jimmy's forearm as he reached for his coffee. She reached out and touched the tattoo gently. "It's beautiful."

He rolled up his sleeve, revealing the new tattoo on his forearm—a simple but elegant design of yarrow flowers. "This? It's from Leo's journal too. He drew it the day before he died. My aunt says it's an old symbol for resistance, for fighting back against forces that would destroy our sacred spaces. The whole community's getting them now. Leo's last stand, living on our skin." Jimmy covered the artwork carefully.

"The last entry," he said, "it's different from the rest. More personal. He wrote about Vincent, about wanting to protect him. And about you."

Elizabeth looked up sharply. "Me?"

"Said you reminded him of someone. Someone who stood up against powerful people years ago." Jimmy's dark eyes met hers. "He was talking about your parents, wasn't he?"

Elizabeth's eyes welled over at Jimmy's words. She stared at the translated pages, her vision blurring slightly as memories of her parents rushed back. The ache of their loss mixed with fresh grief. Her fingers traced Leo's words, marveling at how he'd hidden such vital information in plain sight. The old man had been cleverer than anyone realized. She thought of the nights spent talking with him on the trailer's porch, how he'd share stories about the land while subtly observing the increased activity across the ridge while sipping his tea.

"There's more," Jimmy said, flipping to the final pages. "Leo mapped out underground water channels, places where the chemicals would spread fastest if there was a breach. Or a flood."

Elizabeth's coffee went cold as she absorbed the implications. Her mind raced, connecting the dots between Leo's documentation and the devastating flood that had torn through town. The timing of his death, the destruction of the community center, the push for rapid development - it wasn't coincidence.

"Did your aunt say anything else about these symbols?" She tapped a recurring pattern that appeared throughout the journal pages.

Jimmy nodded slowly. "She said it's an old warning sign, means 'poison in the water.' Leo used it whenever he recorded chemical dumps or contamination sites."

Elizabeth pulled out her phone, comparing Leo's mapped locations to photos she'd taken of the construction zones. Everything lined up - the shipping containers, the late-night truck routes, the dead wildlife. Uncle Leo had created a detailed record of environmental violations, knowing exactly how to preserve the evidence where few could decipher it.

Her hand shook slightly as she gathered the pages. "Jimmy, this is exactly what we needed. Leo left us a roadmap."

He nodded, helping her with gathering the papers back into the folder. "But Elizabeth..." He hesitated, lowering his voice. "These people, they already killed Leo. You need to be careful."

"I know." Her fingers brushed over the precious ink strokes. "But he trusted us with this information. And we can't let it die with him."

"What are you going to do?" Jimmy asked, sliding the folder across the table to her.

"What Uncle Leo would have done. Tell the truth, no matter the cost." She paused, looking out the window at the ridge where Leo had once gathered his healing plants. "We owe him that much."

"True," Jimmy said, standing up. "We owe it to everyone who'll come after. Leo used to say our ancestors didn't preserve this land for us—they preserved it for our grandchildren's grandchildren."

The diner's bell chimed as new customers entered. Elizabeth glanced up, tensing slightly before recognizing the elderly couple who walked in. Uncle Leo's warnings about being watched still nagged at her.

"Meet me at Harper's place tonight. I'll text you the address," she said, keeping her voice low. "It'll be safer than discussing this at Echo Ridge."

Jimmy stood. "What about Councilman Montgomery? He should know about this."

Elizabeth's stomach tightened at the mention of Noah's name. The memory of him with Victoria in that alcove flashed through her mind, along with his repeated calls for "patience" with the investigation. A new wave of suspicions arose. He had secrets, things he hadn't shared with her yet, a whole universe of thoughts and experiences that were hidden beneath the surface of them both. Was it enough to break them? Time would decide but for now...

"Not yet," she said firmly. "We need to verify everything first. Make sure we understand exactly what Uncle Leo was trying to tell us."

Elizabeth watched Jimmy leave the diner, her mind filled with the weight of Leo's evidence. She pulled out her phone, typing a quick message to Harper about meeting later. The screen lit up with another incoming text from Noah - his third attempt to reach her since their night together. She clicked the phone off without responding.

The waitress stopped by to warm up her coffee, but she barely noticed. Her attention kept drifting to her messenger bag, knowing the translated pages inside could completely change the course of the investigation. Uncle Leo hadn't just been making wild accusations - he'd methodically documented everything, creating an environmental impact report that no one could ignore.

Elizabeth took a final sip of coffee and laid some cash on the table. As she stepped out into the afternoon sun, a familiar ache settled in her chest. Uncle Leo had trusted her to carry on his work, to expose the truth about what was happening to their town. She wouldn't let him down.

The bell chimed behind her as someone pushed past her through the diner's door. She dodged them and stepped onto the cracked sidewalk, headed to her next meetup. She had work to do, and for the first time since returning to Sweetwater Springs, her path forward was clear. The truth had cost Uncle Leo everything, and now she had to decide if she was willing to pay the same price.

*　*　*

Elizabeth drummed her fingers against the old wooden picnic tabletop at Sawmill Park, checking her watch for the third time. Maya was late, which wasn't like her. The lunch crowd had thinned, leaving only a few regulars nursing their afternoon coffees.

Finally, Maya rushed over, her reporter's notebook clutched to her chest. Her dark curls were windswept, and she hadn't bothered with her usual polished appearance.

"Sorry I'm late." Maya slid into the chair across from Elizabeth. "But this couldn't wait. Remember that inspector they're trying to pin the levee failure on?"

Elizabeth leaned forward. "Charles Jackson? The one who signed off on the structural inspection?"

"He reached out to me." Maya's voice dropped to a whisper. "Says he never conducted that inspection. Any documents showing his approval are forged."

Elizabeth's pulse quickened. "He's willing to go on record with us?"

"Yes and get this. He's ready to testify." Maya flipped open her notebook. "Says they're setting him up to take the fall for the flood damage. He's got proof that he wasn't even in Sweetwater Springs the week that inspection was supposedly done."

"Why come forward now?"

"Because they're closing in on him. The county executive's office is building a case, painting him as negligent. He says he'd rather face the public than be railroaded for something he didn't do."

If Jackson was telling the truth, this wasn't just about a failed inspection —it was about deliberate fraud. Someone had forged those documents, knowing the levee wouldn't hold.

"Where is he now?" Elizabeth said.

"Staying with family in Cincinnati. He's willing to meet, but only off the record first. Wants to make sure we can protect him before he goes public."

Elizabeth raked her fingers through her hair. Jackson's testimony could break this case wide open -connecting the forged documents to Uncle Leo's environmental findings. She pulled out her phone, checking the signal strength before responding.

"Tell him I'll drive up to Cincinnati tomorrow. We need to document everything before the county office moves against him."

Maya nodded, scribbling in her notebook. "I'll set it up. But Liz…" She glanced around the café. "There's something else. Jackson mentioned pressure from above - way above the county level. Said some state officials were involved in fast-tracking permits for the concrete plant."

Elizabeth thought of Noah's recent behavior, his closed-door meetings with Victoria and the county executive. The pieces were starting to align in ways that made her question everything.

"Did he name names?"

"Not yet. Says he wants to meet in person first." Maya tore the page from her notebook and slid it across the table. "Here's his contact info. He's staying at his sister's place near Mount Adams."

Elizabeth tucked the paper into her bag alongside Uncle Leo's translated journal pages. Between Jackson's testimony and Leo's documentation, they finally had solid evidence of wrongdoing. But she needed to move fast, before anyone realized what they'd uncovered.

"I'll head up first thing tomorrow," Elizabeth said. "Better if I go alone - less conspicuous that way."

"Be careful," Maya warned. "If Jackson is right about state-level involvement, these people won't hesitate to protect themselves."

Elizabeth thought of Leo's final warnings, of Vincent's concerns about her safety. But she'd come too far to back down now. "I'll check in every few hours. If anything feels off, I'll pull out."

She gathered her belongings from the table and headed back toward town, her mind sorting through the possibilities. Maya's revelations about Jackson had shifted the investigation into new territory -one that required careful legal navigation. The weight of Uncle Leo's journal pressed against her hip through her messenger bag, a constant reminder of what was at stake. A county works truck rumbled past, kicking up dust from the ongoing flood cleanup. The sight of it made her pause, considering the layers of bureaucracy and legal red tape she'd need to cut through to protect Jackson's testimony.

Her phone felt heavy in her hand as she scrolled through her contacts, thumb hovering over Noah's number. The memory of Victoria at the fundraiser, standing too close to him in that alcove, made her hesitate. But personal feelings aside, Victoria was one of the sharpest legal minds in the county. She'd know exactly what protections whistleblowers could expect, especially when going up against state-level officials.

Elizabeth found a quiet spot on a bench outside a café, watching people hurry past. She reached for Uncle Leo's journal again and leafed through the pages. She needed to understand the legal landscape before heading to Cincinnati. One wrong move could spook Jackson or, worse, leave him vulnerable to retaliation. The question was whether she could trust Victoria to give honest advice without tipping off Noah or the county office about Jackson's willingness to talk.

She found Victoria's social media profile and started composing a message, keeping it vague:

> **Need your expertise on whistleblower protections in Ohio. Private citizen seeking information about county inspection processes. Can we meet?**

Each refresh of the page made her stomach tighten. Would Victoria ignore her? Report back to Noah? Go public with the request? Her heart jumped as Victoria's response appeared:

> **I assume this is about more than general legal advice. 937-555-0142. Call don't text. Available after 8 PM.**

Elizabeth let out a breath. Victoria's response was careful, professional—but the fact that she'd shared her telephone number spoke volumes. She understood the need for privacy. She saved the number under a fake contact name: "Garden Center." She glanced at the time: 6:47 PM. Just over an hour to prepare her approach. Everything would depend on this conversation—not just the evidence, but how she presented it.

She looked at Uncle Leo's journal on the table, then back at Victoria's message. The Acting DA's reputation for pursuing justice despite political pressure was well known. Elizabeth just hoped that reputation would hold true if the evidence implicated Noah Montgomery. And if her heart could survive it.

19

Uneasy Alliance

Elizabeth's car wound through Cincinnati's Mount Adams neighborhood, the late afternoon sun casting thick, dark shadows between historic buildings. The quaint Victorian homes and renovated row houses reminded her of a European village, their weathered brick facades glowing amber in the fading light. She double-checked the address on her phone before pulling into a spot near a small coffee shop, its chalk-written menu board visible through steamy windows. The aroma of fresh-roasted beans drifted inside, momentarily distracting her from the purpose of her visit.

Charles Jackson sat at an outdoor table, his fingers drumming nervously against a ceramic mug. She recognized him from Maya's description - mid-fifties, salt-and-pepper hair, wearing a plain button-down shirt with the sleeves rolled up. As she approached, she noticed the tattoo on his forearm - a delicate spray of yarrow flowers, identical to the ones that grew wild around Leo's trailer. And matched the tattoo on Jimmy's forearm.

"Mr. Jackson?" Elizabeth kept her voice low, professional. "I'm Elizabeth Nelson."

He nodded, gesturing to the empty chair across from him with a slightly trembling hand. "Call me Charles. I recognize you from the protests." His eyes darted around the nearly empty patio, scanning each corner as if expecting someone to emerge from the shadows. A light breeze rustled the umbrella over their table as he leaned forward, his voice dropping even lower. "I worked with Leo, you know. Before…"

Elizabeth's throat tightened at the mention of Leo's name. "The yarrow -is that for him?"

"Yeah." Charles traced the outline of the tattoo. "He taught me about the local plants, their meanings. Said yarrow was for healing and protection." He let out a shaky breath. "Fat lot of good that did him."

Elizabeth pulled out her recorder but kept it off, waiting for his signal. "Maya said you had information about the levee inspection?"

"OVAC pushed it through." Charles leaned forward, lowering his voice. "They needed that inspection passed to start construction on schedule. The new expansion would require the build of a diversion channel, it would redirect the flow from a barrier up river sending more pressure against the levee. The paperwork came back approved, but I never set foot on that site."

"Someone forged your signature?"

He nodded. "Found out later the levee had major structural issues. Should've been completely rebuilt, not just patched." His hands trembled as he reached for his coffee. "When I tried to report it, suddenly there was pressure from above to keep quiet."

Elizabeth's heart raced. "Was anyone from Sweetwater Springs involved?"

"Not that I know of. The orders came straight from OVAC's corporate office." Charles shrugged. "Local officials probably didn't know the specifics. They just saw the approved paperwork."

Elizabeth felt a small wave of relief wash over her. She'd been dreading the possibility of finding Noah's name connected to this. Her hands shook slightly as she tucked the recorder back into her bag, her fingers fumbling with the zipper as the impact of Charles's revelations settled over her. "I understand your concerns, Charles. Your name won't appear anywhere until you're ready. We can use 'anonymous source' in the initial reporting." She knew firsthand how crucial it was to protect whistleblowers, especially in cases involving powerful corporations like OVAC.

Charles nodded, his shoulders relaxing with a sigh. "Just... be careful who you trust with this. These people, they don't play fair."

"I know exactly who to take this to." She stood, offering her hand. "Thank you for coming forward."

Back in her car, Elizabeth pulled out her phone and dialed Victoria's number, her thumb hovering over the call button for a moment. The image of Victoria and Noah in that intimate moment at the fundraiser flashed through her mind again, making her think twice. But this was bigger than personal drama.

Victoria answered on the second ring. "Elizabeth?"

"Can you meet me for drinks? Outside of town - the Boat House in Clover City?"

A pause. "Give me an hour."

* * *

The Boat House's bar area hummed with late evening energy, a low thrum of conversation and clinking glasses. Elizabeth, nursing a club soda, chose a corner table away from the crowd, the dim lighting offering a small sense of anonymity. She watched Victoria stride in, her honey-blonde hair styled in loose waves, a stark contrast to her own dark mane. Victoria wore a perfectly tailored blazer, deep crimson, that probably cost more than her friend Stacy's monthly rent. It was a power move, she recognized, the kind of outfit that said, "I'm in control." Her heels clicked purposefully across the hardwood floor, each step a declaration of her arrival. Elizabeth smoothed down her simple jeans and chambray shirt, a flicker of self-consciousness rising within her. This meeting was important, bigger than petty wardrobe comparisons, she reminded herself. She had information that Victoria needed to hear, information that could change everything for Sweetwater Springs.

"This must be important," Victoria said, sliding into the seat across from her.

Elizabeth studied the woman's composed expression, searching for any hint of duplicity or hidden agenda. Was this the woman who had been so secretive with Noah that night? The same one who might still harbor feelings for him? Or did she create different versions of herself depending on who she was talking to? There was only one way to find out. *Get straight to the damn point.*

"I have evidence about the recent levee inspection." Elizabeth kept her voice low. "Someone with direct knowledge of the forgery of county documents."

Victoria's professional mask slipped for a moment, her eyes alight with a flicker of genuine interest, like a predator catching the scent of prey —hungry to know more. "Admissible evidence?"

"With the right legal protection for my source, yes."

Victoria leaned forward, all business now. "I'm listening."

As Elizabeth laid out Charles's information, she watched Victoria take precise notes in a small leather-bound notebook. There was no trace of the woman from the fundraiser - this was a lawyer laser-focused on justice.

"This could bring down half the county board," Victoria said finally.

"We'll need to move carefully."

"'We?"

Victoria met her eyes directly. "Yes, we. You need legal backup, and I need a journalist who isn't afraid to ruffle feathers. Personal feelings aside, we both want the truth exposed."

Elizabeth felt her shoulders relax slightly. Whatever Victoria's relationship with Noah might be, her commitment to this case seemed genuine. She recognized the same fire in Victoria's eyes that she often saw in her own reflection when pursuing a story - that unwavering determination to expose corruption. It was oddly comforting to find an unexpected ally in someone she'd initially viewed with such suspicion. Maybe their shared dedication to exposing the fraud could overcome any personal tension between them.

Victoria closed her notebook with a decisive snap and slid it into her designer executive tote bag, a sleek leather number that was probably worth more than Uncle Leo's trailer and its entire contents. "I'll need forty-eight hours to review everything and create a strategy. No one else can know about this yet -not anyone else at the DA's office, not the press." Her green eyes fixed on Elizabeth with an intensity that left no room for argument, a hint of something deeper, almost personal, flickering in their depths. "And especially not Noah." The way she emphasized his name made Elizabeth wonder just how complicated the relationship between Victoria and Noah truly was.

"Agreed. But I need your word, Victoria. Complete confidentiality."

"You have it." Victoria pulled out a business card and wrote something on the back. "This is my personal cell. Not my office line, not my assistant's number. If anything comes up, you contact me directly." She slid the card across the table. "I'm putting my career on the line here too. We both know what OVAC is capable of."

"And you'll protect my source?"

"Charles Jackson's name won't appear in any documentation until we're ready to move forward with formal charges." Victoria's voice carried the weight of legal authority. "I'll draw up confidentiality agreements first thing tomorrow. You have my word as an officer of the court."

Elizabeth studied Victoria's face, searching for any hint of deception. But she saw only determination and professional resolve. This wasn't about Noah or their complicated history - this was about justice.

"Then we have a deal." Elizabeth extended her hand across the table. Victoria's grip was firm as they shook on it. "We have a deal."

20

Heart vs. Head

Elizabeth sat at her laptop, staring at the blank document where her latest article should have been. Uncle Leo's journal lay open beside her, his careful documentation of environmental damage a testament to his dedication. Her phone buzzed with another message from a local editor asking about her next piece.

"You don't need to worry about deadlines anymore." Noah's arms slipped around her shoulders from behind. "I told you, I can take care of everything."

She tucked away the journal and closed the laptop. "My career matters to me, Noah. I can't just give up everything I've worked for."

"Think about it differently." His lips brushed her neck. "You'll be helping shape policy, making real change right here. Isn't that better than running around the world digging up stories about people you don't know? And with people who don't care about you?"

The faintest hint of a smile played on his lips as his fingers traced light, seductive circles on her skin. "My mayoral campaign needs you. I need you."

Elizabeth leaned back into his embrace, conflicted. As much as she tried to block it, the thrill of investigation still pulled at her, but

Noah's vision of their future together tempted her with its stability and purpose. There had to be a way to have both. She was determined to find it.

"Trust me," he whispered, turning her chair to face him. "Let me handle things."

His kiss was persuasive, demanding. Elizabeth yielded to it, letting him pull her up and guide her toward the bedroom. His hands slid under her shirt, erasing her doubts with each touch.

"You're meant to be here," Noah whispered against her skin. "With me."

Elizabeth surrendered to his certainty, to the heat building between them. His body covered hers, familiar and insistent, his weight pressing her into the softness of the mattress. She wrapped herself around him, trying to believe that this was enough, that she could be content in the role he'd designed for her. Her fingers traced the muscled planes of his back as doubts flickered at the edges of her consciousness, but Noah's passionate kisses pushed them away, replacing her uncertainty with a desperate need for connection. Still, somewhere in the back of her mind, a small voice whispered that passion alone couldn't fill the void left by abandoned dreams.

His lips trailed heat along her neck, his hands caressing her curves with slow tender motion.

"Is this what you want?" he murmured against her skin, his breath warm. "Tell me how it feels."

Elizabeth shivered at his touch, a moan escaping her lips. "It feels good," she breathed, trying to be present.

Noah's rhythm faltered slightly. "Just good?" He pulled back to meet her eyes, seeking reassurance. "I need to know I'm giving you what you want. What you need from me. That I'm satisfying you, Lizzy."

She cupped his face in her hands. "You are," she assured him. But even as she said it, a flicker of irritation passed through her. Couldn't he just lose himself in the moment like she was trying to?

His fingers danced lower, teasing and exploring. As Elizabeth yielded to his demands, she felt her arousal beginning to deepen within her. But instead of intensifying their lovemaking, Noah paused again.

"This okay?"

"Yes," Elizabeth snapped before she could stop herself. Noticing him flinch at her harshness, she softened her voice. "Everything's fine."

She guided one hand between them, showing him where to touch. But he didn't seem satisfied by her answer. His movements became hesitant now, as if every caress required permission first. She felt tension coiling within him instead of passion.

"Do you want..." Noah began hesitantly.

"Wait," Elizabeth interrupted impatiently before he could ask another question that would kill the mood entirely. Rolling over, she took a dominant position, her legs straddling his hips.

"What are you doing?" Noah asked in confusion.

"I'm showing you what I want," Elizabeth retorted sharply before capturing his lips with hers and kissing him hard and deep until questions became impossible for them both. He froze.

She rolled off Noah with an exasperated sigh, pulling the sheet around her body. The heat of passion had cooled to lukewarm frustration.

"Did I do something wrong?" Noah propped himself up on an elbow, his brow furrowed with concern.

"No, it's just..." Elizabeth stared at the ceiling, trying to find the right words. "You just need to trust that I'm enjoying myself without asking for constant confirmation."

Noah's hand reached for hers. "I want to make sure you're happy.

You seem distracted..."

Elizabeth withdrew her hand and sat up, keeping the sheet wrapped around her. This was exactly why she avoided relationships - the constant need for reassurance, the emotional demands, the expectations. Give her a quick hook-up any day over this complicated dance of feelings and validation.

But Noah was different, wasn't he? He genuinely cared about her happiness, even if his methods were suffocating. She glanced at him - his warm brown eyes filled with genuine concern, his strong jawline tense with worry. He was stable, successful, kind. The type of man her parents would have approved of.

"I know you mean well," Elizabeth said softly. "But sometimes being with you feels like I'm filling out a satisfaction survey."

Noah sat up, hurt flashing across his face. "I just want to be sure I'm doing right by you. I know what I've asked you to give up for me, Lizzy. I don't want you to regret anything."

Elizabeth's chest tightened with guilt. Here was a good man trying his best to make her happy, and she was pushing him away. Maybe the problem wasn't him - maybe it was her inability to accept genuine care and affection.

"I need some air," she said, gathering her clothes from the floor. "We can talk later."

As she dressed quickly in the bathroom, she caught her reflection in the mirror. The woman staring back looked torn between flight and settling down. Noah represented everything she should want - stability, devotion, a future. So why did his attention make her feel like she was suffocating?

She slipped into her jeans and pulled her wrinkled blouse over her head, her movements quick and efficient. Her reflection in Noah's bathroom mirror showed dark circles under her eyes - evidence of too many late nights poring over Uncle Leo's journal. She splashed cold water on her face, trying to wash away the lingering frustration from their failed moment of intimacy. The expensive hand soap next to his sink smelled of sandalwood and success - everything in Noah's life was carefully curated, even down to the smallest details. Everything here was so pristine, so perfect - from the carefully arranged family photos to the precisely aligned throw pillows on his leather couch.

In the bedroom, Noah had already dressed in pressed khakis and a polo shirt. He stood by the window, his jaw muscles tense as he stared out at his manicured backyard.

"I've got some work to catch up on," Elizabeth said, gathering her laptop and purse. The lie felt foul in her mouth, but it was easier than explaining the restlessness crawling under her skin.

Noah turned, his expression carefully neutral. "The campaign meeting's at 6:30 tonight. Will you make it?"

Elizabeth paused at the bedroom door. "I'll try my best." She forced a smile. "I'll call you later, okay?"

His answering smile didn't quite reach his eyes. "Sure, babe."

The pet name made her wince - it reminded her too much of those corny rom-coms. She hurried down the stairs of Noah's townhouse, her footsteps echoing in the empty space. As she stepped outside, the evening air, warm and sweet with the scent of freshly cut grass, caressed her face, bringing with it a sense of freedom. She took a deep breath, letting the tension ease from her shoulders.

"I'll call you," she repeated, more to herself than to Noah who watched from the upstairs window. Her keys jingled in her hand as she walked to her car, promising herself she would follow through this time.

* * *

Elizabeth pulled her car into the parking spot at Harper's condo complex, grateful for the spare key her friend had given her. The scent of jasmine from the climbing vines near the entrance welcomed her as she made her way inside. She kicked off her heels and pulled up the delivery app on her phone, ordering her usual - kung pao chicken and crab rangoon from Golden Palace. Her laptop whirred to life as she settled onto the couch, the blank document still mocking her with its emptiness.

Her fingers hovered over the keyboard, but instead of typing, she touched her lips where Noah had kissed her earlier. He was attentive, successful, and genuinely cared about her happiness. Maybe too much, but wasn't that better than not caring at all?

The doorbell chimed - her food had arrived faster than expected. She grabbed her wallet and paid the delivery guy, then settled back on the couch with her takeout containers. She flipped through the premium channels, landing on something steamy and mindless - exactly what she needed to quiet her thoughts.

As she stabbed at a piece of chicken with her chopsticks, she forced herself to focus on Noah's good qualities. He was steady, unlike the chaos of her usual lifestyle. He wanted to build something real with her. And most importantly, he saw a future for them in Sweetwater Springs.

"Give it time," she muttered to herself, reaching for another crab rangoon. "Good relationships take work." The words felt rehearsed, but she repeated them anyway, trying to convince herself that her restlessness would fade if she just gave them a chance.

* * *

Elizabeth adjusted her navy blazer one last time in her car's rearview mirror. The tailored jacket paired perfectly with her cream silk blouse and pencil skirt - the epitome of a politician's partner. She'd spent an extra hour that morning smoothing her black hair into elegant waves and perfecting her makeup to appear both polished and natural.

The morning sun caught her pearl earrings as she stepped out of her car in front of Sweetwater Springs City Hall. Her heels clicked against the concrete, each step measured and graceful. She'd practiced her walk, her smile, even the way she'd hold Noah's arm later during the press conference about the flood recovery efforts.

Her phone buzzed with a text from Noah:

Can't wait to see you. You're going to blow them away!

Elizabeth's stomach fluttered. This was different from her usual camera-ready preparations for field reporting. Back then, she'd thrown on whatever was clean and functional. Now each detail mattered - from her subtle lipstick to her perfectly manicured nails. The transformation felt strange, like trying on someone else's skin.

She checked her reflection in a window, ensuring her appearance matched the vision of the potential future Mrs. Montgomery that Noah's constituents would expect. The woman staring back at her looked elegant, refined -nothing like the scrappy journalist who'd dodged bullets in Venezuela just months ago.

Inside City Hall, the marble floors echoed with her footsteps. She'd memorized her talking points about Noah's dedication to the community and his vision for Sweetwater Springs' future. The note cards in her purse were just backup -she wouldn't need them. She was ready to play her part.

Elizabeth's phone buzzed with a text from Jimmy:

They're selling the trailer park. 14 days to clear out

Her stomach dropped. Echo Ridge Trailer Park sat well above the flood zone, making it prime real estate after half of Sweetwater Springs had been underwater. She should have seen this coming - developers had been circling like vultures since the waters receded. Her hands trembled as she read Jimmy's text again. The residents of Echo Ridge - they were her people now. Uncle Leo's people. Her throat tightened as she pictured their faces, their homes about to be ripped away.

She glanced at the imposing wooden doors of the council chamber, where Noah waited to rehearse their press conference. The pearls around her neck suddenly felt like a chokehold. She pounded out a text:

I'm sorry, something urgent came up. Family emergency.

She spun around, her carefully practiced walk forgotten as she rushed back through the marble halls. Her heels clattered against the floor, drawing stares from the city employees, but she didn't care.

Outside, the morning sun felt harsh and accusing. Elizabeth yanked open her car door, not bothering to check if her skirt caught. The elegant outfit that had felt so important minutes ago now seemed ridiculous. She kicked off her heels, fishing her flat shoes from under the passenger seat. As she peeled out of the parking lot, her phone lit up with Noah's face. She hit ignore and pressed harder on the gas.

The road to Echo Ridge stretched before her, winding up into the hills above town. She saw the trailers, their windows reflecting the sun, a defiant glimmer in the face of the surrounding desolation. Uncle Leo's words reverberated through her mind, as if she could still hear his gravelly tone: "This ain't just property, Elizabeth. It's community. It's family."

The air was warm and still as she pulled up to Uncle Leo's trailer, the sun casting long shadows across the overgrown grass. The garden they'd planted together was still thriving -herbs and medicinal plants that he'd taught her about during those quiet afternoons. She couldn't bear the thought of bulldozers tearing through them, destroying one of the last living connections to him.

She grabbed a small shovel from the side yard, determined to save what she could. The pungent scent of sage and yarrow filled her nostrils as she kneeled in the soft earth. Uncle Leo's voice echoed in her memory, she whispered his words aloud with tears welling in her eyes, "Every plant has a purpose. Nature doesn't waste anything."

"You'll need these."

Elizabeth startled at Vincent's voice behind her. He stood there holding two clay pots, his face unreadable in the fading light. She hadn't heard him approach.

"How did you know?" she asked, brushing dirt from her hands.

"Jimmy texted me too." Vincent kneeled beside her, carefully working a trowel around a cluster of echinacea. "Uncle Leo used to say these flowers were warriors -fighting off sickness, healing the body." His fingers traced the purple petals. "Seems fitting they survived the flood."

Elizabeth watched him work, his movements gentle despite his strong hands. The same hands that had fought his way through political uprisings and natural disasters now moved swiftly and delicately to preserve his uncle's legacy.

"You remember what he said about transplants?" Vincent asked, not looking up.

"Take the roots deep," Elizabeth replied softly. "Or they won't survive the move."

The double meaning hung heavy in the air between them. They worked in silence, the setting sun painting the sky in shades of orange and pink. Each plant they saved felt like a small victory against the developers, against time itself.

"I found something," Vincent said finally, reaching into his jacket. He pulled out another worn leather journal. "Was checking the trailer before they could clear it out. Look at the last few entries."

Elizabeth's hands trembled slightly as she took the journal. She knew whatever was in those pages would change everything - her relationship with Noah, her future in Sweetwater Springs, her understanding of Uncle Leo's death.

The choice loomed before her like a storm on the horizon. She could feel Vincent's eyes on her, waiting, as the last rays of sunlight filtered through the trees.

"You have twenty-four hours," he said quietly. "To decide if you're ready to dig deeper or if you'd rather let sleeping dogs lie."

Elizabeth looked at the journal, then at the uprooted plants waiting to be saved. Sometimes, she realized, preserving what matters meant having to tear everything up first. She watched as Vincent vanished around the trailer's edge, Leo's diary still clutched in her hand. The wind whispered through the surviving flora, raising goosebumps on her skin despite the pleasant temperature.

On autopilot, she bundled the rescued greenery in wet newsprint, nesting each inside cardboard containers. She brushed a hand across her skirt, leaving streaks of dark soil on the fabric, and hurriedly tucked a stray hair behind her ear. Kneeling on the ground, she felt the gritty earth cling to her fingertips, and as she adjusted her shirt, more dirt flaked off her arms, swirling around her in her hasty movements. Each smudge was a physical reminder of her divided life.

The car's trunk squeaked as she loaded it, carefully positioning the cartons to avoid tipping. Her fingers lingered on the last pot of echinacea, its bright blossoms vivid in the crowded box. *The warrior flowers.* She gently nestled it among the others and closed the trunk.

She climbed the worn steps of the mobile home, each creak a comforting sound after her time there. Her heart hammered against her ribs as she reached for the doorknob. Through the frosted glass, she saw Vincent's silhouette moving in the kitchenette.

The door creaked as she stepped inside. Vincent didn't glance from the countertop, his posture rigid beneath his well-worn jacket. An uncomfortable quiet settled between them, heavy with unspoken feelings and a past they couldn't escape. She closed the door; the sharp snap reverberated in the confined space.

Vincent walked out of the kitchen into the living room, his frame stark against the setting sun streaming through the window. She followed him like a lost ghost, her footsteps silent on the worn linoleum floor. An undeniable tension filled the small space, its presence palpable and weighty. He stood motionless, his gaze fixed on the chipped paint peeling from the windowsill. Elizabeth stopped a few feet away, her hands clenching and unclenching in her pockets. The silence stretched between them, thick and suffocating. It was the same silence they'd wrestled with at every painful crossroad of their friendship, the silence that spoke volumes about the unresolved chasm between them.

Finally, Vincent turned, his eyes meeting hers. They were dark pools reflecting the fading light, an intensity that both ignited and frightened her. He was the storm she both craved and dreaded. He took a step toward her, then stopped, his expression indecipherable. He reached out a hand, his fingers hovering just inches from her cheek.

Elizabeth held her breath, her body instinctively leaning into his touch. But he didn't touch her. Instead, he withdrew his hand, leaving

HEART VS. HEAD

her aching for a connection she wasn't sure she deserved.

21

Breaking Boundaries, Tangled Hearts

Elizabeth watched Vincent move methodically through Uncle Leo's belongings, sorting what to keep and what to leave behind. His movements were precise, almost mechanical, like he was trying to distance himself from the emotional weight of the task. He paused at the shelf above a small metal cabinet, reaching for something half-hidden behind a stack of worn paperbacks. The old digital camera emerged, covered in a thin layer of dust. Elizabeth recognized it immediately - the Canon Rebel she'd helped him carefully package and ship out years ago as a gift for his uncle.

"Can't believe he kept this," Vincent muttered, turning the camera over in his hands. His thumb brushed across the scratched LCD screen. "I'm sure it still has the same memory card in it. Probably didn't even use the thing."

Vincent popped open the card slot and extracted the tiny SD card. He studied it for a moment before slipping it into his pocket. The camera itself got tossed into his bag with barely a second glance. The casualness of his actions made Elizabeth's chest tighten. That camera had been Vincent's first step toward becoming a photojournalist, and seeing him handle it so dismissively felt wrong. But she kept quiet, understanding that everyone processed grief differently. She watched as he stuffed more clothes into his duffle bag, her heart heavy. The dry, musty trailer air brought back memories of their time together in foreign lands. Each item he packed felt like another thread snapping off their shared life.

"You know this isn't you, Liz." Vincent zipped the bag closed with a harsh finality. "Small town life, playing politics -this place will suck the life right out of you."

Her eyes welled over. He wasn't wrong. The thrill of exposing bad actors, of feeling the adrenaline rush of the chase, was a part of her life she couldn't easily give up. But something had changed in her during these weeks back home. The flood, Uncle Leo's death, the community's fight to survive -it had awakened a different kind of purpose.

"I need to see this through, Vin." Her voice came out steadier than she felt. "These people, they're not just a story anymore."

Vincent stepped closer, his dark eyes searching hers. "Then this is where our story ends."

His fingers brushed her cheek, sending a familiar spark through her skin. She closed her eyes tightly, trying to hold back the hot tears that threatened to spill. The choice before her felt impossible -stay and build something solid with Noah, fight for this town that had both wounded and healed her or return to the exciting but rootless life she'd shared with Vincent. Her career, her identity as a journalist, had been her shield against vulnerability for so long. Laying it down terrified her.

The power of Vincent's presence, so close yet already feeling distant, made her chest ache. Tomorrow he would leave, taking with him a piece of who she was, who they'd been together. The thought of never again sharing a laugh over bad coffee in some remote village or feeling the electric current of their partnership in the field cut deep into her heart.

"I'll be gone by tomorrow night," Vincent said, zipping a side pocket of the bag closed. "There's something brewing in Colombia that could use my eyes."

The familiar pull of adventure tugged at her core —the thrill of chasing leads, dodging danger, capturing truth through their lens. But something else held her in place now, roots she never expected to grow in Sweetwater's soil.

"The town needs help rebuilding," Elizabeth said, her voice barely above a whisper. "They need someone to tell their story."

Vincent stepped closer, his familiar scent of leather and spice filling her senses, drawing her in. "They have Noah for that. You're meant for bigger things, Kitten"

Hearing that nickname this time brought a rush of memories she wasn't prepared for. How many times had he whispered it in bombed-out hotel rooms or hidden jungle camps? The images flooded back —their first meeting in that Cairo marketplace, teasing kisses in Vietnamese safe houses, the way he always had her back when things went sideways. But Sweetwater had changed her. These were her people now, their pain was her pain. The thought of walking away made her feel empty somehow.

"I can't leave them," she said, meeting his intense gaze. "Not now."

Vincent nodded slowly, understanding and disappointment warring in his expression. "Twenty-four hours. If you change your mind, you know how to find me."

Elizabeth wrapped her arms around herself, fighting the urge to grab that duffle bag and run with him toward their next adventure. Instead, she watched him, her eyes brimming with tears, as he walked toward the trailer's door, each step seeming to widen the chasm between their lives.

"Wait."

She could feel the blood rushing in her ears, a loud, throbbing pulse, as she took a deep breath and made her decision. With trembling fingers, she reached for the buttons of her navy blazer, slowly undoing them one by one. Vincent's eyes widened, a flicker of desire mingling with confusion in his eyes. She slipped the jacket from her shoulders, then moved to the delicate buttons of her silk blouse. With a deep breath, she unfastened them, letting the blouse fall open. Her fingers found the zipper of her pencil skirt, the sound of metal teeth parting seemed loud in the quiet room. The skirt slid down her legs, pooling at her feet. She stepped out of it gracefully, standing before him in only a pair of her favorite lace panties and matching bra, the pearl necklace and earrings catching the light. The air between them pulsed with an almost palpable intensity. as she hooked her fingers into the sides of her panties and slid them down her legs, revealing herself to him inch by tantalizing inch.

Just one last time. One last memory before I lock away this part of myself forever.

Vincent swallowed hard, his Adam's apple bobbing as he took in the sight of her naked body. He hadn't seen her like this in months —lean and lithe from their nomadic lifestyle, but still curved in all the right places. His gaze lingered on the small tattoo on her hipbone—a reminder of their time together deep in the Amazon rainforest— before meeting hers again. Her hands trembled as she reached behind her back to unclasp her bra, letting it fall away from her full breasts. Her nipples hardened under his heated stare, betraying the desire coursing through her.

Vincent's chest rose and fell erratically as he took in every inch of her exposed skin —every freckle and scar that told a story of their shared past adventures. The tent of his pants revealed his arousal, and Elizabeth felt a surge of power, knowing that even after all this time apart, she still held this control over him. *Every scar, every mark on my body –he was there. He knows the story behind each one. We wrote those stories together.*

She stood before Vincent, her heart pounding as she bared herself completely to him. The cool trailer air caressed her naked skin, sending a shiver down her back. Her mind raced, a jumble of emotions warring within her –desire, uncertainty, a deep ache at the thought of losing him. She reached for him instinctively, craving his touch. *Maybe this isn't goodbye. Maybe it's my body telling me what my head won't admit.*

Her fingers found the hem of his t-shirt, ready to tug it over his head and explore the planes of his chest. But Vincent caught her wrists in one large hand, holding them still. His eyes met hers, dark and stormy with conflicted emotion. For a moment, they stood like that, the tension between them nearly unbearable.

Then with a low growl that sent heat curling in Elizabeth's belly, Vincent pulled her to him. One strong arm banded around her waist while he cradled the back of her head with his other hand. He lifted her effortlessly against his chest as he carried her toward the bedroom door.

She wound her arms around his neck on instinct, pressing closer to soak up his heat. She buried her face into the crook of his neck as he shouldered open the door and kicked it shut behind them. The room was dimly lit by the setting sun spilling through the sheer curtains, casting shadows over the simple bed and dresser.

Vincent laid Elizabeth down on top of the quilted coverlet with surprising gentleness for such a big man. She watched from beneath lowered lashes as he straightened above her, drinking in every detail of his rugged features - strong jaw clenched tight, dark eyes burning into hers with barely restrained hunger. Slowly he stripped off his shirt first and then pants until he loomed naked over her - all chiseled muscle, and scarred skin telling stories of their shared battles overseas.

Elizabeth's breath hitched at the sight of him.

Her body trembled as she felt Vincent's warm breath on her thighs, inching closer to the source of her desire. His eyes met hers, a mix of hunger and dominance in their depths. He kissed his way upward, his tongue flicking out to taste every inch of her skin. She arched her back, moaning softly as he finally reached his destination. His tongue delved into her folds, teasing and probing with a skill that left her breathless.

"Oh god," she gasped as his tongue swirled around her clitoris, expertly coaxing forth a pool of wetness. Vincent looked up at her, a wicked grin on his face, then he continued to feast on her. He knew exactly what buttons to push to send shivers of pleasure coursing through her body.

Her fingers dug into the sheets as the pressure built within her core. "Vin," she moaned louder this time, unable to contain herself any longer. "I... I need you inside me."

He stopped and looked up at her with a mischievous glint in his eyes before shaking his head slowly. "Not yet," he said, returning to his task with renewed vigor. His fingers joined his tongue now, plunging inside of her while he continued to tease and suckle on her clitoris. Elizabeth's hips bucked against his face, her back arching off the bed as the pleasure intensified.

"Vincent, please," she begged, her voice a desperate whimper. "I can't... I need... I need you—"

He pulled away, leaving her gasping and aching for more. "Not yet, Kitten" He stood up, his own arousal commanding her attention. "I want you like this."

My god, the way he looks at me - like he can see straight into my soul. He always could.

She exhaled a deep sigh in frustration as he lowered himself back down between her legs, this time focusing on her other entrance. His tongue teasing and exploring before slipping a finger inside, eliciting a moan from deep within her chest.

"Vinny!" she cried out, clutching at the pillows above her head as he added another finger to the mix, stretching her in preparation for what was to come. "Please... I can't... I'm going to..."

Vincent removed himself once more and climbed up the bed to join her. His eyes were filled with desire as he positioned himself at her slick folds, looking into her eyes as he slowly pushed himself inside of her. Elizabeth gasped as their bodies connected once more after so many weeks apart; it felt both familiar and new all at once. He moved in and out of her slowly at first, their bodies learning each other's rhythms anew before picking up speed until they were both lost in a frenzy of passion. *Yes! Oh fuck yes! That's it!*

Her body trembled as his tongue and fingers electrified her in ways she had only ever dreamed of. He knew her body better than anyone else, and he was using that knowledge to drive her wild with desire.

"Vincent," she panted, "I... I can't... much more."

He groaned low in his throat before picking up the pace even more, driving himself deep within her with abandon. "Let go for me," he said between clenched teeth. "I want to watch you come." His words were like gasoline on the fire raging within Elizabeth's body, and with a helpless cry, she shattered apart, her climax tearing through her like a wildfire. Vincent's name was torn from her lips as wave after wave of pleasure washed over her, leaving her spent and trembling in his arms. He didn't last much longer; with a final, guttural moan, he joined her in the throes of ecstasy.

They lay tangled together for several moments, their breathing ragged and their hearts pounding in time with one another. He must have sensed her inner turmoil because he gently brushed a stray strand of hair away from her face before leaning down to press a chaste kiss to her forehead. "I know this complicates things," he said softly, "but I've never stopped wanting you."

Elizabeth looked up at him, searching his eyes for any hint of deception or regret. Instead, she found only sincerity and desire. His gentle caresses were like balm to her aching body, his hands tracing soothing patterns across her skin. She leaned into his touch, savoring the comforting heat of his palms against her fevered flesh. His fingers danced along her curves, stroking away the residual tension that lingered in her muscles from their passionate encounter.

"Shh," he murmured against her hair, "Everything's alright now." The deep rumble of his voice vibrated through his chest, providing an additional source of relief as she pressed herself closer to him.

Elizabeth knew that this moment wouldn't last - they were worlds apart in more ways than one, and the reality of their situation would soon intrude upon the cocoon they'd created for themselves. But for now, she wanted nothing more than to lose herself in Vincent's powerful presence, to let his steady heartbeat and solid warmth chase away any lingering fears. She buried her face in the crook of his neck, inhaling deeply of his scent. His arms tightened around her reflexively as he continued to stroke her back, each touch sending little zings of sensation along her nerve endings.

"You good?" he asked after a moment, tilting his head so that he could look into her eyes.

She nodded mutely, not trusting herself to speak past the lump forming in her throat. She knew what this meant - or rather, didn't mean - but right now it was enough to simply be here with him like this. To bask in the aftermath of their shared passion and pretend that there was no tomorrow waiting beyond the bedroom of that old trailer. He seemed content with that answer because he merely hummed lowly before shifting them so that she was tucked securely against his side once more. His hand settled on her hip possessively as if worried she might try to slip away during the night. Little did he know just how much she wanted to stay right here as long as possible.

Tomorrow he'd leave, taking with him the only person who truly understood her hunger for adventure, her refusal to look away from hard truths. The only one who'd never asked her to be smaller, safer, more predictable. She could pretend all she wanted that staying in Sweetwater Springs was the right choice, the mature choice. But lying here, feeling Vincent's heartbeat against her palm, breathing in his scent that reminded her of a thousand shared stories, she knew she was only fooling herself. Each tick of the clock felt like a betrayal, another moment closer to goodbye. Another step toward becoming someone she wasn't sure she wanted to be.

As sleep began to steal over her limbs and drag down their heavy lids, Elizabeth pressed a soft kiss to Vincent's jawline before nestling closer still into his warmth. Tomorrow would bring its own challenges - questions and complications that would have to be dealt with sooner or later. But for now? Now it was enough simply to be together like this.

As Vincent closed his eyes and his breathing became deep and hypnotic, she slipped away to the bathroom, desperate for a few minutes alone with her racing mind. She turned on the shower and stepped under the spray, wincing slightly as the warm water hit her tender body. Closing her eyes, she tried to process the whirlwind of emotions and sensations coursing through her. It had been years since she had felt so alive, so desired, so... wicked in all the right ways.

As she lathered up with soap, she relived every single moment of their encounter: Vincent's skilled fingers teasing her most sensitive spots; his thickness stretching her; his low growls and dirty talk pushing her over the edge into an abyss of pleasure she had never known. Lost in her thoughts, she didn't hear the bathroom door open or the sound of the shower stall door sliding open. It wasn't until a strong arm wrapped around her waist that she realized she was no longer alone. She gasped and turned around to find Vincent, naked and erect, a sly grin on his face.

"I thought you could use some... company," he said, his voice dripping with sarcasm as he pressed himself against her damp backside. "Let me help you with that."

Without waiting for a response, he took the soap from her trembling hand and began to lather up his own palms before starting at her ankles. His touch was firm yet tender as he massaged the tension from her sore muscles, working his way up her calves and thighs. Elizabeth bit back a moan as he reached the junction of her thighs, his fingers teasingly circling her swollen folds. She shuddered as his fingers trailed up her sides, his calloused hands rough against her soapy skin. She pressed into his touch, a breathy sigh escaping her lips when he cupped her breasts, his thumbs teasing her hardened nipples.

As Elizabeth moaned into the steamy air, Vincent reached for the showerhead, twisting the knob to adjust the water pressure. He set it on a gentle spray before guiding the nozzle down her body, washing away the soapy suds that clung to her skin. The warm water felt like a thousand tiny fingers caressing her from head to toe, but it was when he angled the stream between her thighs that Elizabeth's knees nearly buckled.

He chuckled at her reaction, his breath hot against her damp neck. "Like that, Kitten?" he whispered, and she could only manage a breathless nod in response. He knew exactly what to do, and he wasn't afraid to use that knowledge against her. To wreck her.

The water danced across her skin, teasing and taunting as it circled closer and closer to her clit without ever quite making contact. Her frustration bubbled over as she sucked in a breath, pushing back against his chest with a desperate arch, urging him to move faster. But Vincent was in control now - and he seemed intent on drawing out her pleasure as long as possible.

"Patience," he whispered into her ear before nipping at her earlobe playfully. "We've got all night."

His words sent a shiver down her spine even as they inflamed her desire. She gripped the shower rod for support as he continued his torturous maneuvers, alternating between broad sweeps of the nozzle across her thighs and stomach with more focused attention on her aching center. He continued his sensual massage, his strong hands guiding the shower nozzle across her quivering body. His voice, deep and husky in her ear, only served to heighten her arousal.

"You're so beautiful, Kitten," his breath hot against her shoulder as his teeth nipped at her skin. "Look at you. So hungry for it."

She gasped, arching her hips into the delicious torment. He chuckled darkly in response, clearly enjoying every second of her undoing. Embarrassment and arousal warred within her at his blunt words, but it only served to further stoke the flames of desire raging within her core. Her breath came in short pants as she struggled to maintain some measure of self-control. But with each pass of his hand and shift of the water's stream, that control slipped away just a little more.

"Vincent," she whined, gripping the shower rod tighter as he circled closer to where she needed him. "Please..."

He nipped at the shell of her ear before whispering, "Show me how much you want it." as he slipped a hand downward to cup her mound possessively. His fingers slid through her slick folds easily, finding that bundle of nerves that had her hips bucking back against him. Vincent groaned lowly at the sensation before slowly sinking two fingers deep inside of her.

"Oh god," Elizabeth panted out, her walls clenching down on him greedily.

"Ready for round two?" he whispered in her ear, sucking her earlobe gently as he withdrew. His hands glided upward along her body with a possessive caress, cupping and cradling the fullness of her breasts as if reclaiming something he had cherished long ago. "What else you want me to do to you? Tell me."

Lost in their heated embrace and entranced by the shower's rhythmic drumming, Elizabeth found herself voicing fantasies she'd never dared speak aloud before. With each request, Vincent's eyes gleamed with a competitive fire, his jaw tightening with each new challenge he accepted. He reached out and turned the knob, shutting off the rushing water.

"Make me feel dirty again," she breathed, her cheeks flushing with desire and shock at her own boldness.

Vincent's low moan sent shivers down her spine, and she felt him harden even more against her. His hands left her breasts and traveled down to her hips, guiding her onto her knees in the shower stall. He positioned himself in front of her, his erection mere inches from her face.

"Is this what you had in mind?" he said, running his fingers through her wet hair before gripping it firmly.

Her heart raced, a frantic drumbeat against her chest, as she met Vincent's intense gaze, his eyes smoldering with an unspoken hunger. She felt a thrill run through her at the command in his voice when he growled out, "Open wide."

Without thinking, she obeyed, parting her lips for him. The tip of his member brushed against them teasingly before he pressed forward, slipping past wet lips and over her tongue. Elizabeth moaned around the thick intrusion, tasting salt and musk that only made her crave more. He groaned out above her as she began to suckle him slowly. One hand cradled the back of her head while the other gripped her shoulder possessively squeezing her flesh between his fingers.

"That's it," he praised huskily urging her on, "That's a good girl."

A low purr escaped her, the vibrations tingling along his length as she took him deeper. He hissed in pleasure when she relaxed her muscles, allowing him to push further until her nose was nestled in his curly pubic hair. *I can feel his pulse in my mouth. He's so hard and needy right now. And I'm the one making him like this.*

Elizabeth's head swam with a mix of sensations as Vincent abruptly pulled out of her mouth. Before she could catch her breath, he hauled her up to her feet, spinning her around to face the shower wall. His hands found her breasts almost instantly, kneading and pinching with a rough urgency that made her gasp and press into his touch. She raised her arms above her head in total surrender, fingers wrapping around the showerhead for support.

"Tell me you want this," he commanded, eyes blazing with lust as they locked gazes.

Her heart fluttered at the power in his voice -but so did the desire that coiled tightly in her center. She wanted him more than air right now.

"I... I want it," she panted out finally, shamelessly pushing back against him.

Grabbing a towel from the rack beside them without warning, he twisted her wrists above the shower bar, securing them in place with a few swift turns, leaving her arms stretched high and granting him access to every inch of her body. She hesitated for a beat before acquiescing, parting her legs to give him total dominance over her pleasure. *This is new territory... I've never let anyone take control like this before.*

He wrapped his arms tightly around her, his hard body against hers, setting her aflame with desire once again. Elizabeth gasped as she felt Vincent's hot length pressing against her lower back, his chest warm against her skin.

"You're so goddamn beautiful, Liz."

His hands roamed over her body possessively, cupping and caressing every inch of exposed skin. He tweaked a nipple between his fingers before trailing down to tease at the junction of her thighs once more. And when Vincent found that spot that drove her wild, she curved her back and let out a needy cry, unable to resist the overwhelming sensations coursing through her body. A part of her wanted to push back, to assert her control. But another part... a stronger part... wanted to give in completely.

"Yes, please..." she breathed out shakily, a thrill of excitement running through her at being bound and completely at his mercy. She had never been one for restraints before, but something about the way Vincent touched her made everything feel right.

"I love it when you beg for it." He said. To emphasize his point, he pinched that bundle of nerves hard enough to have her seeing stars. "I'm going to fuck your ass after I pound this sweet pussy." She felt the heat of his body against her back as he positioned himself between her legs and spread her ass cheeks apart.

"Are you ready for me?" he said in her ear, his hot breath sending tingles across her skin.

"Yes," she whispered on a shaky exhale, pressing back into his touch as much as the towel would allow. She couldn't deny the desire pooling low in her belly, begging to be sated.

"Good girl."

She heard the shower door open, followed by the sound of a zippered pouch. Then Vincent returned to her, his hands pressing against her hips as he positioned himself at her entrance. She felt the head of his penis brush against her opening, sending shockwaves through her body in anticipation. "Lubed," he said lowly, biting down on the cradle of her neck. He looked into her eyes one last time for confirmation before slowly pressing inside of her tight opening, stopping every so often to ensure she was alright. A grunt escaped her lips at the initial burn of being stretched so suddenly around his thick girth. The sensation was a delicious mix of pressure and pleasure that had tears pricking at the corners of her eyes.

"Oh, fuck yeah," she pleaded, her arms straining against the towel that bound her, struggling to adapt to the fullness of his size within her. Her body tensed as Vincent's full length penetrated her, the sensation unlike anything she had ever experienced before. It was both intense and overwhelming, the unfamiliar sensation sending jolts of pleasure and discomfort through every inch of her being. *Relax girl, you said you wanted to try new things. You can do this... Breathe, just breathe through it. He'll stop if you ask him to.*

"Vinny," she sighed, unsure if she should tell him to stop or to continue. His movements were slow and deliberate, as if he could sense her hesitation. He moved in and out of her, each stroke sending a bolt of white-hot heat straight to her core.

"Relax," he breathed in her ear, his hot breath fanning across her neck. "I got you, Kitten." His words were both a comfort and a command, and she relaxed into his arms as he continued his slow, measured strokes. He set a steady rhythm, hips snapping forward to hit a spot deep inside that had her toes curling against the slick shower floor. *It's easing up a bit now. The burning is going away and...*

"Vinnnny," she breathed, her voice ragged, her arms trembling as she fought against the towel's restraint, desperate for him, always wanting more. "Oh god, yes..."

Vincent responded by continuing to penetrate Elizabeth's tightness with a relentless rhythm, his thick shaft stretching her to her limits. His other hand left her clit, instead squeezing her full breasts from behind, pinching and twisting her hardened nipples between his fingers. The duality of pleasure and pain sent conflicting sensations coursing through her, eliciting a stifled yelp from her lips. *My whole body is on fire. So deep and full and aching...*

"That's it, Kitten," Vincent whispered in her ear, his deep voice sending shudders across her writhing body. "You're so damn tight." His words were punctuated by his thrusts.

She gritted her teeth as waves of pleasure swelled inside her. She began to spiral. The combination of sensations was overwhelming—it was all too much.

"Not yet," Vincent insisted, biting down on the shell of her earlobe before soothing it with a hot kiss. "I'm not there yet. Hold on."

Elizabeth cried out, every nerve ending alight with an electric current begging for release.

"You feel so good," Vincent murmured words of admiration, his tone honey-sweet as his lips brushed against the delicate curve of her neck. "I wanna fuck you all night."

His words inflamed something within her -she felt wild and wanton under his touch. Desperate to savor these extraordinary sensations, she fought to hold back, but it was futile -as Vincent drove into her one last time with powerful force, everything unraveled in a blinding release. Her body convulsed as the most intense orgasm of her life ripped through her body, her nails digging into the towel above her head as she arched her back in ecstasy.

"That's it," he encouraged, his fingers gripped her flesh like a vice. "Take all you want. All of it."

Vincent didn't relent, continuing to lavish attention on her sensitive parts until she was reduced to a quivering, spent mess. A broken scream tore from her throat as the pleasure hit her like a tidal wave pulling everything under. And leaving behind a limp rag doll wrecked in its aftermath, with aftershock upon aftershock until her hoarse whispers finally faded away into blissful silence.

As the waves of pleasure finally began to subside, Vincent withdrew and turned her around to face him. She opened her eyes to find him watching her with a smug grin on his face. "I always knew you had it in you, Kitten."

Her breath came in short, ragged gasps as she stared up at him in wonder. "I... I never..." She trailed off, shaking her head in disbelief. *Why did I wait so long to try this?*

He pulled her close, pressing his forehead against hers. "I may not know everything about you," he said, "but I know when a woman wants to be ravished."

A deep flush crept up Elizabeth's neck and across her cheeks at his words. She couldn't deny the truth of them - she had wanted exactly that for so long.

"How can you know me so—?" she whispered softly, her words trailing off in a confused haze.

The question seemed to catch him off guard as he blinked down at her with a furrowed brow before shrugging slightly. "I knew you from Day One," he continued as one large hand cupped the back of her neck possessively while the other gripped her mound, "it was your scent on my fingers after I touched you that first time."

Heat flared low in her belly as the memory of that moment caused Elizabeth to clench around his fingers suddenly.

"You remember that, don't you?" he smiled, noticing the effect his words had on her as her body reached for more of him.

"Yes," Elizabeth admitted breathlessly watching his pupils dilate with desire.

"Bangladesh," he said with slow gentle strokes, caressing her womanhood as she tried to gather herself back to earth, with his cooling kisses up the column of her throat. "The inauguration photoshoot for President Farzana Karim." More soft caresses. "The monsoons came, washed out the roads..." More caresses and quick kisses. "We were trapped alone that night. Remember that night?" His teeth nipped her lower lip.

"Yes." A guttural moan escaped Elizabeth's lips, her thoughts cloudy and disoriented in an intoxicated haze. Her limbs felt utterly useless, dangling limply against the restraints still fastened around her wrists, leaving her body completely exposed and helpless, open to Vincent's every whim as he explored the tantalizing curves of her figure, trailing his fingers along the valley between the swell of her ample breasts, playfully circling her navel before caressing the fullness of her wide hips.

"Oh god, Vin." she swooned needily, writhing under the sensual cravings of her body.

"You emptied my tank," Vincent chuckled and untied her wrists. "That was the last round for tonight." He pressed a soft kiss on her lips and wrapped his arms around her. "You alright?"

"Yeah, I think..." She laughed weakly as she looked up at him, her eyes dazed and blurry from the intense pleasure they had just shared. Her satiated body leaned against his strength, her fingers digging gently into his skin, not wanting the moment to end. She savored the serenity of this moment -a physical closeness that satisfied all of her basic human needs for touch, affection, sex, and emotional connection.

Vincent kissed her tenderly, coaxing her lips open with his own. She tasted the minty freshness of his mouth as he swiped his tongue along her teeth before delving deeper. Their tongues tangled and danced slowly, sweetly, and passionately, as if to claim ownership and stake his mark on her soul, body, and heart. They stayed like that for several minutes; catching their breaths and coming down from their respective highs before Vincent reached for a nearby towel and handed it to her without a word. She accepted it, using it to dry herself off before handing it back to him. They shared a charged look in the steamy mirror, before starting to make their way out of the bathroom.

"That... that was...," Elizabeth started to say, struggling to find the right words to describe the intensity of her emotions.

"Yeah," Vincent finished for her, running a hand through his damp hair. "About that..."

Her heart sank, certain that he was about to drop the "it's been fun but" line. Unexpectedly, he continued speaking, turning to face her and gazing into her eyes, searching for a reaction of either acceptance or refusal. "I know we both have our own lives and commitments. Seems like you've walked away from our work and I'm trying to understand that, but... either way, I never want this to end." He lifted her chin with his fingertips. "Come with me."

Taken aback by his admission, Elizabeth didn't know what to say at first. Part of her wanted nothing more than to throw caution to the wind and dive headfirst into whatever this newfound connection between them could be; another part of her urged caution, reminding her of the last time they tried this whole relationship thing and how it ended in heartbreak for each of them. Their boundaries were safe, necessary.

"Vincent," she started cautiously, "I... I don't know what to say." It wasn't a no, but it wasn't a yes either; she needed time to process everything that had just happened between them before making such a life-altering decision. "Can I think about it?" she asked finally, hating herself for sounding so wishy-washy but unwilling to make any rash decisions she might regret later on down the road. Vincent nodded curtly as if he had expected as much and guided her back to the bedroom.

Elizabeth lay in the afterglow, her body still humming. The persistent jingling of her phone from the living room kept breaking through their intimate silence. Vincent cursed under his breath.

"That damn thing's been going off non-stop."

"Just leave it," Elizabeth murmured, not wanting to disrupt the closeness between them.

"No way. It'll run down your battery, and you'll be bitching about it later." He pulled away from her, the bed shifting. "I'll grab it."

He rolled out of bed, his muscular frame silhouetted in the subdued light as he padded toward the living room. The jingling stopped as he retrieved her phone. She closed her eyes, savoring the lingering sensations on her skin, the tender aches, and muscle spasms within. The bed dipped as he returned, tossing her phone onto her stomach.

Her heart dropped as she looked at the screen. Noah's text glowed bright:

Let's set the wedding date, babe. We need to make it official.

"Vin —" Elizabeth started, pushing herself up on her elbows, but he was already reaching for his clothes. She expanded the message to see:

What do you say? Will you —? followed by a diamond ring emoji.

Cursing herself for not setting a passcode on her new phone, she looked up at Vincent, who had clearly seen the first notification. His face hardened, jaw clenching as he stepped back from the bed.

"I've got to take care of something." His tone was clipped as he pulled on his jeans and grabbed his shirt from the floor. Without another word or backward glance, he stormed out of the bedroom and moments later, the front door slammed shut.

With a sigh, Elizabeth collapsed on the bed, replaying his words in her mind over and over again. The fire between them was still there, as potent as ever; but could they really make it work this time around? They were both different people now; more guarded and world-weary than they were just starting out in the field. Could they put everything behind them and give this a shot? Or would it be nothing more than a temporary distraction before reality came crashing down around them again?

Elizabeth stared at the ceiling fan spinning lazily above Uncle Leo's old bed, the sheets still warm from their bodies. Her phone screen glowed accusingly - Noah's proposal text unanswered. Vincent's abrupt departure left a hollow ache in her chest that she wasn't ready to examine too closely.

"Dammit, Vin," she whispered to the empty room. They'd always been good at the physical part, maybe too good. It made it easy to ignore the deeper currents running between them. But this time felt different. His words about leaving together, about starting fresh - they weren't just post-coital sweet nothings. She rolled onto her side, inhaling his lingering scent on the pillow. Vincent as a partner had always represented freedom, adventure, the thrill of chasing the next big story. Noah meant stability, respectability, a chance to finally belong somewhere. But belonging felt a lot like compromise lately. Her fingers traced the indent where Vincent's head had rested just hours ago. He'd looked at her with such intensity when he'd made his offer, like he was memorizing her face. Like he truly believed she might choose him.

"What if he's right?" The words escaped her lips before she could stop them.

The silence of the trailer offered no answers, only the distant sound of crickets and her own racing thoughts. Vincent could be halfway to anywhere by now, charging headfirst into the next crisis zone. It was what they both did best -run toward danger rather than deal with their feelings.

But something about his parting look nagged at her. It wasn't anger she'd seen in his eyes. It was resignation, like he'd finally accepted what she'd been too afraid to acknowledge all these years. That one day things would end between them, forever.

Elizabeth sat up, wrapping the sheet around herself. Noah's text still waited for an answer. The safe choice. The smart choice. The choice everyone in Sweetwater Springs would understand. So why did it feel like she was about to make the biggest mistake of her life?

As she drifted off to sleep; one thing was for certain though: their night together had changed everything between them - for better or worse remained to be seen.

* * *

Elizabeth sipped her lemon water, her eyes darting around the diner as if she were a spy in enemy territory. Katie's Diner was a popular spot for gossip, and she didn't need her indiscretions with Vincent to become fodder for Harper's column.

Harper sipped her latte, her eyes boring into Elizabeth's with that intensity she used when hunting down a juicy story. The magenta streaks in her hair caught the diner's fluorescent lighting as she leaned forward. "Spill it, girlfriend. You look like you swallowed a whole cactus."

"Noah proposed. By text. Who does that?" Elizabeth's stomach churned just thinking about the message that had popped up on her phone screen last night.

"Shut up! What did he say exactly? Did you accept? Oh my God." Harper's nails drummed against the ceramic mug, her gossip reporter's juices flowing.

"The worst part, Vincent saw it." Elizabeth's voice dropped to barely above a whisper, remembering the look of betrayal that had flashed across his face. "And now he's gone, forever this time."

"Wait, what? Girlfriend." Harper's eyes widened to saucers as she pushed her half-finished latte aside, giving Elizabeth her full attention. "How?"

Elizabeth sighed, setting down her glass with a clatter. "Last night, Vincent and I, we—"

Harper read between the lines immediately. "You two hooked up last night. Wow, Liz. I mean, how did that happen?"

Elizabeth felt the heat creeping up her neck as she recounted the events of the previous evening. "I went out to Uncle Leo's trailer to pick up a few things after I got a text from Jimmy and Vincent showed up for the same reason. One thing led to another and—"

Harper raised an eyebrow, leaning in closer over the table. "Was that the first time you guys—?"

"No, no," Elizabeth stammered, shaking her head. "We've gone at each other before. No big deal, you know, with all the time we're stuck together on field assignments and all. Sometimes you just need to blow off some steam." She shrugged, hoping to convey a nonchalance she didn't feel. "You gotta shake yourself loose a little now and then. You know what I mean."

Harper tilted her head thoughtfully as she stirred more sugar into her drink. "Is that what last night was about? Blowing off a little steam?"

"No," Elizabeth said slowly, picking at a loose thread on her jeans. "No, that's what's bothering me. It wasn't the same, the usual, whatever you wanna call it." She took a deep breath and exhaled. "We did things last night that I — Well, to be honest, woman to woman—" Elizabeth's cheeks flushed at the thought of the different experiences they had explored during sex.

"You don't have to tell me the details if you're not comfortable sharing that part." Harper sipped her latte, a little grin arched at the corner of her mouth.

"It was," Elizabeth said, making a gesture like her mind was blown.

The waitress arrived with a mug of dark roast. "No cream, no sugar." Elizabeth acknowledged it with a distracted nod, her thoughts clearly elsewhere.

Harper held her breath until the woman was out of sight, then leaned forward and whispered, "So, it was different, and you enjoyed it. Two consenting adults. What's the problem?"

"Noah, Noah is the problem." Elizabeth said and planted her face in her hands. "I mean, maybe last night was nothing. Vincent is leaving today. It was just sex, right? Right?"

Harper shrugged and sipped her latte.

Elizabeth rubbed her fingers across her forehead and exhaled heavily, scanning the café to make certain no one could overhear her pathetic confession. "What was I thinking?"

"Let's start there. We'll leave Noah out of it for now. What *were* you thinking when you were with Vincent last night?"

"Nothing, that's the thing. Nothing at all." Elizabeth sighed and stared into her coffee cup as if the answer lay at its murky depths. "It's like my brain shut off completely and I was just—." She confided, her fingers tracing the rim of her coffee mug, as the images from last night flashed before her eyes. "It was like that time we were on assignment on the Big Island," she said, snapping her fingers as the memory surfaced. "Remember when you tried to convince me to try surfing? But I refused."

Harper nodded with a knowing smile. "Girl, you were terrified of the ocean."

"I was, wasn't I?" Elizabeth chuckled, the tension easing from her voice. "But years later, I was in Hawaii with Vincent, and he kept saying, 'You can do it, Liz. You're stronger than you think.'"

"I'm sure he was looking some kinda fine in those swim trunks. Or is he a Speedo kinda guy?" Harper commented, her eyes twinkling. "Asking for a friend."

"Anyway," Elizabeth continued, swirling the coffee in her mug, "after a few weeks of lessons, the instructor, this old Hawaiian guy named Kai, took us out to catch a real wave. A Pōniu, he called it. Said it was a mythical wave, ridden by the gods." A shiver ran down her spine, remembering the sheer power of the ocean that day. "It was huge, Harper. A wall of water. I nearly chickened out."

"But you didn't," Harper said softly, her gaze steady.

Elizabeth shook her head. "Vincent looked at me, right there on the board, with this absolute faith in his eyes. 'You got this,' he said. And I believed him." A small smile touched her lips. "I rode that Pōniu, Harper. Rode it straight through the tunnel." Her voice dropped to a whisper, the memory still vivid. "It was the most exhilarating, terrifying, freeing thing I'd ever done."

She looked up at Harper, the connection between the two experiences suddenly clear. "Last night was like catching that wave. I didn't think, I didn't plan, I just... let myself feel it. Vincent, he knows what I—." She sighed, the weight of her confession settling in her chest. "It's just... with Noah, it's always... different."

Elizabeth hunched closer, searching her confidant's face for understanding. "I didn't have to choreograph or figure things out and help land the plane, you know? Anything he wanted to try, I was up for it. And even more, if he'd asked, to be honest." She took a shaky breath before continuing. "Last night. It was Pōniu all over again."

Elizabeth came back to the present, lifted her cup to her lips, and let out a soft chuckle, shaking her head. "I'm sorry. I know that sounds so silly."

Harper leaned back in her chair with a playful smile on her lips. "Do you know what it *really* sounds like?" she asked in a conspiratorial tone.

Elizabeth searched her friend's face, her brow furrowed in concentration as she sought to understand. "No, what?"

"Trust."

The word hit Elizabeth like a thunderbolt. She sat back, her mind reeling. Trust? With Vincent? Okay sure, he was the best field videographer in the business without question. And she couldn't imagine traveling with anyone else. He'd gotten her out of more than a few sticky situations abroad, advised her on some career moves, and always had her back. Of course, that level of trust was no problem. But with her heart? The concept seemed like a fairy tale, yet it resonated deep within her.

"I... I never thought of it that way," Elizabeth admitted, her voice softened at the revelation.

Harper nodded, the smile still radiating from across the table. "It's rare, Liz. To find someone you can completely let go with, someone who makes you feel safe enough to just be."

Elizabeth's thoughts drifted back to the previous night. The way Vincent's hands had moved over her body, how she'd surrendered to his touch without a second thought. It wasn't just physical; it was emotional, raw, and real.

"But what about Noah?" Elizabeth said, more to herself than to Harper. "What he has to offer... it makes sense. I thought I was building something with him."

Harper's expression brightened. "Honey, building and being are two different things. With Noah, you're always on, always trying to fit into some mold that this town needs you to be. But with Vincent..."

"I'm just me," Elizabeth finished, the realization dawning on her like the first rays of sunrise.

She thought about the ultimatum Vincent had given her. Twenty-four hours to decide if she wanted to leave Sweetwater Springs with him. The clock was ticking, and suddenly, the decision didn't seem as clear-cut as it had before.

"I don't know what to do," Elizabeth confessed, running a hand through her hair.

Harper reached across the table and squeezed her friend's hand. "Listen to your gut, Liz. It's gotten you safe this far, hasn't it?"

Elizabeth nodded, her mind a beehive of conflicting emotions. Trust. Such a simple word, yet it held the immense power to transform everything.

22

Vincent's Last Stand

Elizabeth stood frozen, her champagne flute trembling in her hand. The glittering chandeliers of the Sweetwater Springs Country Club ballroom seemed to mock her. The latest fundraiser for rebuilding their flood-ravaged town had been going so well. Noah's charm was in full force as he worked the room, building up to his big announcement. She had carefully evaluated the opportunities presented by a life with Noah. Stability. Roots. Legacy. It was the confluence of those three factors that prompted her decision, setting in motion a series of promises that irrevocably sealed her fate. She had felt a sense of pride as the campaign plans that she proposed were beginning to take shape already. And she was starting to feel optimistic about their shared future. It was the only logical path forward. The conclusion was uncomplicated.

Then Vincent walked into the room.

Her stomach dropped as soon as she saw him, his face set in grim determination. Before she could react, his voice thundered across the room, silencing the chatter and clinking glasses.

"Noah Montgomery is a goddamn fraud!"

Elizabeth felt the impact of those words like the ground shifting under her feet. She watched, helpless, as Vincent strode through the room and joined them on the platform, brandishing a folder.

"Whoa, hold up, playboy. You don't belong up here." Noah's voice, though laced with annoyance, held a smooth, adept calm as he waved off the intruder. Elizabeth felt his hand tighten on hers.

"Don't tell me where I fucking belong—" Vincent lunged. Elizabeth instinctively stepped between them.

"Liz, I need to talk to you." The desperation in Vincent's voice made her wince.

"If this is about last night, I'm—I'm sorry... I'm so sorry, but—" She shook her head. *No. Not here. Not now.*

"Wait, what happened last night?" Noah's tone sharpened.

"Nothing," Elizabeth said quickly, her cheeks burning.

Vincent's face crumpled. "Oh, it's like that. Okay." His eyes turned dark. "Well, while you were cozying up to this piece of shit, I was doing your damn job."

"This isn't the place, Vin. I know you're upset, but—"

Victoria, sleek and composed, materialized beside them. A sense of dread knotted in Elizabeth's stomach. A showdown was not on the agenda. But what could she do?

"He's in OVAC's pocket, the bastard. He knew about the illegal dumping and toxic spills. He did nothing about it and helped silence the whistleblowers. His constituents need to hear about this." Vincent's words tumbled out, fueled by rage. He held up the tiny memory card from Uncle Leo's camera.

"Wait a minute, you're flirting with a defamation lawsuit." Victoria's voice was ice. "I suggest that you—"

"Who the hell are you?" Vincent snapped.

"I'm the current Acting District Attorney and future Law Director here in Sweet—"

"Oh, I get it. You're part of this mess."

"And who are you?" Victoria said, unmoved.

"He's just a cameraman." Noah said, regaining his composure. "Full of bogus claims, apparently. Cite the sources of your allegations or get the—,"

"I am the goddamn source, mutha-fucker." Vincent grabbed Noah again. Elizabeth struggled to shove them apart, her heart hammering. The crowd below buzzed, a hive of confused murmurs.

"Noah has a point, Vin." Elizabeth said, her voice soft, filled with empathy. "Before we can share any of this publicly, we have to vet the information and verify its credibility. You know that."

Murmurs rippled through the crowd, a growing restlessness, as more eyes focused on the unfolding drama between them. Elizabeth felt lightheaded, struggling to process Vincent's words. It couldn't be true. Noah wouldn't... would he?

Victoria's voice cut through the chaos, sharp and accusing. "Is any of this true, Noah?"

Elizabeth turned to Noah, desperately seeking denial in his eyes. But what she saw there made her blood run cold. Panic, anger, calculation—but not innocence.

"He's lying," Noah said smoothly, but she heard the tremor beneath his words. He pivoted and shifted his attention to the onlookers. "Mr. Rivera has always been jealous. He's trying to sabotage my success."

She wanted to believe him. god, how she wanted to. But a nagging doubt lingered, as Vincent's words had taken root within her soul.

"Noah wouldn't do those things," she heard herself say, her voice sounding distant and hollow. "He cares about this town. And the people in it."

Vincent's eyes softened as they met hers, a mix of pity and frustration in his gaze. "'Keep your friends close and your enemies closer,'" he quoted. "That's his fucking game, Liz. As long as you know what you know, you'll never stand a damn chance with him."

Her world tilted on its axis as Vincent's next words sank in. "You want that asshole? You can have him, or you can have the truth, but you'll never have both."

Elizabeth felt tears burning her cheeks, her certainty crumbling around her.

"With me, you'll always have the truth," Vincent continued, his voice gentler now. "You know where my heart lands. You never have to guess with me, for fuck's sake."

Her breath caught in her throat as she realized what was coming next.

Vincent's shoulders slumped. "Here, do whatever the hell you want with it." He shoved the envelope and memory card into her hands, his touch lingering for just a moment. Then he was gone, leaving her standing amid the wreckage of her carefully constructed plans. She clutched the envelope, feeling the effect of its contents—and the life-altering choice she faced. The truth or the life she thought she wanted. Vincent or Noah.

A storm of confusion swirled around her, she stood still, her heart pounding. She had a decision to make, and for once in her life, she wasn't sure she was ready to face the truth. Her fingers fumbled with the clasp, her eyes quickly scanned the documents. Pictures of Noah with the heads of OVAC and their consortium members. Financial records. Emails.

"You're an investor in OVAC…and Ridgeway Development, and Blackwood Holdings. They're the biggest donors for your mayoral campaign. These are major global polluters on environmental watch lists across every continent. Noah, you knew." The words were barely a whisper, but the accusation hung heavy in the air. "Everything."

"Again," Victoria's eyes were sharp, assessing. "Is this true?"

Noah turned to Elizabeth, his voice a low plea. "Babe, all of that can be explained. But right now, everyone is waiting for our important announcement. Let's not keep them waiting any longer. It's time to kick off my campaign and —our engagement." He took her hand. "I need you by my side. Lizzy— "

"Where's all the money coming from?" The question was out before she could stop it.

"Don't worry about that. I told you I would handle everything. You'll learn how we do things here in Sweetwater. Everything's going to be fine."

Elizabeth turned away and immediately, her gaze locked with Maya, who was surrounded by her team of student reporters, her phone was pointed directly at them, recording every second of her emotional train wreck. She shoved the folder into Victoria's hands, her eyes never leaving the woman's face. Turning away from the stage, she walked into the throng of people, pushing through the crowd and out the door, her footsteps racing down the mud caked, gray-green streets of Sweetwater Springs.

23

The Price of Truth

Elizabeth tossed the last box into her trunk, the cardboard container heavy with Uncle Leo's journals and the potted plants she'd managed to save. Her phone buzzed with another message from Noah, but she left it unread like the dozen others from last night.

The morning sun cast long shadows across Stacy's driveway as Elizabeth slid into the driver's seat. She adjusted her rearview mirror, catching a glimpse of the packed backseat -her life condensed into bags and boxes once again. Her fingers gripped the steering wheel, knuckles tight. The key hung suspended in the ignition as memories flooded over her -of late-night stake-outs with Vincent, quiet gardening sessions with Uncle Leo, stolen kisses with Noah in his office. Each memory felt like a photograph burning at the edges, curling into ash.

Uncle Leo's voice, rough as sandpaper, resurrected in her thoughts, his words as clear as day: "Truth ain't always pretty, but it's the only thing that will last." She remembered his weathered hands showing her how to plant sage, the same hands that had documented every toxic spill and illegal dump in his journal. The same hands they'd found cold and lifeless.

Noah's promises of stability and belonging rang hollow now. His smooth words about handling everything, about teaching her "how things work in Sweetwater" made her nauseous. She thought of Vincent's face at the fundraiser, raw with hurt and betrayal when she'd dismissed their night together as nothing. The folder he had shoved at her sat on the passenger seat. Inside were copies of the photos, documents, and proof of everything - Noah's investment in OVAC, the coordinated effort to silence environmental alerts, the money trail leading straight to Uncle Leo's death. All of it. Her instincts had been right all along, but she'd let Noah's charm blind her to the facts. She glanced at her phone. Maya's unanswered text was still visible on the screen:

Footage from yesterday is ready to go. How do you want me to handle it?

As Elizabeth closed her eyes, the pressing needs of Sweetwater Springs settled upon her, making her heart feel heavy. She'd come back to step into the shadows for a rest, but somehow found a renewed sense of home, the feeling that she finally belonged somewhere. But with a wicked twist of fate, she'd found herself caught between two versions of truth - Noah's carefully constructed facade and Vincent's brutal honesty.

Her hands trembled as they moved from the steering wheel to her lap. The morning light caught the potted echinacea in her boxes on the floorboard next to her feet - warrior flowers, Uncle Leo had called them. Fighting off sickness. Healing what was broken. She typed out her response to Maya, took a deep breath, and steered the car onto the road.

Run it. All of it.

Main Street looked surreal in the harsh morning light. Construction crews were already at work, the sound of hammers and saws filling the air as they rebuilt what the flood had stolen. She drove past the Centennial Community Center -or what remained of it. The place where she'd danced at Stacy's wedding just weeks ago was now a skeleton of wooden beams and memories.

Her phone buzzed again -Stacy's smiling face lighting up the screen. She let it ring, her throat tight. She hadn't said goodbye to her best friend. Couldn't face those kind eyes, that forgiving smile, her sympathetic words that would defend Noah and try to explain away his actions as necessary compromises in small-town politics. But Elizabeth had spent too many years tracking down the culprits at the core of corrupt centers of influence to accept comfortable lies now, even from the people she loved. Her last conversation with Stacy played back as if she were still there -sitting on that worn couch, sharing coffee and swooning over her wedding photos. "Noah really loves you," Stacy had insisted. "He's trying to take care of this town, protect all of us." Her friend's words had been so earnest, so hopeful.

Elizabeth thought of the translated pages of Uncle Leo's journal. Those pages held more truth than all of Noah's eloquent speeches. She imagined each of the medicinal plants dying off one by one, of Leo carefully documenting each loss while the town officials turned a blind eye. Of Vincent, raw and honest, laying out evidence while she'd chosen compromise.

Stacy's voicemail notification pinged. Elizabeth's hand hovered over the phone, then dropped. Some goodbyes were better left unsaid. Some friendships couldn't survive the harsh light of conflict. She held onto the hope that time and distance would act as a buffer while the wounds of their relationship healed.

As she drove past the "Sweetwater Springs Historic District" sign, she felt a sorrowful sense of loss deep within her chest. Vincent had been right - she wasn't meant for cute planning committees and charity galas. Her lens had always focused on hunting down corruption, not concealing it behind polite smiles and partisan handshakes. The image of his face sent a fresh wave of guilt. He'd seen through Noah's facade while she'd been busy trying to reshape herself into someone who could fit into Sweetwater's narrow definitions. Her hands tightened on the steering wheel as she recalled their last night together in Uncle Leo's trailer. The way his touch had awakened something she'd buried deep inside - not just desire, but a fierce hunger for authenticity. With him, she hadn't needed to calculate her words or measure her responses. She'd been free to be herself, messy and imperfect and real.

Noah's carefully crafted life of publicity events felt damning in comparison now. She'd tried so hard to fit into that world, to believe that settling down meant trading her analytical disposition for garden parties and polite conversation. But every time Noah had smoothed over her concerns about OVAC with stale talking points and empty promises, a part of her had died inside.

The magnitude of Uncle Leo's steadfastness, his detailed notes stood as testament to the integrity she'd almost betrayed - that some stories needed to be told, no matter how uncomfortable they made her feel. That's who she was - not Noah's perfectly poised politician's wife-to-be, but a seeker of truth, even when that truth hurt - The Truth Mercenary, for God's sake. What happened to that woman? *Damn it. What a fucking mess I've turned out to be.* She choked back a sob mounting in her throat.

The rising sun painted the sky in beautiful shades of pink and gold along the highway, but Elizabeth barely noticed. Her mind was too full of Vincent's last words at the fundraiser: "You want that asshole? You can have him, or you can have the truth, but you'll never have both."

Noah had shown her two versions of himself: the charismatic politician who could charm a crowd with ease, and the man who whispered promises in the dark. But both versions, she realized, were equally shallow. His world began and ended at the city limits, and he'd never understand why that could never be enough for her.

The "Now Leaving Sweetwater Springs" sign whooshed past, its fresh paint gleaming. Elizabeth slowed down as she approached Echo Ridge. The bulldozers were already there, tearing through the trailer park like hungry beasts. Uncle Leo's garden was gone, reduced to churned earth and broken stems. Soon, there would be nothing left to show he'd ever lived there, nothing but the roots of what he'd died protecting. Elizabeth pressed her foot to the accelerator, leaving behind the dust and destruction.

Oak Grove Cemetery came into view, its iron gates stark against the morning sky. She pulled her car over. Her weary eyes located her parents' headstones positioned on the gentle slope, worn marble marking where they'd been laid to rest after the train derailment. The company had claimed all safety protocols were followed. The government inspectors had signed off on everything. Yet twenty-three people had died that day because someone had cut corners, falsified reports, chosen profit over lives.

Her mother's voice whispered in her memory: "Always ask questions, mija. Even when no one wants to hear the answers."

The cemetery's oak trees cast dappled shadows across the graves, their branches reaching toward heaven like supplicants. How many others lay here because of similar choices? Because people like Noah decided to "handle everything" rather than face uncomfortable confrontations?

Her tears broke free as she thought of Uncle Leo joining her parents beyond this world, another victim of the corrupt culture of silence. His death had been ruled suicide, neat and tidy - just like the railroad investigation, just like the county flood damage reports. Each tragedy wrapped up in bureaucratic ribbons, filed away and forgotten. The pattern was there for anyone willing to see it. *But nobody gives a damn.* Tears streamed down her face, her head pounding with each agonizing sob. She noticed how the morning sun caught the granite angels standing guard over the graves, their faces serene and blind to the corruption rotting their town from within. How many more would join them here, sacrificed to maintain Sweetwater Springs' picture-perfect disguise?

Elizabeth glanced up and noticed storm clouds gathering over the horizon across the bluff behind the cemetery, their dark masses heavy with unshed rain. The wind picked up, rustling through the oak trees and sending dead leaves skittering across her parents' graves. Nature itself seemed to mirror her emotions - turbulent, threatening to break. The approaching clouds reflected on her windshield as they rolled across the darkening sky. How fitting that rain would accompany her departure. Sweetwater Springs had always been good at washing away its inconvenient truths, letting the flood waters carry away evidence of its sins. Just like the train derailment that took her parents, just like Uncle Leo's suspicious death, just like the toxic dumping that Noah had helped cover up. Each time she replayed these deadly scenarios, the sting of grief intensified, and her eyes filled with more tears. The tragedies haunted her, playing on repeat in her mind, each one a broken record stuck on the same agonizing tune. *I've got to get out of here, before I...*

She drove on.

Heavy droplets of rain began to fall, leaving trails of water mirroring her own tears across the windshield. Behind her, the cemetery's iron gates stood sentinel, guarding generations of secrets buried beneath manicured grass and polished stone. How many other stories lay drowned beneath Sweetwater's surface, masked by rehearsed excuses and affected smiles from those in power. A gust of wind rocked her car, and thunder rolled across the sky. The storm was moving fast, just like the floods that had swept through town, suspicious in their timing and devastating in their impact. She switched on the wipers, watching them sweep away the rain just as efficiently as Noah's smooth words had tried to sweep away her doubts.

She accelerated onto the highway, her windshield wipers fighting against the downpour. The sudden storm matched her true self - wild and untamed, refusing to be contained by Sweetwater Springs' neat boundaries. Her hands turned the steering wheel as she merged into traffic, muscle memory taking over while her mind tumbled through more regrets and what-ifs. The folder of evidence shifted in the passenger seat, as the car hydroplaned, and she maneuvered it back onto the road. She brought the documents to her lap, committed to ensuring that the official report would not suppress the details of Leo's death. The facts would come out, not through Noah's expertly manufactured press releases, but through her own words - unfiltered.

Her phone buzzed again. Noah's name flashed on the screen, but she didn't need to read his message. She could already hear his smooth voice trying to explain everything away, making promises about their future together. But she wasn't that person anymore - if she ever had been.

The highway stretched before her, a ribbon of asphalt cutting through the Ohio countryside. Each mile marker put more distance between her and the lies. The rain pelted her car harder now, but Elizabeth punched the accelerator, feeling a surge of adrenaline - the same rush she got from pressing beyond the gaggle of reporters and landing the exclusive that broke in the opening credits, capturing international attention. Her rear-view mirror showed only gray sheets of rain, obscuring the town she was leaving behind. Sweetwater Springs grew smaller, its rebuilt facades and carefully maintained illusions shrinking until they disappeared completely.

24

Epilogue: A New Chapter

Elizabeth leaned back against the faux leather seat of the shuttle van, her eyes fixed on the small screen of her phone. The landing strip of the Ohio Valley Regional Airport rolled by outside the window, but her attention was captivated by her own image on the screen, delivering what would be her final report from the town that had both broken and restored her.

"As Sweetwater Springs begins to rebuild and heal," her recorded voice echoed from the phone's tinny speakers, "we're reminded of the resilience of this community and the impact of those who fought to protect it."

A lump formed in Elizabeth's throat as she watched herself speak about Uncle Leo's legacy. The absence of Vincent's steady camerawork was painfully apparent in the shaky, self-recorded footage. She had grown dependent upon his presence, his silent support behind the lens. Now, watching herself in the awkward framing, she felt truly alone.

The van hit a pothole, jolting Elizabeth back to the present. She glanced around at her fellow passengers—strangers heading to the airport, each lost in their own world. None of them knew the gravity

EPILOGUE: A NEW CHAPTER

of the decision that sat heavy on her shoulders.

As the video concluded, Elizabeth's finger hovered over the screen, hesitating before she finally closed the browser. The reflection in the darkened screen stared back at her—a woman caught between worlds, between the truth she'd uncovered and the relationships she'd left behind.

Her phone buzzed with a text from Stacy:

Are you really leaving? Please call me.

Elizabeth released a heavy sigh. Sad that she had slipped away without goodbyes, unable to face the disappointment and hurt in her friend's eyes. And her naïve optimism that she had grown to disdain. The truth had come at a cost, and that cost was the life she'd begun to imagine for herself in Sweetwater Springs.

Another message popped up, this time from Noah:

We need to talk about your video. What you've done...
It's causing more harm than good. Was that your intent?
Are you—

She couldn't bring herself to read the rest. The pain of his betrayal was still raw, the memory of his duplicity still bitter. She could feel the shockwaves hammering against her soul since she posted her report across social media and local cable. She had chosen truth over love, over the comfort of belonging. But as the van carried her further from Sweetwater Springs, she wondered if she'd made the right choice. The faces of her friends, of Stacy and her son, flashed through her mind—innocent bystanders caught in the blast radius of exposed corruption. Yet deep down, she knew that the pain of truth, however sharp, was better than the slow poison of lies that had been killing the town she once called home.

Elizabeth stepped into the airport terminal, her carry-on bag slung over her shoulder, dragging the storage box of memories behind her. The familiar odor of jet fuel and overpriced coffee filled her nostrils as she made her way to the check-in counter. Her mind was already sprinting ahead to her next assignment in the Republic of Congo, a world away from her shattered hometown.

While waiting in line, she pulled out her phone and scrolled through the briefing on the upcoming story. The standoff between UN peacekeepers and protesters over the use of child labor in cobalt mines was a powder keg waiting to explode. It was exactly the kind of hard-hitting journalism she had built her career on, but one nagging concern crept into her thoughts: her new cameraman, Sean. They had worked together before, but the memory of their lackluster coverage at the Cannes Film Festival did little to instill confidence. The shipyard workers' strike had barely made a ripple in the news cycle, and Sean's inexperience had shown through in every poorly blocked frame. Elizabeth sighed, running a hand through her hair. The Congo was a far cry from the glitz and glamor of Cannes. Volatile situations required a steady hand and nerves of steel behind the camera. She wondered if Sean was up to the task.

As she approached the counter, her thoughts drifted to Vincent. His absence felt like a physical ache, a void where his reassuring presence should be. She had grown dependent on his intuitive understanding of her needs in the field, the way he could capture the heart of a story without a word passing between them.

"Next, please," the airline attendant called, snapping Elizabeth back to the present.

She stepped forward, fishing out her passport and ticket. As she handed them over, Elizabeth pushed aside her doubts about Sean

EPILOGUE: A NEW CHAPTER

and the lingering thoughts of Vincent. She had a job to do, and she would do it to the best of her ability, regardless of who was behind the camera.

Elizabeth settled into her seat on the plane, her mind already formulating plans for her new field assignment. She'd make a few calls during her layover in Florida and maybe get a massage. Her muscles throbbed with the strain of the tension she had been holding onto. As she reached up to stow her carry-on luggage, a familiar hand intercepted hers.

"I got it," Vincent said, effortlessly lifting the bag into the overhead compartment. "Take the window seat."

Stunned, Elizabeth slid into the seat, her heart pounding as Vincent sat down next to her. She fumbled for her phone, quickly tapping out a message to Fred's cellphone at the assignment desk:

What is Vincent Rivera doing on this plane?

The response came almost immediately:

Ask him

She turned to Vincent, her brow furrowed. "Did you watch my wrap-up on the news from Sweetwater Springs?"

Vincent's eyes remained fixed ahead. "No. All I cared about in that town was scattered over Togan's Bluff," he said referring to Leo's ashes.

The bitter acknowledgment filled the space between them with unspoken grief. *Rest in Power, Uncle Leo.* Elizabeth swallowed hard. "That's fair. But then, how did you know that I was—?"

"That you'd be headed to Tallahassee on the next flight out?" Vincent finished for her. "I trusted that you'd do the right thing."

Her gaze lingered on his profile, searching for clues in his expression. "Have you taken on a new assignment?"

"Yep."

"The UN peacekeepers?"

"That's the one."

Confusion flickered across Elizabeth's face. "I thought Sean was on my team."

"I convinced him to change his mind."

As the plane began to taxi, Elizabeth felt a mix of relief and tension as she settled into her seat next to Vincent. His unexpected presence both comforted and disturbed her. She turned to him, a nervous smile playing on her lips. "You're good at that, convincing people to change their mind," she said.

"You don't need anyone to help you with that, Liz." Vincent's eyes met hers for the first time, his expression noncommittal. "You know what's best for you."

Her smile faded, still trying to gauge how to navigate the conversation. "You mean 'who' is right for me. Right?"

Without responding, he signaled the flight attendant and requested a blanket for her. As the attendant draped the soft fabric over them, Elizabeth seized the moment, sliding her hand along his thigh beneath the cover.

Vincent's body tensed. "It's a short flight," he murmured, his voice low.

"I like the pressure," Elizabeth replied, her tone playful yet charged. "It's when I do my best work." She paused, her expression growing serious. "I never thanked you for all the work you did to uncover the plans Noah and his people had for Sweetwater. I know it had to be tough for you. I owe you, Vin."

Vincent's hand clamped down on hers, arresting its movement. "Does the sun owe the shadow?" he asked cryptically.

EPILOGUE: A NEW CHAPTER

She frowned, her eyes full of questions. "What- what are you saying?"

His grip hardened, unyielding as iron, holding her hand firmly in place, unwilling to let her pull away. "I'm saying you don't owe me anything," Vincent replied, his voice firm.

Elizabeth's heart ached, her hand still resting on his thigh beneath the blanket. His scent, a mix of spice and musk, mingled with the stagnant airplane air, bringing back vivid memories of their intimate time together. She felt a desperate need for reassurance that their friendship hadn't been lost in the mess of Sweetwater Springs. Her eyes searched his face, trying to gauge his feelings. The tension between them was palpable, electric. In that moment, she understood just how deeply she needed him, how essential he was to her life, in whatever way that might unfold. She had abandoned and betrayed him. And yet, despite everything, here he was, a reassuring presence in the face of uncertainty. The fissure in their relationship worried her, leaving her feeling exposed and uncertain, like a raw nerve.

As if reading her insecurity, Vincent lifted her hand to his lips and placed a soft kiss into her open palm. The tender gesture sent shivers through her body. He then rested her hand on his chest, over his heart. She could feel its steady rhythm beneath her fingers.

"I'm asking for an upgrade," he said, his voice both hushed and forceful. "I don't ever want to get that close to losing you again."

Elizabeth's heart swelled, threatening to burst through her chest. Before she could respond, he leaned in and captured her mouth in a deep, passionate kiss. Everything beyond their embrace disappeared as Elizabeth surrendered to the tenderness of his lips. Breaking the kiss, Vincent spoke in a husky whisper, "Tell me I'm that guy, Liz, or I'll jump out this mutha-fuckin' plane."

Elizabeth's lips curved into a smile, her eyes sparkling. "Is that right? Should I alert the pilot that we've got a jumper?"

Vincent's jaw, tight with a fierce protectiveness she'd only glimpsed before, relaxed as his thumb brushed a stray tear from her cheek. His eyes, usually guarded and intense, softened with a helplessness that disarmed her. A flicker of vulnerability mirrored her own as he held her gaze. The iron grip on her hand relaxed, replaced by a gentle caress that spoke volumes of the depth of his affection. For the first time, Elizabeth saw not just the hardened adventurer, but the man beneath, the one who would risk everything for her. A boyish smile spread across his face.

"Well, if you're a jumper," Elizabeth murmured, leaning in closer. "I'm a mutha-fuckin' parachute."

Love danced in his eyes, a chuckle struggling to escape. "So, we're in this thing together for real this time?"

Her spirit soared as she kissed him again, pressing soft, sweet kisses while pouring all her love and commitment into each touch, whispering tenderly against his mouth. "Together. Forever."

The words lingered between them, heavy with promise and electric with excitement. She felt a rush of warmth spread through her body, a sense of rightness settling over her. Vincent's arms tightened around her back, pulling her closer in the confined space of their airplane seats.

She inhaled deeply, something uniquely him that made her feel grounded. Her heart raced, not from the anticipation of their upcoming assignment, but from the realization that this was it. This moment, the culmination of a silent longing, was finally here, and she felt a sense of exhilaration that she couldn't explain.

The flight attendant's voice crackled over the intercom, reminding passengers to fasten their seatbelts for takeoff. Elizabeth reluctantly pulled away from Vincent, her fingers lingering on his chest as long as possible until she finally reached for her seatbelt.

As the plane began to taxi down the runway, she glanced out the window at the receding airport. Sweetwater Springs and all its complications seemed to shrink away, becoming nothing more than a distant memory. She turned back to Vincent, finding his eyes already on her, warm and full of assurance. She intertwined her fingers with his. The enormity of their commitment settled over her, not as a weight, but like a comforting blanket. She knew there would be challenges ahead—dangerous assignments, long separations, the constant dance of balancing their personal and professional lives. But for the first time in a long while, Elizabeth felt truly anchored.

She turned back to Vincent, studying his face. The lines around his eyes, the set of his jaw - it all felt like coming home. But there was something new there too, an openness she hadn't seen before. Vincent held his phone out to her, the screen displaying the breaking news headline from Reuters. Her eyes widened as she read about the investigation launched by Global Environmental Justice Watch.

"Three states?" she breathed, scanning the article. "They're going after the whole Ohio River Valley Aggregates Corporation and their partners."

Vincent nodded, scrolling to show her more details. "Look at this - over two hundred FOIA requests filed in the past 24-hours alone. Environmental agencies, zoning boards, county commissioners - they're hitting everyone involved."

Elizabeth's pulse quickened as she recognized several names from their Sweetwater Springs investigation. Officials who had stonewalled her requests for comments were now facing scrutiny from international regulators.

"The consortium's gone dark," Vincent said, his voice a strained whisper against the engine noise around them. "Not a single statement from any of the major players. Even their PR firms are declining to comment. They're all running scared."

Elizabeth smiled as she spotted Noah Montgomery's name among the local officials dodging interview requests. Her decision to pass Vincent's evidence to the activists had sparked exactly the kind of investigation she'd hoped for - one too big for local politics to sweep under the rug.

"Maya must have connected with the right people," she said. "This is way bigger than just Sweetwater Springs now."

"You did that, Liz. You gave them the match to light the fire."

"Noah," she whispered, shaking her head. Her words were almost drowned out by the hum of the engines. "So many red flags. How could I be so stu—"

"You don't have to talk about it." He squeezed her hand gently.

She nodded, grateful. Her return to Sweetwater Springs had been a rollercoaster of emotion and revelation. She had thought she was ready to settle down, to become someone else. But sitting here next to Vincent, she realized she had been running from herself.

Elizabeth pulled up a video on her phone, this one from Maya. The young reporter stood in front of the Historic Community Center construction site, her confidence evident in her steady delivery.

"In a surprising turn of events," Maya reported, "LM Enterprises, a newly registered Ohio corporation, has proposed an innovative reconstruction plan for Sweetwater Springs. The company, named in honor of the late Leonard Montoya, aims to implement sustainable building practices using designs originally created by journalist Elizabeth Nelson's father, the esteemed local architect, Henry Nelson."

The camera panned to show Jimmy White Cloud reviewing blueprints with a group of community members, his new role as local agent for LM Enterprises bringing a sense of purpose to his stance. The yarrow flower tattoo on his forearm, his tribute to Uncle Leo, was visible as he pointed out details in the plans.

"The proposed designs incorporate solar power and renewable materials," Maya continued, "marking a dramatic shift from traditional construction methods. Local resident Jimmy White Cloud explains the significance."

The footage cut to Jimmy, his expression both solemn and hopeful. "These plans honor two legacies," he said. "The innovative spirit of Henry Nelson and the environmental wisdom of Leonard Montoya. We're not just rebuilding –we're healing."

Her eyes filled with emotion as the video showed Stacy standing among the community members, her little boy perched on her hip. "The community will heal," Stacy's words echoed in Elizabeth's memory. "We always do."

The final shot panned across Uncle Leo's garden, now preserved as part of the reconstruction project. Maya's voice carried over the image: "As Uncle Leo often said, 'The earth will reclaim what was lost if we give it a chance.' With these new initiatives, Sweetwater Springs is doing just that–giving the earth, and this community, a chance to heal and grow stronger."

Elizabeth clicked off the video, her vision blurring with tears. She had done what she could to help Sweetwater Springs move forward, even if she couldn't stay. The paperwork she'd filed in Columbus with the Secretary of State before leaving felt like her final gift to the town–a way to honor both her father's legacy and Uncle Leo's kindness toward her.

Vincent's fingers intertwined with hers beneath the blanket, his touch grounding her in the present moment. "You did good, Kitten," he said. "Real good."

"I'm sorry," she said, daring to make eye contact without breaking down again. "I'm sorry I tried to be someone I'm not. I thought... I thought I could make it work. But you were right. That's not who I am." She brushed back a tear. "Or could ever be."

Vincent's eyes softened. "You don't need to apologize. We all get lost sometimes."

Elizabeth felt a weight lift from her shoulders. She had been carrying the guilt from reporting her expose on Sweetwater Springs knowing the fallout would be swift and severe, the pain she caused Stacy by running off without a sideways glance, the betrayal she felt from Noah. But here, thousands of feet above the ground, she felt like she could finally breathe again.

After the death of her parents, she had fought her way through life with a fierce determination to approach everything as black or white, right or wrong, truth or lies. She had refused to live in the gray places. And it had worked for her. Until the return to Sweetwater Springs revealed that real life happens in the shadowy spaces where her insecurities continually battle against trust. Uncle Leo had opened the door for her to look inside her own heart. It forced her to finally gather up her fears and step in with both feet, feeling her way through the fog and rubble, bumping into past versions of herself and false identities she had worn like armor. She was in that space now and there was no going back. Today, as she stepped inside another chamber, there was someone already there, waiting to help her feel safe and surround her with his light whenever she lost her way.

"So," she said, a hint of her old mischief creeping into her voice. "The Congo. You ready for this?"

Vincent grinned, the familiar spark of adventure lighting up his eyes. "With you? Always."

Cast of Characters

Elizabeth Nelson
a.k.a. The Truth Mercenary

Brave and Fearless: Elizabeth thrives in high-pressure environments and her journalistic career has exposed her to numerous dangerous situations, from war-torn countries to natural disasters. Her bravery is not just about physical safety; it's also about emotional courage. She often faces societal norms and personal risks head-on, whether it's standing up for a vulnerable witness in an interview or challenging established narratives in her reporting. However, this bravery does not translate to her personal life. She's often paralyzed by insecurities when confronted with vulnerability in intimate relationships. Insecure when approaching romantic relationships, does not commit easily, prefers casual sexual encounters but inwardly wants to settle down in monogamous marriage.

Resourceful and Adaptable: Constantly on the move, she possesses a quick wit and is capable of thinking on her feet. Whether it's troubleshooting a problem with her equipment or navigating a challenging cultural landscape, she finds creative solutions.

Curious and Inquisitive: A driving force in her personality is an insatiable curiosity about the world. She seeks to understand different cultures, societies, and the complexities of global issues, leading her to ask insightful questions in her interviews.

Empathetic and Compassionate: While she is tough and gritty, she deeply cares about the people whose stories she tells. This empathy enables her to connect with sources on a personal level, making their stories more compelling.

Passionate and Driven: Elizabeth's professional life is characterized by an unwavering commitment to journalism and a desire to shine a light on under-reported stories. She believes in accountability and the importance of truth, which fuels her drive to uncover injustices and expose corruption. This passion, however, can also be a double-edged sword. It often leads her to sacrifice her personal life for her work. While she cherishes the impact her reporting can bring, the toll it takes on her relationships and well-being raises questions about her priorities. Her ambition is not merely for recognition, but rather stems from a deeper desire to effect change in the world around her. As she grapples with her own desires for stability and familial connections, her quest for meaning is reflected in the complexity of her personality.

Vincent Rivera

Adventurous: Vincent isn't just comfortable in high-pressure situations—he thrives in them. The adrenaline rush of documenting breaking news in dangerous or unpredictable environments fuels him. He views each assignment as a new adventure, embracing the unknown and the challenges it presents. He's drawn to stories that others might shy away from, driven by a need to witness and record history as it unfolds, no matter the personal risk. This thrill-seeking tendency also extends to his personal life—he enjoys pushing his own boundaries, whether it's through extreme sports, exploring new cultures, or taking spontaneous trips.

Resourceful: Given his role in managing complex technical gear, he is adept at problem-solving on the fly. Whether it's fixing equipment, finding alternative routes for safety, or troubleshooting technical issues under pressure, he displays quick thinking and ingenuity.

Observant: He has a keen eye for detail, both in his work and in his surroundings. This trait allows him to capture raw, authentic moments on camera and also helps him anticipate potential dangers, making him an essential safety partner for the correspondent.

Supportive: While Vincent enjoys the thrill of the job, he is also deeply committed to the safety of his colleagues, particularly the foreign correspondent he works alongside. He acts as her protector and confidante, anticipating risks and offering support in stressful situations. This protective nature stems from a combination of genuine care for her well-being and a sense of responsibility for their shared mission. He balances being a reliable partner in the field with being someone who encourages her to take risks and push her limits. He is deeply protective of Elizabeth, making her safety a priority.

Charming and Charismatic: His attractive presence and engaging personality make him easy to connect with. He often forms relationships with locals and sources, helping to gather information and secure insights for their reports.

Passionate: He cares deeply about journalism and believes in the power of storytelling. This passion drives him to produce compelling videos that accurately reflect current events and issues around the world.

Stacy Harris

Friendly and Outgoing: Stacy has a natural ability to connect with others, making friends easily wherever she goes. Her warm demeanor and genuine interest in people draw others to her.

Nurturing: As a professional registered nurse, she is caring and empathetic, often going the extra mile to support her patients and their families. This nurturing aspect extends to her relationship with her son.

Family: Stacy is engaged to be married, which adds to her happiness and stability. She is also the mother of Pierson, her neuro-divergent son, whom she loves deeply and advocates for, ensuring he receives the understanding and support he needs.

Interests and Hobbies:

Singing: Stacy has a passion for singing, which she often indulges in during her free time, whether alone or with friends.

Community-Oriented: She loves living in a small town, where she enjoys being part of a close-knit community. Stacy often participates in local events and is dedicated to fostering a sense of belonging among her neighbors.

Stacy Harris embodies the spirit of resilience, love, and connection, making her a pivotal character in her world, both as a mother and a community member. Her journey showcases the balance she seeks between her professional responsibilities, her personal life, and her advocacy for her son, Pierson.

Noah Montgomery

The small-town councilman possesses a personality that is a blend of charm, tradition, and ambition. Having grown up in the town, he carries a strong sense of loyalty and pride toward his community. His deep roots and generational wealth grant him a level of prestige, allowing him to navigate social dynamics with ease. He is well-liked, a trait he cultivated during his popular high school years, and this charm translates into his political career.

His desire to maintain the status quo reflects a cautious nature; he values stability and the familiar rhythms of town life. While he is open-minded, he often leans toward conservative approaches in policy to protect the community's historical character. He is clean-cut and photogenic, which accentuates his public appeal; he is often likened to a classic, small-town hero.

Noah, at 30, retains the athletic build honed from his years as a star quarterback. Standing tall at 6'1", he possesses broad shoulders, muscular arms and legs, and moves with an easy grace. His dark brown hair is styled impeccably, framing a face marked by full lips, expressive brown eyes, and a disarming smile. He favors tailored suits, crisp shirts, and expensive accessories, projecting an image of success and sophistication. His grooming is meticulous - always clean-shaven, with a subtle cologne hinting at his refined taste. A hint of a dimple appears in his left cheek when he smiles genuinely.

Though he is single, his attractiveness often draws attention, but he is focused more on his political aspirations than romantic entanglements. He can be charismatic, using his good looks and affable demeanor to foster connections with constituents. However, beneath his polished exterior, he may grapple with the pressure of maintaining his family's legacy and the expectations that come with it, making him somewhat guarded about his personal life and emotions.

Noah's relationship with Elizabeth is complex, tinged with unresolved feelings and the allure of a shared past. He is drawn to her independent spirit and her unwavering commitment to truth, qualities that both attract and intimidate him. His on-again, off-again relationship with Victoria reflects his fear of commitment and his tendency to prioritize his political aspirations over romantic entanglements. He maintains cordial relationships with his constituents, using his charm and affability to build connections and solidify his position within the community. His interactions with his family are marked by a sense of duty and the pressure to live up to their expectations. He is secretly a hopeless romantic.

Leonard "Uncle Leo" Montoya

Physical Appearance: Leonard "Leo" Montoya, Native American and Hispanic heritage is a rugged and weathered man in his late 70s. Standing at 5 feet 8 inches, he has a stocky build, shaped by years of physical labor and the demands of rural living. His skin is a warm, sun-kissed brown, a testament to his mixed Native American and Hispanic heritage. Leo's hair is long and silvery gray, often tied back in a simple ponytail. Deep-set, dark brown eyes reflect a blend of wisdom and suspicion, holding countless untold stories and a guarded nature. His face is marked by deep creases and wrinkles that tell the tale of a life filled with hardship and resilience. He typically dresses in comfortably worn flannel shirts and sturdy work boots, often layered with a weathered denim jacket that has seen better days.

Mannerisms: Leo is a man of few words; his demeanor is quiet and contemplative. He has a habit of pausing before he speaks, choosing his words carefully. He has a steady, deliberate gait, moving with a calm assurance born from years of living off the land. Leo often finds comfort in routine; tending to his small vegetable garden, or observing the changes in nature around him, while his brow furrows in thought. When he does speak, his voice is low and gravelly, often carrying a tone of authority that demands respect.

Dreams and Desires: Leo dreams of preserving the legacy of his ancestors and the solitude that the land provides. Having raised Vincent as his own after the loss of his brother, Leo desires to impart wisdom and strength to his nephew, hoping that he will appreciate the connection to their heritage and the importance of family despite the challenges they face.

Harper Martinez

Harper Martinez is a 29-year-old Latina journalist with a dynamic spirit and a nose for sensational stories. Her striking appearance is characterized by jet-black hair streaked with vibrant magenta, a look that reflects her bold personality. Ambitious and driven, Harper works for the **Crimson Call-Out**, a local gossip newspaper where she has quickly climbed the ranks. At 27, she became the youngest managing editor in the county, a testament to her talent and relentless pursuit of scoops. Harper's success extends beyond traditional media; she boasts a substantial social media following of 100,000, where she dishes out celebrity gossip, local news, and even exposes criminal activities. This online presence has amplified her voice and influence, making her a force to be reckoned with in Clover City.

Beneath her tough exterior lies a loyal and courageous heart. She is fiercely protective of her loved ones, especially her fiancé, renowned chef Raphael Parera. Her love for Raphael is a driving force in her life, and she is devoted to their relationship. However, she also grapples with insecurities stemming from her lack of formal education and perceived biases due to her ethnicity and age. She believes these factors are holding her back from further advancement at the **Crimson Call-Out**, specifically a promotion to national director, despite her impressive track record. Harper lives in her condo in Clover City, a space that reflects her modern and independent lifestyle.

Skills and Abilities

- Bilingual (speaks Spanish and English)
- Skilled investigative journalist
- Adept at social media and building an online presence
- Strong writing and reporting abilities
- Natural talent for uncovering stories and exposing wrongdoing

Goals and Motivations
- Professional advancement at the Crimson Call-Out
- Building a successful relationship with Raphael
- Proving herself in a challenging industry
- Creating her own platform ("Behind the Hype with Harper")
- Breaking important stories and maintaining journalistic integrity
- Overcoming prejudice and stereotypes in her profession

Victoria "Tori" Caldwell

Distinguishing features: A small, crescent-shaped scar near her left eyebrow from a childhood accident

Style: Polished and professional, favoring tailored blazers and pencil skirts in muted colors

Personality Traits: Ambitious and driven. Intelligent and analytical. Outwardly composed but internally passionate. Fiercely loyal to those she trusts. Competitive, especially when it comes to her career and relationships. Prone to jealousy, which she tries to mask with cool indifference. Resourceful and quick-thinking in high-pressure situations. Struggles with vulnerability and opening up emotionally.

Career: Victoria is a rising star in the District Attorney's office. Her sharp mind and dedication to justice have put her on a fast track to success. She specializes in white-collar crime and has a reputation for being relentless in pursuit of the truth. Her career often puts her in dangerous situations, as she's not afraid to take on powerful adversaries.

Background: Victoria grew up in Sweetwater Springs and has known Noah since high school. They reconnected after college when she returned to work for the DA's office. Their relationship blossomed over shared ambitions and a mutual understanding of the pressures of public service. However, Victoria's intense focus on her career and Noah's commitment issues led to an on-again, off-again dynamic. Victoria is in love with Noah and doesn't tolerate competition. She sees Elizabeth as a threat not only to her romantic aspirations but also to the careful plans she's made for her and Noah's future in local politics.

Jimmy Whitecloud

Physical Appearance: Jimmy is a man of strong presence, with dark eyes that reflect a deep focus and determination. His copper-toned skin shows the signs of years spent laboring under the sun, particularly from his extensive work on construction sites. His black hair, showing streaks of early gray at the temples, is meticulously pulled back into a neat braid that reaches past his shoulders, often a symbol of respect for his heritage. A new tattoo graces his forearm—a simple yet elegant design of yarrow flowers, inked in remembrance of his friend Uncle Leo. His apparel typically consists of sturdy work clothes, a testament to his hands-on lifestyle, often layered to accommodate the varying climates of their rural setting.

Mannerisms: Jimmy possesses a calm and steady demeanor, often taking time to listen more than he speaks. He tends to roll up his sleeves while discussing or demonstrating something, revealing his tattoo, which serves as a point of pride and connection to Uncle Leo.

Dreams and Desires: Jimmy dreams of protecting the land and the community he deeply cherishes, influenced by his conversations with Uncle Leo about the importance of heritage and resistance against those who threaten it. He desires to carry on Leo's legacy, preserving both the physical and cultural landscapes he holds dear. His tattoo symbolizes this fight—the resistance against forces that could disrupt their sacred spaces. Jimmy's ultimate aim is to build a better future for the community, ensuring that the legacies of their ancestors remain alive and respected.

Book Club Discussion Questions

1. Discuss Elizabeth's initial portrayal and how her experiences in Venezuela shape her character throughout the novel.
2. How does the setting of Sweetwater Springs contribute to the overall themes of the story? Consider its small-town dynamics, history, and the impact of industrialization.
3. Analyze the love triangle between Elizabeth, Noah, and Vincent. How do these relationships reflect her internal conflicts and evolving priorities?
4. What is the significance of Uncle Leo's character and his role in Elizabeth's life? Discuss his influence on her investigation and understanding of Sweetwater Springs.
5. How does the concrete batch plant project serve as a catalyst for conflict and change within the community? Explore the different perspectives on economic development versus environmental preservation.
6. Discuss the role of investigative journalism in the novel. How does Elizabeth's profession shape her interactions with other characters and influence the unfolding events?
7. Discuss the theme of community and belonging. How does Elizabeth's return to her hometown challenge her sense of identity and connection to her roots?
8. How do the flashbacks to Elizabeth's childhood and adolescence

inform her present-day struggles and relationships?

9. Analyze the symbolism of the flood. How does this natural disaster mirror the emotional and social turmoil within the community?
10. Discuss the novel's exploration of environmental themes. How does the concrete plant project raise questions about the balance between progress and ecological responsibility?
11. How does Elizabeth's relationship with Stacy reflect the complexities of female friendships and the challenges of balancing personal loyalties with differing viewpoints?
12. Discuss the use of suspense and mystery in the novel. How do the unfolding revelations about Uncle Leo's death and the sabotage maintain reader engagement?
13. Discuss the theme of family legacy. How does Elizabeth's relationship with her father's past influence her actions and decisions in the present?
14. Analyze the use of vivid imagery and descriptive language in the novel. How does the author create a sense of place and atmosphere?
15. Discuss the pacing of the novel. How does the author balance moments of introspection with action and suspense?
16. What are the ethical dilemmas faced by Elizabeth throughout the story, and how does she navigate them?
17. Discuss the significance of the title, Sweetwater Springs. How does it relate to the themes and events of the novel?
18. Analyze the ending of the novel. Did you find it satisfying? How does it resolve the central conflicts and character arcs?
19. If you could ask the author one question about the novel, what would it be?
20. How did this book make you feel about the importance of community engagement and speaking truth to power?

About the Author

Barbara Howard, a storyteller and tech-savvy gardener, pens enchanting mystery series with diverse characters and a dash of romance. Author of "Finding Home" and "The Clover City Files," she brings her extensive experience as a Department of Defense Project Manager, KPMG Eastern Region Project Leader, and Corporate Sales Representative for Borders Books & Music to her writing. Now back in her Midwestern hometown, Ms. Howard spends her days treasure hunting, spoiling her fur-babies, growing veggies, and plotting captivating whodunits.

You can connect with me on:
- https://www.barbarahowardbooks.com
- https://www.facebook.com/barbarahowardauthor
- https://www.instagram.com/bhowardphipps

Also by Barbara Howard

Traditional and romantic suspense mystery stories featuring a strong female protagonist, a diverse cast of characters, and a dash of romance.

Lost History Between Us
https://www.barbarahowardbooks.com
When history teacher Olivia James inherits her grandmother's remote cabin, she expects nostalgia, not danger. Arriving during a storm to find the cabin ransacked and boot prints in the mud, Olivia uncovers ties to a decades-old museum robbery and the Civil Rights movement. Unexpectedly reunited with Park Ranger Cameron Ellis—the man who broke her heart three years earlier—they delve into hidden journals, coded messages, and Underground Railroad safe houses. As their investigation draws the attention of a dangerous trafficking ring, and Cameron battles a secret illness, Olivia must decide if pursuing the truth is worth risking their safety—and their second chance at love.

The Taste of Rain, The Clover City Files, Book 1

https://www.barbarahowardbooks.com

A mystery that explores the themes of trust, aging, and justice. It is a heartwarming tale of the unlikely friendship between a young college student and an elderly resident, as they work together to uncover the truth, and solve a decades-old murder.

The Spice Code, The Clover City Files. Book 2

https://www.barbarahowardbooks.com

Raphael Parera, a restaurant owner and chef, is ensnared in a perilous web of deceit that jeopardizes both his culinary career and his life, enchanted by his girlfriend Isabella, unaware of the sinister secrets concealed behind her captivating façade.

A Match Made in Murder, The Clover City Files, Book 3

https://www.barbarahowardbooks.com

In the heart of Clover City, love is a grand affair orchestrated by matchmaker extraordinaire, Fiona Murphy. But this Valentine's Day, her twelve perfect weddings become a chilling mystery. As the Boat House restaurant transforms from a haven of romance to a crime scene, 'A Match Made in Murder' unveils a tale where love and betrayal intermingle, and uncovering the truth becomes the ultimate act of love.

A Royal Twist, The Clover City Files, Book 4

https://www.barbarahowardbooks.com

When renowned chef Raphael plans an extraordinary proposal for his girlfriend Harper under the guise of a royal event, misunderstandings and secrets threaten to derail his perfect plan. As Harper's suspicions grow and her nemesis returns with sinister plots, their love faces its ultimate test. In a heartwarming twist, Raphael's true intentions are revealed, promising a fairy tale proposal if they can overcome the looming dangers together.

Stitched in Secrets

https://www.barbarahowardbooks.com

Harper Martinez, now an independent journalist, becomes suspicious when her boyfriend, celebrity chef Raphael Parera, gets involved with Robert Gaines through a high-profile cooking show. After receiving an anonymous tip about Gaines' fashion empire, Harper uncovers a dangerous conspiracy. With the help of her best friend Amira, a health aide, Amira's lawyer boyfriend Lionel, and Raphael, Harper discovers that Gaines is using nanotechnology in his clothing and media to manipulate people. As the investigation deepens and a major fashion show approaches, the group must risk everything to stop Gaines' sinister plot before it's too late.

Final Harvest, Finding Home, Book 1

https://www.barbarahowardbooks.com

Amidst the chaos of job loss and the looming threat of homelessness, Traci Simmons discovers an unexpected purpose when her neighbor's death sparks a crusade for justice and preservation. As she navigates the challenges of urban farming and unravels the mystery behind the tragedy, Traci not only fights for her neighbor's legacy but also confronts her own insecurities, redefining the true meaning of home in a world overshadowed by homelessness, anxiety, food insecurity, and gentrification.

Charlotte's Revenge, Finding Home, Book 2
https://www.barbarahowardbooks.com
Traci Simmons' story, two years later, her relationship with Officer Randall Wells deepens as they face a malicious scheme from their past, putting both their lives and Randall's career in jeopardy and testing their love and loyalty to the limit.

Milo's Journey, Finding Home, Book 3
https://www.barbarahowardbooks.com
Experience the heartwarming journey of Milo, a rising star in the small town of Faucier County. With the support of his friend Traci, he has overcome a troubled past and is now on the path to success as an aspiring chef with a bright future ahead. But just as things seem to be falling into place, a reopened cold case threatens to unravel everything he has worked for. As he struggles to maintain his identity and relationships, will he be forced to leave behind the people who have become his family? And will Traci and Randall's relationship survive the turmoil that threatens to tear them apart?

Cup of Secrets - Trace of Lace
https://www.barbarahowardbooks.com
As Jules prepares for college graduation and Milo builds their new catering business, their lives are further complicated by murder investigations that engulf their small hometown of Keeferton.